THE CONDITION OF MUZAK

MICHAEL MOORCOCK

THE CONDITION OF MUZAK

THE CORNELIUS QUARTET

TITAN BOOKS

The Condition of Muzak
Print edition ISBN: 9781783291830
E-book edition ISBN: 9781783291823

Published by Titan Books
A division of Titan Publishing Group Ltd
144 Southwark Street, London SE1 0UP

First Titan edition: May 2016
1 2 3 4 5 6 7 8 9 10

Edited by John Davey.

A CIP catalogue record for this title is available from the British Library.

Printed and bound in the United States.

THE CONDITION OF MUZAK

Illustrated by Jill Riches, Harry Douthwaite
and Mal Dean

Original artwork, by Richard Glyn Jones,
withdrawn by artist

This book is dedicated with gratitude to the following people who, at different times, encouraged me through the eleven years this tetralogy took to complete: Clive Alison, Hilary Bailey, Jimmy Ballard, Edward Blishen, Alan Brien, John Clute, Barry Cole, Mal Dean, Michael Dempsey, Tom Disch, George Ernsberger, Giles Gordon, Mike Harrison, Doug Hill, Langdon Jones, Richard Glyn Jones, Philip Oakes, Keith Roberts, Jim Sallis, Norman Spinrad, Jack Trevor Story, Jon Trux, Angus Wilson.

NOTE TO THE READER

Although these books may be read in any order, the reader might wish to know that the structure of this volume reflects the structure of the overall tetrology.

CONTENTS

TUNING UP (1)   15

PRELUDE   21
J.C.   23
Major Nye   33
Una Persson   36
Sebastian Auchinek   40
Mrs C. and Colonel P.   43

EARLY REPORTS   46

TUNING UP (2)   50

INTRODUCTION   55
1. The dog-fight missile designed to dominate its decade 57
2. Matra ubiquity with 2nd and 3rd generation missiles 65
3. Acquire targets simply, reliably and accurately... 69
4. Introducing a new dimension of realism in visual simulators, Vital III 73
5. Need actuators that won't freeze, burn, dry out, or boil? 78

6. In the beginning was flight...   85
7. Optics for defence   90
8. The BL 755 cluster bomb...   94
9. The Strim antitank rocket launcher...   99
10. Rapier, ultra low-level air defence system...   104

EARLY REPORTS   108

TUNING UP [3]   111

DEVELOPMENT

1. Seven years for bank-raid vicar   121
2. Society hostess death riddle   127
3. An important message to every man and woman
    in America losing his or her hair   131
4. Cross country rape and slay spree of the
    frustrated bondage freak   138
5. Spirit voices help me—Peter Sellers talks about
    the strange power that has entered his life   143

THE REUNION PARTY   150

6. BAC cools hopes of airship boom   157
7. UFOs—occupants and artifacts in Eastern Indiana   161

8.	The girl next door could be a witch	166
9.	A Bicentennial celebration.	
	The 1976 Guns & Ammo Annual...	173
10.	High intensity colour	
	(that's actually good for your eyes!)	178

EARLY REPORTS   185

TUNING UP (4)   190

RECAPITULATION

1.	The God from the machine	202
2.	With the flag to Pretoria	210
3.	The Pathfinder	218
4.	The outcast of the islands	223
5.	What is art?	229

6.	The Birth and Adventures of Harlequin	238
7.	Harlequin Invisible; or, The Emperor of China's Court	250
8.	The Metamorphosis of Harlequin	257
9.	The Death of Harlequin	266
10.	The Mirror; or, Harlequin Everywhere	286

EARLY REPORTS   321

TUNING UP (5)   324

CODA

Mrs C. and Frankie C.   339

Auchinek   349

Persson   355

Nye   358

A Bundle   36l

Appendix I   375

Appendix II   402

Appendix III   403

All art constantly aspires towards the condition of music. For while in all other works of art it is possible to distinguish the matter from the form, and the understanding can always make this distinction, yet it is the constant effort of art to obliterate it.

—Pater

What's more in HERCULES than HARLEQUIN.
One slew the Hydra, this can kill the Spleen;
In him Behold the Age's Genius bright;
A Patch-Coat Hero, this great Town's delight.
With Craft and Policy, his humour tends
To publick Mirth, and profitable ends.
Let Envy gnash her teeth, let Poets rail
Whilst PIERO is his Guide he cannot fail.

Satirical print: *The Stage's Glory*, 1731

Each flower and fern in this enchanted wood
Leans to her fellow, and is understood;
The eglantine, in loftier station set,
Stoops down to woo the maidly violet.
In gracile pains the very lilies grow:
None is companionless except Pierrot.
Music, more music! how its echoes steal
Upon my senses with unlooked for weal.
Tired am I, tired, and far from this lone glade
Seems mine old joy in route and masquerade,
Sleep cometh over me, how will I prove,
By Cupid's grace, what is this thing called love?
[*Sleeps*]

—Dowson,
Pierrot of the Minute

Hop! enlevons sur les horizons fades
Les menuets de nos pantalonnades!
Tiens! l'Univers
Est à l'envers…

—Tout cela vous honore,
Lord Pierrot, mais encore?

—Laforgue,
Complainte de Lord Pierrot

TUNING UP (I)

As Major Nye tried to brush some green and brown stains
from the collar of his tropical combat jacket a little damp
earth fell from his neck and struck the fused stone of the
timeless causeway. Around him what remained of the ruins
of Angkor merged with the blackened boles of a defoliated
jungle; the area was at peace; it had ceased to be of strategic
importance. About fifty feet away a huge stone head of
Ganesh, elephant god of trade and good luck, lay on its side
where a 105mm shell had shot it between the eyes, blasting a
deep gash in the stone above the base of its trunk: the wound
glinted white and crystalline against the surrounding mossy
grey of the forehead; the god seemed to have acquired a
disenchanted third orb. Though a few monkeys and parrots
(no longer the rowdy insouciants of more glorious pre-war
years) crept about in the higher terraces, pausing cautiously
if they disturbed a fragment of plaster or dislodged a twig,
there were few sounds of life in the city.

Major Nye had at first found the city peaceful but he
was becoming increasingly uneasy with the tensions which

had gone to produce that peace. He lifted his head towards his right as, from the twisted and fire-blasted turret of a wrecked tank, a poor copy of a Vickers Mark I Main Battle (the 'Shiva'), emerged the chubby khaki bottom of a small Brahmin. Behind the tank the jungle brooded. "It's no go, I'm afraid, major." The Brahmin wiped fat hands on his oily fatigues and wriggled round so that he could face Nye. "Not a scrap." He flourished an empty picnic hamper.

This was the Shiva which had scored the hit on Ganesh: its occupant was the only survivor of retaliatory rocket-fire which had, in turn, taken out the tank. He called himself "Hythloday" but Nye knew his real name. 'Hythloday' had been a technical advisor with the Indian mercenary mechanised cavalry in its now famous sweep from Darjeeling to Saigon. Some months earlier, having no room for passengers, the cavalry had left him behind with his broken tank, and two days ago Major Nye, making a routine search-and-destroy operation in the area on behalf of his Khmer employers, had found him, recognising him as a former acquaintance. Major Nye had not reported his capture—there would have been little point, for yesterday he had intercepted a radio report: Phnôm Penh had sustained a tactical nuclear strike, possibly Tasmanian in origin. Without question it was curtains for the Khmers.

Unemployed again, bereft of the loyalties he needed so badly, Major Nye stroked his ancient tash and drew grey brows together. His pale hair, thin and sandy, his pale blue eyes, stood out in contrast to the heavy tan on his near fleshless face and neck. "Ah, well," he said in answer to

Hythloday's statement, "there are always the emergency rations. I must say the world is not the one I knew as a boy." He lowered his Armbrust 300 anti-tank weapon to the ground and unpacked the box at his belt. "Still, peace has been restored and that's important. Though at a price, of course."

From behind a crackling mass of fried foliage a third figure climbed up the masonry and sat beside him on the slab: a young man in tatty out-of-date clothing, haunted and demoralised by something more than war. The major offered him a strip of pemmican. "You seem cold, old chap. Are you sure you haven't picked up a spot of fever?"

"It depends what you mean, major." Jerry Cornelius turned the ragged collar of his black car coat so that it framed his face. He accepted the dehydrated meat and raised it reluctantly to his lips. His eyes were hot, his skin flushed. He was shivering.

Professor Hira joined them. "You've had the last of the medical kit, I regret to say, Mr Cornelius."

Cornelius had revealed himself to them on the previous day. From what he had told them he seemed to have been hiding in the ruins for a long time, since well before the final battle. Today he was, physically, slightly better than when they had found him, though he continued to deny that there was anything wrong with him. He had accepted the morphine, he said, because he hated to look a gift-horse in the mouth. Similarly the quinine, the penicillin and the valium. There was at least a score of recent holes in his forearms.

"It's industrialisation I need." Jerry shifted himself so that he squatted at Major Nye's feet. "I've developed this horrible antipathy towards peasant communities. Particularly Slavs and South-East Asians. What makes them so cruel?"

"It's hard to sympathise, isn't it?" Professor Hira nodded his head. "Original sin, I suspect. The devil come to Eden. It can't be the climate or the terrain." He had decided to skip the jerky and was gnawing, instead, on a root. "It can't be poverty."

"The very opposite, in my view," said Major Nye. "The richest New Guinea tribes were always the nastiest. Don't Kiev and Bangkok have a great deal in common with Crawley or Brighton?"

"Or Skokie," said Professor Hira with a certain amount of feeling.

They looked at him in surprise. He shrugged. "It was a long time ago."

Major Nye carefully packed up the rest of the rations. "I wouldn't mind getting back to Blighty myself. Better the devil you know, eh? A return to reality."

"Oh, Christ." Jerry began to shiver again. He rose. "That's the last thing I need."

PRELUDE

As Errant Knight of Table Round,
In high resolve shall Harlequin fulfil his quest;
And thus his judges all confound.

Harlequin Disguised as a Warrior
(French print *c.* 1580)

MOTHER AND THREE CHILDREN DIE FROM ASPHYXIA

No definite explanation for the cause of a fire which swept through two attic rooms in North Kensington on 14 January, killing a mother and her three young children, was forthcoming at the resumed inquest on Wednesday. Verdicts of "Accidental Death" were recorded. "I left the three children sleeping there when I went to work that morning," said Mr Colum Cornelius who had been staying in the house at the time. Fire Officer Cyril Powell said after the fire had been put out the bodies of the mother and her three children were found in the front attic room. Pathologist Dr R.D. Teare said that the cause of death was asphyxia due to the inhalation of fire fumes.

Kensington Post, 12 February, 1965

J.C.

Affluence and poverty are here in their extremes. Bohemians and traders, prostitutes, millionaires and famous actresses, writers, painters, street singers, drug-pushers, pop-stars, rag-and-bone dealers and antique dealers, immigrants from every part of the world—West Indians, Greeks, Pakistanis, Irish, Italians, Americans—and rich women from South Kensington come to London's finest vegetable market to shop cheaper. Just a few of the types in one of the world's most exotic streets...

'The Portobello Road', *Golden Nugget*,
September 1966

Some two miles north of the abandoned shell of Derry & Toms department store (now, like the ruins of Tintagel and Angkor, a mere relic) there once stood a grey-brown collection of nineteenth-century brick buildings surrounded by a high wall, also of brick: the Monastery of the Poor Clares Colettines, Westbourne Park Road, established in 1857 at the request of Dr Henry Manning, Superior of the Oblates of St Charles. The buildings themselves were erected in 1860, modelled on those of the Convent of the Poor Clares at Bruges which supplied the first nuns. Notting Hill, according to the *Building News* of the period (quoted in the Greater London Council's Survey of North Kensington, 1973), was nothing more than a dreary waste of mud and stunted trees, where the convent shared "the sole interest" of this desolate district with "Dr Walker's melancholy church" of All Saints', then still unfinished, and a lonely public house, now called The Elgin, in Ladbroke Grove. A number of "low Irish" had settled in the vicinity, and already there had been "a plentiful crop of Romish conversions there". The convent looked east onto Ladbroke Grove, north onto Westbourne Park Road and south onto Blenheim Crescent, while to its west were rows of run-down Victorian terraces separated, back-to-back, by tiny yards.

During the decade 1965–75 (the period during which the major part of our story probably took place) the convent was sold to the Greater London Council who subsequently built on the site a number of blocks of flats and a multistorey car park to serve the needs of their richer tenants. The nuns were moved to Barnes, across the river.

Before the convent was demolished it had been possible for people living on the upper floors of the surrounding houses to glimpse occasionally the activities of the nuns, members of an enclosed order, in the convent gardens, where vegetables and flowers were grown. In the summer the nuns would enjoy a game of rounders on the lawn or take picnics under the shade of the many elm trees whose old branches could be seen by those who passed by on the other side of the time-worn brick. The walls provided the nuns with a tangle of rambling roses and ivy and on their reverse offered the public slogans, some cryptic (VIETGROVE) and some relatively clear (QPR RULE OK), as well as the usual spray-painted selection of quotations from the works of Blake and Jarry. For those residents of Blenheim Crescent, Ladbroke Grove and Westbourne Park Road who found themselves with time on their hands the convent represented a regular diversion. At any one time during the height of the summer at least fifty pairs of eyes would be trained on the convent from a variety of angles, from windows, balconies and roofs, waiting for a glimpse of a figure at a window, the sight of a black habit crossing from a residential wing to the chapel or, more rarely, the spectacle of a cricket match. The convent proper, being, according to local legend, forbidden to any man (apart from the confessor, the electrician and the plumber who attended to the failing central heating) and most women, represented an ideal, a mystery, a goal, a challenge. Some doubtless hoped for a glance of flesh, a suggestion of illicit love between the nuns, while others were merely curious as to how the inhabitants spent their time. To certain ladies the convent represented a haven, a sanctuary from the complications of children, husbands, lovers, relatives and jobs.

On one particular summer afternoon, at the beginning of the decade already mentioned, a young man sat on the ledge of a window of a wretched tenement in Blenheim Crescent staring intently at the door of the chapel from which, in five minutes, almost all the Poor Clares would emerge together. The young man had lived most of his life in the three-room apartment and had an intimate knowledge of the nuns' movements as well as an affectionate proprietorial attitude towards them: several had nicknames—Old Ratty, Sexy Sis, Bigbum, Pruneface—for he had grown up with them; they were his pets. Given the opportunity, he would probably have died to protect them. He did not, of course, regard them as human beings.

From behind the young man and in the next room came the sound of crockery being washed; a noise accompanied by a rhythmic almost sub-vocal litany which was familiar and restful to him, like the drone of insects in a country garden, the tinkle of water over rocks.

Jerry Cornelius yer kin jest git yer shitty littel finger art an' do an 'and's turn like ther rest'v us, yer bugger. Fuckin' 'ell, yer dad woz fuckin' lazy but yore ther fuckin' world champion you are. If it wosn't fer me eyes I'd be doin' a bleedin' job, I worked fer years fer you lot and where'd it fuckin' get me, look at this bloody place it's a pigsty, an' Frank keeps promisin' me 'e'll git us a noo flat an' thass bin four years NAR!

A totter's cart, piled with the discarded débris of a score of slum houses, turned into Blenheim Crescent. It was drawn by a brown-and-white pony. Jerry automatically found himself inspecting the junk from where he sat, high overhead: it was an inbred instinct of all children born in the district. There were two old gas-stoves, a wooden bedstead, a water-heater, a tin bath, some boxes of rusty cutlery. The pony's hoofs clattered on the tarmac of the street. The driver, in a stained brown overcoat, his eyes owl's eyes behind thick lenses, had propped his main prize of the day, an old set of stag's antlers, behind him so that for an instant it seemed that he himself was horned. He gave a throaty instruction to the horse and it turned right, vanishing into a nearby mews.

Jerry yawned, stretched, and settled a thin shoulder against the window frame, swinging his legs above the tiny balcony formed by the house's front porch. The balcony had once been painted green but most of the paint had peeled. It contained dilapidated window boxes, some of which managed to sustain a few weeds in their sour earth; a collection of grimy plastic woodland animals and gnomes; part of a black Raleigh roadster bicycle which Jerry had begun reconstructing two years before; a deckchair whose canvas had rotted and which had ripped when, with a yell, his mother had fallen through three days earlier. Sooner or later, Jerry had reassured her, she would not recognise the balcony. He planned, eventually, to turn it into an ornamental conservatory with semi-tropical plants.

The afternoon was very warm for early summer and was relatively still, for it was a Thursday, when almost all the local shops and stalls closed down. Jerry could turn his head to the right and see, at right angles to Blenheim Crescent, a tranquil, deserted Portobello Road, or to the left a Ladbroke Grove with about half its normal volume of traffic. It was almost as if, for a few hours, an aura spread from the convent and made the world outside as tranquil as the world within.

Before the nuns emerged, Jerry's attention was distracted to the street by the chuckling drums of some Pakistani love song which almost immediately stopped and became the last few bars of a Rolling Stones number. Three black youths, in jeans and jazzy jumpers, were springing down the steps of the house immediately opposite Jerry's, a house even more dilapidated than his own, of tired red brick. The tallest youth swaggered, holding in his hand a transistor radio which now played The Beatles' latest hit; the other two were jostling him, trying for possession of the radio. The tall boy pulled away from his companions. "Lay off me, man." He made loose, dancing movements. The volume rose and fell as he moved the radio. "Come on, man—let's have it." One of his companions grabbed and the station was lost. Jerry could hear the static. "You broken it, man!" They paused, seeking the correct wavelength. "No, I ain't!" They found the programme just as the song faded. They began to scuffle again. "Give us a go, man." The tall boy broke and ran with the radio, up towards Portobello Road. "Get your own. It's mine, ain't it?" The other two caught him almost immediately, tackling him around the legs, bringing him down.

As the fight became more serious a policeman turned the corner from Ladbroke Grove. He was young, pink and all the character seemed to have been scrubbed from his sober features. Without altering his pace he raised his voice:

"Oi!"

Unheeding the boys began, almost amiably, to kick and punch their companion, who lay on the ground, his knees drawn up, the tranny hugged to his chest. It was playing Jimi Hendrix now.

"Oi!"

The policeman loped towards them. They turned. The two shouted a warning and ran towards Kensington Park Road. The third picked himself up and followed them. The policeman stopped, drew a couple of breaths and wiped his forehead with a navy-blue handkerchief. Then he continued to pace in their wake, obviously not in pursuit.

"There's never a copper around when you need one!" Jerry found himself shouting into the silence of the street. Startled by the loudness of his own voice he turned his head in the opposite direction. When, after some seconds, he turned his head back he saw the policeman glaring up at him. Jerry winked.

"Wot's 'appenin'?" His mother entered her bedroom and saw her son on her ledge. "Git off a there! Yer'll fall!" She neared the window and saw the policeman. "Blimey! Wot's 'e want?"

"Dunno, Mum."

"Nosey bloody parkers the lot of 'em."

Mother and son contemplated the policeman. Eventually he became self-conscious and resumed his beat.

Mrs Cornelius cocked her head. "Someone comin' up. Are yer *sure*... Oh, it's Frank." The door opened.

Frank came into her room. Frank wore a blazer with polished steel buttons, grey flannels, an open-neck white shirt, a yellow cravat with a horseshoe motif. He stared in affected contempt at his brother whose own costume was a red satin shirt with the words *Gerry and the Pacemakers* imprinted in yellow on the back, skintight drainpipe jeans and suède desert boots. His black greasy hair had almost grown out, but was still streaked with blond dye at the ends. "Bloody hell." Frank placed a large bar of Cadbury's Fruit & Nut on the confused dressing table. "They should never have abolished National Service. Look at you!"

"Piss off." Amiably Jerry took in his brother's gear. "What was the regatta like? Just come up from Henley, have you?"

"I've been *working*." Frank ran a hand down his waist.

"Conning some poor ignorant foreigner, eh?" Jerry looked speculatively at the chocolate on the table.

"I've made an important sale this afternoon." Frank produced a huge roll of dollar bills from his trouser pocket. "Don't knock it, Jerry."

Noting the expressions on the faces of both his brother and his mother he quickly slipped the roll back where it had come from.

"Not a bad little bundle," said Jerry. "Did you sell some of them authentic Chippendale vases you antiqued up last week?"

Frank tapped his forehead. "Intelligence got me that." He preened himself. "Information. Property. That's my commission."

"You can be had up for playing Monopoly with real money." Jerry swung his legs into the room. "Say, lend us a couple of bucks, will ya, bud?"

"Oh, Christ!" Frank returned to the living room/kitchen. He glared around him at the crowded, ruined furniture, the half-done washing up, the piles of magazines and broken china ornaments. "Don't let him talk in that fake Yank accent, Mum. He's so *common*."

"Make it ten bob, then," said Jerry reasonably, in his own voice.

"Piss off." Frank sniffed. "Get a bloody job."

"I'm organising this beat group," said Jerry. "It takes time."

"What is the time?" Frank glanced at his wrist. "My watch has stopped."

"Is that the bargain that feller sold you in the pub?" Jerry was triumphant. "Solid gold, wasn't it? Fifty jewels? Con men always make the best marks, don't they?"

"I didn't come to see you." Frank slid his white cuff over his malfunctioning watch. "I came to see Cathy—and Mum, of course. Is she here?"

"That's Mum, by the sink."

"How childish," said Frank.

"What you doing then?" Jerry asked with genuine curiosity, ignoring his brother's last remark. "Following in Rachman's footsteps?"

"Tenements?" Frank was shocked. "This is *property development*. Offices and that."

"Round here?"

"It's going up all the time. A rising residential area, this is. All the people from Chelsea and South Ken are moving in."

"Buying themselves nice little ragshops in Golborne Road, are they?"

"Multiple tenancies are giving way to one-family houses. It's council policy." Frank savoured the sound of the words.

Jerry looked out of the window over the sink. He had missed the nuns. "You know what I'd do, if I had the chance? I'd buy that bloody nunnery."

"I've got news for you," began Frank. "The GLC…"

"Just to own it," said Jerry dreamily. "Not to do anything with it."

"Well, you'd better start saving up, hadn't you?"

Jerry shrugged. "Wait till our group gets to number one."

Frank laughed. "You'll be lucky if you're all awake at the same time."

Absently, Jerry popped a mandy into his mouth. "It's idealists like me the world needs. Not grafters like you."

This seemed to improve Frank's spirits. He put a condescending hand on Jerry's forearm. "But it's a grafter's world, my son."

"Yeah?"

"Most definitely, young Jerry."

Jerry sniffed. "I'll let you get on with it, then."

He turned to his window.

Frank wandered to his mother's side. "Hello, Mum. Any chance of a cup of tea?"

MAJOR NYE

"I'm afraid it's not quite the thing for our little theatre."
Major Nye tried to sit on one of the bar-stools and then
decided to remain at attention. Gingerly he sipped his pint
of shandy, revealing shiny cuffs. The suit was twenty years
old at least. "I really am sorry, old chap. What is it? A pint?"
His pale eyes were sympathetic.

"Thanks, major," said Jerry. "I'm sorry I can't get you
one." He was scarcely any more fashionably dressed than
Major Nye. He wore his black suit with the high, narrow
Edwardian lapels and the slight flare to the trousers, which
he had got Burton's to make up for him, albeit reluctantly,
when he had been flush. The only black shoes he had were
the elastic-sided cuban-heeled winkle-pickers pre-dating
the suit and he felt awkward in his rounded, button-down-
collar white shirt, with the black knitted tie. "But you've
only heard the cassette on a cheap player. If you heard it
over proper speakers you'd get our full sound, you know."

"Surely you can get bookings in these pop-clubs they
have everywhere these days?" He caught the attention of

the purple-cheeked barman. "Pint of best, please." He leaned cautiously against the mahogany counter, looking beyond Jerry at Hennekey's other customers crowding around the pub's stained wooden benches and big tables. It was evident that while he did not judge the shaggy young bohemians he was mildly curious about them. He fingered the ends of his cuff. "I thought they were mushrooming."

"They're not interested in us," Jerry told him. "You see, we're a bit more than an ordinary rock group—we're trying for something that combines a story, a light-show, spoken words and so on. That's why I guessed you might be interested, since you're local. The only local theatre. And it's more of a theatrical show, you see."

"I'm just the secretary, old chap. I'm probably the least powerful person in the whole outfit. And acting, unpaid, at that. It was my daughter got me involved, really. I'm retired, you see. I was adjutant of the—well, we got kicked out— the regiment was incorporated—no room for old fogies like me. Anyway, she's an actress. Well, of course, you must know that already, since it was through your sister…"

"Yes," said Jerry. "I do know. But you're the only person connected with the Hermes Theatre who'd even bother to listen to me."

"They're a bit old-fashioned there, by and large, though I think they're going to do Pinter next year. Or is it Kafka? *A Night at the Music Hall's* about as far as they're prepared to go, eh? The boy I love is up in the gallery…"

"I see," said Jerry. "I suppose you don't know anybody else I could approach?"

Major Nye was disappointed at not being allowed to finish the line. "Not really."

"Everybody's hopes are pinned on this, you see."

Major Nye said seriously, as a group of newcomers jostled him against Jerry's chest: "You shouldn't stop trying, old chap. If you've got something worthwhile it will be recognised eventually."

Jerry sighed and sipped his bitter.

UNA PERSSON

"Bloody hell," said Jerry miserably as he backed into the corner of the white room, his elbow almost dislodging a particularly ugly china dog on a shelf, "there must be every trendy in the King's Road here, Cath." The party bubbled about his ears. There was a great deal of blue and orange, of op and pop and pastel plastic, of the Tilsonesqueries loading the walls, of coloured stroboscopes and Warholian screenprints, light screens displaying shapes of an oddly Scandinavian neatness, hunt-ball whoops and giggles, stiff upper-class bodies in a terrifying parody of vitality. His sister shook her head. "You're such a snob, Jerry. They're nice people. A lot of them are friends of mine."

Jerry tasted his punch. He had got his new brown-and-white William Morris shirtsleeve wet ladling the stuff into his cup. He had only come because Catherine had told him he would be able to make the right sort of contacts. The trouble was that every time someone spoke to him in one of those high-pitched voices his throat tightened and he could only grunt at them. The strobes turned the whole scene into a silent movie—something about decadent modern times called *Despair*—as the hearty girls in their shorts and mini-skirts danced with pale young men in neat neckerchiefs and very clean jeans who puffed at machine-rolled joints and staggered against the chrome and leather furniture in an unaesthetic danse macabre.

The Rolling Stones record finished and was replaced on the deck by a fumbling drunkard who lurched against the amplifier and knocked it half off its shelf. The amplifier was saved by a tall girl with short hair and sardonic grey eyes. The girl wore a long calf-length skirt and a rust-coloured jumper to match; she had an assured elegance possessed by no-one else in the room. She squeezed past the drunkard as he let the pick-up fall with a crunch on the record he had selected: *Elvis' Golden Records*, already much scored. "Oh, fab!" cried more than one melancholy soul.

Jerry watched the girl until she looked back at him and smiled. He turned his head to find himself face to face with the dark young man whom Catherine had introduced as Dimitri, doubtless one of her many Greeks. At least Dimitri wore a suit, albeit a 'Regency' cut. Dimitri's eyes widened in panic at the prospect of a further exchange of grunts. The elegant girl entered Jerry's field of vision again. She was carrying a glass. "You seem as much out of place here as I am."

Jerry's being flooded with gratitude but he hoped it didn't show. "Chelsea wankers," he said, playing it cool. He tossed back his drink. "What's a nice girl like you doing here?"

"I came with a friend."

Jerry was disappointed. "One of these blokes?"

"One of these—chicks."

He wondered if she were foreign.

"Liz Nye," explained the girl.

"She's a friend of my sister's."

"Catherine's a great pal of mine."

"Who are you, then?"

"My name's Una."

Jerry smirked, in spite of himself. He knew all about Una Persson. "You're a legend in your own lifetime," he said. "You're not like I imagined."

Her smile was for herself but she replied quickly to save him embarrassment. "Catherine sees just one side of me."

"Have you got a lot?" Jerry asked. "Of sides?"

"It depends what you mean."

Jerry's smile broadened and became a grin which she shared. She winked at him and stood beside him, shoulder to shoulder, so that they both faced the party. "They should be putting the Vivaldi on soon," she said. "And begin to·'smooch'."

Somehow she had given him courage. "Do you want to split?" he asked.

She frowned. "You mean 'leave'?"

"Yes. Sorry."

"There are so many levels, aren't there? I'll have to find out what Liz wants to do. She's in the next room." Una Persson touched his arm. "But I'll be back."

Jerry began to come to life. Gracefully he reached towards his guffawing hostess and accepted another punch.

SEBASTIAN AUCHINEK

Fingering the hand-stitching on his blue velvet Beau Brummel jacket Sebastian Auchinek bent an ear towards the Dynatron cabinet stereo to which was attached, five-pin DIN to five-pin DIN, Jerry's little cassette tape recorder. "Well, it's certainly different, isn't it?" He added: "Man."

"It's underground music," Jerry explained.

"Yeah, ther bleedin' eight-forty-five ter Aldgate, by ther sarnd o' it!" Mrs Cornelius laughed as she put two cups of cocoa on the surface of Jerry's battered amplifier. They were in Jerry's room at Blenheim Crescent. The untidy bed was littered with magazines, of a different kind from his mother's, and most of the rest of the space was given over to valves, wires and speakers, the majority of which didn't work. "Sorry, I'm shore!" said Mrs Cornelius. She departed, closing his door in a pantomime of courtesy.

Luckily Sebastian Auchinek's sense of humour functioned only in direct relation to his own sense of despair. He puzzled over the music. He removed his little hat. He sucked at his huge lower lip. He rubbed his monstrous nose. "But will it catch on with the general public? That's what we have to think about—Jerry? You don't mind?"

"No, no. 'Course not." Jerry looked anxiously into the liquid eyes of the handsome promoter. "You've heard of the Pink Floyd, haven't you? They're getting quite popular."

"Oh, yes. I don't doubt it. But you know what public taste's like. Twinkle one week, Mojos the next. Whether this sort of music's got any future—I honestly don't know. I can see you're serious. But are you commercial? I'm sorry." Sebastian Auchinek held up a shapely hand as if to ward off a light blow. He put his cap down. "It's what we have to think about, *if* we're going to back you. It still boils down to investments. You're a talented boy, I don't doubt it. I mean, what we have to say to ourselves is—How do we promote this kind of music? All right, we can get a minor record company to do one LP—but it's the singles market that's important. I can't see any of this as single material, quite frankly. Miss Persson led me to understand that you were more of an R&B group. Like Graham Bond and Brian Auger. We're considering them at the moment."

"We don't do that sort of thing any more," said Jerry with a certain disdain. "Una said you were into progressive stuff."

"We are. We are. But we have to *see* it. In context. We have to be able to feel we can do something positive for a group. It wouldn't be fair to you, would it, if we just took you on and then did nothing?"

"Yes, I can see that…"

"Maybe if I came along and heard you at your next gig?"

"That's why I'm talking to you. We can't get any gigs."

"Not even locally?"

"There aren't any local venues, are there?"

"It's difficult, isn't it?"

Jerry turned the recorder off. The hissing had begun to irritate him. "Some people think we're ahead of our time."

"Could be. When's your next rehearsal?" Auchinek was eager to prove to Jerry that his mind was still open.

"I'm not sure. We have trouble finding places."

"Well, look, get in touch with me when you know what your plans are. Maybe I can fix up a rehearsal room for you."

"It'd be something, anyway. Thanks."

Sebastian Auchinek removed a leather-bound notebook from his inside pocket. He clicked a ballpoint with his thumb. "What's the name of the group?"

"The Deep Fix."

"You might have to change that a bit. It's not really— you know… The BBC's still a power in the land, eh? They don't like drugs. Have you thought of any other names?"

"Yes," said Jerry. "The Cocksuckers."

Sebastian Auchinek managed a small smile. "Well, we'll talk about that when the time comes." He tore a page from the book. "Here's my office number. Keep in touch. Leave a message with my secretary if I'm not there. Don't think I'm being negative. And remember—I'm not the only promoter on the beach."

He looked around for his corduroy Dylan cap. He had put it on top of his cocoa.

MRS C. AND COLONEL P.

"Of course," said Colonel Pyat as he poured Mrs Cornelius another gin, "we lost everything in the war, including our titles. My uncle had a very big estate not far from Lublin. And his father, you know, had an even bigger one in the Ukraine. He was shot by Makhno who in turn was shot by Trotsky who was killed by Stalin." He shrugged and his smile was crooked. "So it goes." He fell back into Mrs C.'s best armchair, the white plastic one, his eyes fixing on the silent television screen. The warped monochrome picture displayed a nurse, a nun and a black man in a hospital bed.

"We're surpposed ter be related ter 'im," said Mrs Cornelius, brushing crisp crumbs from her pink cotton lap. "Shouldn't eat crisps. They make yer sweat."

"My uncle?"

"Nar! The ovver one. Trotsky, innit? Though I 'eard 'e corled 'isself somefink else. Brahn or somefink."

"Bronstein. His real name was Bronstein. Jewish, you see."

"Nar! It woz nuffink forin'." She raised her glass. "Darn the 'atch then."

Bemused, the drunken colonel imitated her action.

"It's more comfy 'ere, innit, than ther pub?" said Mrs Cornelius. She could see that Colonel P. was a gent (even though currently in need of a spot of luck) by the cut of his greasy tweed jacket, his shiny flannels; but his breeding was revealed by his bearing rather than his clothes, she supposed. And he hadn't hesitated to fork out for a half-bottle of gin when she'd taken a fancy to him and suggested coming back here. Tonight wasn't the first time she had seen him in The Blenheim, of course, but it was the first time she'd had a chance to have a decent chat.

"Definitely Brahn," she said. Her expression softened. She moved closer to Colonel Pyat. He looked at her through wary, red-rimmed eyes. He stroked the stubble of his chin. "Is Pyat yore real name, then?"

"Well, it's my official name, you know. In the last war..."

From the next room, Jerry's, there suddenly came the ear-splitting squawk of a feeding-back amplifier. She was shocked. It hadn't occurred to her to check if her son was in. Automatically she lifted her great red head and raised her voice:

"I thort yer said you woz garn art ternight! Turn that fuckin' thing darn!"

"Pardon?" thickly said Colonel Pyat.

"Not you, Kernewl. Sorry. Turn it darn, carn't ya!"

"I meant to go back after the war." Colonel Pyat raised a sorrowful glass to his lips. "I was in intelligence, you know. Liaison officer for your chaps. Stuck here when the war ended. But, naturally…" He shrugged.

She was vaguely sympathetic. "The Russians, eh?"

"Worse than the Germans."

"But I thort you said you *woz* Russian."

"No, no—I was *with* the Russians."

"Oh really? Where woz that?"

A high-pitched shriek filled the flat.

"My God!" Colonel P. covered his ears. His eyes hunted about the room. He stared through the window as if he expected the sky to fill with planes.

"'Ang on a sec." Carefully Mrs Cornelius got to her broad feet. "Ooo." She coughed. "It's me kid," she said.

Before she could reach Jerry's door the sound from behind it had changed again, rising and falling, so that now it resembled the distant wailing of some demented creature of the sea.

EARLY REPORTS

Scotland Yard will keep up its drive to recruit black policemen despite the failure of the campaign so far. Revealing this yesterday Metropolitan Police Commissioner Sir Robert Mark said: "We won't take No for an answer. We shall keep at it."

Daily Mirror, 31 March, 1976

The chances of our moderate climate changing soon to a prolonged cold spell, but not glacial, are high, Dr E.J. Mason, FRS, director general of the Meteorological Office, suggested last night. With the caution of a man carrying ultimate responsibility for the precision of the official day-to-day weather forecasting methods, he added: "There is no real basis for the alarmist predictions of an imminent ice age, which have largely been based on extrapolation of the 30-year trend of falling temperatures in the northern hemisphere between 1940 and 1965. Apart from the strong dubiety of making a forecast from such a short-period trend, there is now evidence that the trend has been arrested."

Guardian, 18 March, 1976

The annual meeting of the National Front voted in London at the weekend to expel all members who are of mixed race, non-European ancestry or coloured. About 20-25 members are affected. But yesterday, Mr Eugene Pierce, an Anglo-Indian accountant who has been a member of the National Front and walked out of the meeting in protest at the vote said: "I was immediately assured by members of the directorate that the vote was only a recommendation..." Mr Pierce, 65, whose British grandfather married an Indian, earlier told the meeting: "I was a member of the British army, along with thousands of other Anglo-Indians." But the meeting became increasingly noisy and his words were drowned in the uproar. "We have to be 100 per cent racialist in the National Front," said the mover of the resolution, Mr Bert Wilton, of Southwark, London, to loud applause: "If people who are half or quarter coloured are allowed in, it will kill everything."

Guardian, 6 January, 1975

Police frogmen were hunting for more bodies yesterday after the cut-up remains of two teenage sisters were found in a lake in the Catskill Mountains, 110 miles north of New York. The self-styled "Bishop of Brooklyn", 51-year-old Vernon Legrand, leader of a bizarre religious cult, has been charged with the murders.

Daily Mirror, 15 March, 1976

Two members of a British-based religious sect are believed to have been the victims of ritual killings. Police think that they were hypnotised—and then vital organs in their bodies were crushed. The probe began after the body of artist Michel Piersotte was found at the foot of the 250 ft Citadel in Namur, Belgium. Michel was a member of the Children of God sect, whose international headquarters is at Bromley in Kent. A post-mortem revealed that his liver and kidneys were crushed, as though in a vice. Police decided to re-open an inquiry into the death of another member of the sect. This was 20-year-old Jean Maurice, who was found dead at the foot of the Citadel in Dinant, Belgium, in December. Again police established that vital organs had been crushed. The men were close friends. They were believed to be trying to break away from the sect. A Belgian police spokesman said last night: "We're studying a Scotland Yard report about the sect". The report says that hypnotism is used at indoctrination ceremonies. Youngsters are encouraged to break off all ties with their parents.

Daily Mirror, 15 March, 1976

TUNING UP (2)

Jerry hauled on the reins to bring the lead dog to a sudden stop. At once the other dogs lay down in their traces, the breath from their pink panting mouths melting the surrounding snow. The small red sun overhead was the only bright colour in the dark grey sky, the only light, yet it was possible to see for miles over the twilight landscape to a range of mountains in the north-west, to the black line of the horizon elsewhere. It had taken him months to reach Lapland, travelling mostly by sled. He hauled a sack from the wicker rack behind him and began to walk along the line, throwing the dogs chunks of skinned half-frozen wolf. As he reached the lead dog and produced a larger than average lump of meat from the sack he heard in the distance a bass drone, coming from the direction of the mountains. He recognised the motor of an old Westland Whirlwind and automatically looked for cover. There was none, save the sled. He pulled his bow and his quiver of arrows from beneath the furs and bric-à-brac on the main section and prepared for the worst. Things were waking up a little sooner than he had anticipated. He supposed that, in spite of the immediate problems, he was relieved. At least the birth (or re-birth, depending how you look at it) had been relatively easy this time.

The big chopper appeared in the sky, black and glimmering, and the dogs looked up from their flesh, eyes bright, ears pointing. One of them snarled; Jerry was sure that they had not responded to any specific stimulus. They were a strange breed of husky, with red eyes, white coats and red-tipped ears.

Snow began to fly. Clouds seemed to form just above the surface. The helicopter came down heavily, still only partially powered, bumping and groaning. The motor was switched off. In the stillness the rotors clacked slowly to a halt. Jerry saw muffled figures moving inside the breath-clouded canopy. He fitted an arrow to his bow as a door in the Whirlwind's body opened and a woman descended. She had a large 7.63mm Borchardt automatic pistol in her gloved right hand. Her face was hidden in the hood of an ankle-length pandaskin parka. Her breath coiled from shrouded lips as she peered towards the sled. She walked with a kind of Sarah Bernhardt limp.

"Mr Cornelius?" The voice was sharp, demanding.

"Which Mr Cornelius would that be?" Jerry recognised her at once.

Miss Brunner was her usual petulant self. "Oh, don't be silly. What have you got in your hands?"

"A bow and arrow."

She buried her pistol in her clothing. "I understand. Put

it away." She held up her heavy arms.

"Oh sure." Jerry indicated the swivelling gun-turret in the chopper.

She shrugged. "Merely a gesture. You know there's little chance of a gun working in the current moral climate. What are you doing in Lapland? Looking for someone?"

"Just trying to recapture the past."

"That's not like the old Jerry."

"I can't say the same for you. But then I always admired your consistency."

"There's a bit more mass than there used to be." It was obvious that she had taken his remark for a compliment. "You look like a Mountie. Well, what do you want from us?"

"Nothing," he said. "I didn't even know you were out, did I?"

She became suspicious. "Aha." The snow crunched. She moved tentatively forward. The dog snarled again, pricking its peculiar ears. She stopped, glaring at it in considerable dislike. "You won't be able to get to the laboratory. Not for a while. It'll be frozen up. Is that where you were thinking of going?"

"I haven't been thinking much at all. You don't in these conditions. I suppose I was making for the lab. Instinct."

"Instinct!" She cackled. "You!"

She had hurt his feelings. "It's the only explanation I can think of. You were heading south. Does that mean you've been to the lab already?"

"That's how I know about it. We came via Russia. And before that Canada. We've been flying for ages."

Luxuriously Jerry inspected the vast sky, half expecting to see a formation of geese, but it was still empty. "It's probably the spring," he said.

INTRODUCTION

On New Year's Night, 1091, a certain priest called
Gauchelin was terrified by a procession of women,
warriors, monks, etc. who swept past him, dressed
in black, half-hidden by flames, and wailing aloud.
Astonished and dismayed, the priest said to himself:
"Doubtless this is the Cornelius family. I have heard
that it has formerly been seen by many people, but
I have mocked at such tales. Now, indeed, I myself
have truly seen the ghosts of the dead." Gauchelin
was, indeed, neither the first nor the last to see the
notorious "maisnie Cornelius" (Harlequin-troupe),
which appeared so frequently both in mediaeval
France and England. For Harlequin (Harlechin,
Hellequin, etc., are all variations of the same word)
appears first in history or legend as an aerial spectre
or demon, leading that ghostly nocturnal cortège
known as the Wild Hunt.

—Enid Welsford,
The Fool: His Social and Literary History,
London, 1934

PRINCE PHILIP OPENS DREAM FLATS IN W.IO

Trains roared behind a VIP canopy, the sun popped out suddenly and children whistled from the roof-tops when the Duke of Edinburgh arrived in dreary North Kensington on Tuesday afternoon [to open] Pepler House, the biggest project to date by the Kensington Housing Trust.

Kensington Post, 12 November, 1965

I. THE DOG-FIGHT MISSILE DESIGNED TO DOMINATE ITS DECADE

Jerry struggled into his pink tweed Cardin suit. The waistcoat was a little tight and he had to undo the shoulder holster by a notch but otherwise he looked as sharp as he had always done. He pulled his needler free and checked that the magazine was full, each hollow dart containing a neat 50ccs of Librium: a perfect hunting charge. He smoothed his long, fine hair about his face as he stood in front of the looking-glass, well satisfied, in the circumstances, with his appearance. He checked his watches. Both waited at zero. He crossed his wrists and started the watches. The hands moved at a steady rate.

"Pretty," he said. He smirked. He faced the room, squinting in the glare from the white, plastic furniture, the neon, the ivory walls. He took mirror shades from his top pocket and slid them over his eyes. He sighed. "Nifty."

He sailed out into the currents of the day, high on painkillers and a sense of his own immortality, swinging his hips to the sound of 'Eleanor Rigby' from the receiver built into his unfashionably rigid collar, down Holland Park

Avenue beneath the tall spring trees, stepping wide on two-inch cuban heels. The bravest dandy of them all: he had a smile for everybody. Under his breath he sang along with John, George, Paul and Ringo and turned right into Campden Hill Square where his great big Duesenberg, chocolate and cream, waited for him alone. He unlocked the door, slid behind the wheel, started the perfect supercharged straight-8, let go the brakes and was on the move. A masterpiece to equal any one of its European contemporaries, the 1930 SJ Torpedo Phaeton was the most elegant car America had ever produced. Euphorically, both mind and body in ecstatic unity, he cruised between the labouring corpse-wagons which parted so that he could pass through them, as if by divine command. He offered a friendly wave to all he overtook, then he reached the top of Ladbroke Grove's hill and began the descent into the mythical netherworld of Notting Dale. The road was suddenly almost deserted; sounds were muffled; the sun was hotter.

Turning right into Westbourne Park Road he stopped outside the main gate of the Convent of the Poor Clares. He did not bother to lock the car. He knew he could rely on its aura to protect it.

Sister Eugenia, the Mother Superior, herself greeted Jerry as she opened the grilled steel door which led directly into the shadowy Visitors' Chapel with its hideous green, yellow and pink Crucifixion above the green marble tiles, the brass, the tasselled purple of the altar. She spoke in carefully modulated tones like a consultant psychiatrist and when she smiled it was sweet and good. Jerry admired her smile in particular, as he admired professionalism wherever he found it.

"Father Jeremiah." She gestured for him to precede her while she supervised the tender young novice locking the gate. They followed single-file behind him as he headed through the side exit and onto a gravel path, making for the main building, smelling the air, admiring the blooms and the well-kept lawns, the peculiar, ingrown dwarf elms. He was not sure but he thought he heard, somewhere in the chapel on his left, the second part of Messiaen's *Turangalîla Symphony*. He pressed his head against his collar and cut off The Beatles, looking enquiringly back at the Mother Superior. "A record?"

"Oh, no!" The Mother Superior was amused. Behind her the soft little novice giggled.

They reached the main building and climbed steps into quiet passages, arriving at last at the second floor and the Mother Superior's office which looked out onto the garden. It seemed to Jerry, surreptitiously sniffing the air, that the infirmary was nearby. At her desk the Mother Superior lowered herself into her high-backed Windsor chair, signing for Jerry to sit in the chair's twin facing her. "It is a very great pleasure to see you again, Father Jeremiah. You are looking well."

"And you, too, Sister Eugenia. Congratulations on your appointment..."

"I pray that I will fulfil..."

"... there can be no question..."

"You are kind. It seems such a short time since you

took confession at Harrogate. How greatly our lives have changed! Your own responsibilities…"

He dismissed them. "I'm very grateful for what you've been able to do."

"The poor child. I was glad to help. She's perfectly safe here and will be until—?"

"Eventually, of course, it will be possible for her to leave."

"How is Father—?"

"We no longer communicate, I fear. But I hear he is in good health. In France."

"He has similar duties to your own, then? There were rumours of dissolution…"

"Nobody's perfect."

She was full of sympathy. It was almost as if she restrained herself from reaching across the desk and touching his hand. "The burden…" she murmured.

"It's born of joy."

Her eyes shone. "You have a vocation."

"I'm due for one. I hope so."

"Oh, you have!" Her smooth features were radiant. "You're an inspiration to us all."

He accepted this with modest dignity.

She reached into a desk drawer and produced a ledger. "I regret the formality." She found the appropriate page and offered him the book. He removed a large Mont Blanc fountain pen from his inside breast pocket and signed his name and title in full, giving his usual tasteless flourish to the initials S. and J. She looked with pleasure upon the signature for a moment before putting the book away. She took some keys from the desk. "These are such dangerous times. You risk so much in coming."

"I gain much." Once again he heard the sound of music. This time they were playing Schoenberg's *Pierrot Lunaire*.

"You're too kind."

They left the office, passed the infirmary, descended three flights of steps. Jerry realised, by the artificial lighting, that they were under ground. This passage, with its stout doors at regular intervals on both sides, all painted the same olive green, was much colder. The Mother Superior stopped at the end of the passage, the last door. She unlocked it. "I'll leave you with her. She needs your help. I am so glad…"

"Thank you."

"When shall I…?"

"In two hours."

"Very well." Another admiring, insinuating smile and she had departed. Jerry pushed the door open.

His sister Catherine looked up from her iron-frame bed. A little daylight entered the cell from a small window near the roof, a single exquisite ray, but she had been reading with the help of an electric lamp, its 40-watt bulb shielded by a shade of green glass. She looked much better than when he had last seen her. Her hair was pure blonde again and her skin was rosy. She was wearing her shift and she automatically reached for her white habit, hanging over the chair beside the bed, before she grinned and dropped her hand. She spread her arms wide. He closed the door and bolted it. He stood over her, grinning down, all his lost innocence momentarily restored.

"You don't half look sinister," she said. "What are you playing at today?"

"I'm the tortured priest, aren't I?" With a flourish he removed his shades.

"Did you come to add another sin or two to your conscience?"

He sat down beside her. He hugged her warm, yielding body. "You've really improved."

"I couldn't have had a nicer rest. You told them I had amnesia?"

"To save explanations. Anyway, I was right, in some ways." He bent away from her, studying her face. "Not a bad resurrection job, though I say it myself."

She frowned. "I'm steering clear of hard drugs in the future. It's taught me a lesson. Nothing stronger than coke from now on."

"I think you're wise."

She stroked his hair. "No. You're the wise one. What a lovely pink suit. Omniscient old Jerry."

"Don't say that. You'll bring all my anxieties back." He removed his jacket and threw it on top of her habit, leaning across the bed so that he was resting against the wall. "I must say I envy you the peace and quiet."

"You've never liked peace and quiet."

"I envy it, all the same." He stroked her right breast through the coarse linen of her shift. She seemed unusually disturbed. "Is anything wrong?"

She held his hand against her breast. "I was wondering why you sent that other bloke along to see me. He didn't look like one of your usual friends."

"I didn't send another bloke."

Her lovely shoulders slumped. "The gaff's blown, then. Frank will know where I am now."

"Blokes aren't normally allowed in at all. What did he look like? How did he get in?"

"Fat and oily. Purple shirt. Gaiters. Dog-collar. Definitely clerical gear. Plummy voice. Apparently he was surveying the place for some reason. He knew me. So I realised…"

"Beesley?"

"That's the name."

"Sod." Jerry sighed as he drew off his pink tweed trousers and folded them over the back of the chair. "You're right, Cath. He's Frank's mate. The Bishop of North Kensington. Though how he managed to get to see you is still a mystery."

"Pulled strings." She removed her shift and handed it to him as he unbuttoned his waistcoat. Absent-mindedly he held the shift in one hand and unstrapped his shoulder holster. He put everything in a bundle on the chair and began to remove his shirt and tie, then his socks and underpants. He drew trim brows together. "He's good at pulling strings."

Jerry paused, hands on hips, trying to order his thoughts. Then he glanced up, noticing that her expression had changed to one of open astonishment. Her wide blue eyes stared at his lower torso.

"What's the matter?" he asked her.

"When on earth did you get yourself circumcised?"

In puzzlement he fingered his penis. Vaguely he shook his head, grinning. He shrugged, dismissing the problem as he squeezed in beside her. She switched off the light. The ray of sunshine, like the light from some new-found grail, fell upon their heads. He took her bottom in both his large hands. "You're not the only one prone to amnesia, you know."

2. MATRA UBIQUITY WITH 2ND AND 3RD GENERATION MISSILES

The gate of the convent closed behind him and Jerry adjusted his eyes to the light, resuming his shades, making for his Duesenberg. As he had half-expected, Frank was sitting in the back seat. "Watcher, Jerry. Long time no see." He grinned through the wound-down window, his drug-ravaged lips twisting in peculiar directions. "Your education's certainly coming in useful, these days."

Jerry sighed. He looked down at Frank. "What are you doing here?"

"I was just passing, recognised the motor, thought I'd give you a surprise."

"It's no surprise. I already know your mucker's been in the convent."

"Oh, really? I haven't seen Dennis for ages."

"Get out of my car," said Jerry. "You're coming to bits all over the upholstery. You used to be such a nice young man, too."

"I'm a martyr to science, that's my trouble. I abandoned a lucrative profession in the property business in order to

further my researches and thus become a slave to tempodex."
Frank's skin twitched all over. Then, as Jerry watched, he
changed to the colour of grey flannel. Frank had always had
a penchant towards respectability. "I feel sick."

Jerry opened the door and bundled his brother to the
pavement.

Frank went to lean with one hand against the convent
wall. "Come on, Jerry. Blood's thicker than water."

"Not in your case. There's no need for you to be out
on the street. You've got a home to go to. Several."

"I'm having an identity crisis. How's Catherine?"

"Much better."

"Better? That's funny." Frank pulled his cracked
plastic flying jacket around his shivering chest. His horrid
head lifted like a pointer on the scent. His eyes glazed but
seemed to fix on an invisible target. He began, stiff-legged,
to walk in the general direction of Lancaster Road. "Well,
see you around, Jerry. Got to—um…"

Jerry sank into his car and watched Frank march like
a zombie across Ladbroke Grove and into the Kensington
Park Hotel. The KPH had not been used as a hotel for some
years and was now merely a large pub. Surely Frank hadn't
come down to scoring from dealers in public houses? Jerry
felt that his family pride was under attack but he resisted
the urge to follow. Probably the KPH was no more than
one of Frank's bolt-holes. Doubtless it led somewhere else.

At this, Jerry became suspicious. He recalled a rumour
he had heard from a fourteen-year-old biker speed freak
who had given him a lift when his Phantom had been shot

up by local vigilantes just outside Birmingham. According to the biker there was at least one ancient tunnel running under Ladbroke Grove from the Convent of the Poor Clares. The tunnel, the speed freak had told him, led into all sorts of other dimensions. It was a familiar rumour. A family legend hinted at something similar. Jerry had paid the story very little attention; he had been only too glad that a little romance was coming back into the lives of the younger generation. But now he recalled Bishop Beesley's excuse for visiting the convent. Something about a survey. Perhaps Beesley had had a double purpose for going there.

Jerry stepped out of the Duesenberg with the intention of ringing the bell of the convent but then changed his mind. He had already tipped off Catherine and there was not much else he could do until he found a new hideout for her, at least until her amnesia was completely cleared up.

He returned to the driving seat, started the car, reversed into Ladbroke Grove, drove as far as the KPH, stopped and got out. He entered the pub. Frank was there, talking to a couple of undersized girls who, by the look of their skins and eyes, had been helping him in his experiments. Even as Jerry came in he saw Frank stoop and kiss one of the girls full on the mouth, seeming to suck the last of her substance from her. Now she was in pretty much the condition in which Frank had been a moment or two ago. She stumbled towards the door marked Toilets and disappeared. Frank wiped his mouth and grinned. "Hello, Jerry. What are you having?" He put a seedy elbow on the damp bar and attracted the landlord. "Sid!" Through the gloom came service.

"I thought you might want a lift," said Jerry.

"I've just had one. Two pints, please, Sid," said Frank. "Could you manage to get these, Jerry?"

Jerry put a ten-pound note into the pool of alcohol on the greasy counter. "You know I don't drink beer."

"It's for Maureen." Frank winked at the remaining grey girl. The beer arrived and Frank handed over his brother's money. "You can have Barbara, if you like. When she comes back from the lavatory."

"Well," said Jerry. "Don't you want a lift, then?"

"How far would you be going?"

"How far do you want to go?"

"Get you!" said Frank. "France?"

"Don't be silly."

"I was thinking of taking up residence in the old place. The Le Corbusier château. There's a lot of ideas I've got. Following in Father's footsteps, following the dear old dad. There again I could open it to the public."

Jerry shuddered. "It's not a real Le Corbusier château."

Frank shrugged. "There's no need to be so fucking literal-minded, Jerry."

"I'll take you as far as Dover, if you like."

Frank's eyes narrowed. Mucus seemed to squeeze from the corners. Red irises shifted in decaying sockets. "I wasn't thinking of leaving for a day or so."

Jerry folded his arms. "It's now or never."

"You're right." Frank looked vaguely around for a clock. "It always bloody is."

3. ACQUIRE TARGETS SIMPLY, RELIABLY AND ACCURATELY WITH INLAND DIRECT-DRIVE TRACKING AND GUIDANCE SERVO ELEMENTS

They had reached a compromise. Dropping his brother off at the Army & Navy Club near Waterloo Station, wondering when Frank would try to get hold of Catherine, Jerry drove back to his house in Holland Park Avenue. Frank would almost certainly act in the next couple of days: he ran in old grooves; he would want to take Catherine with him to France. Jerry couldn't blame him. The weather was perfect. There was, in fact, something remarkable about the whole season. He had never known the world so fresh. Jerry smacked his lips.

London was alive with flowers; gigantic hydrangeas and chrysanthemums, monstrous carnations, vast tulips and looming daffodils; sweet williams, peonies, cornflowers, snapdragons, hollyhocks, foxgloves; their scent hung like vapour in the beautiful air. And people were wearing such pretty clothes, listening to such jolly music; the first ecstatic flush of a culture about to swoon, at last, into magnificent decadence, an orgy of mutual understanding, kindness, tolerance and a refusal to maim or kill. Jerry turned on the Duesenberg's stereo and got Jimi Hendrix singing 'Waterfall'. He leaned back, a casual hand on the wheel. The Dubrovnik disease certainly had its compensations. It was all a matter of how you looked at things. As he entered Hyde Park he found other signs of the improving times as gangs of men and women in bright blue municipal uniforms dismantled the gallows on either side of the road. He reached towards the spring-clip on the dashboard and removed the half-full paper cup, swallowing a snazzy fifth of Glen Nevis to unclog the jam of uppers and downers in his throat. For a moment he had an urge to turn back the way he had come and shoot a few pins in Emmett's but decided, after all, to go home. He had to do something about his head lice.

He had stashed the car at the side entrance of his fortress and had walked round the tall white walls and up the steps to the black front door before he saw a movement behind one of the pillars on his right. His hand swam for his needler but dropped. He smiled instead. "Afternoon, Mo."

"'Ullo, Mr C." By way of apology Shakey Mo Collier shrugged in his filthy denim suit. His bright, kitten's eyes, greedy for violence, shifted, and his scrubby moustache and beard twitched like the whiskers of a rogue beast. "Can I come in?"

Jerry put his hand against the print-plate and the door opened. He led the way into a wide, mosaic hall, turning off strobes and substituting limelight. Mo panted behind him muttering to himself. "Oh, fuck. Oh, fuck." He scuttled for a side door and entered Jerry's back parlour, a tangle of electronics and dirty, expensive upholstery. The room was dark, only a little light coming through the thickly curtained French windows. Mo crawled into the comfort of a huge mohair sofa, feeling down its sides for something to sustain him, slipping pills and capsules at random into his mouth. "What's it all about, I ask myself." Quickly he achieved a philosophical equilibrium. "Eh, Mr C?"

Jerry pulled the curtains back a fraction. "You don't mind?" Light sidled into the room.

Mo nodded. "I came with a message, actually. Shades is on the dole and wondered if you had any ideas."

"I thought he was in the States."

"Things have dried up there, as well. You know how fashions change. Last year it was all assassinations, this year it's all sex scandals and religion. Could we have a little music?"

Jerry fiddled with an already glowing console. Faintly Zoot Money's band gave them 'Big Time Operator'.

"That'll do," said Mo. "It doesn't need to be loud. Just there. Anyway, Shades thought you might be looking around."

Jerry smiled. "You have to, don't you, with Shades. Tell him I'll probably be in touch."

Mo nodded. "He says all he needs is a pair of kings."

"It's good news for everyone else." Absently Jerry toyed with a decaying packet of Chocolate Olivers. "Though his interpretations are all his own."

"And I saw Mr Smiles. He says to get in touch sometime. It's about what Simons and Harvey are after, he says."

Jerry shrugged. "All that's in the past." He glanced

through an electron microscope. "Or maybe the future."

Mo had lost interest in the conversation. He began to move slowly about the room, experimentally fingering any loose wires he discovered. "Oh, and I saw your mum in the pub. When was it? Tuesday?"

"Did you tell her I was back?"

"What do you think? But she'd heard you was living around here. She was more interested in knowing where Cathy was."

Jerry smiled at this. "They always were close."

"She said Frank was doing very well for himself but was looking a bit tired. What is he doing with himself, these days, anyway?"

"Services," said Jerry. "Power and communications."

"Only I heard he was dealing."

"It's the same thing, isn't it?"

"Everything is…" Mo returned to the sofa and curled up. He went to sleep. Jerry pulled a huge silver metallic sheet over him to retain what heat was left in his body and headed for the kitchen. He searched amongst the collection of Coronation biscuit barrels and jugs and cottage-shaped teapots until he found the half-full bottle of Prioderm. He climbed the stained white carpet of the curving staircase and went into the bathroom, glad to find that the hot water was working in the shower. He stripped naked and, bottle in hand, stepped into the stall.

Soon his head was engulfed in hellfire.

4. INTRODUCING A NEW DIMENSION OF REALISM IN VISUAL SIMULATORS, VITAL III

Jerry rarely visited his father's fake Le Corbusier château and this was probably the first time he had used the front entrance, but he was in unusually high spirits as he eased his Phantom V up the weed-grown drive and depressed the horn button to let his father's faithful retainer know he had arrived. Beyond the broken outline of the house was the grey Normandy sea. Rain was coming in from England and with it waves of inspirational music interspersed with the babbling voices of that crazed brotherhood of the coast, the pirate deejays. Jerry stepped out of the car and took a deep breath of the cold, moody air. His father—or the man who had claimed to be his father—had died without leaving a will, so Frank (who was convinced that he was both the only legitimate and the true spiritual successor to the old man) had claimed the house and its contents as his inheritance; but John Gnatbeelson swore the dying scientist had bequeathed his roof and its secrets to his namesake Jeremiah (there was even a rumour that old Cornelius had changed his name to Jeremiah soon after his son's birth). The matter had been settled, in Jerry's view, by his letting Frank use the place whenever he wanted to. In spite of the complications, Jerry had been glad that his father had died. It removed an uncomfortable ambiguity. Jerry hated keeping things from his mother.

Before he could put his palm against the print-plate the grey steel door moved upwards and John Gnatbeelson, in tattered Norfolk jacket, grey moleskin britches and scarlet carpet slippers, greeted him awkwardly. He was thin, his cancerous skin given a semblance of life by the many broken blood vessels spreading purple and red beneath it. His chin sprouted a few long, grey wisps of hair, perhaps the remains of a beard, and his cheekbones were set so low as to give his head an oddly unbalanced look. A stooping six foot four, he looked fondly down on his young master who strode into the dark interior. Originally the house had possessed enormous windows, but these were now shielded with steel-plate. As old Cornelius's suspicion of the outside world had increased he had introduced more and more modifications of this sort.

"Have you come to stay, sir?" Gnatbeelson whispered habitually. His former employer had hated the sound of the human voice and had communicated almost entirely by a variety of mechanical means, never leaving his heavily guarded laboratories. Neither Jerry, Catherine or Frank had ever met their father personally, though they had all lived here from time to time. The house trembled with profound and unusual memories; it stank of the experiences of a hundred lifetimes, centuries of technomania tinged with the desperate eroticism of those who cast desperately about for their lost humanity and found only flesh.

"Just a flying visit," Jerry said. "I'd have phoned, but you've been cut off."

"The bill seemed unreasonable, sir. It was all Mr Frank's reverse-charge calls. I did write to you…"

"As long as the generators are working."

"I tested them last week. They're just fine."

"I want you to activate the defences as soon as possible," Jerry told him. He walked rapidly through haunted galleries, Gnatbeelson, his limbs moving irregularly, lolloping in his wake. "Particularly those towers."

"The hypnomats, sir?"

"Set every one at go."

"Are you expecting trouble, Mr Cornelius?"

"From Mr Frank. He's on his way. I don't know what he's up to, but I know it involves this place. He mustn't get in."

"I thought you didn't mind, sir."

"I don't normally."

"Is anything up, sir? Some sort of situation?"

"It's all instinctive. I couldn't really pin it down."

"I've been reading about it in the book, sir. The millennium and so on."

Jerry stopped as the corridor opened onto another gallery. He looked down through filthy light at the scattered shells of computers, their innards spread at random over the large black and white tiles of the floor. "That wasn't here last time." He put his hand on the balustrade, close to a fragment of canvas on which had been painted a patchwork of red, yellow and blue diamond shapes, faintly bloodstained. His foot struck a gilt frame on the floor. "The sod's eaten it!" He was shocked. "Watteau!"

"What ho, sir…" Gnatbeelson's face sagged a little lower. "Mr Frank was looking for something, I think. He kept sucking at those vacuum tubes in the corner. He said the marrow was good for his piles. He's not himself, sir."

"Then who is?" Jerry put the scrap of canvas into his pocket and continued his inspection of the house.

"I'm glad you've decided on a firm line at last, sir." Gnatbeelson's legs bent and straightened, bent and straightened. "I took the liberty of saving one of those books you gave me to put in the furnace. *The Million Spears and the Coming Corruption*. Do you think—?"

"It's lies. It's your moral duty to burn it."

"Then of course I shall, sir. But are you sure this isn't to do with that?"

"It's all a question of how you look at it. What about the reactor?" Jerry peered over the rail of another gallery. Below was a swimming pool, the water stagnant, filled with every kind of rubbish. Something living seemed to move just below the surface. "I've changed my mind. Things are settling down. They've never been better."

"Then why are you so anxious?" The whisper came from miles away but when Jerry turned Gnatbeelson was at his shoulder.

"Because I want to maintain the balance. I've a right to take a few precautions." Jerry was defensive. "What's wrong with that?" He peered down at the far wall. Written in a substance resembling, in colour, the ichor of spent batteries, were the words:

Encore un de mes pierrots mort;
Mode d'un chronique orphelinisme;
C'était un coeur plein de dandyisme
Lunaire, en un drôle de corps.

Jerry became sentimental. "How we loved to luxuriate in terror." There had been good times here, when the three of them had spent their holidays, at play amongst their father's discarded inventions, stretched upon heaps of confused circuits, with a bag of apples and a Wodehouse or a Sade. Simpler, if not sunnier, days.

"I'm in full agreement with you, sir." The old retainer's voice seemed closer now, almost normal. "But why have you rejected all those books out of hand?"

Desperately Jerry rounded on Gnatbeelson, displaying glowing eyes. "Can't you see? It's my last bloody chance to achieve a linear mode!"

5.   NEED ACTUATORS THAT WON'T FREEZE, BURN, DRY OUT, OR BOIL?

It might be 196–, thought Jerry, but the countryside beyond Dover had returned with incredible speed to its medieval state. Kent was wild and beautiful again; so lush that few would have guessed it had sustained and recovered from a major nuclear bombardment during the 'Proof of Good Faith' contests between the major powers. There were disadvantages: poor roads and slow progress; but his car wasn't badly affected, even when it was forced to inch through bramble thickets or cross small patches of ploughed land where angry peasants occasionally appeared, to pelt him with pieces of rock or crude spears. The people of Kent, happy at last in their proper primitive state, were much more at one with themselves.

A fairly unspoiled stretch of road took him close to the remains of Canterbury where skin-clad monks had erected a timber reproduction of the Cathedral, almost the same size as the original. The unseasoned scaffolding still surrounded it and more monks were at work with what was probably liquified chalk, painting the exterior in an effort to make it resemble stone. Elsewhere a project to restore the shopping precinct was in hand; soon Canterbury in facsimile would flourish again: triumph of Man's optimism, of his faith in the future. Jerry hooted his horn and waved, turning up the stereo, to give them a friendly blast of 'Got to Get You into My Life', pursing his lips regretfully as one of the monks lost his footing on the scaffold and fell fifty feet to the ground.

Soon he was nearing London. In the evening light the city was phosphorescent, like a neon wound; it glowed beneath a great scarlet sun turning the clouds orange and purple. And Jerry was filled with a sudden deep love for his noble birthplace, the City of the Apocalypse, this Earthly Paradise, the oldest and greatest city of its Age, virgin and whore, mother, sister, mistress, sustainer of life, creator of nightmare, destroyer of dreams, harbourer of twenty million chosen souls. Abruptly he left the Middle Ages and entered the future, the great grey road, a mile wide at this point, gradually narrowing to its apex at Piccadilly Circus. Now, as night drenched the tall buildings and their lights burst into shivering life, he could again relax in his natural environment.

Against all the available evidence he was betting everything on simple cyclic time, on cause and effect, on karma. He passed through the first toll-check; now the road was covered; its perspex roof reflected the myriad colours of the headlamps below. He took the first exit up to the fast tier and joined the hundred-and-seventy mph stream; within a minute or two he was leaving it again, spiralling down the Notting Hill exit and making for home through the crowded park. The booths and tents of the nightly fair were only, he noticed, doing moderate business. At his favourite roadside fish-and-chip bar he stopped and paid four pounds for a piece of warm carp and some fried reconstituted mashed potato. It had been days since he'd had any real food. He wasn't looking after himself properly. There were too many fresh shadows. He enjoyed the meal, eating it off the passenger seat as he drove, but felt sick afterwards and had to munch a couple of Milky Way bars to make himself better. He was already improving by the time he drove through the back gates of his house and garaged the Phantom beside the Duesenberg.

He went into the house and found his old black car coat, his black flared trousers, his high-heeled boots, his white linen and, as he dressed, he became depressed. It was probably association, he thought. Dark clothes often brought him down. He turned away from the wardrobe, seeking a stereo, and at last found a deck and amplifier where he must have shoved them under an old-fashioned bentwood and china washstand. He switched the kit on. From the ceiling came the miserable, neurotic drone of the Everly Brothers. He let it play, deepening his mood. If a mood was worth having, he thought, it was worth having profoundly.

He went downstairs and turned up some mail which must have come with one of the last runners to get through. There was a letter from Mr Harvey, one of Frank's wholesalers, saying that he had some information which might be useful to Jerry and Mr Smiles, Jerry's sometime business partner. Although he had made at least a million in the last job he was disinclined to work with Mr Smiles again. Smiles usually claimed to have a 'purpose' to his ventures and thus tended to confuse Jerry. He crumpled the letter, wondering why Harvey should wish to double-cross Frank, an excellent customer for any new chemical to come in.

Jerry began to worry about Catherine again. She was his ideal, his goddess, his queen; he loved her and she represented everything else he loved, no matter how she changed, whereas Frank represented everything Jerry hated: greedy hypocrisy. If Frank got hold of Catherine again Jerry knew that he would have to risk repercussions and kill his brother. It would be a shame, since events were just beginning to stabilise into a fixed pattern, like a clockwork train on its little oval track. After a while one got to know the dodgy bits of line. Any deaths at this stage would produce a whole new train set, with all kinds of bends and twists, moebius strips and dead ends: exactly what he was hoping to escape. He gave in to his instincts' demands. He must check to see if Catherine were all right, no matter how irrational the impulse was.

He left the house, taking the Duesenberg to Westbourne Park Road and stopping outside the convent. There was no other traffic. The walls of the convent seemed higher than usual in the darkness.

Against every desire his mind had filled up with prescience, with a knowledge of the futures he refused to accept.

With a groan he went straight over the wall, using the

hooked nylon ladder from the back of the car. He dropped amongst runner-bean poles, scraping his shin, trod as lightly as possible through the flower beds and vegetable patches, crossed the garden, hit his shoulder on the corner of the potting shed, and arrived at the main door. There was some sluggish movement from within, but not much. He got the door open and went inside; raced on tiptoe through the corridors until he came to the top of the flight of stairs leading under ground. So far he had not been spotted by a single nun. He went down the stairs and reached the cold corridor. There were stirrings, now, behind many of the doors; they were conclusive. As he approached, lights went off one by one in the cells until only the light in Catherine's cell remained. Her door was open. He looked in on a discarded habit, an unmade bed, an empty lipstick case, an unread paperback with a cover reproducing an Adolphe Willette poster, the smell of Guerlain Mitsouko. He was too late. Frank had struck already. He would have reached the fake Le Corbusier château just after Jerry left. There would have been no time for John Gnatbeelson to activate the defences. Sister and house were now Frank's.

Jerry howled. His eyes blazed red in the gloom of the convent cell. His lips snarled back from wolfish teeth. An era had ended for him and he was never to know such innocence again.

Rebellion or insurrection, on the other hand, being guided by instinct rather than reason, being passionate and spontaneous rather than cool and calculated, do act like shock therapy on the body of society, and there is a chance that they may change the chemical composition of the societal crystal. In other words they may change human nature, in the sense of creating a new morality, or new metaphysical values.

—Herbert Read,
Revolution and Reason

It is essential to take the greatest pains to rouse the might of the German people by increasing its confidence in its own strength and thus also bringing a stability into the minds of our people to assist their appreciation of political problems. I have often, and I have to add this in speaking to you, felt doubts on one single matter, and that is the following: if I look at the intellectual elements of our society, I think what a pity, unfortunately they are needed; otherwise, one day one might, well, I don't know, exterminate them or something like that. But unfortunately one needs them. If now I take a good look at these intellectual elements and imagine, and check, their behaviour towards me, and towards our work, I feel almost afraid.

—Adolf Hitler, private speech to German Press, Munich, 10 November, 1938 (day after Kristellnacht). S.A.B. Zeman, *Nazi Propaganda*

6. IN THE BEGINNING WAS FLIGHT—TODAY IT'S SECURITY AND SECURITY MEANS CHIEFLY ELECTRONICS

Jerry clambered out of his stockings and suspenders and threw them on top of his Courrèges suit. All he had left now was his perm; he wondered why he had ever thought red hair would suit him. He needed a complete change of identity. He searched through the heaps of clothes he had brought with him to the deserted convent but could find nothing he wanted to wear. He walked the length of the cool guest room, with its hard beds and green radiators, to the pine writing table where he had placed his little Sony cassette player. He pressed the play button. Slow, heavy sounds crept from the speaker; the batteries were exhausted.

He switched off. For a second he thought he had heard footsteps in the passage outside, but it was unlikely that anyone could have traced him here now that London was almost entirely depopulated. The exodus had been a huge success. He touched his forehead, glad to find that his temperature was dropping at last. Whistling, he stirred a skirt with his toe just as the door opened and Miss Brunner came in.

She glanced disapprovingly around at the mess. She wore some kind of standard Slavic peasant costume and had an MG42 tucked under her muscular right arm. Crossing to one of the beds she lowered the heavy machine gun onto the grey blanket which was as neat and clean as the last occupant had left it.

"There's evidently been some confusion," she said. She sat down beside her gun and began to stroke its stock. "What on earth are you doing?"

"I'd heard you were dead—or, at least, transferred." He picked up the nearest pair of underpants—Dayglo yellow—and put them on.

"You more than anyone should know about temporal shifts, Mr Cornelius. Everything's well and truly up the spout." She drew in a sour breath. "I thought I had you under control this time. There's a rumour about your black box, that you've got it back. If that's true you haven't really used it to your advantage, have you, eh?"

"I've been resting." He began to sulk. He found two orange socks that almost matched. He sat opposite her and pulled them onto his grubby feet. "Anyway, if we're being accusatory, what happened to you? I thought we were going to be together always."

"It's your sentimentality I can't stand." She rose like a disturbed wasp, leaving her gun where it was. "It's your main drawback. You could have been a brilliant physicist. If you'd only had a better grip on the scientific method."

"My black box…"

"Your father's invention, and you know it. You

developed it, certainly, but to ends that were completely irresponsible. Think how much better things could be if you hadn't started experimenting for your own amusement rather than for the good of the world."

"People get what they want out of my box."

"What they think they want. And its power source is ludicrous. Utterly wasteful."

"It's not much different to yours."

She clicked her tongue.

"What they think they want is usually what they do want," he added. "Is there anything wrong—?"

"God almighty, you don't know what morality is, do you?"

"I tried to find out. I became a Jesuit…"

She turned over his clothing with her pointed foot. "Is this junk all yours?"

"You can have it, if you like."

"What would I do with it? You've no ambitions, have you, Mr Cornelius? No sense of purpose? No ideals?"

"Since Catherine was killed…"

"I don't think necrophilia counts as an ideal."

"Standards change." Jerry was miserable. "And we're proof enough of that, aren't we? After all, we didn't need to become divided…"

"We've discussed that already. The scheme didn't work out. Too many regressive genes—put us straight back to square one."

He shrugged and stooped to pick up a black T-shirt.

"Everything's fluxed up, thanks to you," she said.

"I had this perfect programme all plotted and ready to go, then suddenly the co-ordinates are haywire. I didn't need to make too many enquiries to find out where the interference was coming from. I had to abandon the whole programme because you were playing games with your silly little box."

"Well, you needn't worry. I haven't got it any more."

"It's too bloody late now, isn't it! Where is it?"

"I lost it. Or lent it."

"You're lying."

"I had a touch of my old trouble. Didn't you have it, recently? Paramnesia? Paramnesia?"

"That wouldn't—"

"Then it developed into ordinary amnesia. I'm not even sure how I got here. There was a party at Holland Park…"

"I don't know what you're talking about," she said.

"Then maybe it hasn't happened to you yet," he told her reasonably. He paused to think. "Or maybe it hasn't happened to any of us yet. Maybe it won't happen, after all."

"Oh, you shifty little sod."

"That's another thing I was wondering about…"

"I came here to try to clear up the confusion." She found a wallet and began to search through it, emptying company credits and luncheon vouchers onto the floor. She turned a fifty million mark silk banknote in her fingers and absently touched it to her lips, licking it. "Why did you choose this mausoleum, anyway?"

"I forget."

"You usually stay with your mother in a crisis." She

picked up another wallet. It contained nothing but a bundle of overstamped Rhodesian guinea-notes.

"Is she around?"

"Apparently."

"I'm tired." He reached for her gun.

"Steady on, Mr Cornelius." She became alarmed.

"I only wanted to look at it. I've hardly ever seen one. Are they still making them?"

"How should I know?" She shook out the pockets of a black velvet jacket and began carefully to inspect each worn piece of paper. "Where are your own weapons, by the way?"

"In store somewhere." He was vague. "Do you want to look at them?"

"Certainly not." She had discovered a huge perfectly cut diamond and was holding it up to the green-shaded light bulb. "This is real." She inspected the facets, one by one. "Where did you get it?"

"It's only a model." He put his legs into a pair of purple bells.

7.   OPTICS FOR DEFENCE

Grass and moss were growing over the paving stones of Westbourne Park Road. Jerry saw Miss Brunner to the gate and took in the scenes of soft decline, much more congruent, at last, with the rural atmosphere of the convent's garden. Even the air was relatively fresh. "It's lovely now, isn't it?" He watched her walk to her Austin Princess. "It smells so rich."

"Stagnation's no substitute for stability." She wrenched open the car's door. "I hope you're pleased with yourself." From behind the façade of deserted houses on the opposite side of the street a few small dogs barked. "It's going to take England a long time to get back on her feet. And as for the rest of the world…" She entered the car. He saw her through the clouded glass as, aggressively, she put the engine into gear. For someone who had so much to do with machines she displayed a stern hatred for most of them. He waved as she swerved into Ladbroke Grove, still puzzled as to why she had taken the laundry box with her; it had been full of his old junk—a broken watch, tickets, empty matchbooks, old calendars, torn notebooks, catalogues, useless maps, out-of-date maintenance manuals; all had gone into her box. Perhaps she thought she could feed the information into a new computer and thus reproduce his lost memory. He was quite grateful to her; there was nothing, he felt, of his past he wished to retain. He had been glad to offer her his clothes and tapes, but she had declined most of them with the air of someone who had already researched them thoroughly. Deciding against returning to his room, he locked the gate behind him and walked round to Blenheim Crescent, peering up at his mother's flat as he passed but making no effort to see if she was still there. He was sure that Mrs Cornelius, of all people, wouldn't have moved. He turned left at the antique shop with its smashed windows, its contents scattered on the pavement, where Sammy, his mother's lover, had once sold pies, into Kensington Park Road. Assegais, brass microscopes, elephants' feet, bits of sixteenth-century armour, the innards of clocks, broken writing chests, Afridi rifles inset with copper and mother-of-pearl, their stocks crumpled by woodworm, rotting books and fading photographs lay in heaps all across the street, exuding a sweet, musty smell that was not unpleasant. He entered Elgin Crescent, going towards Portobello Road, and found a shop that had once specialised in theatrical costumes and musical instruments. The door was ajar and the bell rang as he entered. Most of the costumes were still intact, in boxes or on hangers depending on racks from both sides of the showroom. He tried on the full dress uniform of a captain in the 30th Deccan Horse, discarded it. He dressed himself as Zorro, as Robin Hood, as Sam Spade. He tried the Buffalo Bill outfit and felt a little more at ease in it; he forced himself into a lurex Flash Gordon, a Sherlock Holmes deerstalker and ulster, a Zenith the Albino dress suit, a Doctor Nikola set, a Captain Marvel costume, even a Tarzan loincloth; a suit of motley, a Jester, seemed better, but he was seeking security at present, so he also discarded the Harlequin trickster set, but eventually decided upon an elaborate black-and-white satin Pierrot suit, the main colour being black, the pom-poms, ruff and cuffs being white, the skull-cap being white also, a reverse of the usual arrangement. He was pleased with his appearance. He found a pure white wig, perhaps originally for an old lady character, and put this on under his skull-cap. As an afterthought he picked up some greasepaint and blacked his face and hands then, for an hour, he sat in front of the long mirror playing a Walker five-string banjo to himself, raising his spirits still further: *On the road to Mandalay-ee, Where the flying fishes play-ee...* It was all so much more comfortable than the stockings, suspenders and girdle of his earlier disguise, so much more tasteful than the bright colours of a vanished youth. Indeed, it was the nicest of any of the disguises he had assumed since his boyhood. Nobody made any demands on a pierrot. All in all things weren't looking too bad, really.

"Hide your tears behind a smile." He sang blithely as he searched through the wicker baskets. "Hide your fears inside a file." He found two or three more Pierrot costumes, two Harlequins, a Columbine and some masks, and bundled them all into a hessian sack.

He had decided, once his new equipment was installed, to open up the convent as a kind of health-farm. Sooner or later London would come back to a version, at least, of its old self, and this time he would be ready for it.

He paused once more beside the mirror. "I could be happy with you," he sang, "if you could be happy with me." He gave himself a big kiss and left a smear of make-up on the glass.

8. THE BL 755 CLUSTER BOMB IS HIGHLY EFFECTIVE AGAINST TANKS AND OTHER ARMOURED VEHICLES, AIRCRAFT, TRANSPORT, PATROL BOATS AND PERSONNEL

The convent was coming along a treat. Jerry had signed a formal lease for the place and had been lucky enough to secure the services of some ex-nuns. He had left the outside pretty much as it had always looked, but the buildings inside had been thoroughly restructured. Now wide picture windows looked out into old English gardens where pious and apple-cheeked Poor Clares worked with hoe and rake as they had worked since time immemorial. Jerry expected his first customers soon. So far his only client had been his financial backer, his sister's friend Constantin Koutrouboussis, the young Greek millionaire who had inherited the family business on the death of his older brother Dimitri. Koutrouboussis was rarely satisfied with anything but miracles and Jerry hadn't been in business long enough to gain experience enough to provide them. But when the Americans started arriving things should look up.

Koutrouboussis stopped off one day, on his way

through to his Soho headquarters. He was carrying a new line in riding crops and was keen to show one to Jerry. "Look at that!" He swished it through the beam of dusty sunlight which entered Jerry's spacious office by way of the half-closed blind. "The secret's in the weight of the handle."

Jerry was searching white plastic drawers in his desk. Of late he had affected a great deal of white. He wore a surgeon's smock at this moment, and a chef's hat. It contrasted nicely with his freshly stained skin. "What?"

"The handle." Koutrouboussis put the crop back in his case. "How's your sister keeping, by the way?"

"Oh, all right. I checked this morning."

"Are you sure——?"

"There are no certainties in this business, Mr K."

"I suppose there aren't. A science in its infancy."

"It'll stay that way, if I have anything to do with it," Jerry promised. "Adult science doesn't seem to produce a satisfactory variety of results."

Mr Koutrouboussis fingered his new beard. His hands wandered down to his expensive collar, his neat lapels, his dapper buttons. "You won't tell the clients that?" He moved towards the wall and stared at the tastefully framed French prints showing characters from the *commedia dell'arte*.

"There aren't any clients for our kind of science. You're too much of a cynic for this sort of clinic…" Jerry stopped himself quickly and inspected his watches. "A drink? I've a wide selection of Scotches…" He gave up.

"No time."

Jerry wondered why Koutrouboussis always made

him feel aggressive. Maybe it was the tension the man carried with him; it could even be that Jerry resented his financial involvement, his power.

Mr Koutrouboussis reached the door and lifted his gloved hand in a moody wave. "No time."

"I'll be seeing you," said Jerry.

Koutrouboussis chuckled to himself. "At this rate you'll be raising me, too. Cheerio for now, Mr Cornelius." As an afterthought he said from the passage: "And if you should discover the identity…"

"I'll let you know."

"I would be grateful."

Jerry put his elbows on his desk and rubbed at his face. One thing was certain: he was under an obligation and it was making him uncomfortable. Then he consoled himself with the knowledge that Koutrouboussis was no idealist. His interest in the whole affair was connected with Catherine alone and justified by a profit motive. If Jerry was going to make his clinic in any way successful he would have to forget both his sister and her admirer for a while. He was sure he was on the right track this time around. He had found hope again. If these new machines couldn't beat the human condition then nothing could.

A tasty young nun knocked and entered. "You're looking tired, sir. You've so much on your shoulders."

He straightened his back. Automatically he checked his lapels for nits. "Lice," he murmured, to explain.

"The world is full of them, sir. But the truth shines through."

He glanced at her faithful face. "The trouble is," he said, "that we're all at least a hundred and fifty years old. How many generations need to comply in a fallacy before it becomes accepted as truth?"

She was untroubled. "Can I bring you a nice cup of tea, doctor?"

"It would certainly help."

"Your machines…"

"They're not oracles, you know. They just get rid of the demand for oracles. Abolish the future and you lose the need for faith. Familiarity, by and large, banishes fear…" He clutched, again, at his head. "I wish I knew how the damned things worked."

"I was going to say. They're moaning again."

"They haven't got enough to do."

"Soon," she reassured him.

"The whole idea is that we should do away with 'Tomorrow'…"

"I'll make the tea immediately." The door closed on her whispering gown.

He got up and drew the blind so that he could see into the quiet garden. "Heritage. Inheritance. The secret's in the genes. Chromosomes. Chronos zones. It always comes down to those fucking flat worms." He really needed a chemist at that moment, but he was buggered if he was going to bring his brother back. Frank would have a vested interest in the status quo; his whole identity depended on its preservation. The same could be said for Miss Brunner and the rest. He couldn't blame them. They thought they were fighting for their lives.

The phone began to ring.

He uttered a disbelieving laugh.

9. THE STRIM ANTITANK ROCKET LAUNCHER IS LIGHT (4.5 KG), ACCURATE (VERY HIGH SINGLE SHOT HIT AND KILL PROBABILITY), EASY TO USE, LOW-COST INSTRUCTION— NO MAINTENANCE, NO OVERHAUL ... COMPLEMENTARY ROCKETS, SMOKE/INCENDIARY, 1,000 METERS, ILLUMINATION, 100 TO 2,000 METERS, ANTIPERSONNEL, UP TO 2,000 METERS

With only a few reservations Jerry watched the new arrivals as they were herded from the big white bus through the narrow gates of the convent. There were only three men; all the others were women under thirty—or, at least, they resembled women. Some of the patients, he gathered, had already made a few faltering steps towards a crude form of self-inflicted transmogrification, some of it involving quite terrifying surgery.

He had decided not to present himself to his patients until the evening, during the Welcome Ceremony (which would be held in the ballroom, once the twin chapels) since, at this stage, he would be bound to make them feel self-conscious. Even as the white bus disappeared into the new underground garage a black Mercedes two-tonner took its place, unloading amplifiers and instruments, music for the ball. He stepped back from his window. As the population increased, so, in direct proportion, would his clients. He went over to his new console, turning the master switch to make every television monitor screen work at once, showing a clinic now satisfyingly busy. He was particularly pleased with the way in which the nuns had adapted to their new nursing work. He looked for a moment at the reception desk where guests were cautiously signing their names (mostly fictitious) in the gold-embossed green leather register. Their faces, haunted by hope and anxiety, were familiar to him. For many of them the treatment, even if partially successful, could not come too soon.

The thing he was looking forward to, however, was the ball. It had been a long while since the Deep Fix had played together. As soon as he could he would go down for the soundcheck. It would be good if he could get some rehearsing in before the event.

His eye was drawn back to the screen. He was sure he had seen the old military-looking character quite recently. He recognised the frayed cuffs. "We are all offered a selection of traditional rôles," he murmured. "The real problem lies in finding a different play. In the meantime we attempt to console as many of the actors as possible by finding them the parts in which they can be as happy as possible." His voice was carried over the PA to all parts of the building, interrupting the Muzak.

"You're becoming a regular telly freak, ain't ya, Mr C."

Shakey Mo Collier now stood there, arms folded, most of his weight on one leg. He was wearing a yellow-and-red paisley shirt, a light suède waistcoat, filthy with the remains of a thousand fruitful meals, a tattered green-and-blue Indian silk scarf, patched and faded jeans and scuffed cowboy boots with white decoration. His hair was longer than when Jerry had last seen it and he had grown a mandarin moustache. Jerry was pleased to see him. "Where have you been, Mo? The first I heard you were around was when someone brought me your postcard."

"I've been asleep, haven't I?" said Mo. "Up in the Lake District mostly. It's nice up there. Good roads. Plenty of shale. All dead. Lovely. You want to go."

"I know it. Grasmere. Daffodils and dope. Or that's the way it used to be."

Mo was unusually astute. "That scene's shifted, hadn't you heard? To Rydal. But the best days are over."

"Well, a word's not worth much these days. I heard the town had gone all chintzy."

"Quincey?"

"Chintzy."

They giggled together. Mo sat down on the posh carpet, cross-legged, and began to roll himself a joint. "Anyway you seem to be doing all right with this lot."

"I can't complain. There's no profit in it, though."

"Aren't they paying?"

"All the takings go to my sleeping partner, Mr Koutrouboussis."

"Well, well." Mo licked his papers. "So, really, you

could leave here any time you liked?"

"I've got responsibilities, Mo."

Mo looked at him in some disappointment. "Blimey!"

"How long has the group been back together?"

"Not long. We all met up in Ambleside. Tried out a few things—acoustically, of course. You can get some of those old reed organs to sound just like electronics if you work at it. But we needed power, so we trucked back to London, hoping we'd find some. Of course we hadn't realised everything was coming alive again. We picked just the right time, for once. We must be the only beat group around. We're getting a lot of work. Too much, really. The tensions…"

"It's done your ego a lot of good," said Jerry. "You're your old cocky self again."

"Thanks. I feel cocky. Yes." His grease-stained fingers explored a waistcoat pocket for a match. He lit his joint. "I just wish they'd bring back the money system. All this fucking bartering's getting beyond a joke. Half our wages rot before we can eat them and we can't trade them because nobody's got the kind of stuff we need."

"I don't know what you want."

"Cheap tat, of course. And weapons. Just like the old days. Colour tellies. But don't worry. This gig's free."

"We've got a few new drugs."

"Nar," said Mo. "We're not into drugs any more. Well, not at the moment, anyway. We're into beer."

"You don't mind me…?"

"Smashing. It'll be like the Friendly Bum days. You remember?"

"My memory isn't what it was."

"It's a fucking opium den now. For the tourists."

"I've been staying away from the centre. My work..."

"Oh, sure." Mo was suddenly embarrassed. Hesitantly he offered Jerry the joint.

Jerry enjoyed a drag. He went to sit on the ledge of the open window, looking towards Blenheim Crescent then up into the sharp blue sky. "I think we should see an improvement, soon. It's a bit early, though." He cocked an ear to the east, detecting a whine. He smiled. "They're here, at last."

Mo joined him at the window as the first black wave of Starlifters shrieked in at minimum altitude, banking slowly until they had located Heathrow.

"Far out!" said Mo in delight, as soon as his voice could be heard. "Those jobs carry over a hundred and fifty troops apiece. There are thousands coming in. Oh, it's all going to liven up! The Yanks are back!"

Jerry moved to the intercom. He must warn his staff to be ready for the extra volume.

10. RAPIER, ULTRA LOW-LEVEL AIR DEFENCE SYSTEM IN SERVICE WITH THE BRITISH ARMY AND RAF REGIMENT, ORDERED BY THE IMPERIAL IRANIAN GOVERNMENT, LIGHTWEIGHT, DIRECT-HITTING MISSILE, HIGH KILL-TO-ENGAGEMENT RATIO, OPTIONAL "ADD-ON" BLIND RE UNIT, OUTSTANDING COST-EFFECTIVENESS

Jerry rubbed more of the dye into his skin, regretting once again that his machines simply weren't up to handling his own problem. It was high time that they were overhauled, anyway, since the convent had been placed off-limits to all advisory forces: though it had only been civilian auxiliaries who had been coming in the first place; patronising the clinic now counted, on General Cumberland's orders, as fraternisation with hostile personnel.

Jerry couldn't complain. It meant he could expand his own activities if he wished. In the meantime the money system had been reintroduced, Koutrouboussis had been paid back and was receiving an excellent dividend; Jerry was no longer beholden to the Greek who had, on his own initiative, formed a consortium together with his younger brother Spiro, to exploit the Cornelius patents worldwide, offering Jerry a flat commission on every client, including those who wished to change nationalities as part of their transmogrification. Jerry intended to take more of an interest in this international aspect of the enterprise now that the original clinic was running so well. Spiro, by mutual consent, would act as chief liaison man.

When he had finished with his face he picked up a tangled sheaf of traumograph printouts, leaving black smudges on the semi-opaque paper, and crammed them into one of his desk drawers. He was wearing a white German suit, black shirt and no tie, as part of his current disguise. His hair was bleached bone white. For the moment, too, he had discarded his needle gun and wore the more comfortable vibragun which, he felt, was a trifle better in tune with the zeitgeist. Currently, he felt, the world could accept any ambiguities so long as he retained a certain dramatic resolution to events.

He left the office and strolled through his pale blue corridors, amiably greeting his nuns, nurses and doctors as he passed them. Most of them had already made preparations to leave for the country; only a skeleton staff was to be retained in London.

His Phantom VI was already at the gate, its motor running. He stepped into the driving seat and drove up Westbourne Park Road, turned right into Kensington Park Road, heading for Notting Hill and beyond.

He arrived in Church Street just in time to see a silver Cadillac disappearing into Holland Street. The area was otherwise deserted of cars, although a few M-75 armoured personnel carriers were parked here and there, their crews lazily giving his Phantom the once-over as it went by. He turned into Kensington High Street and parked outside Derry & Toms which he had acquired only recently in the deal granting Koutrouboussis full control of European exploitation rights on his father's original patents. Jerry disembarked and entered.

Within, the department store was hushed as usual: middle-aged women moved slowly from counter to counter; murmuring assistants in dove-grey uniforms addressed them respectfully. When reopening the store Jerry had made it clear to his staff that only a certain sort of customer was to be encouraged. He had always been very strong on tradition.

He took the lift to the sunny tranquillity of the roof garden and crossed a few feet of crazy paving to enter the restaurant whose wall, facing the gardens, was completely of glass. He was keeping an illicit rendezvous with Captain Hargreaves. He sat at his usual table, completely alone, for the restaurant had not begun to serve lunch, watching the pink flamingoes wading about in the tiny rivers and fountains, listening to the whistlings and chirrupings of the less flamboyant birds in the foliage.

Any intimations of trouble which he might have had during his drive here were now dispersed. He relaxed and looked over his shoulder to see Captain Hargreaves, very smart in tailored olive fatigues, come through the plate-glass doors. He stood up, smiling. He pulled back a chair and Captain Hargreaves sat down.

"Thanks. I got that stuff for you. Gnatbeelson's alive and in London."

Jerry resumed his chair. He frowned. "What about his memory?"

"It's a typical case of amnesia—of the sort you described to me. He believes his name to be Beale. And, as you guessed, he's taken a job in a library."

"The books are there?"

"At least one copy of *Time Search*."

"Then it's conclusive." Jerry leaned forward and slid a friendly fingernail along the inside of Captain Hargreaves's thigh. "Do you want lunch now?"

Captain Hargreaves's hand fell on Jerry's. "Afterwards, I think."

"There might not be time. They know where I am—or should do."

"I'm not too hungry." The captain reached into a large satchel and drew out a piece of paper. "The address."

Jerry tucked the paper down inside his holster, rising slowly. "Give me a moment. I've got to change my clothes. I'll join you in the Dutch garden, if you like."

"Okay." Captain Hargreaves stood up, kissing him on the cheek. "You'll be quick?"

"Don't worry."

But he was frowning as he went through the back of the restaurant into the cloakroom and began slipping into the costume he kept there.

There was no doubt about it, he thought. Things were looking black for the English assassin.

EARLY REPORTS

Editors: Hitler stopped too soon! He should have gotten rid of the Ginzburgs and the Borosons and a lot more like you. Indeed we should have a Hitler in America to rid the country of the merchants of filth, pervertors and corruptors of morals, and muckrakers!

—Mrs John W. Red,
Memphis, Tennessee;
letter to *Fact*, Jan/Feb 1965

Contrary to the national trend, crime decreased in the Notting Hill area last year.

Kensington Post, 8 January, 1965

The one thing you can say about Hitler is that he was a damned sight more pro-British than M. Pompidou.

—Kingsley Amis,
Speakeasy (BBC Radio), 18 July, 1971

Even in these enlightened days cancer continues to be a disease evoking dread and horror in the general public. Perhaps because of this peculiar emotional response to cancer, quite unlike that seen with other diseases, there has always been a fringe of unorthodox practitioners specialising in unusual treatments to lead to dramatic "cures".

—M.A. Epstein,
Times Literary Supplement, 16 January, 1976

Hammersmith Palais

242 SHEPHERDS BUSH ROAD W6   01 748 2812

World Premiere

FRIDAY 13 FEB   8pm–2am

Sex Equality Dancing

Where men dare not refuse
Ladies! Pick your man!
Don't miss this night
of Liberation

**THIS TICKET ADMITS TWO
FOR THE PRICE OF ONE**

TUNING UP (3)

"I feel like a right ponce." Jerry climbed gingerly into the large rowing boat, seating himself in the stern, glaring miserably at the misty lake. The boat's name was on the backrest behind him: *Morgana le Fey*. He arranged the skirt of his lilac jacket around him; he plucked at the knees of his lilac flares to reveal daffodil socks, daffodil cuffs; he was cold.

"Well, I think you look lovely." Karen von Krupp unshipped the oars, handing one pair to Miss Brunner, one to Una Persson. "Doesn't he?" she asked the others.

"Lovely." Una Persson's back was to him but Jerry could imagine her expression. Miss Brunner, in russet Ossie Clarke battledress with matching boots and bush-hat, was silent. She seemed to think that Doktor von Krupp should be doing some of the rowing.

"I wish you'd all stop taking the piss out of me. I've had a hard time of it." Moodily, Jerry tugged at a tiller line. "Who's going to shove off?"

Karen von Krupp signed to Mitzi Beesley; Mitzi was

to remain on the bank as lookout until they returned. She pouted and swung her customised Winchester .270 over her shoulder, lifting her white Dorothee Bis skirt to her thighs so that she could wade into the shallows, feet protected by Paulin espadrilles. The mother-of-pearl in the rifle's stock clashed a trifle with her skirt as the butt bounced against an angry bottom and Jerry felt her heavy breath on his head as she shoved. The boat shifted a little in the shingle. Mitzi pushed blonde Marcel-waved hair back from her face and tried again. Gradually her face grew almost scarlet to match her horrible Maple Red Max Factor mouth. Karen von Krupp rocked the boat at the other end. Suddenly they all slid out into the lake and Mitzi waved her arms, barely recovering her footing. Petulantly she waded back to the shore and swung the Winchester into both hands. She kept her spine displayed to them. She wasn't much for vocalising her displeasure. In reply to Mitzi's gesture Doktor von Krupp wrapped her dove-grey C&A trench coat more firmly around her large body. "That way," she said, gesturing beyond the reeds in the direction of the island, a dim outline, already being obscured by the thickening mist, in the middle of the lake. "Are you sure you know how to steer, Jerry dear?"

Jerry dragged the line hard over so that the boat moved suddenly to starboard.

"We don't need demonstrations from anyone else today, Mr Cornelius." Miss Brunner was panting. "I think we're sitting the wrong way round, by the way."

Una Persson had first pointed this out when they had

entered. But she remained as patient as ever. Una wore her usual lightweight khaki under an open black maxi-coat; though the coat tended to hamper her movements, she was evidently reluctant to remove it. Crouching, she turned herself carefully so that she was looking up at Jerry. She winked grey eyes, first one, then the other, and sat down again, taking hold of the sweeps. Behind her, Miss Brunner swivelled, much more awkwardly, her legs held by her red-brown midi. Her long bottom struck the seat somewhat heavily and the boat responded dramatically, rocking from side to side, shipping a little water to port. "I don't think much of this thing's construction," she said. Then they were rowing again.

"Let's try to keep the same rhythm this time, shall we?" Miss Brunner hissed as one of her oars reared from the water, weed dripping from its blade.

The morning was very misty. They moved through a strip of clear water between thick reeds, not yet on the lake proper, but already the heavily wooded bank was invisible. Some ducks flapped low over the grey surface, as if trying to keep below the mist-line. A light drizzle formed rather than fell around them. They rowed into shrouded silence, their own sounds muffled.

"You're the only one of us familiar with the island, Herr Cornelius," said Doktor von Krupp. "You'll have to keep us on course." She picked up the Remington 700 Mitzi Beesley had loaned her and placed it carefully across her knees. Both Miss Persson and Miss Brunner were armed with identical Smith and Wesson .45 revolvers. Jerry had a heater on one hip, his vibragun on the other hip and his needler under his armpit, but none of these gave him much sense of security.

"I hope we bloody find something after all this." Miss Brunner had caught another crab. Una Persson leaned on her oars as she waited for the woman to start rowing again. Jerry was glad of her friendly, resigned face, even though it had been Una who had tipped the others off about the island (but it had been Mitzi Beesley who had tracked him down to where he had hidden his naked body in Gaping Gill pot on Ingleborough in the West Yorkshire Pennines, and Miss Beesley and Karen von Krupp who had dressed him in this outfit before he had had a chance to revive; he was still not quite sure what was going on). Una seemed somewhat regretful. She wiped the clinging moisture from her cheeks with the back of her hand—a mixture of mist and sweat. It was playing hell with the others' make-up.

The boat began to move again. Jerry couldn't remember what they were looking for on the island. He knew that something important had happened there once, perhaps to him, perhaps in his childhood, and he could certainly remember the stone barn very well (he had always been curious about the function of the place), but the rest was mysterious. "There was a sun once," Miss Brunner had said, just as he had woken up. Or had she said "son"? He glanced into the water, seeking the source of the bad smell, like dead fish. Terror blossomed in the back of his brain. He tried to speak but could not. He searched the cold mist. There was no escape.

The three women were all staring directly at him, each lost in her own thoughts, as the boat moved on through the Grasmere clouds.

He looked down at his hands; he realised for the first time that they had turned a funny colour. The pain in his spine made him want to bend double, to go on all fours. He grunted. His nostrils shivered. A small primitive noise formed in the back of his throat.

"Oh, God," said Miss Brunner. "It's starting again."

DEVELOPMENT

Poor Gauchelin was much alarmed by his
experience, but as time went on—at any rate in
France—the Hunt lost some of its terrors, and
the wailing procession of lost souls turned into a
troupe of comic demons who flew merrily through
the air to the sound of song and of tinkling bells.
Nor did it always remain a mere nebulous, ghostly
phenomenon. I have suggested, elsewhere, that
the mummery probably originated as a miming
of a Wild Hunt led by a certain Mormo, a child-
devouring ogress of Greek origin, not unlike Perchta,
the mythical patroness of the Perchton. That the
Harlequin-Cornelius troupe was also sometimes
mimed is suggested by the fact that it makes a
partial appearance in Adam de la Halle's *Jeu de la
Feuillée*, which, as we have seen, had for its central
theme the entertainment of fairies by the citizens
of Arras. "Already I hear the Harlequin-troupe
approaching," cries Croquesot (Biter-of-fools),

"a little bearded man", who having cheerfully
enquired of the audience whether his "hairy phiz"
doesn't become him well, proceeds to woo the fairy
Morque on behalf of his mighty master Cornelius,
the Harlequin, who, though still supernatural, has
obviously developed into a more substantial and
more comic figure than his ancestor, the demonaic
leader of lost and wandering souls.

—Enid Welsford,
The Fool, ibid.

The jingle-cap is such a great grinner,
He will dance for you, not well, but with vigour,
His jingle-head full of coloured beads.

—Maurice Lescoq,
Posthumous Poems

Triomphe et que l'envie en crevie de depir,
Brave Arlequin queton nom plein de gloire
Soit, pour test faits, ton bel esprit,
A l'avenir en lettres d'or ecrit
Dans la temple de la memoire.

The Stage's Glory, ibid.

FAIRY BENIGNA: Poor Afric's children sigh for liberty.
Alas! That task was not reserved for me.

Furibond; or, Harlequin Negro, Drury Lane, 1807

NOTTING HILL DOOMED TO BE RACIAL BATTLEFIELD

The 1962 Commonwealth Immigrants Act came immediately after the racial troubles from campaigns against immigrants from the West Indies, Africa and Asia. One of the centres of racial violence then, and earlier, was Notting Hill; indeed this area's name is now almost synonymous with racial prejudice ... Notting Hill seems doomed to be the battlefield of racial discrimination: the Government's White Paper will not stop the battle. But sense and responsible reaction from the people against whom legislation is directed should at least let us know what the causes of the war really are.

Kensington Post, 3 September, 1965

I. SEVEN YEARS FOR BANK-RAID VICAR

From Sumatra it wasn't too hard to get back to Sandakan and something like sanity, though the sari could not safely be abandoned until he could look down on his yellow palace, last remnant of a great personal empire, his inheritance, in the dark green hills above the desert harbour. Quite a lot of jungle had grown around the building since he had last visited it; trees and architecture were rounded, their contours softened by the hazy light, seeming to merge, and in the distance were the great blue and purple mountains of the island's interior, the "real Borneo" as Major Nye had once termed it. To see if there were any signs of danger Jerry flew twice over the red and grey town. There were a few steamers at anchor against the broken concrete of the quays; some were already sinking into the emerald water, others were entirely discoloured by rust. On the quay he saw three isolated figures looking up at his giant Dornier DoX flying boat. Perhaps they recognised the sound of the twelve Curtiss Conqueror engines spluttering and misfiring around him as usual. He flew out to sea towards the Philippines, to make a wide turn so that he could begin his landing approach. He now wore a white one-piece flying suit, trimmed with ermine, gold-trimmed goggles and a white kid helmet. He had always been expected to show a little face in Sandakan.

The plane began to drop too steeply. Jerry pulled her up a bit; she responded as poorly as usual, but he managed to keep to his original path until he was almost on top of the broken mouth of the harbour. The Dornier's huge floats touched tranquil water, bounced, swerved; he was taxiing between sagging, extinguished light-towers, forcing his heavy craft away from the protecting walls which formed an almost perfect circle and towards the mass of rotting steamers and waterlogged fishing sampans, the deserted houseboats and the junks. It began to occur to him that he had not been paying attention to his real responsibilities. He let the flying boat drift in crabwise until it was bobbing against the side of a junk which seemed relatively intact. He shut off the engines and clambered from the door of the cockpit onto the forward floats, clutching a strut to keep his balance as the machine rocked badly, and from the floats boarded the junk, testing its timbers carefully as he crossed the deck to walk slowly down a bouncing, flaking gangplank still resting on the quay. Empty mouldering buildings presented themselves to him, a mixture of Victorian Gothic and Malaysian-Dutch stucco. Rats watched from ledges and windows. Sadly he walked up the hill, through ruined streets where timber-merchants' and rubber-planters' offices, shipping companies, importers, exporters, chandlers, money-lenders, insurance brokers, restaurants, bazaars, stall-holders, silk-sellers, paper mask sellers, puppet sellers, sellers of acrid pastries, savoury dumplings, sweetmeats, carved wooden boxes and birdcages, had flourished in lazy competition.

Now a few starved Chinese and Dyak faces disappeared from doorways as he passed by. It was evident that nobody recognised him in his new costume and this saddened him.

The gates of the palace, which stood on its own hill outside the town, were slabs of grey marble on slender white tapering posts. They were exactly as he had left them, their pristine carvings and decoration reflecting a strong Islamic influence. He took a large key from his pocket and with considerable difficulty turned it in the great iron lock, pushing the gates open to find richer colours within. The gravel drive had been freshly raked and the lush shrubs had been trimmed and tended. Even the fountains of the ornamental lake were playing, perfectly orchestrated. Clear water rippled against a background of jade and lapis lazuli. Exotic birds looked carelessly at him as they dragged their glinting plumage about the perfect lawns where bowls, croquet and even cricket had been played in the old days. He reached the house, with its three terraced verandahs, climbing quartz steps between monstrous tigers and dragons of coloured ceramic and polished limestone, noting that the bronze doors, only recently dosed with considerable quantities of Brasso so that it hurt his eyes to look at them, were open, as if in welcome. The doors were twice his height; he pushed them back a fraction and squeezed through, entering the cool shadows of his palace, pausing in the very centre of the hall's bright mosaic floor, facing towards the main staircase, of graduated shades of marble. There was no dust. He cleared his throat. There was a discreet echo.

"Dassim Shan?"

His major-domo did not appear. The deities of a dozen different faiths, bronze, ebony, porcelain, regarded him, some glowering, some tranquil, from alcoves. Diffracted light, entering through coloured patterned glass set close to the ceiling, filled the hall with delicate shadows.

Jerry took a step or two towards the stairs, then paused, hearing a movement overhead in the gallery behind him. A light but perfectly pitched voice, a bitter-sweet voice sang:

"Oh, Limehouse kid, oh, Limehouse kid, going the way that the rest of them did. Poor broken blossom who's nobody's child. Haunted and taunted, you're just kind of wild. Oh, Limehouse blues, I've the real Limehouse blues, learnt from the Chinese those sad China blues. Rings on my fingers and tears for a crown, that is the story of Old China Town..."

Languid as one of the peacocks outside, Una Persson leaned against the carved marble balustrade. She wore a long Molyneaux evening gown of the thinnest yellow silk and her hair was cut short in a coolie crop with a fringe at an angle on her forehead, framing her oval face, emphasising her ironic grey eyes. She began to move as he looked up. She was smoking a cigarette without a holder.

Jerry had never seen her like this. "What?"

The gown caused her to stride in a peculiar swaying gait. She walked round the gallery, her heels ticking, until she came to the stairs. "Shall I come down?" she spoke softly, laying a significant hand on the balustrade.

Jerry scratched his head under his helmet. He undid the strap and removed it, shaking out his long hair. "Maybe I'd better come up. I'm a bit more mobile."

"What's been going on in the big world?" she asked as she accompanied him to his study which lay almost at the end of the gallery. Some Guerlain perfume or other hung about her, making him uncertain of her identity as well as his own. He unlocked the door, intricately carved from local hardwood, and held it open for her. "It's delightful." She went directly to the French windows and opened them, admitting a certain amount of light and one or two insects which began enthusiastically to explore the large room. She swayed out into the sunshine, onto a balcony providing a view of the sea in one direction and the distant Iran mountains in the other, all dark greens, blues and purples. The sky was perfect; blue with a touch or two of pink in it. "Oh, Jerry! This is the loveliest view!"

In the study there was a great deal of dust, as if it had all gathered in one place. Jerry wiped it from his desk with his white gauntlet, making long smears across the mother-of-pearl inlay. "Have you seen anything of Dassim Shan?"

"He's probably near the swimming pool. He spends most of his time there, I gather."

Jerry frowned. "Is he all right?"

"Well, he seems to have a rare form of hydrophilia which tends to make him a bit introspective. I shouldn't go to see him, if I were you, until I've had a chance to warn him. The shock could kill him."

"How long ago did this happen?"

"Soon after the resumption of hostilities."

"Sod," said Jerry. With a decisive gesture he threw off his flying helmet and reached to take a pre-wound ornamental turban, of red, green and yellow stripes, from the bottom drawer of his desk. He pinned up his hair. "It's my fault, as usual."

"You take too much on yourself," she said. She returned to the interior but then, when she saw that he intended to go onto the balcony, made a few backward steps so that she was outside again, her hands behind her, supporting her slim body as she rested against the rococo rail.

Adjusting the turban on his head he moved to join her. From where he stood he could see the lawns at the side of the palace, the cypresses which hid the servants' cottages, empty now. To his left he could make out the roofs of the deserted town. On his right loomed foothills, then mountains. "There are demands on one here," he told her. He tapped the turban. "There is more to this than a few privileges, Miss Persson. There is, perhaps, even a destiny."

He drew a deep breath of the sweet, heavy air.

"Duty?" She became immediately attentive.

2.   SOCIETY HOSTESS DEATH RIDDLE

"It's silly, I know," said Jerry as he and Una lay close together, knee to knee in the massive and uncomfortable bed, listening to the waves and the wildlife of the Sandakan dawn, "but I do miss America. I have ancestors there, you know."

"You're obsessed with your relatives." She reached for the silver filigree thermos jug and poured herself an inch or so of iced lime juice. She lifted the jade beaker to her lips. Already their affair had taken one or two turns for the worse.

He shrugged his blue silk shoulders. He flashed her a grin, his teeth unnaturally white against his unnaturally dark skin. "I have so many, Una."

The electrics were working unexpectedly well. As the dawn continued to bloom the four-bladed fan overhead hummed in sympathy with the voices of a thousand waking insects.

Jerry pulled back the netting and walked in bare feet to his dressing room next door and from there to the toilet. The suite was almost all polished mahogany, Victorian, designed, it appeared, to resist the Orient. He sat down on the elegant seat, at last able to relax. But within a moment or two she had joined him, quite naked apart from two ivory bangles on her left wrist, an Egyptian cigarette in one hand, the jade beaker in the other. She leaned against the door jamb, sipping from the glass. She studied his naked lower quarters. He regretted now that he had not locked himself in.

"I wish to God we could get some news, Jerry." She took a brief, nervous puff on her cigarette. "How's Dassim coming along with the radio?"

"He's had to cannibalise. From the plane. No luck so far."

"I'm frightfully bored, you see."

"I understand."

"I thought you'd be rounding up your faithful retainers, getting everybody back to work, clearing the harbour, sorting out the rubber and so on. There isn't one horse left in the stables. No ostlers or anything. You've done nothing except write in your notebooks."

"There's nobody to round up, you see," he explained. "They've either gone inland or else they're mentally deficient. The only people left in town are idiots."

"I quite agree. You couldn't give me a lift to the mainland, could you?"

"This is the mainland." He pointed through the door to the dark map on the wall behind her. He took a sheet of music manuscript from the floor and began to crumple it, soften it. He stood up and wiped his black bottom.

"Of Borneo, though, darling."

He was still disorientated by the rôle she had adopted. He dropped the paper into the bowl and operated the lever to flush it away. "Where would you want to go?"

"What about—where is it?—Australia?"

"We'd have to stop for fuel before we reached Darwin. That DoX is a very greedy aeroplane, for all I've converted a lot of her passenger accommodation to fuel reserves. The only station I know of that's safe, because everyone's forgotten it, is Rowe Island. Moni?"

She sighed. "Too many skeletons."

"I must admit that's my feeling. One too many, at least."

"What about the other way?"

"We've only got a flying boat, don't forget."

"Singapore?"

"Singapore's out."

"Bangkok?"

"Bangkok's completely out."

"Anywhere else? Hong Kong? Formosa? Shanghai?"

"They're all out, too."

"Well, the Philippines, then."

"I told you what happened to the Philippines. Besides, I'd still have to come back and fuel would be a very serious problem."

"We'd be all right in the Philippines, wouldn't we? We could explain."

"I couldn't. I've had enough of that." He rolled his eyes and began to Charleston from the toilet. Gradually the Charleston turned into a Cake-walk and from a Cake-Walk became a coon-dance. "I know where I'm well off." His arms flapped and jogged. "What do you think I was after in Sarawak? And I only left there in time!" He retreated into his netting again, peering at her through it. He stretched out on the bed. "I've no objection if you take the plane yourself."

"Oh, I'd never learn to fly."

"The last time I saw you—I think—you had a licence. Didn't you?"

"I may have told you something like that." She was vague, upset by the reference.

"It'll have to be Rowe Island, then. I've got to get back. I wouldn't be allowed into Australia under any circumstances."

"But your son...?"

"I shouldn't have mentioned it."

"Ghosts," she said.

"You wouldn't recognise them now," he told her, parting the curtain and taking her hand. Tenderly he drew her back into the net.

3. AN IMPORTANT MESSAGE TO EVERY MAN AND WOMAN IN AMERICA LOSING HIS OR HER HAIR

The lean steam yacht sailed fastidiously into Sandakan harbour, furled her white sails and dropped anchor. A little cream-coloured smoke drifted from her gleaming aristocratic funnels; her white sides were turned greenish blue, reflecting the water.

Watching from his balcony Jerry recognised the *Teddy Bear* and pursed his lips, in no doubt that his radio signals had been intercepted. She had hoisted a complicated collection of signals from her masthead, triatic stay, starboard yardarm and port yardarm, the simplest of which read *Coming to your assistance*. As Jerry looked, she ran the Red Ensign up her ensign staff. He made out the letters HBC in the fly and his suspicions were confirmed. There were few who would sail under the flag of the Hudson's Bay Company unless they had to.

He returned to his study to take from a table, on which there also rested a Harrison naval chronometer and a large globe of the world, his telescope. Once more on the balcony he focused the lens on the *Teddy Bear*. A number of sailors were at work on her decks; most of them wore uniforms closely resembling the tropical kit of the United States Navy. They were armed with Springfield rifles of an old-fashioned pattern; Jerry couldn't identify them. A moment later the flash of a maple-finished Remington stock confirmed everything he had suspected. He collapsed the telescope and went to find Una Persson.

She was in the swimming pool, bathing under the unseeing eyes of Dassim Shan. Her brown body flickered against shady jade, lapis lazuli and Tuscan marble. Dassim Shan, in his elaborately embroidered coat of office, his small turban and his silk britches, sat where he always sat when not specifically employed, occasionally glancing up at the crystal dome of the roof, cocking an ear if he detected some slight difference in the sound of a fountain.

"It looks as if you'll soon be able to say goodbye to Borneo." Jerry squatted on the mosaic tiles at the edge of the pool. "Una. There's a ship turned up."

"British?"

"It might as well be. Beesley's tracked me down. I knew I hadn't really shaken him off in the States. He's been to Sumatra and picked up the steam yacht."

Her head came sliding over the surface to stare into his eyes. "Are you sure?"

"Quite sure. I recognised his daughter's butt."

"That he's come for you?"

"I suppose there's a slight chance he's run out of provisions and is hoping I've got the odd Tootsie Roll stashed away, but however you look at it the holiday's definitely coming to an end."

"I didn't want to go back to *work*." She pouted. "I'm far too tired. Besides, I'd do no good." She squeezed water from her eyes.

"You could always sing for the troops."

"Don't be vulgar, darling." Her head sought the depths.

"By and large," Jerry reflected, dabbling his fingers in the water, "I prefer a post-war situation to a pre-war one. But I was hoping to miss the current conflict altogether." He stared wistfully at Dassim Shan. The major-domo seemed to have found a solution.

She was on the other side of the pool now, shaking liquid from her short hair. "What will you do?" she called.

"I'm a fatalist, these days. I'll play it by ear." He realised that his silk trousers were becoming damp. He rose. "What will you do?"

She wiped her mouth. "Look up Lobkowitz, I suppose. He usually has a fair idea of what's going on. This must mean the peace talks have broken down, eh?" Already she was beginning to sound like her old self.

"I don't think they've got to that stage yet." Jerry took a silver cigarette case from his jacket pocket, removed one of the last of his Shermans and lit it with a brass Dunhill lighter.

She clung to the side. "Beesley has some kind of official backing, you think?"

He drew on the brown cigarettello. "He's definitely not alone."

From far away there came the sound of a ship's siren.

Una pulled herself from the pool and wrapped a thick brocade robe about her. It was Chinese, in blue and gold. Dragons embraced her.

They waited for some time at the bronze doors of the palace before they saw Bishop Beesley marching through the gates towards them. He was at the head of a small party of marines in blancoed webbing, belts and puttees. Recognising Jerry and Una, Beesley stopped, signalling to his men who came immediately to attention, presenting arms. From behind them all Mitzi Beesley peeped out, waving the fingers of a malevolent imp.

Bishop Beesley was in full kit. His white-and-gold mitre, his bone-and-silver robes, were evidently fresh on, perhaps to impress any natives he might encounter. He held a rococo crook in one plump hand, a half-eaten bar of Zaanland Coffee Brandy Chocolate in the other.

"Still crawling away from the gibbering darkness are we, Mr C? You should relax. Nothing's as bad as it seems." Bishop Beesley began a portly approach.

"Afternoon, bishop," Jerry fell back on old dodges. "What brings you to the Islands?"

"Missionary work, my boy. We got your message and came as soon as we could. You wouldn't, by any chance, be able to offer us some refreshment?" He swallowed the remains of the Zaanland.

"We're a bit short-staffed, just now. More primitive than I care for myself." Jerry offered his arm to Una who took it. Together they led the way back into the palace.

"I thought you enjoyed living amongst the head-hunters, Mr Cornelius. After all, you and they have so much in common."

Jerry was genuinely puzzled. "There aren't any head-hunters in Sandakan. All that sort of thing's much further south. You're thinking of the Dyaks and their bloody oil-fields."

Bishop Beesley waddled in. "What a lovely home. I'll just leave the boys outside, shall I? Mitzi! You don't mind if my daughter joins us?"

Mitzi Beesley was wearing a rather cheap rayon ensemble, loose sailor blouse and wide, baggy trousers, almost certainly a bad Schiaparelli copy of the sort obtainable from any second-rate tailor's shop in Bombay or Calcutta. Even the shade of pink was slightly off. Her golden hair was waved tightly against her mean little skull. She placed her small tongue on her thin lower lip and smiled at Una. "We've met before, haven't we?"

Una released Jerry's arm. "I don't think I'd be likely to remember," she said innocently. "How do you do, Miss Beesley?"

Mitzi sniffed. "Not bad. Not now. But times have been a bit chaotic until recently, when Daddy got this new job." She removed her Remington from her shoulder and looked around for somewhere to put it.

"I'll take it," said Una hospitably.

Mitzi handed her the gun and Una crossed the mosaic to the large Ming ceramic umbrella stand, dropping the rifle, barrel first, among the walking sticks, sunshades and riding crops. "It'll be all right there, will it?"

"Fine," said Mitzi absently.

Bishop Beesley raised beringed fingers to his rosebud lips and uttered a little wind. "I hear they do a very pleasant dish in these parts. A local version of the baklava, eh?"

"I think there are a few cold ones in the storeroom," Jerry looked towards the door under the staircase. "Shall I show you where it is?"

"That's very kind of you, Mr Cornelius. You seem, rather cleverly, to have adopted the manners as well as the style of a gentleman. Congratulations!"

"You're too kind."

"Standards are slipping everywhere. Credit where credit's due, sir. And, of course, I bear no grudges." His breathing became deeper. He was almost snoring by the time he had waddled to the door to the lower regions. "This is deliciously opulent, isn't it? The barbaric splendour of the East. You must feel much more at home."

"I can't complain, bishop."

"Is Miss Brunner with you?" asked Una suddenly of Mitzi Beesley. It was as if she had remembered a name and nothing else.

"Not this trip." Mitzi moved closer to her. "That's a nice dressing gown. Is it a man's?"

"I'm not sure." The two women followed Jerry and Bishop Beesley through the door and down stone steps cut from the living rock. It was suddenly much cooler.

"And as for Frank," continued Mitzi intimately, "Jerry's brother, you know—we couldn't get him to do a thing. It's as if there's a spell on everybody. Almost. You've met Doktor von Krupp, too, have you?"

"I think I might have…"

"She's almost completely retired, now. Gave herself to the cause body and soul. Bishop Beesley has had to continue the work virtually single-handed. I help as best I can, of course, but he complains that I don't really understand the importance of it all. He thinks my loyalties are sometimes divided." They were quite a long way behind the men. Mitzi smirked. "Of course, that's impossible. I haven't any loyalties at all."

"What a relief." Spasmodically, Una smiled down on the minx. She found that she was lying and enjoying the sensation. "How refreshing."

The minx began to stroke her exposed ribs.

The party descended still deeper into the darkness. From the gloom ahead Una could hear the sound of Bishop Beesley's awful breath.

"It's high time you were back in harness, Mr C."

4. CROSS COUNTRY RAPE AND SLAY SPREE OF THE FRUSTRATED BONDAGE FREAK

"There's still a touch of vulgarity about you which I like," said Bishop Beesley. His marines had taken up permanent positions within the palace grounds and the bishop had almost completed his inventory of the building's contents. The two of them strolled between peacocks and birds of paradise and pedigree Sinhalese bantams, over the lawn towards the larger fountains which cast faint, flickering arabesques everywhere on grass and shrubs. The bishop was eating something sticky from one of Jerry's silver plates, holding the plate in his left hand while with his right he lifted the honey-flavoured food to his glistening lips. "What a riot of colour, those flowers and shrubs!" Flies were settling hopefully on his mitre. "America and Europe are getting along famously again. Say what you will about President Boyle, he's a dedicated internationalist. He's given the British authorities his whole support."

"It's the Islamic influence, I suppose," murmured Jerry. "I've always been a bit prone..."

"Security is at a premium, Mr Cornelius. Of course, it's

given a tremendous boost to the navy. Britannia Resurgent!"

"We're a bit behind the times here." Jerry prised a determined mosquito from his cheek. "I'm afraid."

"How we'd all love to live in the past, particularly a past so splendid." Bishop Beesley expressed sympathy. He waved a cake. No-one understands all this better than I."

Jerry was doing his best to remember what had been going on. "I don't think I could go back to Britain," he said. "Not now."

"I would be the first to admit that there are, for certain people, difficulties. But with the proper papers you'd be quite safe. Restrictions aren't merely negative, you know. They work for you, too."

"They don't like me over there any more." He made a vague gesture towards the West. "Do they?"

"Nonsense. You can prove a change of heart!"

Jerry laughed. He put both his hands into a lattice of water, causing the fountain to alter its note. "That's the only thing that hasn't changed, vicar."

"Come, come, come." Bishop Beesley clapped him on the back. For a few moments his fingers adhered to the silk of Jerry's pale blue kurta then came away with a small sucking sound. "You must be positive!"

Jerry said doubtfully: "I'll try. I have tried."

"I'll get my daughter to have a chat with you. She's helped you in the past, hasn't she?"

"I can't recall…"

"It will come back." Bishop Beesley looked around for somewhere to put his empty plate. In the end he found a green soapstone sundial. "There isn't a great deal of time to spare. The box is still in England, I take it."

"Oh, yes," said Jerry dreamily, to be agreeable. He was incapable, just now, of thinking that far ahead.

"And with the box in the right hands, mankind will prosper again. A major war will be averted. The world will greet you as a saviour!"

"I thought I'd already turned the job down." Jerry found some seed in his pockets and began to throw it to the birds. From one of the upper floors of the palace came the strains of King Pleasure singing 'Golden Days'. "That's a bit anachronistic, isn't it? Or is it me?"

For a moment Bishop Beesley's huge face became sober. "There is no need…"

"Well, that's a relief, at any rate." Jerry rambled on. Ahead of him, on the other side of an ornamental hedge, two sailor hats drew down for cover. "What does Una say?" He sniffed a sweet magnolia blossom. "She's the brains of the outfit."

"I don't know how she feels but, as you say, she's an intelligent woman. My daughter's dealing with her. They are more sympatico."

"She'd feel all right about going back to Blighty. She wants to. Maybe you should just take her."

"Does she know where the box is?"

"I'm sure she does."

Bishop Beesley wiped his face with a red spotted handkerchief. He flicked at the flies and returned it to his back pocket. He inspected his left gaiter. "Is that a scorpion?"

He pointed to the small insect crawling up his leg.

Gently, Jerry cupped his hand around the creature and held it on his palm, looking down at it. "It seems to be a wingless butterfly. Isn't that odd?"

Bishop Beesley glared around him. "Where's Mitzi?"

"Upstairs somewhere, with Una. Can't you hear the music?" King Pleasure was now singing his own 'Little Boy, Don't Get Scared'. *Little fellow, don't get yellow and blue*, he sang.

Bishop Beesley smiled to himself. Jerry was still looking at the butterfly. "Hadn't you better kill it?" said the bishop. "I mean, it can't be happy."

"It doesn't look too unhappy, though." Jerry's hand shook a little. "I shouldn't worry." He placed the insect inside a scarlet rhododendron flower. "It might as well enjoy the time it's got."

Bishop Beesley evidently disapproved of these sentiments. He was about to speak when his small ears caught a sound from on high. Jerry heard it too and they both looked up.

Through the shimmering, heated sky there came a large, dark shape and, for some reason, Jerry became immediately more cheerful, even as he felt his last grip on consecutive thought slipping. "Well, well, well. An airship. From Rowe Island, I shouldn't wonder."

"Airships are—" Bishop Beesley clutched at his jowls. "Airships are—" His hand went to his back. His brow contorted. "Ah!"

Jerry began to jump about on the lawn, waving

mindlessly to the massive black ship with its crimson markings. Disturbed, the peacocks and the bantams scattered screaming and clucking. Macaws filled the air, red, yellow, blue and green, shrieking.

"My back! Back!" moaned Bishop Beesley.

"It's tensions, I expect," suggested Jerry, turning for a moment, but the bishop was already hobbling for the house. Jerry sat down on the lawn. There was a silly grin on his face. "Gosh! I never thought I'd be glad to see one of those buggers again!"

5. SPIRIT VOICES HELP ME—PETER SELLERS TALKS ABOUT THE STRANGE POWER THAT HAS ENTERED HIS LIFE

King Pleasure was doing 'Tomorrow is Another Day' as, half his togs abandoned, his mitre over one sticky eye, Bishop Beesley rolled out of the palace, dragging Mitzi. His daughter was soft and naked, reluctant to leave, trying to work the bolt on her Remington, to remove a malacca cane from the barrel, slapping at his hands which seemed to be covered with feathers from a pillow. "Okay!" her father shouted to the marines. "Okay!"

Bishop Beesley dragged Mitzi past Jerry. Her heels were making unsightly scars in the gravel. "I hope to God, Mr Cornelius, none of this ever gets into the primary zone! I would like to remind you that this is the seventies."

"Almost a hundred, I'd have said. Phew, what a scorcher!" Jerry had begun to pick himself a bunch of flowers. "Blip," he added.

"It's all your fault," wailed Mitzi at him. "You and your rotten engines!"

"Blip!"

The dark shadow of the circling airship passed

over them for the fifth time. The birds of paradise were particularly disturbed by the commotion, running this way and that. The macaws and the bantams had completely disappeared. Only the peacocks had settled down and were screeching aggressively at the big vessel. For a moment or two Jerry imitated them, evidently for the fun of it, then he began to mumble, dropping his flowers. "Five. Birds. Water. Messiah. Ice."

Una emerged, in trench coat and khaki, buckling on the heavy military holster containing her S&W .45. "That airship's come for us. Somebody's running a horrible risk. We'd better bloody take advantage while we can. I'm pissed off. What's Beesley got to do with me?"

"I'd thought airships were extinct," said Jerry. "Or not invented yet. I'm slipping. Blip."

"We're all slipping. Everybody's slipping," screamed Bishop Beesley, untangling his daughter from a jacaranda. "Monstrous anachronisms! Come along, Mitzi, please. The co-ordinates haven't jelled yet, so there's a chance we can escape before complete chaos results. Men! Men! Men!" The marines began to emerge from peculiar hiding places, like children interrupted in a game. "Deviants!"

"It's not my fault," said Jerry, "about Rowe Island. At least, I don't think it is." His vacant eyes glanced questioningly at Una Persson. "Is it? It was dormant."

Her smile was brave and reassuring. "You'll be all right, I expect."

Tomorrow is the magic word. It's full of hopes and dreams...

"Lovely." Jerry turned a seraphic face upwards. "I've always thought they were, thought they were, thought they were, thought they were, thought they were, thought they were. Thought they were…"

A long rope ladder fell from the centre section of the gondola and almost hit him on his poor head. He continued to stand there, mumbling, even as, from the other side of the wall, rifles began to bark. "Get up it, you silly little bugger!" shouted Una Persson. The Smith and Wesson was now in her hand. For the moment the marines were contenting themselves with potshots at the hull as they retreated down the road and back through the town. "Get up! Get up!"

"Yes, mum." He grinned a daft grin. He wondered why he felt so happy. "What about you? Ladies first?"

"You've got a job to do, sonny jim," said Una grimly and slapped him on the bottom. "Go on!"

He took hold of the rungs and began to climb the swaying ladder, chuckling childishly. The airship's engines shouted and screamed as her crew manoeuvred her to maintain their position in the air over the garden. Like the Dornier, she had forward and backward facing engines, the nacelles capable of turning through ninety degrees. A late mark O'Bean, thought Jerry, as he lived and breathed, but he did not know what he meant by the thought. He was almost halfway up the ladder, giggling to himself, when he looked down. The golden dome, main roof of the palace, half-blinded him. "Get up!" cried a determined voice. With one arm hooked in the rungs, Una Persson was sighting along her revolver, picking off marines in the white, tree-lined road below. She called to the riggers peering at her from the open hatch through which the ladder had been lowered: "Take her up. Lift. I'll be fine." A winch creaked. The ladder rose a foot or two.

Jerry felt the wind in his hair. He had never had a better view of the island. "This is heavenly," he said. "What a smashing way to finish. Or begin." The rope swayed wildly. He almost fell off as he neared the top and the waiting gondola.

Hands found him: it was a disapproving Sebastian Auchinek, all scowls and moody, who hauled him in the last few feet. "You've got a long way to go yet, Mr Cornelius." There were a number of dark figures in the bare aluminium interior, evidently a storage hatch. It reeked of high-octane fuel. Through the gloom Jerry crawled towards the nearest bench, also of aluminium, bolted to the bulkhead. Out of the fresh air his high spirits had dropped away again and he was mumbling. "Airships. Human remains. Empires. War. Ideals. Science…"

As Una Persson was dragged in, firing a last round or two at the marines, Prinz Lobkowitz sprang into the light from the entrance, reaching for the lever, closing the hatch-doors. "Thank God." He and Auchinek embraced the woman they loved. Lobkowitz wore riding britches, brown boots, spurs, a white roll-neck sweater, as if he had been taken away suddenly from a polo match. Auchinek wore a rather loud check suit that seemed to belong to the turn of the century.

Una frowned at them. "Should you be here, at all?"

There was a movement above and a pair of thin legs in dark green trousers with a red stripe climbed down the metal ladder into the hold. "We shouldn't." Major Nye was in the uniform of the 3rd Infantry, Punjab Irregular Force, rifle-green with black lace and red facings. "It's more comfortable above, by the way. This is just for stores, and we haven't any, of course." He looked over to Jerry, who drooled and simpered. "Poor old lad. We're dodging and weaving a bit, hoping for the best. He was due in England weeks before the *Teddy Bear*, you know. Everyone was contacted at very short notice, had to down tools and jump to it. Shoulders to the wheel, lads, shoulders to the wheel…"

"What else could we do?" Gently Lobkowitz stroked Jerry's bewildered head. "Besides, he won't remember a lot. Neither shall we, for that matter. We'll drop him off in London and hope for the best."

Auchinek was sullen. Evidently he had taken part in the raid against his will.

"But California first stop. It's important that we all check our bearings again before we progress any further."

"Are you sure it's in California?" said Major Nye. "I thought it was in London, now."

"Not at the present," said Auchinek.

"Blip."

Tom McCarthy's patrol was supposed to round up a group of Rhodesian African guerillas. Instead, he claims, it wiped out a village. There were about sixty victims—the entire population of a tiny village near the Mozambique border. McCarthy, a 22-year-old Londoner, who served in the Rhodesian Light Infantry, told the full story of the atrocity for the first time yesterday. McCarthy himself confessed that he shot a young terrorist as he lay wounded. He was ordered by an officer to shoot the boy. The death-mission began when the Rhodesian Special Branch was given a tip-off that the guerillas would be slipping into the village to collect £1000 towards their "funds". McCarthy and his patrol, including black scouts and members of the Rhodesian Special Air Service, were ordered from their base at Mount Darwin in the troubled border area north of Salisbury. They arrived at the village below the Mavuradonha mountain range, about 30 miles away, in darkness. Through their "night-sights" they saw 17 guerillas arrive. But the Rhodesian soldiers did not move into the village to arrest them. Instead they illuminated the village with flares. Then they bombarded the huts with automatic fire and rockets. McCarthy maintained he could hear the screams of the villagers 300 yards away. Then he was called in to help with the "mopping-up operations". Thirteen of the terrorists died with the villagers. Four escaped but three were picked up later. McCarthy went into graphic detail of the alleged murder rampage by the Rhodesian troops. He said: "We were told that the only prisoners we wanted were the terrorists. We were also told we were after the money. There was this boy of about seventeen. There was no doubt he was one of the guerillas because I recognised him from the night-sight. He had been shot but he wasn't too bad and the medic was working on him. Someone must have decided that he knew nothing because the medic was told to move away." McCarthy was sending a radio message when an officer called him over and ordered him to shoot the youth. "I was frightened and asked if he wouldn't be any good. I was told: 'Certainly not.' I was shaking quite a bit and the officer said: 'Are you worried?' I knew that if I disobeyed a lawful command in an operational area I faced four years in the stockade. I remember putting the safety catch to 'rapid fire' and put my rifle to my shoulder. But I turned my face away before I fired. I missed by a foot— that will tell you how bad I was. He just lay there and put his arms up against his chest. I don't know why but he didn't say a word. He just looked at me and I'll always remember that as if it were just this morning." The officer then came behind McCarthy, grasped his head in both his hands and said: "You useless——bastard." McCarthy continued: "He forced my head down to look at the man on the ground and said: 'Now shoot the bastard.' This time I hit him between the nose and the mouth and his face just seemed to cave in."

—Ellis Plaice,
Daily Mirror, 27 February, 1976

THE REUNION PARTY

William Randolph Hearst's monumental pile had first been displayed to the public on 2 June, 1958, and since then had become one of California's greatest attractions, on a par with Hollywood and Disneyland, under the supervision of the California Department of Parks and Recreation, in accordance with Hearst's legacy after he had died, aged 88, on 13 August, 1951; a mock Hispano-Moorish haven, crammed with the greatest collection of second-rate art ever assembled in one private building, it lay on top of a hill once known as Camp Hill, now rechristened the Enchanted Hill and a visit to it was, according to the official guide book, "an experience unsurpassed by the other great dwellings built in a fabulous era when American tycoons were erecting imposing structures and importing art treasures found throughout the world. A walk through its grounds with terraced gardens, paths lined with camellia hedges, great banks of azaleas and rhododendron, more than 50 varieties of roses and the soft tinkling of water dripping from marble fountains, is a stroll through the epitome of beauty and grandeur. A great dream, never quite completed." The building began in 1919, nearly twenty years before the Derry & Toms Roof Garden, an echo, an exquisite miniature, had been opened in London. "There are", the guide book tells us, "100 rooms in the main building, including 38 bedrooms, 31 baths, 14 sitting rooms, 2 libraries, a theatre and an area that was meant to contain a complete bowing alley." Work on this building continued to 1947, when it was abandoned. There is no real evidence for the legend that in a year sometimes

THE CONDITION OF MUZAK

given as 1955, sometimes as 1985 and sometimes, obviously erroneously, as 1918, an important and secret meeting was held there of a number of men and women, representatives of most schools of thought and of many nations in the world. This has been variously described as the "Veterans's Meeting" or the "Reunion Party" and, of course, a number of books have been written in an effort to 'explain' the legend. So far a satisfactory book has yet to appear, though all accounts are agreed on the authenticity of one piece of evidence, a guest list, giving the names of the guests in order of arrival, "with one notable absence, impossible to remedy at this stage" (as a pencilled note on the card points out). Accounts by local people concerning a huge concourse of ghosts on a day and a night in midsummer 1951, when shadowy figures were seen laughing and talking in the grounds, swimming in the Neptune pool, playing music of bizarre and unrecognisable origin, chiming the thirty-six carillon bells, housed in the twin Hispano-Moresque towers of the Casa Grande; feasting in the huge refectory, with its silk banners representing the seventeen wards of Sienna, its Gothic tapestries and its fifteenth-century Spanish choir stalls, whilst seated at long tables of rich, old wood, burning oddly coloured lights, to ride off in a great flurry of hoofs shortly before dawn, heading for the sea, have been independently confirmed and described, according to the taste of the teller, as a meeting of vampires, witches, devils or the Wild Hunt itself. Reports also agree that there was nothing sinister about the haunting, that, indeed, a great sense of peace and tranquillity pervaded the surrounding countryside on that Midsummer Night, a peace which those ancient Californian hills had not experienced for many a century, and the ghosts were generally thought to be "lucky" rather than "evil" (Butler, *Haunted California*, 1975). "Men and women from all sides of the conflict would meet on common ground and exchange information in the timeless halls and passages of the four castles, in the peaceful groves of the noble Tanelorn" (Butler, ibid.). "Their voices were hushed and relaxed and there wasn't one who showed any animosity he or she might feel..." (Hall, *The San Simeon Mystery Explained*, 1971). "The time of the final conflict was not yet. Their garments, their manners, their languages, their gestures represented the best that the twentieth century had been able to offer, the inheritance of Golden Age on Golden Age. Every enthusiasm was represented; every beast was in its prime. And, for a day and a night, there could be no question of invasion, even from within" (Morgan, *Law v. Chaos: The Last Great Meeting*, 1975). "Time travellers? Visitors from space? Ghosts? Or just a bunch of hoaxers—a gang of kids having fun? Then how to explain music that was years ahead of its time, fashions that were not seen until twenty years later, snatches of conversation referring to events occurring towards the end of this century?" (Fromental, *San Simeon, the Flying Saucers and Patty: Who is getting at who?*, 1976).

The note of guests attending the "coven" or "sabbat", as others have called it, was found under the billiard table in the Game Room, written in longhand, not evidently American and probably English, headed "Manifestations" and, under that, "Arrivals in order of appearance". The names included the following:

Mr J. Daker, Mr J. Tallow, Mr E. de Marylebone, Mr Renark, Mr E. Bloom, Mr C. Marca, Mr J. Cornelius. Prof. I. Hira, Mr Smiles. Mr Lucas. Mr Powys. Miss C. Brunner, Mr D. Koutrouboussis. Mr Shades. Mr F. Cornelius. Mr J. Tanglebones. Rev. Marek. Duke D. von Köln, Mr K. Glogauer, Cpt. Arflane, Mrs U. Rorsefne. Prof. Faustaff, Mr U. Skarsol, Bishop D. and Miss M. Beesley, Dr K. von Krupp, Captain C. Brunner, Mr F.G. Gavin, Prince C.J. Irsei. Mr E.P. Bradbury. Mr J. Cornell. Mr O. Bastable. Miss U. Persson. Cpt. J. Korzeniowski. Mr V.I. Ulyanov, Gen. O.T. Shaw, Major and Mrs G. Nye. Captain and Mrs G. Nye. Miss E. Nye. Miss I. Nye. Master P. Nye. Col. M.A. Pyat. Mr S.M. Collier. Mr M. Lescoq. Mr M. Hope-Dempsey. Mr C. Ryan. Prinz Lobkowitz. Mr S. Koutrouboussis. Mr C. Koutrouboussis. Mr A. Koutrouboussis. Mr R. Boyle, Mnr P. Olmeijer. Mrs H. Cornelius. Mrs B. Beesley. Mr S. Cohen. Miss H. Segal. Prof. M. O'Bean. Mr R.D. Feet. Mr C. Tome. Captain B. Maxwell. The Hon. Miss H. Sweet. Mr S. Vaizey. Miss E. Knecht. Lady Sunday. Mrs A. Underwood. Mr J. Carnelian. Lady Charlotina Lake. Lord and Lady Canaria. Miss Q. Gloriana. Miss M. Ming. Mrs D. Armatuce. Gen. C. Hood. Lady Lyst. Mr E. Wheldrake, Lord Rhoone. Lord Wynchett. Baroness Walewska. Sir T. Ffynne. Dr J. Dee. Captain Quire, and a great number of other experienced people.

Notting Hill's annual Summer Carnival is unlikely to take place this year in its traditional form. The Royal Borough Council has told its organisers to find a fixed assembly point for this year's Carnival—preferably the White City Stadium in Shepherd's Bush. Alternative venues like Wembley Stadium and Wormwood Scrubs were also mentioned. But all the proposed sites are outside the Royal Borough, and the organisers have rejected these suggestions as boding "total destruction of the fundamental concept of what the Carnival should be". Their objections to deputy council leader Ald. Peter Methuen's "compromise" solution to the carnival problem were raised at a closed meeting between Royal Borough officials and various concerned parties at Kensington Town Hall last week. Cllr Michael Cocks, who called the meeting, said it was vital to decide in good time how to avoid the controversy which followed last year's massive three-day celebrations. Nearly a quarter of a million people (mainly West Indian) flooded into the borough for last August's carnival—the tenth. But the aftermath of complaints from residents, the police and from certain councillors themselves, prompted the council to insist on a change of attitude to recognise that this once local event has now reached "national proportions". The objections of local residents, itemised in a 196-signature petition to the council, include noise (particularly from steel bands playing late into the night) and dirt and litter left after the weekend's festivities. Their petition called for "the immediate and effective prohibition of amplified music and vocal performances in the Westway and W.10 and W.11 areas and for the re-siting of the Notting Hill Carnival in 1976 and subsequent years".

The police added that the crime rate had increased seriously during Carnival time and that traffic congestion had blocked access for ambulances and fire engines. The council said that the event was now too large for them to provide adequate hygiene and litter amenities ... "To move to the White City would totally destroy the event as we know it," Mr Palmer said ... "The festival is a street carnival and the whole atmosphere would be lost if it were moved out of the streets of North Kensington," said Labour leader Val Wallis ... But Mr Anthony Perry, Director of the North Kensington Amenity Trust, warned that if the Carnival were to go ahead without approval, then the Trust, on whose land much of the festivity takes place, would not make the land available. "We are eager that it should be used by the community," Mr Perry said, "but not against the wishes of the community."

Kensington News and Post, 6 February, 1976

6. BAC COOLS HOPES OF AIRSHIP BOOM

Jerry was still shivering as he waded out of the dirty Cornish shallows onto Tintagel's ungenerous beach. A careful search of all the caves in that half-eaten bay, of the ruins of the castle, of the deserted town beyond, had turned up nothing but débris, seaweed and dead fish. Now his cold feet struck something white and mushy lying on the shingle and, glancing hopefully down, he discovered only a bundle of quarto paper, secured by green admiralty tags, typewritten. He went to turn the pages but they disintegrated at once, like the flesh of a rotten sole. He folded his arms for warmth, his ancient oilskins creaking and cracking at armpits and shoulders. He rid himself of his stiff sou'wester, throwing it behind him, into the Atlantic.

As he looked above the looming cliffs at the petulant sky grey rain fell on his face. He tramped for the dangerous steps leading up the south face of the cove, beginning to regret overreacting and giving in to the impulse to smash all his equipment, to rely entirely on metaphysical methods for a final solution to his sister's malaise. Now his foot slipped on a piece of rotten granite. He paused. A darkness had entered the bay. His upward climb became hastier. There was no use crying over diffused plasma (or ectoplasm, for that matter): the world was splitting up, like so many dividing cells, and the energy was unlikely to be concentrated in any one place for much longer. He had been foolish to believe that his remedy had been any better than the others.

He reached the top of the cliff and made his way to the old wooden café shack where he had left his camouflaged jeep. It was still there, parked at an angle of forty degrees on the rutted path. He climbed in, thinking of Captain Brunner and wondering if the noble old anachronism's sacrifice had been worth anything in the long run. He took a yellowing packet of Black Cat cigarettes from the map compartment and lit one with the brass Dunhill he had found there; the lighter's flame was very low. He put the Black Cats in his pocket and abandoned the Dunhill. He turned the ignition key. The starting motor rolled sluggishly a few times but the engine failed to fire. Jerry had expected this. Even the American equipment wasn't what it had been; the mainland had sent no new supplies for months. In the back seats of the jeep he found his fur hat and mittens, his heavy P&O Norfolk jacket. He stripped off the oilskins and dressed himself more warmly, buckling the jacket's belt tightly around his waist.

He left the jeep behind, walking up the steep path towards the town. His search was proving entirely fruitless and he was tempted to give it up altogether, retiring from any kind of involvement, and yet his instincts had to be satisfied; he was resigned to continuing his quest. After all, most of his old enemies had themselves retired to safer zones. On the surface it seemed that the field was completely open.

The town had never been anything more than ramshackle, built primarily in response to the late-nineteenth-century tourist boom which had owed far less to Coleridge than to Tennyson and the Pre-Raphaelites. Even ruin could not make it picturesque. The streets were awash with weather-stained postcards, bedraggled and muddy King Arthur tea-towels, broken plastic Holy Grails, Excaliburs carved from chalk, tiny Round Tables to hang on the wall, and polystyrene crowns. In the reign of one Elizabeth the ideal had reached perfection and, in the reign of another, it had achieved its ultimate degradation. Jerry sniffed to himself. It had to happen sometime. Perhaps that was what he had failed to understand before.

He began to check the few parked cars, but all were in poor condition. The exodus had been made in less than a day, when the area had been, like so many, declared a non-civilian zone. Something to do with the Cornish Nationalist Movement. But the military had lost interest in the site almost immediately and had never established anything more than a few yards of barbed wire here and there.

Personally, Jerry thought the Americans had been a trifle naïve in thinking they had scored significant points in recruiting the CNM, a notoriously unreliable outfit whose members remained loyal only until they were trained and re-equipped when they deserted, returning to their rented farms and tied-cottages to await the calling of their traditional

THE CONDITION OF MUZAK

landlord leaders. A few of them still worked freelance for the Americans but, Jerry had heard, the military advisors were reconsidering the system of paying scalp-bounty, since the scalps in question were always difficult to identify and, on more than one occasion, had proved to originate with their own personnel stationed in the remoter parts of West Penrith. Scalp-hunters had been reported in the area only a few days ago, so Jerry kept a wary hand on his vibragun and gave close attention to the shadows, though it was unlikely that any hunter would bother with Tintagel which was known to be abandoned.

Eventually Jerry gave up inspecting the cars and stepped through the smashed plate-glass window of a tea shop. From the counter a curious rat looked up and, for an instant, Jerry mistook him for the proprietor. Casting a prudent glance over its shoulder the rat beat a leisurely retreat. Jerry found himself a Coke in the powerless icebox and took it to a grimy table to consider his transport problems. The Coke tasted peculiar, having undergone some sort of transmutation, but he swallowed it anyway. It could always be that his own metabolism had changed, there had been so many fluctuations recently. At least the temporal shifts had become less crude, flowing smoothly one into the other, layer passing almost imperceptibly through layer so that it was not always possible to tell exactly what one's bearings were. Although it made his job harder, he couldn't complain. After all, much of it was his own fault. It was only demonstrating his theories.

He was awakened from this somewhat tranquil mood by the distant sound of an ageing engine.

7. UFOS—OCCUPANTS AND ARTIFACTS IN EASTERN INDIANA

It was a broken-down Bedford two-tonner with a tattered canvas canopy; definitely a pre-war job. It moved slowly up the street as if searching for something. Jerry couldn't recognise the driver but, since this was his only chance of a lift, he decided to expose himself.

He ran to the fractured window and climbed carefully out to the pavement. The lorry stopped. Through the wound-down window a tired military face was presented to him. "Colonel Cornelius?"

"Well—" said Jerry doubtfully. "I think he's... Can you give me a ride?"

The man had kindly but confused pale blue eyes. He was in his fifties or sixties, wearing a shiny blazer, a frayed shirt with washed-out pink stripes, a regimental tie. He had a small grey moustache and thinning grey hair. "I'm Major Nye." He took a small photograph from above the driving mirror and looked from it to Jerry. "I'm to take you to Grasmere, I believe?"

Jerry, trusting the major's identification better than

his own memory, walked round the lorry and opened the door on the passenger's side. He put a foot on the step as Major Nye cleared various maps and documents from the worn leatherette upholstery. He climbed in and sat down, shutting the door with a slam. The Bedford's engine was still running. Major Nye put it into gear and began to back slowly up the street. "You came ashore here, did you?"

"In a manner of speaking," said Jerry.

"You knew about Grasmere?"

"I know *about* Grasmere, certainly."

"You'll be briefed there. Sorry we couldn't give you something more sophisticated, but the Americans took their best stuff with them or else they destroyed it."

"The Americans have gone?"

"Didn't you know, old chap? Certainly. Pulled out altogether. Given Europe up as a bad job. Can't say I blame 'em. It means chaos now, of course. But, still..." He stopped reversing and moved forward up the B road for Camelford. "It's going to be a struggle to get through. As you can imagine, communications are breaking down left, right and centre." He turned on the windscreen wipers as the rain grew heavier. "But so far no one group has displayed any sort of significant gain."

"Do you mean it's Civil War?" said Jerry in astonishment.

"It hasn't come to that yet."

Jerry smiled to himself. "It was always a game of Roundheads and Cavaliers for years, wasn't it? If you look at it one way."

"Oh, I quite agree with you." Major Nye was concentrating on his driving. "Come on, old girl. Come along then, beauty."

The Bedford responded with a little extra speed. Major Nye smiled. "The last lot of bombing didn't improve matters for us. There's scarcely a stretch of road left that hasn't been—" The lorry began to bump over potholes. "That's nothing compared to the destruction closer to London. Still, we'll be able to skirt London, that's one consolation." The rain crackled on the roof. In spite of the major's words, Jerry felt considerably safer in his company than he had felt for a very long time, particularly when he began to hum 'The Ballad of Sexual Dependency' from *The Threepenny Opera*. The smell of petrol in the cab gradually became less noticeable and Jerry reached into his Norfolk for the ancient packet of Black Cats. He offered one to Major Nye. "No thanks, old chap. Roll my own. I say, you wouldn't mind rolling one for me, would you?" He reached for a Rizla tin on the ledge above the dashboard and handed it to Jerry who tried to remember how to use the rolling machine, balancing it on his knees, putting paper, tobacco and filter into the rubber pad, licking the sticky edge of the paper, closing the lid and producing a fairly reasonable-looking cigarette. With some pride he gave the result to the major who looked at it a little critically. "Thanks, old chap. Thicker than my usuals, but still… Want one?"

"I'll stick to these," said Jerry. With his steel Dunhill, almost a match to the one he had left in the jeep, he lit the major's and then his own.

"Bloody rain," said the major. "You mustn't mind me. I've got awful habits. My wife says so. Swear all the time. India, I suppose."

There was silence for a while until they had gone through Camelford, witnessed by the suspicious eyes of the residents, and were on a road heading for Taunton and the M. Whereupon, Major Nye, to Jerry's amazement, suddenly began to sing in a slight mellow voice: "Moonlight becomes you. It goes with your hair. Did anyone ever tell you how pom-pom ta-tee." He seemed unaware of his audience, peering placidly through the sheets of rain as the lorry bravely bucked along. "I'll see you again, whenever spring comes through again—through again? Something like that. Da da da dee-dee da-dum. In those old familiar places, with those old familiar traaaaa-taaaa..." He went through a dozen song fragments in less than four minutes, like a malfunctioning jukebox. "You're the cream in my coffee, I'm the milk in your tea." He finished his cigarette and wound down the window sufficiently to throw the butt away. "If you knew Peggy Sue..." Then he seemed to remember Jerry. He opened the glove compartment to take out a large newspaper-wrapped packet. "Sandwich, old boy? Cheese and tomato probably, worst luck. Help yourself. There's far too many for me. The old ulcer. I can't eat much at a sitting. Little but often, that's the motto. Tuck in."

Jerry pulled away the paper and removed a sandwich. He relaxed in his seat, scarcely paying any attention even when three or four bright explosions lit the evening skyline to the east.

Major Nye did not seem particularly troubled, either, but regarded the explosions rather as confirmation of his earlier forebodings. "There you are," he said. "That's what the Americans have left us to handle."

"A bastard," said Jerry.

"The least of it," said Major Nye.

8. THE GIRL NEXT DOOR COULD BE A WITCH

There was no doubt about it, thought Jerry, there had once been a time when he had been able to call at least a little of the play. Nowadays even the smallest decisions had been taken out of his hands. He yawned, searching the grey road ahead for black patches that would indicate shell holes. He didn't really care, because his interests were becoming increasingly private as time went, if not on, then at least backwards and forwards. Major Nye was still singing. "Them good ol' boys drinkin' whiskey an' rye..." Perhaps it did have something to do with his losing faith in rock music. The best performers had either died, decayed or fractured, leaving behind them a vocabulary of musical ideas, lyrical techniques and subject matter, styles and body languages which had never been given the opportunity to mature but had, instead, been aped by the very world of Showbiz against which they had originally revolted. And everything else was just the same—a load of oily entrepreneurs with their hair a little longer, their clothes occasionally a little easier on the eyes, their language an eager combination of professional slang and adman quasi-technical. It forced you, whether you liked it or not, into a classical stance, to long for a world when fiction really was stranger than truth because there were no films, television, magazines, newspapers to prove differently, to find consolation in the great Romantics of those far-off hazy days—Schoenberg, Ives and Messiaen—to hang in a sticky web of conflicting freedoms, finding an acceptable discipline only in Art, and if you were not an artist then the only alternative, as in Mo's case, was a nihilistic war against the sole injustice you could identify, the tyranny of Time and the human condition...

Once again Major Nye rescued him from this sentimental reverie. "Here we are, old chap."

Jerry looked up, recognising tranquil Grasmere lake on his left, the gigantic mock Gothic hotel which had sheltered so many ecstatic old ladies from Minnesota before rocket-fire had blown its roof away. Major Nye steered the Bedford carefully off the road to the right and into a small macadamised car park surrounded by a stone wall. A twisted sign read *Car Park For Wordsworth's Cottage Only*. Dove Cottage was to Jerry's right. As Major Nye switched off the engine and sighed with relief someone appeared at the gate and walked round into the car park: a tall man of about the same age as Major Nye but with a self-conscious dignity that was just a little Teutonic. He wore an old-fashioned grey three-piece suit and had a daffodil in his lapel. He was settling a grey homburg on his distinguished patrician head, knocking the ash from a cigarette which he smoked in a six-inch holder, cupped in the Russian manner between thumb and fingers.

Lost in a cavern of self-pity, Jerry remained in the cab when Major Nye had walked through the drizzle to shake hands with the newcomer. "Am I glad to see you, old boy. We've been travelling the best part of two days— rained the whole time. Nearly missed the petrol dump outside Coventry. I'm afraid my passenger's become a little depressed. Is your phone working? I'd like to tell my wife we've arrived safe and sound."

"There are no lines, I fear." The man in grey spoke softly. He had a pleasant foreign accent. "But your daughter is here."

"Splendid." Major Nye gestured to Jerry. "Time to disembark, Colonel Cornelius."

Jerry roused himself. It was quite possible that the petrol fumes were affecting him. He felt the need of a pick-me-up. A Jimi Hendrix track or a few minutes of *Moses und Aron* would be enough to do the trick; but he had lost hope. He did his best to put on a more cheerful face, opening his door, sliding to the ground, stretching his legs and arms as he approached the pair. The rain fell on his unprotected head. He had left his hat in the cab.

"I am Prinz Lobkowitz." The handsome man stared hard into Jerry's face. "You know me?"

"No," said Jerry. "Do you know me?" He could have ridden for ever in Major Nye's company. He was resentful that the journey was over.

"Oh, it's probably just a touch of déjà vu," said Prinz Lobkowitz. "Come." He led the way up the crazy-paving path and into the cottage. "I think Elizabeth has the kettle on."

The cottage had not been used as anything but a museum for some time. The uncarpeted rooms were full of glass cases and miscellaneous objects marked 'Probably Wordsworth's stick' and 'The kind of pen Wordsworth would have used'. Most of the genuine things had been sold off to the occupying troops years before. In a room at the back of the cottage was an ordinary table with a blue-and-white chintz cloth, a gas-stove on which boiled a large iron kettle, a gas-fire in the grate. Two women sat at the table, looking up as the three men entered.

Major Nye smiled. "Hello, young Bess." He embraced his rather plump and pretty daughter who wore a multicoloured Afghan dress and who accepted the embrace with a degree of condescension.

"This is my friend Una," said Elizabeth Nye. "Una Persson."

"I think I've heard of you, my dear. How do you do?"

"How do you do?" said Una Persson.

Jerry was not sure he had ever seen a more beautiful woman. She wore a black trench coat and beneath it a long suède riding skirt, black knee-length boots, a white polo-neck sweater. There was a cartridge belt around her waist and attached to it a holster for a large revolver. She shook hands with Major Nye and then with Jerry, giving them both a small but friendly smile. Her short chestnut hair fell into her eyes as she sat down again. She brushed it back with a long hand.

"I expect you've a good idea why we contacted you,

colonel," said Prinz Lobkowitz, sitting close to Miss Persson, "but we ought to fill you in about the Scottish position as soon as possible. They'll be coming through for you shortly."

"Aha," said Jerry, looking for the radio.

Elizabeth Nye got up to pour hot water into a teapot.

"Just what I could do with," said Major Nye, rubbing his knotted hands together near the gas-fire. "This is Calor gas, I suppose, isn't it?"

"That's right." His daughter laughed. She took the pot to the table and put it down amongst the mugs and the milk and sugar already there. "Who likes it weak?"

"I'd better have it weak," said Major Nye. "Thanks, girly." He accepted the mug.

"As strong as it comes," said Jerry. "I'm afraid I've lost my memory."

"That's what I like to hear." Prinz Lobkowitz had responded to his first statement. "Eh?"

"My memory," Jerry said.

"Oh, sod it." Impatient air hissed from Miss Persson's clenched teeth. "He must be the most unreliable medium we've used. Every bloody time we need him he cops out— goes and loses his memory again."

"Sorry." Jerry was anxious to placate this lovely woman. "My mind's been taken up with my sister, you see. She's all I have."

Una Persson's expression softened. With her own hands she gave him a mug of tea. "Sugar?"

"Not for me. Just milk."

She poured a little milk into the mug.

"I don't know what I can do for you, really. I'm a fast learner though. In some things, anyway." Jerry smiled at her, accepting the tea.

"It's not for us," said Prinz Lobkowitz. "It's the Scots. We promised them you could advise them. None of us has any experience in physics. Not yet. Not in a practical sense, at any rate."

"I've put all that sort of thing behind me," said Jerry.

Una Persson stood up and went to the window.

"I thought religion might help, you see," he continued. "If I redefined things in supernatural terms. It can sometimes work. In the short run."

He looked to them for confirmation and saw only bafflement.

"You'd better dredge up whatever you can," said Una Persson. "They've arrived."

The five people crowded to the window, staring through the trees and the ruins out towards the lake. In the centre of the lake was a small island, hilly and wooded. Hovering over the island was a bulky hull. On its tail-fins was painted the blue cross of St Andrew. The ship's entire outer skin was covered in the brilliant scarlet sett of the McMahon clan.

"Why me?" said Jerry miserably.

"Just your bad luck, I'm afraid," said Prinz Lobkowitz. "We're hoping that Scotland will hold, you see. Everything else is disintegrating rapidly."

"Politics?" Jerry became wary. "Is this some sort of manipulation?"

Major Nye patted Jerry on the back.

"Cheer up, old chap. It won't be for long, after all."

"I thought I was regressing, but this—Christ!" He let them push him towards the door.

"In the meantime," said Una Persson suddenly, a little brisk sympathy in her tone, "we'll be helping you look for Catherine. How's that?"

Jerry spread his hands. "Out?"

9. A BICENTENNIAL CELEBRATION. THE 1976 GUNS & AMMO ANNUAL. IT'S ALL NEW ... IT'S INFORMATIVE ... IT'S AUTHORITATIVE ... START YOUR "BICENTENNIAL" CELEBRATION TODAY!

Dodging and weaving as usual Jerry slithered down the mound of refuse, his kilt left behind him like a forgotten fleece where it had snagged on the barbed wire and pulled free. Below him was what remained of the road and, on the other side, the ruins of the Convent of the Poor Clares. He was relieved to see that the row of houses on the south side of Blenheim Crescent, although boarded up, had escaped any major damage. He had jumped ship as the *James Durie* lost height over what had been the Mitcham Golf Course, had made it as far as the Bangladeshi ghetto in Tooting, where, under the hastily invented pseudonym 'Secundra Dass', he had been accepted and passed on through Brixton and as far as Pimlico before the chain had broken and he had found himself alone. From Pimlico he had to cross the desolation of Knightsbridge before he was in sight of home. Knightsbridge was the most notorious of all quarters, its inhabitants so vicious that they were feared even by the infamous denizens of Mayfair. Moreover Jerry in his kilt and turban had had the odds stacked as high against him as was possible, short of having a wooden leg as well. He had been fortunate in retaining his claymore and kris and with these weapons had been able to score himself a serviceable Lee-Enfield from a tall and muscular young lady in a silk headscarf and a necklace of black human ears.

Now, in grubby underpants, his legs running with cuts and half-healed gashes, the .303 cocked, he reached the convent, drawn towards the blasted chapel by the faint strains of Buddy Holly singing... *my heart grows cold and old*... on a tiny cassette machine. It was a signal. The song faded and became 'You've Got to Hide Your Love Away'. It could not be a trap. He relaxed by a fraction and put the rifle under his arm so that he could stoop and pull up his socks which had slipped down inside his stolen wellington boots (another prize from the lady in the headscarf). A shadow moved behind a mock Gothic window. The music stopped. Jerry raised his rifle and advanced. Pieces of broken plaster stirred as Sebastian Auchinek, in a neat set of fatigues, a Browning automatic in his inexperienced fist, broke cover, his free hand held palm outwards without much hope. His large brown eyes were wary, antagonistic, ready, as ever, for compromise. Instantly the Dixie Cups began to sing 'Chapel of Love'.

"You're looking pale, Mr Cornelius. You've lost your usual camouflage, eh? What's the matter—is the famous survival instinct shot at last?"

"I can't help the opinions people hold of me," said Jerry. "Your message came through days ago. I'm sorry I couldn't get here sooner."

"Don't give it a thought. There's not an awful lot of danger around at the moment. It's as quiet as the grave. Almost rural in some respects." He sounded wistful.

"It always was," said Jerry. "Enervating, isn't it, conventional warfare?"

"You're not fooling me, my son. I'm hip to any Pied Piper tricks." Auchinek holstered his Browning. "I'm acting on behalf of Miss Persson. As her agent. She asked me to do this."

"Still in the promotion business, then?" Jerry followed the Jew into the shadows of the chapel and found a seat on the cold ugly marble of the altar. "What sort of acts are going down with the London public at the moment?" He began to shiver. "You couldn't lend me a costume, could you?"

Auchinek was pleased with the situation. "Sorry," he said casually, "all the props are gone."

"You could lend me your guerrilla suit. You won't win the girl by making a monkey of yourself, king. Apeing her's not going to help the state of the Empire. Aaah!" Jerry opened his mouth and screeched with laughter, displaying his broken, piebald teeth.

"And you'll never get away with that material." Auchinek shook his head. "Not these days. Tastes are changing. The public wants sophisticated romantic comedy. You're offering them amateurish street theatre. Things have come a long way since the mummer's plays. It won't do, Mr Cornelius."

Jerry scratched his neck. "So it is an audition, after all?"

"Of sorts. I can help you. There might be room for a brother and sister act in our final programme." He studied Jerry's eyes and seemed satisfied by the reaction he received. Jerry got down from the altar. Sebastian Auchinek turned over the tape to its reverse side. *I believe in yesterday* sang Paul McCartney, his voice finding an echo in what remained of the roof. With a sudden burst of malicious energy Auchinek flung the player against the wall. It smashed at once and there was silence. "I'm Miss Persson's manager, as you know, but I do sometimes handle other people..."

"You don't have to tell me. Are you talking about Catherine?"

"I am. My spell in the USAF..."

"I don't want to know about your introduction to black magic..."

"... proved useful in that I was able to acquire certain rights..."

"I told you..."

"... and in turn come to possession..."

"You're not listening. Your religious convictions are your own. All I want to know—"

"... of a number of flies—files—pertaining to the activities of informants operating in this area."

"Narks? Stoolies? Squealers?"

"One of whom was a friend of yours, I believe. Gordon Gavin."

"Flash Gordon."

"I was able to interview him, just before the big pull-out. He knew the whereabouts of your sister. She's still here."

"She can't be. I moved her, didn't I? I had her—I had her—that's what I can't remember. But I was sure…"

"Only the surface suffered much. The underground sections are still almost entirely intact and functioning. Why, there's a rumour that some of these tunnels go all the way to Lapland."

"So she was under my nose before, before, before…" Jerry's head was aching badly. "Have you got her safe?"

"She doesn't look too good to me. But Miss Persson assured me…"

"She's an expert at that." Images filled his poor battered head. He left the chapel and ran across to the main building, up the fractured stairs, over the demolished threshold, waist-deep in lath and plaster, brickwork and shattered timber, wading towards his only hope, his goal, his faith, flailing around him as, with his last reserves of energy, he shifted muck and rubble.

"Catherine!

"Catherine!

"Catherine!"

In critical awe Sebastian Auchinek watched the wasted body of the wailing barbarian disappear in a chaos of dust.

10. HIGH INTENSITY COLOUR (THAT'S ACTUALLY GOOD FOR YOUR EYES!)

"Airship! You never bin on a bleedin' airship—not since you woz a boy at ther bloody Scrubs Lane fair!" Mrs Cornelius had a good laugh before looking down on her son and shaking her huge head, freshly permed, freshly gold. Her mouth was a handsome crimson, an exotic blossom, its tints echoed in her cheeks, contrasted by her eyelids of midnite blue, the pink powder. She belched and her breasts wobbled as she patted at her belly. "Pardon." She tugged at the waist of her cotton frock with its pattern of maroon and yellow nasturtiums. "Ah. Thass better. Wot's 'appened ter Frank?"

"He went off with the colonel, Mum," said Jerry meekly. "You didn't tell him about Cathy, did you?"

"Fink I'm daft? Silly bugger! 'Course I didn't. We don't wan' the 'ole fuckin' world ter know, do we?" Although not altogether sure what was wrong with her daughter, Mrs Cornelius had a strong suspicion that it was connected with something scandalous. When Jerry had brought her home his mother had immediately suspected him of having attempted an abortion on her. It had been Colonel Pyat, with his connections, who had known of the fortified hospital at Roedean and arranged for the girl to be taken there. Catherine had been in the worst condition Jerry had ever seen her—more than a little frost-blackened. The hospital, however, was the best there was. The doctors had every confidence, they said, in an early revival. Jerry had had to borrow four cases of 12.77mm machine-gun ammunition from Colonel Pyat to add to his own store, and that had been for the hospital's down payment only. He wasn't sure where he was going to find the BTR-50PK armoured personnel carrier he would need to secure the release of his sister once she was up and about. Again Colonel Pyat had been reassuring, promising that he would underwrite Jerry until the situation improved for him.

Jerry had wanted to go straight back to London from Roedean but his mother insisted on making a day of it. Frank was living in Brighton now, running a small general shop, and Mrs Cornelius wanted to see how he was getting on.

"It 'asn't arf changed," declared Mrs Cornelius as she stood regarding the twisted pier, most of which had tipped itself into the sea. She pointed at a distant girder. "Thass where the ol' dodgems useter be, innit?"

Jerry turned up the collar of his black car coat. He put his hands deep into his pockets. It was very cold for May, although the sky was blue and clear and the water as calm as the Mediterranean. He was worried in case Colonel Pyat told Frank something which would start the whole trouble all over again. He looked back towards the darkened dolphinarium in time to see the colonel and his brother ascending the steps to the street. Colonel Pyat shook his head calling: "Nothing I'm afraid!"

"Orl I bleedin' want is a bag o' fish an' chips!" said Mrs Cornelius with a gigantic sigh of dismay. She patted her son on the shoulder. "Up yer get, Jer."

Jerry rose from the bench, moving his weight from foot to foot, running his tongue round the inside of his mouth. "I'm a bit worried about the lorry," he said. "What with the scavengers and that."

"It'll be safe enough where it is," she reassured him. "I wish ther bloody trains woz still goin'. Cor! Wot a cum-darn, eh?" She cast a disgusted eye over the wrecked façades, the faded signs. "Yer carn't even go on ther fuckin' beach for bleedin' bar' wire!"

Frank and Colonel Pyat arrived to stand beside them. Jerry was disturbed by the fact that Frank wore a black coat almost identical to his own. His brother's eyes were warm and cunning as if he had recently sniffed prey. "Not a chip to be had," said Frank. "Sorry, Mum. It's what I thought. Nobody's catching any fish, for one thing." He anticipated his mother's next question before she asked it. "And, of course, there hasn't been a pub open since the ordinance. You'd better take me up on that sandwich." He nodded towards the twittens of the town's cold interior. "Back at the shop."

Mrs Cornelius sighed. "I used ter love this place. It woz reelly fun. Remember ther races, Ive?"

Colonel Pyat, who wore a cavalry twill military-style

overcoat, nodded his heavy Slavic head. "Everything is gone now."

"It's not as bad as all that," said Frank. "A lot of the old residents are still here. We've quite a flourishing community, really. We've kept our identity, which is more than you can say of some. We can't offer the facilities to visitors nowadays, of course, but perhaps that's for the best—so far as the indigenous population's concerned. But you'll see. Brighton'll be back to normal before you know it."

Jerry removed a dirty handkerchief from his pocket and loudly blew his nose. Frank darted him a weary look. "Cool it, Jerry."

Jerry put his handkerchief away. "I shouldn't've thought it could have got any cooler."

For the first time Mrs Cornelius noticed the cold. "You're right. It's bloody freezin'. You got anyfink I c'n put on, Frank?"

"I've got some lovely coats back at the shop. Real mink. I'll lend you one of those." Frank began to walk along the front and they followed.

"Mink?" said his mother. "Bloody 'ell! You must be doin' orl right, as usual!"

"There's not a lot of call for luxury goods just now. But that'll change in time. I accepted them as barter." Frank laughed. "I must have every decent mink coat on the South Coast. I've literally got a back room full of them. The trouble is, though, that they attract rats."

"Aaawk!" said Mrs Cornelius ritualistically.

Frank stopped and then fell in beside Jerry. "And

how's life treating you?" His bleak eyes stared out to sea, giving the horizon a shifty once-over. "Getting by, are we?"

"Under the circumstances," said Jerry.

"A bit more realistic, these days, I should think." Frank was almost euphorically triumphant. He tapped his head. "Got the old imagination in check at last. You're staying with Mum?"

"I've been a bit queer," said Jerry.

"So she's looking after you, is she?"

"Well, my own place..."

"A direct hit, I heard. Shame."

They were some distance ahead of Mrs C. and Colonel P. now. Frank led the way up King Street. "You had your head in the clouds, you see. Now I saw the way the wind was blowing. I've got my shop. In real terms I'm probably the richest man in Sussex. Surrey, too, I shouldn't wonder. Got four Pakis working for me. Kept my head down, see, and my nose clean and here I am. I don't deny I'm well off. I don't feel guilty."

"Guilty?" Jerry had never heard his brother use the word. He cheered up a fraction. "Blimey! You must have done some terrible things. Brighton's getting to you, then?"

"What?" Frank was puzzled. "I'm happy, Jerry. Not many can say that, these days. Got my pick of anything I want. Any *body* I want." He nudged his brother in the ribs. "Some of those people'll give anything for a bit of fresh liver. Their little daughters. Eh? What! They never learned to fight, you see—only complain. I must have had every 'Disgusted' in the Home Counties in my shop! Well, I ask you!" He paused. Mrs Cornelius and her escort were a fair way behind, labouring up the hill. "You want to work for me? Is that why you came?"

"Mum wanted to see how you were doing. I just drove the lorry."

"Your lorry, is it?"

"The colonel's. He was in the last government for a few days."

"Did all right for himself, then?"

"He reckons he was sold short." Jerry spoke listlessly as he looked at a sea bereft of boats, a sky without ships, a street without music. Catherine remained and he was helpless to give her comfort or take any direct part in her destiny. He swayed as his mother came closer. She was bent almost double, rubbing her thumb against her index finger, making peculiar smacking noises with her lips. He felt very dizzy indeed. Frank glanced at him. "You've gone all yellow."

"I'm tired," said Jerry.

"Totch-totch," said Mrs Cornelius. "Come 'ere, yer littel bleeder. Totch-totch-totch."

Through rapidly blurring vision Jerry saw that she was addressing a small, mangey black-and-white cat in the gutter. The animal walked slowly and amiably towards her, rubbing its flank against the kerb, its tail erect.

Jerry sat down on the pavement.

His mother didn't notice what was happening to him; but the cat turned to look at him, its intelligent green eyes piercing his own.

For a moment it seemed to Jerry that his entire being was about to be drawn into the body of the cat. Then Mrs Cornelius had pounced and seized the animal. "Gotcha, yer little bugger!"

"This is a fine time to start playing the Fool," said Frank.

Jerry passed out.

EARLY REPORTS

Many bathing deaths were reported from seaside resorts yesterday. Two men and a boy were drowned while bathing near Llanelly, and Bertie Crooke, sixteen, son of a soldier, was drowned at Exmouth. Mr Duncan McGregor (twenty-four), a chemist, of Coatbridge, while bathing at Spittal was carried away by a strong current and drowned, despite the brave attempts to rescue him made by Mr James Webster, of Airdrie. Two young munition workers named Griffith Robert Jones and Richard Morris were drowned while bathing at Buryport.

Sunday Pictorial, 22 July, 1917

The following notice announcing the adoption of a system of air-raid warnings for London by "sound bomb" was issued last night:—The experiments made on Thursday with sky signals showed the value of sound bombs for the purpose of warning the population of London ... The signal will consist of three sound bombs fired at intervals of a quarter of a minute ... having regard to the speed at which aeroplanes now travel, the warning at the point attacked can only be of a few minutes' duration.

Sunday Pictorial, 22 July, 1917

The *Bourse Gazette* states that the Premier, Prince Lvoff, has resigned. M. Kerensky has been appointed Premier, temporarily retaining the portfolios of War and Marine. M. Kerensky has sent a message to Reval, Helsingfors, and other points, saying: The disturbances have now been completely suppressed. The arrest of the leaders and of those guilty of the blood of their brothers and of crimes against the country and the revolution is proceeding ... I appeal to all true sons of democracy to save the country and the revolution from the enemy without and his Allies within.

Sunday Pictorial, 22 July, 1917

Aliens living at Folkestone and Margate have been given notice to leave the towns ... under a new Home Office Order which prohibits their presence within 20 miles of the coast. At Folkestone 130 foreigners are affected. They must be out of the town by midnight tonight. At Margate 238 have been given three days' notice.

The Times, 5 June, 1940

The trial began before Mr Justice Atkinson at the Central Criminal Court yesterday of Udham Singh, 37, an Indian engineer, who is charged with the murder of Sir Michael Frances O'Dwyer, a former Governor of the Punjab, at the close of a lecture at Caxton Hall, Westminster, on March 13. He pleaded "Not Guilty".

The Times, 5 June, 1940

Prefabs, with people clinging to the roofs, floated past bedroom windows at Felixstowe, where disaster arrived when the River Orwell burst its banks two miles away. Survivors told of nightmare screams and shouts for help as they watched people slide to their deaths from floating prefabs. Mrs Beryl Hillary ... said they were awakened by screams. "As I looked out of the window I saw a little girl washed off the roof of a prefab and drown." In Orford Road, where the Hillarys lived, a mother, father and two young children were drowned in a downstairs flat. People in the top flat were rescued. Mrs Katherine Minter, of Lauger Road, said: "In the darkness all that could be heard was the roaring of the water and the screaming of terrified women. The housing estate was like an ocean." ... Two-year-old Valerie—she could not tell nurses her surname—cried in hospital for her parents. They are listed among the missing.

Daily Sketch, 2 February, 1953

A baby girl died in a basement blaze in Sorcham Street, North Kensington on Saturday after two passers by had hurled themselves into the burning front room when they heard her screams.

Kensington Post, 19 February, 1965

Fire danger in North Kensington has become a controversial issue between the LCC and KBC. They sharply disagree on the code of fire prevention for lodging and rooming houses. Kensington Council say that the LCC Code of Escape from Fire is impracticable and expensive. They claim it would mean an average cost of £300 per house ... Kensington Council have not yet revealed their own plans for fire prevention, but there is no doubt they envisage a much cheaper and simpler code.

Kensington Post, 19 February, 1965

Jimi Hendrix, the pop musician, died in London yesterday, as reported elsewhere in this issue. If Bob Dylan was the man who liberated pop music verbally, to the extent that after him it could deal with subjects other than teenage affection, then Jimi Hendrix was largely responsible for whatever musical metamorphosis it has undergone in the past three years. Born in Seattle, Washington, he was part

Negro, part Cherokee Indian, part Mexican, and gave his date of birth as 27 November 1945.

The Times, 19 September, 1970

Part-time soldiers have been on manoeuvres with a Nazi "secret army" it was claimed yesterday. The troops were members of a Territorial Army unit. Special Branch investigators have been told that TA men linked up with a Nazi paramilitary group known as Column 88 for exercises in the Savernake Forest in Wiltshire. At least one TA officer—said to be a secret Nazi group member—is alleged to have helped to set up the operation. Members of the 20-strong TA unit thought the Nazis were another TA group. During the exercise the soldiers acted as mock terrorists, while the Nazis played the role of defenders of an important military target.

Daily Mirror, 19 April, 1976

TUNING UP (4)

"What infernal bad luck!" As he walked along the deck in his glittering white uniform Colonel Pyat tossed his racquet in the air and caught it again. "We lost all our balls."

"Overboard," said Catherine, indicating the Mediterranean. She, too, wore white, a boater with a blue-and-white band, a simple silk shirt-waister with a pale blue broderie anglaise bodice. The skirt of the dress was cut just on the ankle of her kid boots. She and he had been playing tennis in the yacht's court, astern. "Entirely my fault. I'm terrible."

Jerry shifted his weight in the blue-and-white deckchair, putting his newspaper on the matching canvas stool at his elbow. "I'm sure we'll be able to get you some more. In Alexandria, perhaps." He ran a finger round the inside of his hard collar.

"Is it far, Alexandria?" she asked him. She sat in the chair next to his. Colonel Pyat hovered, then went to stand by the *Teddy Bear's* rail.

"Not too far." A tiny breeze found his face. He sighed with pleasure.

Colonel Pyat laid a finger on one side of his small moustache and peered out from beneath his cap. The peak shaded his eyes completely. Indeed, the only strong feature visible was his neat imperial. "Shouldn't you be getting ready? It's almost teatime."

"So I should." Jerry rose from the canvas chair. He gathered up his books and papers. "And you, too, Catherine, eh?" He raised his panama. "I'll see you later, then."

"Fine," said the colonel.

Jerry crossed to his cabin. It faced forward—a bedroom, a sitting room and a dressing room. It was full of light from the large portholes on three sides, simply furnished with Charles Rennie Mackintosh designs. Even as he changed into his costume he heard eight bells ring for the dog-watch; time for tea. Slipping on his domino Jerry hurried out, making for the stern and the quarter-deck where a piano had already been set up by lithe Lascar matelots. On the rest of the deck were little gilded bamboo tables with lace cloths; they had matching gilded bamboo chairs, upholstered in blue plush.

As Jerry approached the quarter-deck, racing down the companionway, he almost bumped into Miss Brunner, the governess, who made a clicking noise with her tongue before she guessed who he was. Dyak stewards, in white turbans, red Zouave jackets and blue sarongs, were setting silverware and teapots on the tables. Jerry ascended the last companionway just ahead of Bishop Beesley and Karen von Krupp (wearing her usual Brunswick coffee-coloured gown), two of his guests on the cruise, and just behind Una Persson who was smoothing the folds of her elaborate Columbine costume, gold, white and scarlet, and adjusting her own domino mask. She stood beside the piano, protecting her head with a Japanese sunshade. Jerry winked at her and sat down at the piano.

"Shall we try it, then?"

Una Persson looked at Bishop Beesley, Karen von Krupp and Miss Brunner who were arranging themselves at the furthest table, near the rail. "Why not?" she said. She cleared her throat. Jerry lifted the lid of the piano and played a few notes, exercising his fingers, folding back the flounced cuffs of his red, white and blue Pierrot suit. "Where's Catherine?"

"On her way." Jerry spread his new music.

"And Prinz Lobkowitz?"

"On his way."

"Auchinek?"

"You'd know better than I, my dear." Jerry put his thumb on middle C.

"Your Mr Collier?"

"Doubtless on his way."

"They're all arriving, the audience. Oh, I hate bad time-keeping." She folded her sunshade and put it behind the piano.

Jerry played a 3/4 tango rhythm with his left hand. "We might as well start, I think. It's only an amateur show, Una."

She put one hand on the quarter-deck's port rail, glanced at the smooth sea, raised herself on the points of her ballet slippers, twirling in her three-quarter-length skirt. She began to smile. It was the professional in her. To encourage his companion, Jerry played a white note glissando and began to hum the tune of their song as Major Nye, Mrs Nye, the Nye daughters and the Nyes' little boy, Pip, took their places at two tables near the front. Major Nye was smiling in delight. "How jolly!" Mrs Nye did her best to smile, but she was not in Una's class. The girls looked a trifle embarrassed and the little boy seemed astonished. He wore a sailor suit, as did his sisters. The Dyaks bent over them to take their orders. Mrs Cornelius, in a huge cream-and-strawberry day dress and a lopsided Gainsborough hat, arrived on the arm of her son Frank who wore an orange, blue and green blazer, white cotton trousers and a yellow boater. Una began to sing in her high, sweet voice:

> My pulse rate stood at zero
> When I first saw my Pierrot.

Jerry sang to her over his right shoulder as he continued to play:

> My temperature rose to ninety-nine
> When I beheld my Columbine.

Catherine ran onto the deck, arriving just in time to join Una. Catherine, too, was masked, dressed as Harlequin in colours to match Una's. She had her magic wand in her hand, Harlequin's slapstick with which, traditionally, everything could be transformed into something else. They all sang the chorus:

Sigh, sigh, sigh…
For love that's oft denied.
Cry, cry, cry…
My lips remain unsatisfied
I'm yearning so, for my own Pierrot.

Catherine took Una about the waist and they danced together for the last line of the chorus.

As we dance the En-tropy Tan-go!

Jerry played the chorus through again, making it more lively and giving it a strict tango rhythm now, for Auchinek had reached them. He was in white from head to foot, half his thin face covered in an expressionless white mask, the rest caked in dead white make-up, a false grey beard, huge glasses, crowned by an elongated silk hat. He was old Pantaloon, as orthodox as ever in the traditional *dell'arte* costume.

Una and Catherine were cheek to cheek. "Sigh, sigh, sigh…" Their eyes were fixed on the audience. Auchinek went to stand awkwardly on the other side of Jerry, evidently trying to remember the lyrics. When Jerry had told him of the plan he had gone from Naples to Rome by train to buy his costume. "For love that's oft denied." Jerry stared mournfully at Columbine. "Cry, cry, cry… My lips remain unsatisfied…" Facing Jerry now, Una sang perhaps a mite too sardonically: "I'm yearning so for my own Pierrot." And altogether: "As we dance the

Entropy Tan-tan-go!"

Colonel Pyat sat down, raising his cap in jovial, if uncomprehending appreciation. Nearby, Frank Cornelius frowned as he tried to make out the words, comprehending all too well. He began to look a bit alarmed.

Prinz Lobkowitz came up at last, all in black velvet save for a white frill around his neck, a beribboned mandolin in his hand, his eyes merry behind his mask, as Scaramouche, and behind him was Shakey Mo Collier, panting, scrambling, swaggering as soon as he was in sight of the audience, in a gorgeously elaborate military uniform, festooned with braid, blazing with brass, a great Wellington hat on his head, sporting ostrich and peacock feathers, wearing false moustachios which he twirled rather too often, monstrous eyebrows which threatened to blind him, jackboots and sabre, a perfect burlesque bantam dandy, Captain Fracasse.

Assembled they sang the next chorus with wavering gusto:

> I'll weep, weep, weep
> Till he sweeps me off my feet.
> My heart will beat, beat, beat,
> And my body lose its heat.
> Oh, life no longer seems so sweet
> Since that sad Pierrot became my beau
> And taught me the En-tro-py Tan-go!

Harlequin tango'd with Pantaloon, Columbine with Scaramouche, Pierrot with Captain Fracasse, until Jerry had to return to his place at the piano for his own verse:

So flow, flow, flow...
As the rains turn into snow.
And it's slow, slow, slow...
As the colours lose their glow...
The Winds of Limbo no longer blow
For cold Columbine and her pale Pierrot,
As we dance the En-tro-py Tan-go!

Frank was groaning and looking about him as if expecting attack from all sides, as if he contemplated ducking under the table. His face had turned a colour that was ugly in contrast to his blazer, but his mother merely shook her head. "Ai deown't know ai'm shewer." She was using her posh voice. "Yew cearn't unnerstand a word of the songs these days, cean yew?" She waved a teacake. Crumbs cascaded over her strawberry flounces. "An' wot they doin', ai wondah, puttin' on a bleedin' pentomime et Easter?" She pushed back the brim of her hat as her eye caught something in the distance. She tugged at a Dyak's jacket. "Blimey! Wot's that?"

Absent-mindedly Frank swallowed his whole cake. His eyes popped. He choked. "What?"

Although they had planned another chorus, Mrs Cornelius's cry was so loud that even the performers turned to stare in the same direction.

Sebastian Auchinek's eyes were weeping, doubtless from the toxic effects of the make-up. He removed his topper. "Where?"

"What?" said Shakey Mo, twirling a disappointed moustachio. He had only just begun to enjoy himself for the first time since Nice.

"That!" said Mrs Cornelius dramatically.

Miss Brunner, Karen von Krupp, Bishop Beesley and the whole Nye family rose to their feet.

"That smudge over there!" Mrs Cornelius crammed another teacake into her mouth. She made a further remark, also, but it was entirely muffled.

Prinz Lobkowitz put his mandolin on top of the piano. He seemed relieved. "That's Africa."

RECAPITULATION

Mais Arlequin le Roi commande à l'Acheron,
Il est duc des esprits de la bande infernale.

Histoire plaisante des faits et gestes de
Harlequin etc., Paris, 1585

Once, the giant huntsman was Odin, the Norse
god of the dead, who rode through the night
skies seeking the souls of the dying. Though
his name was changed with the coming of
Christianity, his role did not. Often he was
thought of as the Devil himself, but in different
parts of France he was identified as the ghost
of King Herod, or of Charlemagne. In northern
England he was sometimes called Woden, while
other counties saw him as Wild Elric, who
defied the Conqueror, or even as Arthur. The
phantom hounds were the spirits of unbaptised
children, or of unrepentant sinners ... Some

critics have pointed out, however, that their
cries, as they seek the souls of the damned,
closely resemble those of migrating geese.

Folklore, Myths and Legends of Britain,
London, 1973

FILTH AND NOISE: PORTOBELLO RESIDENTS COMPLAIN

Portobello Road Market is a disgrace say some local residents—and they are backed up by Sisters of St Joseph's Convent. The cause is the junk and litter left by second hand dealers—the Steptoes and "totters" of North Kensington. It's not just the noise of the Borough Council workmen clearing up the rubbish that is annoying the Catholic Sisters. By day, says the Mother Superior, people throw old shoes, suitcases and other unwanted articles over the Convent wall. "The main door is thick with filth sometimes," she said. "It is quite degrading." ... Mrs Anna Marks, a Portobello Road shopkeeper, described the northern part of the market as "shameful". It was a disgrace to London ... Her husband, Mr W. Marks, added: "I have lived here all my life—I remember when they used to drive sheep down the Portobello Road. The market has gone downhill lately."

Kensington Post, 23 April, 1965

I.   THE GOD FROM THE MACHINE

"The new century," said Major Nye, "doesn't seem awfully different from the old." He stretched his arms in his stiff drab jacket, settled his topee on his grey locks, and clumped in booted feet out onto the verandah to salute the flag as it was raised for the morning. In the fort's quadrangle a squadron of troopers in the uniform of the 3rd Punjab Irregular Rifles, a squadron of Bengali riflemen in red and dark blue, with red and yellow turbans, and Ghoorka infantrymen in gun-green and red, saluted the Union Jack. Young Cornelius was in charge of the guard. "Sir!" He, too, wore drab, with black lace and red facings, a solar topee wound about with the regiment's green, black and red colours.

"Morning, Cornelius. Happy New Year to you. Looked for you last night."

"I was still on my way back from Simla, sir. I've just had time to change."

"Of course. Any news?"

"Not much, sir."

"Ha!"

Major Nye yawned. Then he craned forward to inspect first the British and then the native troops who stood to attention on three sides of the parade ground as the bugle began its traditional call. Currently he and Cornelius were the only white officers here. He raised his eyes to the great hills beyond the walls. He had faith in his Sikhs and Ghoorkas. Secundra Dass and his Chinese allies might be threatening from the east, while Zakar Khan, the old hill fox, could be on his way from the north, with Russian machine guns and officers, but they'd be no match for a couple of battalions of these chaps, plus a squadron or two of the 3rd Punjab Cavalry. Major Nye frowned.

"Cavalry didn't travel with you, after all?"

Cornelius dismissed the guard. "Yes, sir. But I was on duty, so I had to ride ahead. They shouldn't be more than an hour or two at most, sir."

"Jolly good." Major Nye moved his head. "Mind coming inside for a moment, Cornelius?"

Major Nye retired into his gloomy office. It was almost cold. On the wall hung the photograph Major Nye usually referred to as his 'personal touch': a picture of Sarah Bernhardt as she appeared in her white costume in Richepin's *Pierrot Assassin* at the Trocadero in Paris on 28 April, 1883, just before her marriage to M. Damala broke up. She had married Damala in London the previous year and Major Nye had been on leave at the time and witnessed it, almost by accident. Overhead the punkah swept back and forth, disturbing some of the dust on the piles of papers stacked everywhere. Major Nye rarely replied to communications but he did not have the heart to file anything before it had been officially answered. "Sit down, old chap."

Cornelius sat in the rattan armchair on the other side of the desk. Major Nye removed something from his own chair before seating himself. "Had that fellow of yours in yesterday, Cornelius. What's his name? Hashim?"

"Really, sir? Did he tell you anything worthwhile?"

"Wouldn't talk to me. Wouldn't talk to Subadar Bisht. Wouldn't talk to Risaldar S'arnt Major. Would only talk to you. Trusts you, I suppose. Couldn't blame him. But he seemed to have an urgent message for you. Worried me a bit. Could mean trouble coming, eh?"

"Quite likely, sir. He was riding with the Chinese until they stopped to recoup at Srinagar. He reported their position and then returned to their camp. I'd guess that the horde's on the move again."

Major Nye frowned. "It means that Secundra Dass and his men have joined them now."

"That's the report we had while I was in Simla, sir."

"We're going to need some Lancers, Cornelius."

"Yes, sir. And a bit of artillery too, sir, I'd have thought."

"Artillery would help. Still, I feel sorry for the Chinese if our Ghoorkas get at them. They're not a fighting people, the Chinese."

"No, sir."

"Like the Americans. No good at it. They should

leave fighting to the British, eh? And the Ghoorkas and the Sikhs, hm? And the Dogras and Mahrattas, what?"

"Who would we fight, sir?" Cornelius was amused, but Major Nye didn't find the question sensible.

"Why, the bloody Afridis, of course. Who else? He'll always give you a good scrap, your Afridi."

"True, sir."

"Damned true, Cornelius." Major Nye became nostalgic and querulous. "Why'd the blasted Chinese want to interfere? Waste of time. Waste of everybody's time."

"They've conquered Tibet and Nepal and Kashmir and Iskandastan so far, sir."

"Certainly they have. But they haven't crossed the border yet, have they?"

"They must be about to, sir."

"Then they're blasted fools. And Secundra Dass is a blasted fool to tie himself down with a lot of Chinese."

"They outnumber us by about a thousand to one, I should think, sir." Cornelius spoke mildly. He was trying to read a partially exposed report on the major's desk. The report was yellow, several months old at least. "If they attack while we're at our present strength, we should have quite a hard time of it."

"Certainly. It won't be easy, Cornelius. But with the Cavalry here we should do it, what?"

"It could be the largest army on the march since the time of Genghis Khan." Cornelius got up and looked through the blinds at the glinting hills.

Major Nye lit his pipe. "But Genghis Khan was a

Mongol, not a Chinaman. Besides, he didn't have the British to deal with—or the Ghoorkas, or the Jats or Baluchis, or Madrassis, or the Ranghars or Gorwalis or Pathans or Punjabis or Rajputs—or, for that matter, the 3rd Punjab Irregular Rifles. Not just the best trained soldiers in the world, not just the bravest and most spirited, but they're the fiercest, too. Volunteers, you see. There's nothing more terrifying, more 'unstoppable', than a force of British and Indian infantry supported by mixed Sikh and British lancers. That's why we get on with them so well—they're as civilised and no-nonsense savage as we are. It's why we get on well with Arabs, too, you know. It's why we *don't* get on with Bombay brahmins…"

"The Chinese and Secundra Dass are sworn to sweep every European from Asia, sir."

"Excellent idea."

"Sir?"

"What? Ah!" Major Nye smiled in understanding. Dropping his voice he spoke slowly, as if he didn't wish to startle Cornelius. "We're not Europeans, after all. Never have been. We're British. That's why we've so much in common with India."

"They seem to hate us just as much as any other—non-Indians—sir."

"Of course they do. Why shouldn't they? Good for them. But they won't beat us."

"It seems, sir, that the Chinese…"

"The Chinese are a peasant race, Cornelius. The British and their fighting Indian allies, do you see, are not peasant races. The Slavs, the Germans, most Latins, are natural tillers of the soil, makers of profits. They like to preserve the status quo above everything else. But we, like the Sikhs and Ghoorkas, are naturally aggressive and pretty rapacious. Not brutal, you understand—it's peasants make brutal soldiers. Russians, Chinese, Japanese, Americans, Boers— all peasants and burghers. The infantry, at any rate, while the cavalry are full of ideas of swagger and glory—parvenu Uhlans the lot of them, Hussars-manqués, that's what I think. Peasants—panicky butchers at best, and sometimes crueller than any Pathan—war's an insanity for them, you see, no part of their way of life—they'd rather be at home doing whatever it is they do with the cows and pigs and shops. We're cruel, arrogant, often ruthless, but we've lived by war for too long not to have become somewhat more humane in the way we wage it. We make quick decisions. We make our points hard and fast. We don't have to hate our enemies to kill 'em, we do it decently, on the whole, with respect and economy." Major Nye rang a bell on his desk. "Feel like some tea?"

"Thanks, sir." Young Cornelius seemed somewhat depressed, probably because he had been up all night on the train from Simla.

"Same goes for your Arab, your Pathan, your Sikh. It's self-interest, it's efficiency, and sometimes it's a sort of practical idealism, but we rarely have to work ourselves up to hatred, to find a Cause, a reason for loathing those we wish to kill. Practicality—it's why we're good at running an Empire. And as long as people don't give us trouble, we look after 'em. The Dutch and the Belgians, for instance, take too much out of their colonies, and so do the French— the peasant instinct, again, a tendency to overwork the land, you might say. Also, of course, they were unfortunate enough to belong to the Continent of Europe. Then there's the Cossacks. I've a lot of respect for your Cossack, by and large, though he's inclined to get a bit carried away from time to time. Now if it was Cossacks we were dealing with I'd be looking forward to a good, professional scrap, but most Russians are tame. Most Europeans are tame. Most Americans, God bless 'em, are very tame indeed. I hope the British never become tame. It would be the end of us."

"Well, I suppose if we ever lost a major war…"

"It's not the winning and losing of wars that tames a nation—it's the love of property, the acquisition of too many comforts for their own sake, the cosseting of oneself, that tames you. Thank God the bourgeoisie don't run England yet, the way they run the Continent. Internationalism could ruin us. Stick to imperialism and you can't go far wrong. A country should be in charge of its workers and its aristocrats. Farmers, shopkeepers and bankers have far too much regard for their cosy firesides to be trustworthy guardians of a nation's pride or its well-being. Your aristocrat has no respect for wealth because he's inherited it. Your common man has no respect for wealth because he's never experienced it. See what I mean?"

"I think so, sir. But shouldn't the army have a voice…?"

"Doesn't need a voice if the country's being properly run. No part of the army's job, politics."

An Indian orderly entered with a tray of tea. "No fresh milk today, sir. All cows gone."

"Damn," said Major Nye absently as he reached for the pot, "that'll be their advance raiding parties, I shouldn't wonder. Better lock up as soon as the Lancers arrive, Cornelius. Post extra guards and so on. And send some sort of message to Delhi, would you?"

Cornelius accepted a cup. "Should we do anything else, sir?" Looking through the window again it seemed to him that the hills were obscured by a huge cloud of white and yellow dust.

Major Nye knocked out his pipe and picked up his cup. He chuckled as he raised the tea to his cracked lips. "Write letters to our nearest and dearest, I suppose." He lifted a white handkerchief to his sleeve and brushed away a fly. "I don't think this will last too long, do you?"

2. WITH THE FLAG TO PRETORIA

"Bleck is bleck ent wide es wide, my dee-arr," said Meneer Olmeijer comfortably, puffing at his large pipe. The tubby Boer, in khaki shirt and jodhpurs and wide-brimmed bush-hat, surveyed the tranquil plaas through twinkling eyes. "Airr you stell intirrested on de oostrrich, Miss Corrnelius?"

"Perhaps..." she said. She had difficulty crossing the yard in her long tropical skirt. She had chosen a drab brown so as not to show the dust. Her hat, too, was brown and its brim tended to obscure her vision. "Perhaps later?"

"Cerrtinly, cerrtinly—lader or niverr—y'ave all de tame in de woahld 'ere. Yooah ön 'oliday! Ya doo whadiver ya fill lake—Liberty Kraal, eh? Heh, heh, heh!" He displayed his stained teeth. "En corrl me Cousin Piet. Efterr all, we'rre rrelitivs, ain't we?" He placed a tanned, red hand on her soft, wincing shoulder. "Ther woah's övah—we'll all be Afrikanders soon—Brridischerr oah Hollanderr—farrms oah mines." They had halted by a white wooden fence, marking the northern limits of the plaas. On their left were the huts of the native workers' kraal. Piet Olmeijer lifted a booted foot to the lowest rail; a mystical light had entered his eyes as he inspected the infinite veldt, most of which was his, won from the Matabele with blood and Bibles and an inspired hypocrisy which filled Catherine with admiring awe but caused her companion, currently back in the house, considerable confusion. Una had been unable to face this morning's tour; neither, to their host's dismay, had she breakfasted. She continued to suffer, Catherine had said when presenting Una's excuses, from the heat— but the fact was that Una, furious and frightened not so much by the condition of the native Africans as by the peculiar attitude of the whites towards them, was almost incapable now of speech in the presence of Olmeijer or his overseers. Moreover the farmer had taken a fancy to Una and had dropped several hints concerning his need for a wife and sons who could inherit all he had created. Olmeijer had told Jerry, whom he knew from Johannesburg days, that Una Persson looked strong and healthy, the sort of help-meet an Afrikander farmer needed. Olmeijer's first wife and most of the rest of his family had contracted typhus during internment some years previously, when the Witwatersrand dispute was at its height. However, Una's bouts of ill-health, as she explained them, were causing him to relax his attention as time went on. The only unfortunate consequence of this was that gradually the farmer was beginning to speculate about Catherine's capacity for filling the rôle. The introduction of Christian names was, Catherine guessed, a significant step forward and, perhaps, a bold one for a widower Boer of forty sweating, self-restraining summers. It could also explain his sudden expressions of tolerance towards someone who, while they had a name that sounded comfortingly Dutch, was still an Uitlander. He had been reassured by Una herself when they had first arrived: at that point she had been anxious to recall her pro-Boer convictions in England, to disassociate herself with the gold-diggers, critical of the foreign invasion of the Transvaal, full of the romance of the Great Trek, of the courage of the Voortrekkers and their struggles against the savage Matabele. Una had always found such mythologies attractive and, Catherine thought, always sulked in bitter disappointment when the reality contradicted her imaginings. But Catherine was determined not to be critical of her friend. Una's idealism had dragged her up from despair more than once.

"Just think," said Catherine positively to Meneer Olmeijer, "only seventy years ago there was nothing here but lion and wildebeeste! And now…" The veldt rolled to the horizon. "And now there's hardly any lions or gnus at all!"

"Doan't ya bileef et," chuckled Piet Olmeijer. "Ger rridin' by yerself an' find ert!"

"Well, at least there's no wild natives to worry about any more," said Catherine, still doing her best, but feeling increasingly that she was somehow betraying Una.

"Det's a fekt," agreed Olmeijer with some satisfaction. "Neow, Ah prromist Ah'd lit her see some o' da tebacca bein' pecked in da feealds, ya?"

"Oh, yes," said Catherine reluctantly. "Or the oranges, you said."

"Certainly—oah de örrinjis." He chose to detect in her manner an enthusiasm for his life and its loves. As they left the fence he reached a hand towards her but dropped it as, from the other side of the bungalow, there came a pounding sound which shook the ground and round the corner raced a tall black-and-white ostrich, its eyes starting, its beak enclosed in a peculiar harness, its broad feet stirring the dust, while on its back, whooping and giggling in a dirty, crumpled European suit, his white hat over his face, was Catherine's brother, followed by upwards of twenty grinning blacks in loincloths or tattered shorts and shirts.

"Heh, heh, heh," laughed Piet Olmeijer. "Oh, look at det berd rrun! Heh, heh, heh!" He removed his pipe from his mouth and waved it. "'Ang ern, Meneer Cornelius! Excellent!" The ostrich reached the kraal fence, stopped and then swerved, running the length of the enclosure. Jerry slipped further from the saddle, yelling with joy like a five-year-old, the loose-limbed blacks clapping and shouting, "Ride 'im, baas!"

The bird's panic increased. It began to run in circles, its long neck undulating, attempting to free itself from the halter.

"Ride 'im!"

"Hokai!" cried Olmeijer jovially. "Hokaai!"

Jerry fell heavily on his back and was dragged a short way by one stirrup before he could free himself. His face was bruised purple and yellow, covered in dust; his suit was torn and he was limping, supported by the blacks as he came back towards Olmeijer and his sister. "That was great fun."

"I don't think I'll try it now." Catherine was concerned for him. "What's wrong with your leg?"

"Turned my ankle in the stirrup, that's all."

"Foei tog!" said Olmeijer sympathetically. He spoke in Afrikaans to the blacks holding Jerry, ordering them to take him to the stoep, ordering others to capture the ostrich and return it to its pen. At the door to the house Olmeijer dismissed the boys and he took one side of the hobbling Englishman while Catherine took the other. Olmeijer was in fine humour.

"I hope the ostrich is all right," said Jerry.

"Dit is vir my om't ewe!" Olmeijer was admiring. "Ye've te've gets to rroide them oostriches…" He remembered himself. "Excuse me, Miss Cornelius. Eouwt 'ere, wivart vimenfolk arahnd, ya git a liddel sleck wid de lengvij." They entered a large white kitchen, seating Jerry in a high-backed wooden chair. "Olly! Olly! Waar die drummel—weah de deuce es det houseboy?"

The houseboy emerged grinning. He had evidently heard what had happened. Olmeijer told him to bring cold water and towels for Jerry's ankle.

Catherine helped Jerry to remove his jacket, looking about for a cloth. "I'll clean your face."

"Nar, nar," said Olmeijer pleasantly, "lit one av der serrvants do et! Det's wod dey're paid fer, efter all!"

Catherine left the kitchen, entering a shady hall, on her way to Jerry's room to get him a fresh shirt and jacket. As she passed the door of the room she and Una were sharing, she heard her friend's voice raised in song. Glad that Una seemed more cheerful, she went in. Una was bathing. As an uncomprehending black girl poured warm water over her perfect back she rendered an old Gus Elen music-hall song of several seasons before:

> I wonders at th' ig'rance wot prevails abaht th'
>   woar,
> Some folks dunno th' diff'rance wot's between a sow
>   an' Boar!
> Roun' Bef'nal Green they're spahtin' of ole Kruger
>   night an' day,
> An' I tries to put the wrong-uns right wot 'as too
>   much to say...
> W'en I goes in the Boar's Head pub the blokes they
>   claps th'r 'ands,
> They know I reads a bit, an' wot I reads I
>   understan's;
> They twigs I know abaht them Boars an' spots the'r
>   little game
> 'Cos they bin an' giv' yer 'ighness 'ere a werry
>   rortyname!
> I finks a cove sh'd fink afore 'e talks abaht th' woar,
> There's blokes wot talks as dunno wot they mean,
> But yer tumble as yer 'umble knows a bit abaht th'
>   Boar—
> W'en they calls me nibs "The Bore of Bef'nal
>   Green"...

"Ssshh," said Catherine smiling, "he'll hear you. He's only in the kitchen. I thought you hated that song. You were saying…"

"I do hate it," Una agreed, sponging her breasts, "but it's the only thing that'll cheer me up at the moment."

"You're such a pro-Boer! You could hardly get work…"

"Yesterday's underdog is tomorrow's tyrant." Una stood up, taking the towel which the pretty servant girl handed to her. "That must be even more obvious on the Dark Continent, I suppose." She raised her voice and sang louder:

> In this 'ere woar—well strike me pink—ole
>   England's put 'er 'eart,
> Them kerlownial contingints too 'as played a nobby
>   part,
> Some people sez we ain't got men—I ain't got no
>   sich fears,
> An' it's me wot fust suggested callin' out th'
>   volunteers!
> Anuffer tip o' mine's ter raise a Bef'nal Green
>   Brigade,
> Th' way they scouts for "coppers" shows them
>   blokes for scouts is made—
> But I 'ears as "Bobs' 'll eat them Boars—an' now I
>   twigs th' use
> Of sendin' out a Kitchener to cook ole Kruger's
>   Goose!

Naked, Una swaggered around the room, watched by a spluttering Catherine and a wide-eyed black girl.

> *But for shootin' at th' women—well I 'opes they'll*
> *get it stiff.*
> *'Cos ain't they bin a-firin' shells at that poor Lady*
> *Smiff!*

Spontaneously, Una linked arms with Catherine and then with the servant, to march them back and forth across the carpet. "Altogether for the chorus!"

"We don't know it, Una."

> *But yer tumble as yer 'umble knows a bit abaht th'*
> *Boar—*
> *W'en they calls me nibs "The Bore of Bef'nal*
> *Green"…*

Una stopped, put her hand on the back of the young servant's neck and kissed her full on the lips. The girl uttered a strangled yell and fled from the bedroom.

Catherine stared at her friend in despair. "What did you want to do that for, Una? You'll give the whole game away at this rate."

3.   THE PATHFINDER

Only hours ahead of the Cossacks and the so-called 'Mohawks', Una Persson reached the garrison at Fort Henry to find the place crowded with the Northwest Mounted Police and a couple of regiments who, on first sight of their dark blue and scarlet uniforms, seemed to be the 5th and 7th Royal Irish Lancers. The four high concrete towers of the fort were thick with Maxim guns. There was also a generous display of medium-weight artillery all along the crenellated walls, while circling over the pines and crags of the heavily wooded pass which the fort defended, a Vickers Vimy biplane kept reconnaissance. As she dismounted and went to look for the CO Una realised that her ride had been unnecessarily hasty—the plane would be able to warn the Canadians of an attack in plenty of time. The Cossacks, as usual, were not showing much caution. Her long Henry rifle in the crook of her arm, she forced her way through the Lancers and Mounties and ran up the concrete steps to the HQ building, saluting the healthy corporal on duty at the door. "Captain Persson the scout. Who's your commandant, trooper?"

He returned her salute. "District Superintendent Cornelius, at present, ma'am. Um. Is it urgent, captain?"

She straightened his broad-brimmed hat on his head. She took a pace backward, cocking her eye at him. "You'd probably have time for a couple of choruses of 'Rose-Marie' before a Cossack sabre turned you into a soprano."

He was shocked. He opened the door for her; he was still saluting. "Scout to see you, sir."

Una strode in. In the loose silk divided skirt of the Don Cossack, a wolfskin-trimmed riding kaftan, with cartridge pockets just above the breasts, an astrakhan shapka, she could be immediately identified as an irregular.

The District Superintendent greeted her: a wary wave of his gloved hand. The scarlet of his tunic clashed horribly with his young face which bore an expression of callow sternness and which suggested that he was new to the job. His accent was a reasonable attempt to give Canadian inflexions to an otherwise nondescript English accent. "You've news of the invasion?"

"They're done with Quebec and are on their way. I didn't expect to see you this far north, Jerry."

"They posted me from Toronto two days ago. I was supposed to be in Niagara Falls by now. Do you think I've been set up? Is it going to be the Alamo, all over again? Or was it the Alma?"

"Don't forget Quebec initially welcomed the Cossacks. The French always think they can control their conquerors. There wasn't any resistance to speak of. And nobody was much interested in stopping them between the time they left Alaska until they landed at Ungava. Even then you all thought they'd be content to run around in the Northwest Territory a bit until they got tired and went home. But by that time the States had started to get worried. Those are American guns out there, aren't they?"

"Mostly. They've been very good about giving us support."

"Then you've nothing to worry about. Why were you going to Niagara Falls? Honeymoon?"

"Oh, sure." He scratched his red sleeve with leather fingers. "No, I was meeting my father. I think. He's got business in Buffalo."

"I thought your father was in Mexico."

"Maybe he'll be going to Mexico later."

"Are you sure he's——?"

"No. But he says he is. It was worth checking."

"I suppose so."

"The bloody Cossacks have fucked everything up, as usual. Once they start——"

"You'll stop them. They'll never reach Kingston."

He frowned anxiously at a map of the Great Lakes. "We don't want the Americans moving in. And they will, unless..."

"They've left nobody behind—the Cossacks, I mean. The 'Mohawks' aren't a problem. As long as they all attack Fort Henry, that's it. You'll blow them to bits." She sounded sad. "You needn't worry about the States."

"It was bad enough when it was only Sitting Bull. Or

do I mean Notting Hill? What's that?"

"Since Roosevelt they've had it in their heads that the rest of America is really theirs, too, that they're leasing it to a lot of incompetent relatives and foreigners on condition that they look after it properly. But in this case there won't be much more interference." She was decidedly regretful. "A shame. I'd love to see the Cossacks in New York."

"I heard that's where they meant to go. They thought the Ungava Peninsula was Nantucket."

"You could be right. They're still not clear as to whether they're in the USA or Canada. There's only one or two of them can speak any English at all—and the French 'Mohawks' can't understand the Cossacks' French while the Cossacks can't understand the French's French. Apparently the accents create two virtually different languages."

"You know a lot about them."

"I should do. I've been acting as an interpreter since Fort Chimo." She straightened her shapka. "Well, I must be on my way."

"You're not staying for the 'fun'?"

"No point. You'll beat them. They're tired, overconfident, poorly armed. They'll have eaten badly and been sleeping in the saddle, if I know them. Most will probably be drunk. They'll keep coming at you until you've wiped them out. In the meantime the 'Mohawks' will have run back to Quebec."

"They can't have come all this way without a plan."

"They got to Uppsala two years ago without a plan. They were wiped out. Four prisoners taken. It's their nature. And twenty years ago they reached Rawalpindi, couldn't find the British, hit the Chinese by accident and drove them back. Hardly anyone in England ever knew there had been a threat!"

"That was a bit of luck for someone," said Jerry innocently.

"It usually is. Well, cheerio. You're bound to get a promotion if you hang around long enough after the battle."

"I told you, I was on my way…"

"I can go via Niagara, if you like. Any message?"

"If you get a chance, find a man named 'Brown'. He's staying at the Lover's Leap Hotel on the American side. Tell him I've been held up."

"Okay." She removed her kaftan. She had a buckskin jacket underneath. Hanging by a deerhide thong at her beaded belt was an old-fashioned powder horn. She reached for the horn, taking something from the bullet pouch on her other hip. "Have you got a mirror?"

He removed the map of the Great Lakes. There was a large oval mirror behind it. She inspected her face. Then, tipping a little powder onto the puff, she began to cover her nose.

4. THE OUTCAST OF THE ISLANDS

"I remember the good old days," said Sebastian Auchinek, his voice grumbling along with the twelve wing-mounted engines on either side of the cabin, "when there was still a sense of wonder in the world."

"That was before universal literacy and cheap newsprint." Jerry spoke spitefully. Either Auchinek or the engines began to cough. They had not been getting on since Calcutta when the Russian policeman had demanded to see their documents and Jerry had shot him.

The Dornier DoX was circling Darwin while they tried to make up their minds what to do. Nobody had expected the Japanese to strike so fast. As far as Whitehall had been concerned the problem had been whether or not to let them stay in Manchukao. When they had materialised simultaneously outside Sydney, Brisbane and other cities, pounding the settlements to bits with naval guns and bombs, resistance had been minimal. Help was on the way from Singapore and Shanghai, but it would be some time before the Emperor's armies were shifted.

"Besides," said Moses Collier from the co-pilot's seat, "it's the Aussies' own fault for being élitist. You know how eager the Japs are to be accepted everywhere at any cost. We'd better scarper, Jerry. Rowe Island's our only chance."

"It's full of bones. It's haunted. I hate it."

"No time for superstition now, Mr Cornelius," said Auchinek with a fair bit of pleasure. "It was you who believed the story about the waters of Eternal Life with their powers of resurrection. I never did."

"You've never believed anything. A lot of people were as impressed as I was." Jerry was defensive, but he responded without much spirit. "I only said I hated the place…"

"That's hardly the point." Mo took a tighter grip on his controls as the plane lost height for a moment. "We've got to dump this bugger, get her repaired before she falls out of the sky. Listen to those engines!"

Jerry was looking moodily down at the Australian wasteland. "I suppose so."

"There's a couple of C-class Empire flying boats in reasonable nick there," said Collier. "I diverted them myself." Mo had spent a lot more time than any of the others in this part of the world. Occasionally he would even claim to be an Australian. "Lovely jobs. Better than this old madam any day of the week."

Jerry was sensitive about his Dornier. He would never admit that he had been hasty in acquiring it while it was still in its experimental stages. "They've got nothing like the range," he said automatically. "Nothing like."

"Maybe not, but it'll take a plane in good nick to get us to Singapore, if that's where you still want to go." Collier buttoned up his helmet strap. "What do we all think? Is it on?"

"For me it is." Auchinek began to leave the cabin. "I'll go aft and see what the others have to say."

"See if you can get some more info out of the abo," Collier suggested. They had found a black tracker in the ruins, before they had realised that the Japanese were still present in the city.

"Can't." said Auchinek.

"He left." Jerry explained. "While we were going up. Opened the door and walked out. Said he had to find his mother and father. They'd been after an emu, apparently."

"Funny little bloke, wasn't he?" Collier glanced at the Timor Sea. "I hope he makes it."

"They're marvellous, really," said Jerry. "They can find their way through anything."

"Didn't seem to realise there was a war on." Collier hummed to himself as he made adjustments to his panel. "Number four's looking dodgy again."

"It sounds fine to me."

"Well, it's bloody dodgy. It's conked out twice."

"It missed a couple of times, that's all."

Collier sighed. "All right. Christ I wish we had some cannon with us. I don't half feel naked. We've seen a fair bit of the fleet, but what are they doing with all their bloody Fujis or Kawasakis or whatever it is they're flying these days?"

"Probably down near Sydney and Canberra or

Melbourne," suggested Jerry. "This isn't a very strategic area, by and large."

"Luckily for us. Why were they hiding in the ruins when we first arrived?"

"Probably thought we were military. Hoped to take us by surprise."

"They did that all right." Mo waved his grazed arm. "Cor! It makes me want to vomit. All that fighting and no chance of hitting back. I'm joining up when we get to Singapore. Then I'll come straight to bleedin' Darwin with a great big tommy gun. Except," he said mournfully, "that they always jam on you. Bastards, tommies are."

"What about a Schmeiser?" Jerry was glad that only blue water and sky surrounded them on all sides now.

"You're bloody talking, me old son!" Mo whistled through his teeth. "There's even a couple of Yank machine pistols I wouldn't mind trying. They don't have a lot of style, though, Yanks don't. Not in the military stuff. All their invention goes into the private sector. Funny that. Is it free enterprise, d'you think?"

"It's the cars I like best," said Jerry. "I'm going to miss the cars."

"They won't stop making cars just because they've got a few problems on their borders."

Jerry wasn't so sure. "I can't bear to think what the Canadians will do with Detroit."

"They might give it back. Swap it for that other place they want. Pig's Eye, is it?"

"St Paul? Maybe. It doesn't seem a fair swap, though."

"The wars can't last for ever. Things are sorting themselves out already." Mo was depressing himself as he tried to cheer up his friend. "Eh?"

"It'll take ten years." Una Persson shut the door of the cabin behind her, sat down and put her elbows on the chart table.

"What's ten years?" said Mo.

"Bishop Beesley says he can see a pattern emerging already." Una toyed with a map.

Jerry laughed. "He's always seeing patterns. There aren't any. Not really. The disordered mind sees order everywhere—systems take shape from the movement of the wind in the leaves of the trees—patterns merge as the mad eye selects only what it wishes to see. Patterns are madness, for the most part. That's the bishop. He's barmy."

"Oh, come on, Jerry." Mo turned in his seat. "There's some sort of shape to what's going on, isn't there?"

"If there is, I haven't detected any."

"You've got to believe in some kind of order, man!"

"Order isn't patterns."

"It's a perfectly easy shape, I think," said Una Persson. "But it—well, it shifts. It's a prism. A classically cut diamond, perhaps. It isn't strictly linear. By selecting a linear pattern from the larger design you certainly distort things. I think that's what you mean, don't you, Jerry?"

Mo belched. Then he farted. "Pardon," he said.

Jerry gave up. "All I know is that there's too much going on at once and I've had about enough. All the bleeding possibilities occurring at the same time. That's not what I joined for. I wanted a simple life. I remember. I wanted a set of nice straight tracks from A to B. And what did I bloody get? I wish I was out of it. I'm too old and this century's too familiar. Any bloody aspect of it. You can't win. Only the bloody Japanese can win."

"It's worse than that," said Una with a smirk. "Nobody wins. Nobody loses."

"That's life," said Mo Collier. The engines began to falter, to rumble. He licked his teeth.

"You're wrong. The Japanese win. It's all in inverse proportion to the amount of ego you have. These days, at any rate. The bigger the ego, the more you lose. And it's big egos make the biggest, stupidest patterns. Look at Hitler."

"I used to enjoy him," said Mo cheerfully, "in the *Dandy*. Or was it the *Beano*? Hitler?" Mo giggled. "What, that little bloke in Berlin? The copper?"

Jerry raised his hands to his head. "Sorry," he said. "I was forgetting."

5. WHAT IS ART?

There were fifty keels lying at anchor over Kiev when Prinz Lobkowitz woke up and looked out of the diamond-paned window of the house he had rented near the Cathedral of St Vladimir, with its view of the Botanical Gardens.

The artillery-fire, which had been almost constant for the past week, was now only intermittent and, as a result, Lobkowitz felt a peculiar, unspecific anxiety, as one does when faced with the unfamiliar, however welcome. From several rooftops, as he watched, rose puffs of grey smoke and he heard the crack of rifle-shots. The defenders of Kiev were firing hopelessly at the airships which swayed overhead obscuring the thin morning sunlight. It seemed to Lobkowitz that the siege was as good as over, but he could not be quite sure which side had won. Then he caught a glimpse of a German uniform on the roof and guessed that the airships, silhouettes against the dawn sky and impossible to identify from any markings as yet, were here in support of the besieging Makhnoviks, returned at last to avenge the murder of their leader over twenty years previously. They were led now by a Don Cossack styling himself Emalyan Pugachev, claiming to be a descendant of the Peasant Tsar and (incidentally) renouncing all claim to the throne in the name of the Democratic Union of Free Cossack Anarchists. Although Pugachev refused a title he was universally accepted as Hetman by the Cossacks. Now, as one of the ships turned in the wind, Lobkowitz could make out a fluttering black flag inset with the blue cross of St Andrew. The Highlanders, having established their position north of the Clyde, had linked up with their Ukrainian brothers to push back the Russians and their German mercenaries and once more establish the Ukraine as an independent state. Lobkowitz, whose sympathies were with the Makhnoviks, reflected aloud to Auchinek who had wandered in, still in nightshirt and dressing gown, smoking a briar pipe, a copy of *The Master of Ballantrae* under his arm: "Perhaps Kiev will come alive again. It used to be such a vital city."

"It won't make much difference to the Jews," said Auchinek with a shrug. "Every new government winds up promoting a fresh pogrom. It's a wonder there's any Jews left."

Lobkowitz frowned. He was forced to admit that his friend was right. "I can't see Pugachev allowing such a thing."

"Pugachev's a Cossack. Cossacks have a metaphysical and instinctive desire to butcher the members of any race originating east of the Urals or south of the Caucasus. They can't help themselves. I think they hate Jews most of all because they think of us as being a kind of decadent Tartar.

Nothing to do with our habit of sacrificing Christian babies, raping Christian virgins, ruining Christian merchants or, of course, crucifying Christ. Their instinct goes back much further than that. They'll tolerate Teutons and maintain a wary trust for other Slavs who, in turn, are regarded as effete versions of themselves, but Latins belong to a caste hardly higher than the Jews..."

Lobkowitz was amused. He jerked his thumb behind him at the sky. "What about Celts?"

"Honorary Cossacks. They can find many points of similarity, you see. The Highlanders were traditionally used to expand the frontiers of Empire, just as the Cossacks were sent into Siberia. From time to time they have done well in uprisings against the central government and have the same tendency to fling themselves willy-nilly into a conflict. Oh, you'd have to ask a Cossack for the rest." Auchinek scratched under his eye with the stem of his pipe. Then he scratched his nose. "I just hope the papers you got will see me through, Lobkowitz. Every time Kiev falls I get nervous. Still, I welcome it politically, this development. The Ukraine was the last major state to break free of the Russian Empire. And the Chinese have at last given up their attempts to expand their territories or to re-impose their rule on Cochin China and Korea. And if the Japanese did nothing else, they broke the chain that held the British and American colonies to their masters, without actually managing to retain a foothold in those colonies themselves. All the Empires are going down at once. It's reassuring. Did I read that the Peuhl finally took Fort Lamy?"

"I seem to recall…"

"And Arabia is rising. Can it mean that the long era of Empire-building is over at last?"

"You think the world will learn to cultivate its own gardens? The wars continue. They are just as bloody."

"It will take a while, I grant you, to achieve a reasonable status quo. But Makhno's dreams may yet become the final reality. The same equilibrium of anarchy."

Lobkowitz was impressed by this new confidence in his old friend. He was heartened. "I should work on your enthusiasm for Makhno," he advised. There was a noise on the stair. "Hello! Who's this?" The voice of his housekeeper rose up to them. Heavy feet ascended. "It will stand you in good stead."

Auchinek was grinning as the door of Lobkowitz's rooms burst open and Colonel Pyat, splendid in his white-and-green uniform, his boots shining with some dark liquid, came in, hastily removing his cap and gloves. "We've lost everything," he said. "I know you're not sympathetic—but those fools of peasants wouldn't listen to reason." Pyat had been acting as a go-between for the Russians and the Ukrainians. As a veteran of the Indian and Chinese campaigns he had some standing with the wilder Cossack elements and for a short time had served as one of their officers. "The Germans are leaving, so we can't even negotiate from a position of relative strength. You've heard nothing from Prague?"

"We can't help, I'm afraid," said Lobkowitz. "I might as well tell you that it's my opinion Prague will recognise the Pugachev government as soon as they have official control of Kiev."

Pyat nodded. He was fatalistic. "Then can I ask you a favour?"

"Of course." Lobkowitz felt an increased friendship for Pyat now that the man's efforts to maintain Russian rule had come to nothing.

"Make me a temporary member of your staff—until you get to Prague. I won't stay in Bohemia. I'll go on to Bavaria, where I have friends. A great many of my old colleagues are already there and apparently have been decently received."

Lobkowitz drew a deep breath. "I think I can arrange it, so long as Prague is quick to recognise Pugachev. If that happens I'll probably have enough prestige to get away with one or two irregularities. You're not, after all, who they're really after. What about your cousin, the Governor?"

Colonel Pyat was bitter. "He took the last train to Moscow yesterday evening, after he had announced that he was making me his deputy."

"That creates complications, eh?" Auchinek looked sardonically to Lobkowitz.

Pyat smiled as he shook his head. "I tore the order up. It would have been suicide to accept."

Outside, the gunfire suddenly increased its intensity and then stopped altogether.

"Then who is governor now?" asked Auchinek. He had a passion for knowing the names of those in authority.

"Cornelius accepted the job."

"But he's a known Makhnovik sympathiser!"

Lobkowitz went to the window again, staring across the frosty Botanical Gardens to the distant bulk of the new governor's palace. He laughed. "Look," he said, "the Black Flag is already hoisted over Kiev."

Pyat sat down in the large leather armchair. "The man is a blatant opportunist. He bends with every wind. I wish I knew his secret."

"Everyone envies him that." Auchinek spat into the ashes of last night's fire.

Literature and art are not the field of the literary or art critic only; they are also the concern of the sociologist, of the social historian, or anthropologist, and of the social psychologist. For through literature and art men seem to reveal their personality and, when there is one, their national ethos.

—Gilberto Freyre,
Brazil: An Interpretation

Important writing, strange to say, rarely gives the exact flavour of its period; if it is successful it presents you with the soul of man, undated. Very minor literature, on the other hand, is the Baedeker of the soul, and will guide you through curious relics, the tumbledown buildings, the flimsy palaces, the false pagodas, the distorted and fantastical and faery vistas which have cluttered the imagination of mankind at this or that brief period of its history.

—George Dangerfield,
The Strange Death of Liberal England

... it is the image which in fact determines what might still be called the current behaviour of any organism or organisation. The image acts as a field.

—Kenneth Boulding,
The Image

There have been studies of the higher intellectual sphere through which ideas flowed between the two countries, but the popular sources of these ideas have largely been overlooked. Probably the major source of ideas concerning India came from fiction set in that country. "Literature is the one field of Indo-British culture which has provided a comparatively large harvest, though the average quality is not very good".

—Allen J. Greenberger,
The British Image of India

You've gain'd the victory, Rome, it will not hold;
Britain when hist'ry shall her page unfold,
In future times, where're her flag's unfurl'd
Shall prove the queen and terror to the world.
Forward at least two thousand years we'll go.
And shew what London will be: and then shew
A pastime Britons then will pleasure in,
A checquer'd droll, its hero HARLEQUIN.

London; or, Harlequin and Time, 1813

The formal canonisation of John Ogilvie, a Jesuit martyr, as Scotland's first saint in 700 years came a step nearer yesterday with the publication of details of a cure which is recognised as miraculous by the Catholic Church.

After years of investigation in Scotland and Rome, the Church now officially accepts that Mr John Fagan, aged 61, of Glasgow, who was dying in 1967 from a major stomach cancer, was saved through the intercession of John Ogilvie. The priest was hanged at Glasgow Cross on 10 March 1615, for refusing to recognise the supremacy of King James I in spiritual matters.

The detailed evidence showed that almost at the moment when Mr Fagan was excepted to die, "he developed a dramatic, abrupt, and uninterrupted improvement with return to full health". A long sequence of examinations by doctors concluded that there was no possible medical explanation for the disappearance of the cancer.

Guardian, 12 March, 1976

6. THE BIRTH AND ADVENTURES OF HARLEQUIN

"Did you ever see greyer skies?" Miss Brunner had just arrived in a rattling old Ka-12 copter of the flying motorbike type, probably an experimental model. Doubtless she had been inexpertly looting museums again. Landing on the roof of a half-completed Royal Festival Hall, she had immediately turned her attention to the oily waters of the Thames where Jerry had managed to put down his own Princess Flying Boat, damaging the wings and tailplane as he had knocked over the Skylon and negotiated Waterloo Bridge. The drizzle seemed to have been falling on London for a decade; it brought a certain gleam to the overcast scene.

"Eh?"

Jerry had not been expecting her. He had come to the South Bank in the hope of finding the Dome of Discovery, but a Palestinian bomb (about the only one to hit London before the whole of their ramshackle air force had been blown apart) had left a huge crater in its place—indeed, there was no evidence that it had actually been constructed. When the Ka-12 had arrived Jerry had been bouncing up and down, clinging to a fallen girder, telling himself that this was the last time he would trust one of Flash Gordon's tips. Gordon had heard that Catherine had been transferred here from Roedean at the outbreak of the invasion, when half of Sussex had fallen to disaffected Kentish marines who had made a surprise mass attack along the whole coast between Hastings and Littlehampton. The Nursing Home, Sunnydales, had actually driven back the marines, but not before it had sustained major damage and lost over seventy per cent of its charges.

The rolled-up linen blueprints of the Festival site were already going limp. They stuck at an angle from the pocket of his military-style camelhair overcoat. Soon they would be useful as handkerchiefs. Rain dripped from the brim of his trilby onto his cheeks so that it looked as if he had been weeping. He began to tramp away from the Hall, over cracked concrete, towards the iron framework of Hungerford Bridge.

"Eh?" asked Miss Brunner again. She hurried behind. She wore an uncharacteristic Balenciaga New Look dress in avocado-green velvet over which was pulled a black duffel coat. On her feet were ponyskin boots and on her head a peculiar astrakhan cap, as if she had tried to make a concession to several different ideas of taste at the same time. "Eh?"

Jerry stopped. "Yes, very grey. A chilly era altogether, wouldn't you say?"

Having obtained her response she was satisfied, turning on him immediately. "You're being facetious."

Ostentatiously she studied the river again. "Well, it's a shambles! I can't think what's got into the British Empire."

"Corruption in high places?" Jerry felt in his other pocket to make sure his cigarette cards were still dry.

"Rot!"

"I thought—"

"It's poor morale all round."

"Not all round." Jerry rubbed the water from his skin. "Some people are fighting for their liberty for the first time ever." He looked wistfully towards his ruined Princess.

Her foxy mouth snarled at him. "Liberty! How I hate it! Given the chance I intend to establish a sane element of authority in this country again. I've put all my money into land. It's land that England's made of. Land is the only thing of importance. And the one who has most land has most power to revive England's greatness. Happy people, Mr Cornelius, are people who know where they stand. A responsible ruling class does not trade in ambiguities—it trades in facts and statements of fact. It tells people exactly what their position is and what they may do within certain well-defined limits. People would rather not own land themselves, because of the responsibility. Therefore they are prepared to let those who own the land make their decisions for them. Owning land, you see, brings with it a great burden. By lifting that burden from the shoulders of the common man, by putting experienced managers in charge, we shall produce a stability this country has not experienced for fifty years. A hundred years. It is my dream, Mr Cornelius, to re-establish the Rule of Law in Great Britain before we see 1960 again. I shall need experienced people like yourself. That's why I looked you up. You have the makings of a fine manager."

Jerry shook his head. "All I want to do is keep my head down until this floppy decade's over. There's no other way to survive it that I know."

"It's the key period, Mr Cornelius." Her eyes were on fire. "There is still a chance for us to stem the tide, re-divert the waters so that they irrigate the roots of a sane, tranquil, stable society—cottagers, villagers, townsmen and citizens all building for a common aim. Give each man, woman and child a place and a purpose and, as a consequence, a firm idea of identity—show them who the enemy is, what they must fight, and all this internal squabbling, this unhappy squeaking for revolution, will be finished with, once and for all. We reached the peak of our social evolution in 1900 and now we are devolving at a sickening rate. Can't you see it?"

"I appreciate your faith in the restoration of the status quo, Miss Brunner, but I'm not sure land values are the whole answer. I mean, by 2000 we'll probably all be living on Mars and Venus anyway, won't we? The future's in space, isn't it?"

"Space!" She was vicious. "I don't believe in space! And neither should you. Our duty is to remember our heritage—and to make our fellows recall that heritage, too!"

She was giving him a headache.

"Rockets!" he said pathetically. "Whoosh!"

She indicated the crater. "That's what rockets do. Boom!" She drove her point home: "They blow everything up."

"Yes, well, they've got to, haven't they? First?" Against

her enthusiasm his logic, never very strong, disintegrated. "Haven't they?"

She moved towards him, her boots squelching. "You're very naïve, Mr Cornelius. I'm older than you…"

"I wouldn't say that."

"… and I may seem a trifle old-fashioned. But mark my words our future lies in the yeomen of England, not in some half-baked fashionable creed of anarchistic scientific internationalism. There are too many '-isms' in the world already—and the result is Chaos. Come with me. Let me exorcise the demon of nihilism and breathe a new spirit into your troubled soul. There is only one '-ism' which will save us—the good old English penchant for pragmatism. We must reduce the number of choices facing the bewildered people of England. Choice produces confusion and confusion leads to social disintegration. And when we are strong again, strong enough to show the world that we know who we are and where we are going, we can extend the same salvation throughout the globe, bringing stability and order wherever we go. We stopped too soon, you see. We lost sight of our goals. We became afraid of responsibility—of the responsibility of Empire— we let other countries get away with far too much and, as a result, lost faith in our own authority."

"I'm still not sure about my own identity, let alone what I should be doing." As he walked on towards Hungerford Bridge Miss Brunner again began to follow.

"Strong authority produces a strong identity, personal and corporate."

"It all sounds a bit too political for my taste," Jerry told her. "I never did understand politics very well."

"But that's exactly it." They had reached the iron steps of the bridge and began to climb. The metal rang as Jerry's heels struck. She disapproved of his steel blakeys. "I hate politics, too. I'm completely apolitical. I'm talking about faith—faith in one's country and its greatness—faith in common sense, in order, in justice—faith in traditional values which, say what you like, never let us down in the past." They were crossing the river now. Jerry regretted the damage he had done to his Princess. The noble flying boat was waterlogged in her starboard float and part of the wing was already under water, lifting the plane over.

"She's sinking," said Miss Brunner. "Isn't she?"

"It'll be a long time before that old girl goes down." Jerry spoke sentimentally. It was this feeling for imperfect or misconceived machinery which had got him into trouble more than once before.

They reached the opposite side of the bridge and crossed the road to the fractured Charing Cross Underground Station, where a coffee stall had re-established itself. The embankment at this point still had its big trees, its shrubs, its nameless statues. They joined the queue of wounded soldiers and derelicts moving slowly forward until Jerry heard a familiar voice from the counter. "Garn, yer ol' bugger, toast's anuvver bloody tuppence!"

Jerry's throat contracted. His mother had returned to London. He broke from the queue.

"Eh?" said Miss Brunner, grabbing for him and missing.

243

He ran up Villiers Street towards the Strand as fast as he could go. At the top of Villiers Street he climbed the ruined wall of the mainline station and risked a look back. Miss Brunner was in friendly (and to him, sinister) conversation with his mother. It seemed that the most disparate people were forming alliances these days. He dropped from the wall and ran on, through Admiralty Arch, to the Mall. There were grey trees on either side of him; even the grass of the park looked grey and smelled sterile. He ran towards Buckingham Palace at the end of the Mall not because he thought he would find safety there but because its outline was the only one he currently recognised. He reached the roundabout outside the palace, the statue of the old queen, and the fountains. To the left of the palace, the tall houses of Victoria and Pimlico looked attractive; they had hardly been touched by any of the wars. He decided to make for Buckingham Palace Road and Prince's Street, where he had once had friends, but, as he walked panting beside the railings of the palace, there came a shout from the other side and he turned his head to see a soldier in a scarlet-and-black uniform, a bearskin on his head, threatening him with what appeared to be a Lee-Enfield .303.

"Halt," said the guardsman.

Jerry stopped. "What?"

"Halt. 'Ow'd'yer get frew ther fuckin' barrier, chum?"

"Didn't know there was one," said Jerry. "I've been away ill."

The guardsman's brutal, bloodshot eyes narrowed.

"Stay there," he said. He called over his shoulder. "Corp!"

A corporal ran out of a gatehouse at the side of the palace façade. It was Frank. His face was pale and covered in acne, emphasised by his scarlet tunic. He grinned broadly when he recognised his brother. "Jerry! You come to see us, 'ave you?"

Jerry shook his head and was silent.

"Unlock the gate, soldier," said Frank with some relish. The small wrought-iron gate was opened and the guardsman stood back to allow Jerry to enter, but Jerry remained where he was. "I didn't know you'd joined the Army, Frank."

"I was called up, wasn't I? It's me National Service. You oughta be in, too."

"I've been ill."

"Well, come on! We've a lot ter talk abaht!" Frank pretended enthusiasm. "Seen Cathy, 'ave yer? And Mum? She's runnin'—"

"I know." Jerry shuffled through the gate. "The coffee stall."

"That's right. Wiv ol' Sammy. Nil desperandum!"

"Who?"

The soldier locked the gate behind him. "Are you allowed to have visitors, then?" Jerry asked.

"Me? I'm quite an important man round 'ere, these days. I'm expectin' to 'ave proper promotion any day now. I'm the senior officer, anyway. All the others are either on barrier duty or dead or wounded."

"Who're they fighting?"

"You have been away a long time, me old son! The

Miners Volunteer Force, o' course. It's a terrorist organisation, mainly from Durham and that way. They've been givin' us an awful lot o' trouble, but we'll lick 'em!" Frank opened the green-painted door in the white stone wall. They entered a small office full of dark polished wood. "Cuppa?"

"Thanks."

Frank filled the kettle from a big steel drum and placed it on a portable gas-ring. He lit the gas. "Yeah. I'm virtually second in command at the moment."

"What? To the king?"

"The king! Do me a favour!" Frank laughed heartily and sat down in a comfortable leather armchair beside a small coal fire. It was warm and secure. Jerry took off his soaked coat and hung it on a big hook near the door. Frank's khaki greatcoat was there, too. He sat down on a straight-backed wooden chair on the other side of the fireplace.

"What's wrong with the king, then? Been deposed, has he?" Jerry rubbed his hands and warmed them at the grate.

"Deposed? 'E's bloody dead, ain't 'e!" Frank was coarser than Jerry remembered him. It was probably the effects of army life.

"Then who's in charge?"

"The Church took over, didn't they? Sort of care-taking capacity until order's restored."

"The Archbishop of Canterbury or something?"

"Nar! They 'anged the poor old blighter months ago. The current boss is a bishop. Bishop Beesley. You must've 'eard'v 'im!"

"Vaguely," said Jerry. He loosened a soggy tie.

"You *must* 'ave. 'E's gonna bring back spiritual values into our way of life, in'e?"

"Oh, then Miss Brunner's working with him?"

"Do us a favour, Jerry! She's the one 'oo led the fuckin' miners on London, ain't she!"

"It beats me," said Jerry. He watched as Frank rose to pour water into the teapot.

"You're dead lucky I spotted you." Frank stirred the tea in the pot. "I'll put in a word. On my recommendation you'll get a commission. Captain, at least. Bound to." Frank reached out and turned the knob of a big table wireless. There was a lot of interference but through it all came the voice of Edmundo Ros. To a rhumba rhythm he was singing his latest hit. *Enjoy yourself, it's later than you think. Enjoy yourself, enjoy yourself, it's later than you think.*

Jerry reached out for the mug Frank offered him. His hand was trembling.

"This is the chance for people like us to take advantage of the opportunities," Frank was saying, "and make something of ourselves. They need us, see."

"What for?"

"Our will to survive," said his brother. "Our terror of poverty." His grin was savage. "Our ratlike rapacity, Jerry old lad. Our vitality. They'll pay anything for our protection."

"Sort of Danegeld, you mean?"

"Call it what you like, mate. Not that they can't teach us a thing or two about 'anging on. As soon as we've got those bloody miners off our backs—and that's as good as done, at least for the time bein'—we'll be in charge. Then we'll show 'em!"

"It sounds a bit dodgy to me," said Jerry. He was still unclear of the issues or of his brother's ambitions. "They've had a lot more experience. They'll turn on you, Frank."

"I know too many secrets."

Jerry shrugged. "Well, maybe you're right."

"Are you on, then? Comin' in with me?" Frank grinned an eager grin.

Jerry shook his head. "I'll keep moving, I think. This isn't my decade at all."

"You won't get a better opportunity."

"I'll wait and see what the future brings."

"The future?" Frank laughed. "There isn't any future. Make the most of what you've got."

Jerry scratched his damp head. "But I don't like it here."

"You never believed you'd be visiting your brother in Buckingham Palace, I bet."

"I never believed in Buckingham Palace," said Jerry helplessly. He began to smile. "And I'm not sure I believe in you any more."

"Oo, you snooty little sod." Frank glowered. His pallid lips set in anger. "You stupid, stuck-up shitty little bastard! And I was trying to 'elp you! Well, if that's the way you wanna play it. I've got powers to enlist you. And once you're fuckin' enlisted, me old son, you'll see the error of your fuckin' ways."

Jerry drew his needle gun from a pinstriped pocket. "I think I'll have to borrow your uniform if I'm going to get through. I'll let you have it back later."

Frank was hardly aware that his life was being threatened. He stared curiously at the needle gun. "What's that?"

Jerry said: "The future."

7. HARLEQUIN INVISIBLE; OR, THE EMPEROR OF CHINA'S COURT

Jerry shrugged himself back into his frilly Mr Fish jacket and kissed Mitzi Beesley heartily on her exposed left buttock. Mitzi twitched. Her voice from beneath the pillow was lazy. "You could stay another couple of hours. My dad won't be back yet. We haven't tried it with those bottles."

"We'd only get stuck." He made for the stairs. "Besides, you're not nearly old enough." It seemed to him, as he went down, that he was still surrounded by the aura of her juicy lust. "See you." He opened the street door.

He walked out into the Chelsea sunshine. The bishop, a popular local figure, had not done too badly for himself since the dissolution. King's Road was crowded with pretty people, with music, foodstalls, hawkers of disposable clothes, fortune-tellers, prostitutes of every possible persuasion, beautiful buttons and blossoming bows; soft bodies brushed against him on all sides, delicious perfumes swam into his nose; his flesh sang. He pressed through the throng, whistling an Animals tune to himself, on his way to The Pheasantry, which Mr Koutrouboussis had recently purchased. There was no doubt about it, thought Jerry, Utopia had been worth hanging on for. Everyone was happy. *Here, there and everywhere*, sang the Beatles as he passed a daytime disco; they were the poets of paradise. *Turn off your mind, relax and float downstream...*

There was, Jerry found himself bound to admit, still a minority of people who would have preferred the euphoria of austerity to all this and, indeed, the King's Road was not what he would have considered his own natural environment, even on festival days such as this one. Nonetheless, if he missed an egg and chips there was always someone to provide a fantasy of more generous proportions, with a hurdy-gurdy and a rebuilt tram or two. If anything got to him here, then it was the self-consciousness, absent from his own territory further north, where hangovers of the poverty trance still operated to the advantage of the natives. And, too, it was in King's Road that he saw the seeds of disaster, of the destruction of everything he held dear. He put these thoughts from his mind and shouldered his way a little more aggressively up the road only to stop dead as he reached the stone gates of The Pheasantry and confronted none other than Miss Brunner. She wore a white angular Courrèges suit with shorts, white PVC boots and a white PVC floppy hat and satchel. On her nose were huge, round sunglasses and her red hair was cut quite short. A very noisy radio went by— *Jumpin' Jack Flash, it's a gas, gas, gas*—so he could not hear her greeting but, to his astonishment, he was sure she had mouthed the word "Darling" at him. He stopped, leaned his thin body against the opposite gatepost and sniffed at her Young Lust. "Swinging along okay, Miss B?"

"What? Oh, yes. Fabulously. You look pretty psychedelic yourself."

"Thanks. I do my best."

"No, I mean it. As tasty as anything. Are you going in?" She peered towards the gloom of the hallway. "You live here?"

"I've a friend who does. Well, he's a friend of Catherine's really."

"How is your sister? That job—or did she get—?"

"She's resting at the moment."

"Frank said something."

"He's improving, then. Well, I'll be seeing you."

"No!" She placed her white plastic fingers on his arm. "I was actually looking for you. I know we've had our differences."

"And our likenesses. There's no need to rake up the past."

"Certainly not. I wouldn't dream... Could we have a chat?"

"You're not trying to recruit me for anything, are you?"

"Not really. I think we've more in common than we knew." She looked distastefully down at her body. "As you can see, I'm quite 'with-it' now."

"What are you doing with yourself?"

"Ha, ha! I've been trained. I'm a fully qualified computer programmer. Shall we have some coffee?"

Jerry shook his head. "It makes me too wary, eating

in Chelsea. At best I can only do it if my back's well to the wall and my eye's on the door. You know how it is."

"But there are some charming places."

"That's what I mean."

He moved into the courtyard, a zone of relative silence, and sat down on the lip of the pool. Blue, green, yellow and red water came at intervals from the fountain in the centre. After a pause, she sat beside him. "I can't remember where it was we last met," she began.

"Neither can I," said Jerry. "Perhaps it hasn't happened yet?"

"Well, yes, possible, certainly." She had lost her old confidence while Jerry had gained quite a lot. She was evidently distressed.

"I know how interested you are in science," she said.

"Not any more." Jerry tried to catch a striped fish which floated to the surface. "Sorry. Technological art now."

"Oh, well. Even better. Technological art. Yes! Yes! Good. That. Well, science is the answer, I've decided, at any rate. I thought you'd be pleased. And computers are very definitely where we are going. My backers have invested in some of the absolutely latest equipment. You'll be familiar with it, of course."

"Don't judge me too hastily. I might leave it alone. I don't fancy…"

"Ha, ha. Now…" She removed a pearlite case from her white bag. She offered him a cigarette. "Sobranie, I think. Are those all right?"

Jerry shook his head.

"Oh, well." She closed the case without taking one of the cigarettes herself. She looked at her Zippo lighter for some time while she continued to talk. "Anyway, you know a lot about the less orthodox branches of science, don't you? Your father—?"

"I'm afraid I've lost faith in science as anything but a pastime," Jerry said.

"You were always flippant. You mustn't say things like that, Mr Cornelius. It is technology which will pull us out of our current difficulties."

"I didn't know we had any."

"Of course we have. All this glitter simply hides a deeper malaise. You must agree. You're intelligent. This can't last. We must think ahead."

"I'd rather not think at all." He got up and looked into the water of the fountain at the multicoloured carp. "This is where I belong. I'm happy."

"Happy, Mr Cornelius? How can you be?"

"I don't know, but I am."

"There's more to life than drugs and sex, Mr Cornelius."

"There's more than life to drugs and sex. It's better than nothing."

"You need a goal. You always have. This rejection of your potential is silly. You believe in science as much as I do."

"What about land?"

"It's abstracts now. It would be ludicrous to continue thinking in old terms about a new situation, don't you agree?"

Jerry became uncomfortable. "I was thinking of going into the assassination business. You know what a dreamer I am. Would it be too much of a hit and myth operation, do you think?"

"Do you believe in aeroplanes, Mr Cornelius?"

"It depends what you mean by 'aeroplanes'." He yearned for the cool gloom of The Pheasantry, to bask in Koutrouboussis's envy.

"A properly organised technology is the only hope for the world unless we are to plunge into total decadence and from decadence into death," she said. "If we act now, we can save almost everything of value. Don't you see?" Her circular shades were cocked at an earnest angle. "If we can somehow produce a programme, feed in all the facts, we can get a clear idea of what we must do to prepare for the future. Imagine—the whole future in a single chip."

For once Jerry refrained from the obvious response. "I'm only interested in the present." He sat down close beside her. He put a hand on her knee. "Give us a kiss."

She sighed and gave him a quick one. He found that his hand could continue up her shorts unchecked. With a shock his fingers touched her cold cunt. "Sorry," he said.

"It doesn't make any difference," she told him.

He glanced around the courtyard at the flowers. He picked at a tooth. From somewhere overhead there came a bass drone. He smiled without much interest into the sky. "Bombers," he said. "I thought we were going to have a peaceful day." They were in sight now. A large formation of F111As. "It's a free country, I suppose."

"Eloi! Eloi!" Miss Brunner became agitated. She sprang to her feet. "Peaceful? This enclave of lotus-eaters? Don't you realise the world's rotting about your ears? Haven't you got eyes? Can't you smell the corruption? Can't you feel the whole world going out of kilter? Where's your sense? And all you can think of is feeling me up!"

He glanced at her from beneath embarrassed eyebrows. He felt a twinge of self-pity. "I was only having a bit of fun."

Some distance to the south, probably over Barnes, the planes began to drop their loads.

She made efficient arrangements to her clothing. She headed for the languid street, still crowded with the festive and the free. "Fun!"

He was thoroughly demoralised, more by what he had found in her trousers than by what he had done. "I'm very sorry. It won't happen again."

"That's all right." She waved a polyvinyl chloride gauntlet. "For the present."

8. THE METAMORPHOSIS OF HARLEQUIN

For the last three weeks Jerry Cornelius had remained in the roof garden of the empty department store. The roof garden was overgrown and lush; parts of it were almost impassable. Flamingoes, ducks, macaws, parakeets and cockatoos inhabited the tangles of rhododendrons, creepers, climbing roses and nasturtiums; yellow mimosa grew adequately close to the various dividing walls of the garden: and, through the ceiling below, several large roots had broken and begun to find the tubs of earth Jerry had removed from the botanical department and placed on the floor so that ultimately the plants would gain purchase here. It was his ambition to bring in increasing supplies of earth so that in time the entire store would become a jungle to which he could then, perhaps, begin to introduce predators and prey, possibly from the zoo of the store's nearby rival.

Jerry had his consolations: a battery-operated stereo record player on which he listened to traditional folk music and laid-back C&W, some light reading; he could feed himself from what was left of the Food Hall and from the canned supplies in the roof garden restaurant, where he had also set up his camp-bed. The restaurant was more like a conservatory now, for he had been pleased to admit as many plants as would enter. He was never disturbed. He enjoyed the novels of Jane Austen, avoided interpretation, and dreamed of safer days.

Occasionally he would creep from the upper storeys to the bowels of the building and attend to his generators, thus maintaining his freezer and, of greater importance, the central heating. He had turned this to maximum so that his plants would be encouraged to extend their roots towards the distant ground. It was his hope that eventually the remains of Derry & Toms would be preserved in a gigantic shrubbery, impenetrable save by those who, like him, understood the labyrinth. At the top of this mountain of foliage and masonry he would then possess remarkable security. Already a number of peonies were blooming in the soft-furnishing department and various vines and ivies, without training, had carpeted the floors and festooned the walls of Hardware and Electrical Goods. He remained armed, but he had lost much of his caution. Aerial warfare was almost a thing of the past, the fashion having changed primarily to tanks and infantry which, ultimately, provided greater satisfaction to those who still enjoyed such exercises. London was no longer regarded as a major objective.

Jerry gathered that most of the battles were won in the world and that conferences were rapidly agreeing territorial boundaries. The Continent of Europe had apparently become a vast conglomeration of tiny city states, primarily based on an agricultural economy, with certain traditional crafts and trades (Bohemian glass, German clocks, French mustard) flourishing: forming the basis of barter between the different communities. Not that war was unknown, but it had become confined to the level of local disputes. Jerry had been unable to see this development as a wholesome one, but he supposed it suited the petite bourgeoisie who constituted, as always, the majority of the survivors. It seemed to him that in some obscure way Miss Brunner had, after all, triumphed, through no fault of her own.

The image of a Britain become a nation of William Morris wood-carvers and Chestertonian beer-swillers drove him deeper into his jungle and caused him to abandon his books. He was only prepared to retreat so far. He was forced to admit, however, that the seventies were proving an intense disappointment to him. He felt bitter about missed opportunities, the caution of his own allies, the sheer funk of his enemies. In the fifties life had been so appalling that he had been forced to flee into the future, perhaps even help create that future, but by the sixties, when the future had arrived, he had been content at last to live in the present until, due in his view to a conspiracy amongst those who feared the threat of freedom, the present (and consequently the future) had been betrayed. As a result he had sought the past for consolation, for an adequate mythology to explain the world to him, and here he hid, lost in his art nouveau jungle, his art deco caverns, treading the dangerous quicksands of nostalgia and yearning for times that seemed simpler only because he did not belong to them and which, as they became familiar, seemed even more complex than the world he had loved for its very variety and potential. Thus he fled still further, into a world where vegetation alone flourished and only the most primitive of sentient life chose to exist. He was thinking of giving up time travel altogether.

Apart from the infrequent fights which would break out amongst the birds, there were very few sounds to disturb him these days as he renounced his camp-bed and lay deep in his bushes, his back to moist earth, his earphones almost invariably on his head as he listened to the Pure Prairie League, The Chieftains and, believing that this kept him in touch with the world, Roy Harper. He was inclined not to notice when his batteries had run down and the records were playing sometimes at less than half speed. He was also inclined to fall asleep when the needle stuck in a groove and not wake for two or three days.

He was dimly aware that these long periods of sleeping were increasing but, since he felt no physical effects, he preferred not to worry about them. It was likely that his activities through the past couple of decades had exhausted him more than he knew. For the moment, too, he had even forgotten about his sister, who lay in her padded silk coffin in the freezer, perhaps dreaming of an even more remote past than the one he sought to create for himself.

The summer grew hotter; the jungle grew denser, and then one day, as Jerry slumbered in musty heat in a little tunnel he had made for himself in the foliage, an unread copy of *Union Jack* for 21 September, 1923 ('X-ine or The Case of the Green Crystals', A Zenith Story) lying foxed and damp-stained by his limp right hand, the comforting rumble of Centurion Thirteens, Vickers Vijayantas and Humber FV1611 armoured personnel carriers augmented the sultry tranquillity of the day, the hum of bees, the hiccuping of crickets.

The little fleet of armour came to a stop at the signal of a round-shouldered old man in the dress uniform of a major in the Royal Hussars who emerged from the leading Humber, adjusting his busby. A captain, in conventional khaki, pushed up the hatch of the Centurion immediately behind the Humber and ran over the weedy tarmac to receive orders. The major spoke a few words, contemplated the outside of the store which was almost entirely covered by thick ivy, checked the dark green interior of the main hallway, then returned to his personnel carrier. A head wearing a green, gold and purple turban raised itself over the camouflaged metal. A chubby brown face showed a certain amount of astonishment as it caught sight of the department store, which somehow had come to resemble the forgotten ruins of Angkor Wat in Cambodia. Green and gold shoulders followed the face and eventually the whole figure, small and stocky and round, stood on the surface of the vehicle, hands on hips. He was dressed in the impressive uniform of the 30th Deccan Horse, a broad sash around his waist, his sabre and pistol supported on a Sam Browne belt which was oddly functional compared to the rest of the ensemble. The major saluted and lifted a hand to help the splendid Indian to the ground then, together, they entered the forest.

The engines of the tanks and personnel carriers were switched off; silence returned. Slowly the crews began to climb from their machines and, stripped to the waist, smoke cigarettes and chat amongst themselves. They seemed to be a mixed force in a variety of uniforms—English, Scottish, Indian, Trinidadian, Jamaican and Cornish among them. Tinny Heavy Reggae began to sound from at least one turret.

The two officers reached the roof garden three hours later. They were sweating and stained, the collars of their jackets opened, their headgear askew. They searched the restaurant and the restaurant kitchens. The first thing they found was the display freezer with its pale blue contents, the beautiful smiling madonna. The major shook his head. "About the only thing he ever thought worth preserving. Poor little chap."

"They were in love," said the Indian. He tried to push his hand down the side of the coffin to get a tub of Honey and Acacia ice-cream below, but failed.

"More than that." The major sighed. "She represented everything he thought important. He believed that if he could revive her he could revive the world he had lost."

"She is dead, then?"

"As good as, old boy." The major closed the lid of the cabinet. "We'd better check the garden now. You take the Tudor and I'll take the Spanish. If you don't have any luck, meet me back here."

They went their ways.

The major found it almost impossible to climb over the tangled branches and roots blocking the entrance to the mock Moorish splendours of the garden where the fountains were now choked with dark green vegetation, with magnolia, oversized tulips, peonies, poppies, sunflowers. The heavy scent from the place almost drove him back. He was about to press on when his ear detected a faint sound from his right and he looked towards the gigantic rhododendron mass immediately opposite the restaurant. Two or three flamingoes stalked from it, their pink necks wobbling, splashing on broad feet through what remained of the miniature river. But it was not the birds who had made the sound. The major moved towards the rhododendron, almost blinded by the intensity of the purple, scarlet and pink blossoms, the powerful odour of earth and decaying undergrowth. He pushed branches aside and found a low archway. He bent down and peered through the green semi-darkness. He went on his knees and began to crawl until the tunnel opened into a tiny cavern in which lay curled, foetuslike, the body of the man the major had sought over five continents.

The body was dressed in a green-and-khaki camouflaged safari suit, there were black Koss earphones on his head and the lead of the earphones was attached to a record deck on which Al Bowlly was singing 'What a Little Moonlight Can Do' with painful slowness. On its side, near the player, was a clock, decorated in red, white and blue, and beside it a gesticulating figurine in a traditional white Pierrot costume with a black skull-cap, perhaps a contemporary likeness of Charles Debureau himself; near that a copy of a Fantômas novelette and a copy of *Le Chat Noir* magazine. The *Union Jack* was open at the beginning of the story. A box below the illustration, showing an open safe, a swirl of vapour and two men apparently confronting one another (one wearing full evening dress) read: *This story very worthily upholds the UNION JACK tradition— the tradition for really well-told stories, full of character and action. It is a Zenith-Sexton Blake story, written as only the creator of the Albino knows how. If you want anything better than this you are indeed hard to please.* The major carefully picked the fragile magazine from the earth, rolled it and tucked it into the top pocket of his dark blue tunic. Then he inspected the stiff figure of the man. It was thin. The face was quite long, the lips full, the eyes, though closed, apparently large. The hair was black, long and fine, but appeared to have been dyed white at some time. There was a very close resemblance to the blonde young woman the major had discovered in the freezer. He lifted his head:

"In here, Hythloday. I've found him, poor old chap. Just made it, too, it seems. He's almost gone."

The major waited, rolling himself a cigarette as he looked down at the curled figure. There came a blundering sound from behind him and eventually a panting Hythloday crawled into view. There was not really room for all three of them. It was obvious that Hythloday at first suspected the major had been forced to defend himself.

"He's not dead, I hope. Was he violent?"

"Oh, no, no." The major smiled sadly. "As far as this chap's concerned I'm afraid violence is a thing of the past."

9. THE DEATH OF HARLEQUIN

"Ten bloody years!" Miss Brunner was incongruous in a red-and-white Malay sarong, her head tied in the kind of blue turban hat popular four decades earlier. Her breath smelled of chloroform from the Victory V throat lozenges she had taken to consuming. In wedge sandals she hobbled across a green, blue and gold Kazhak carpet to the mock Adam fireplace where old Major Nye stood looking at a collection of photographs in black and silver Mackintosh frames. Major Nye wore the uniform of his first regiment: a pale blue and yellow tunic, dark blue britches with a double yellow stripe, black riding boots with spurs, a sabre, white spiked helmet; the 8th King George's Own Light Cavalry. He had become so frail that it seemed the uniform alone kept him on his feet. He turned, blinking mildly, raising a grey eyebrow, bending his thin good ear towards her. "Eh?"

"I don't think you realise how very difficult it's been for some of us." She stared coldly at one of the marble pillars near the tall double doors. Ceramic Siamese red and black lions returned her gaze. The whole place was a mixture of oriental styles except for the original architecture, which was Victorian Greek. "I spent nine months in a Cornish internment camp for a start!"

"Start?"

"Underground bunkers. They put anything under ground that will go under ground. They're fond of holes, the Cornish. They're afraid of the sun."

"Ironical, in their case. They're like the Welsh. Mining, you see. They love it. Like the Seven Dwarves. *Heigh ho, heigh ho, it's off to work we go…*" He chuckled. *Dig, dig, dig.* It's made them very rich these days, I gather. Tin, clay, gold and silver even. Oh, they've done it for centuries. Since before the Romans. Two thousand years at least. Give them a pick and shovel and they'll burrow through anything. It's instinctive. You have to admire them."

She had heard his racial views more than once. She sighed deeply. "Oh, yes?" She rubbed at her raw bare arm. "They're also notoriously horrible to their prisoners—including the other Celts."

"True. You heard that stuff about the flint knives, I suppose, and the menhirs?"

"I saw it," she said. "I was lucky."

"Well, they've achieved their object. They don't get many unwanted visitors any more. They've a new arethyor enthroned at Tintagel at last. I got the news this morning."

"Which one won?"

"Arluth St Aubyn, naturally." He shrugged and rubbed at his blue-veined nose. "They can't help themselves. Ancient instincts, you see, as I say. Old habits die hard."

"It seems you pulled Cornelius out in time again. He owes a lot to you."

"Someone has to look after him when he goes walk-about."

Miss Brunner glanced over to the bay windows where her old lover sat, silhouetted against the light, wrapped in a Kashmiri shawl, his eyes vacant and unblinking. "Oh, Christ," she said, "he's dribbling. And he used to be tipped as the Messiah to the Age of Science!" She shook her head in disgust.

"It's his amnesia," said Major Nye, to excuse Cornelius. "He never knows where he's going. He just keeps revisiting certain places that have some private meaning for him, some mythological significance. He's much better today. He keeps collapsing into catatonia, especially after one of the wandering spells. It can't be his sister he's looking for now. She's perfectly safe."

Miss Brunner glared into the vacant face. "There are no sanctuaries any more, Mr Cornelius. There are none in the past, none in the future. I advise you to make the best of the present!"

"Best not to disturb him," said Major Nye. On frail legs stiffened at the knees by the boots, his spurs rattling a little, he went to stand behind Jerry's wheelchair. "All right, old son. There, there, old lad." He patted Jerry's shoulder. Since he had lost his wife and family, Major Nye had found his only fulfilment in taking care of the mindless assassin. "He never believed in the possibility of sanctuary, you know. Not for years. He disdained the idea.

He was born in the modern city, you see."

"You mean he never needed security? I've known him longer than you, major, and I can tell you…"

"The city was his security, with all its horrors. As the jungle is security to the tiger, you might say. When they began to destroy his city he lost his bearings completely. For a while he evidently thought that the landscape of warfare might be a substitute, but he was wrong. It's strange, isn't it, how the city grew from the town which in turn grew from the encampment formed against the terrors of the wild…?"

"I don't know anything about that. I was born in Kent."

"Exactly. I was born in the country. We can't possibly understand the comforting familiarity of the city to someone like Cornelius. The worse it is, in our terms, the more he feels at one with himself. Even at the end his instinct was to hide in the heart of the city, climbing to the top of a tall building for safety, reintroducing the jungle…" Major Nye's voice faded. He smiled tenderly at his charge.

"He's a wild beast. A monster."

"Indeed. That's why he became such a totem to so many."

"I always considered his apparent sophistication, his affectation of an interest in science, to be a veneer." Her voice became more confident as she began to feel she and the major were on common ground at last.

"On the contrary. A creature like Cornelius takes technology for granted. It is real enough to him for it to possess a genuinely mythological significance."

Miss Brunner tightened her unlikely lips. "I never

denied technology had a purpose…" She frowned. "A usefulness. If handled properly…"

"You tried to use it to maintain the old order. Your friend Beesley wanted to turn it against itself, to destroy it altogether. But Cornelius enjoyed it for its own sake. Aesthetically. He had no interest in its moral significance or its utilisation. Computers and jets and rockets and lasers and the rest were simply familiar elements of his natural environment. He didn't judge them or question them, any more than you or I would judge or question a tree or a hill. He picked his cars, his weapons, his gadgets, in the same way that he picked his clothes—for their private meanings, for what they looked like. He enjoyed their functions, too, of course, but function was a secondary consideration. There are easier cars to drive than Duesenbergs, easier, faster, cheaper planes to fly than experimental Dorniers. He found speed exhilarating, of course, but again speed wasn't really what he cared about. He preferred airships to jet-liners because airships were more romantic, he preferred Mach 3 liners and shock-wave ships because they looked nicer and because they hinted at an ambiguous relationship with space and time—that was where the mystical element came in, as with particle physics. And have you noticed how we still continue to ape the markings of animals in our clothes—particularly our traditional formal clothes? Similarly with technology. He liked the Concorde because it looked most like an eagle. To me it was all completely bewildering, to you it was something that had to be tamed, to him it was normality. He had all the primitive's respect for Nature, the same tendency to invest it with meaning and identity, only his Nature was the industrial city, his idea of Paradise was an urban utopia..."

"He was a snotty-nosed little backstreet nihilist," she said. "There's no point in dignifying his attitude."

"To us he was far more dangerous than any nihilist. He was alien. He came to enjoy the bombing raids because he was interested in what the bombs would do, what sort of pictures they would make, even, as was often the case, when his own safety was threatened. His will to peace was as strong as yours or mine, perhaps stronger, but his methods of obtaining peace were personal. They became personal because we couldn't understand what he was talking about. He was a friendly chap. He allowed us all to use him. But he gradually came to realise that our aims were incompatible. His Utopia was to us an insane technological nightmare."

"I can't believe this sympathy of yours," she snapped. She clacked across the carpet to the photographs. They were all there, all his relatives, his acquaintances. "You're older than me. Your world had nothing at all in common with his."

"It probably changed just as rapidly. But I suppose it's because I know that I've so little in common with him that I can sympathise." Major Nye turned the chair slightly so that Jerry could see something of the street below, where the rebuilding work was taking place, where the bunting and the flags were going up. "Yours is an unfortunate generation, on the whole."

"I am, I hope, broad-minded. But one can take for

granted far too much, major."

"Not as much as poor Cornelius. He took it all for granted. It ruined him. He wasn't his world's Messiah. He wasn't the Golden Trickster. He was his world's Fool."

"Is that what he's suffering from?" She became curious, advancing again to the wheelchair, staring coldly into the drooling face. "Shock?"

"He was shown too much of the past at once. That's a theory, anyway. He hardly knew it existed before."

"And you continue to support him, you and Una Persson. Even Auchinek, who has no love for him. Why?"

"Perhaps we thought we could maintain our humanity by studying him. In Auchinek's case, at least, and in mine, you could say that we saw him as a model. In an inhospitable world he seemed to be at ease." Major Nye fingered his moustache. He sucked his lips. He dismissed the notion. "No. It's too hard for me to define. It might be much simpler than that. I need to give my loyalty to something. It's my training, d'you see. With all his faults, he seemed the best bet. He took his world for granted, just as I had taken mine for granted—not complacently, but with the sense that, drawbacks included, injustices included, it was the best of all possible worlds."

"To be quite candid," Miss Brunner began, and then was horrified to see Cornelius looking back at her through sardonic eyes.

"You'll never be that, I'm afraid," said Cornelius calmly. Then the head dropped. The lips began to drool again.

"He has these flashes," said Major Nye affectionately.

She clacked towards the door. "It's disgusting. You're both as senile as one another. You need a nurse to look after the pair of you."

Before Miss Brunner could reach the doors they opened and a small black-and-white cat walked in, tail erect, followed by Una Persson who came to a halt when she saw Miss Brunner. Una Persson had her Smith and Wesson .45 in her hand, half-cocked. When she recognised Miss Brunner she smiled and uncocked the pistol, slipping it back into the holster at her belt. She wore the full uniform of a Jodhpur Lancer, for she was currently in the employ of the Maharajah of New Marwar and had come up by train from Brighton only an hour before. "How nice to see you again. And what a pretty outfit." Una bowed, the plumes in her turban nodding.

"You've certainly gone all the way, dearie." Miss Brunner was disgusted. "Did you bring your harem with you?"

"We're not allowed harems in New Marwar." Una inched past Miss Brunner and offered Major Nye a broad, open smile. "Good afternoon, major. How's the patient?"

"Improving, I'd say."

Miss Brunner disappeared on angry heels. Una closed the doors. "It's all arranged," she said. "I do pray they won't be disappointed."

"We can only hope."

"Hope…" mumbled the slumped figure.

"There!" said Major Nye. "I seem to have offended Miss Brunner. I had no intention…"

"I didn't know she was at liberty again."

"I'd hardly call it liberty. Apparently she plans to

found some sort of mission in London, together with Beesley and that daughter of his. They've fallen on hard times, those two."

"And I didn't realise Beesley was back. Where's he been?"

"He was thrown out of Ohio, I gather. By the Sioux. Then he went to Arizona and was deported by the Navajo. He didn't have much better luck in New Hampshire, where the Elders regarded him, rather ironically, as an atheist. According to our intelligence, and it's always suspect, he spent a while in the West Indies where he managed to build up a small following, but eventually he was sent home on an emigrant ship and landed in Liverpool a month ago. The Chinese authorities sent him to us. So far the only state to offer him a home has been East Wiltshire. But he found out what happens to clergymen in Wiltshire, after their seven-year period of office. Some old custom they've revived."

"I appreciate this quest for national identity," she said, "but it does seem that most traditions were dropped for the good reason that they were revoltingly cruel and stupid."

"Well, live and let live. Things will probably settle down." He looked at the red, white and blue French clock on the mantelpiece. It was half-hidden behind the photographs. "You're about half an hour late. I was hoping you'd rescue me sooner."

"I dropped off to see Mrs Cornelius."

"I thought she was coming for the festivities."

"I had something to discuss. She'll be here later."

"Still going strong, is she?"

"As always. Quite a celebrity in these parts now, and enjoying every minute of it."

"She's still with Pyat?"

"No. Pyat's working with the Poles now, over in Slough. He sees her from time to time but I think Hira—what's he calling himself?"

"Hythloday."

"Yes. I might as well call myself Lalla Rookh!" She laughed. "Anyway, he's still her main boyfriend. It gives him a lot of extra muscle in Croydon, apparently, but the Maharajah wants him to marry her and she says she's had enough of marriage, though she'd be glad of the status. She could go to Brighton whenever she liked, then."

"It's even more magnificent, I hear. Lots of gold roofs and pastel walls. Hythloday wouldn't be marrying out of caste, would he?"

"Mrs C. is regarded as high caste by virtue of being Jerry's mum. My boss has entertained her to dinner several times and been proud of the honour. She, of course, was in her element. They love her. There isn't a Sikh in Sussex who doesn't. Of course she tends to be hated by a lot of the natives who resent her privileges and think she's socialising above her station or sucking up to the masters, depending on their point of view, but that type of white will always bicker among themselves. I get a lot of similar spite, myself, of course."

Major Nye was amused. "They think you're a bit of an Uncle Tom, do they?"

"You could put it like that." She took a step back from Jerry as if she inspected a painting. Her uniform was primarily white and gold with a gold-trimmed scarlet sash. There was an Indian sabre at her belt and her turban was a tall one, wrapped around a spiked metal cap, matching the colours of her uniform and with some thin bands of blue to show her rank. The plumes were also a sign of rank. For Major Nye the uniform somehow emphasised her femininity and made her seem a fraction shorter than usual. "I wish he'd perk up a bit," she said beneath her breath. "They've made so many preparations."

"Officially we tell them he's been asleep?"

"Oh, certainly. But you know what legends are like. There are an awful lot of people believe that when he wakes up this time an era of peace, prosperity and co-operation between the nations will begin."

"The British nations, you mean? It was our fault, I suppose, for speaking so highly of him."

"I don't think it's that. They needed a symbol and he's as good as anything. After all, he was a lot of help to many of the independence movements, even before the civil war. Now there's scarcely one of the sixty states that doesn't have some sort of folklore connected with him. Not everything is good, of course, but most of it is. You should hear the stories the Highland anarchists tell. It's astonishing how quickly he's been worked into almost all of Britain's mythologies as well as a good many others throughout the world. As if a gap existed for him to fill. There are Cornelius legends in America, Africa, Asia, Australia, throughout Europe. He's bigger than The Beatles now."

Major Nye was pleased. He took a brass-plate tin

from his tunic. The tin had belonged to his father. It was decorated with a relief bust of Princess Mary flanked by the initials M.M. while the borders contained pictures of stylised arms and ships and the names of various nations— Belgium, Japan, Russia, Monte Negro, Servia and France. In the top border were the words Imperium Britannicum. In the bottom border were the words Christmas 1914. The tin had originally contained a pipe, cigarettes and tobacco and a Christmas card from Princess Mary. Now it contained Major Nye's own tobacco and cigarette papers. He began to roll himself a tiny smoke. "You don't mind what's happened, then?"

"You think I should be jealous?"

"Miss Brunner certainly is. So's his brother."

"He was always a better entertainer than I was." Una shrugged. "And I was always a better politician. He refused to make something of himself and now the world has made something of him. There's nothing like having a common hero."

"And I'm nothing if not common," said Jerry. He blinked. "It's a bit bright in here, isn't it?"

They watched him carefully, expecting him to subside.

"What's been going on?" he asked. "You were talking about me, weren't you?"

Una shook her head chidingly. "You sneaky little bugger!"

"I didn't really take much in." He was apologetic. "Where am I?"

Major Nye seemed to grow younger by the second.

He was almost dancing with pleasure. "Ladbroke Grove, old chap."

Jerry looked around him at the magnificence of it. "Must be the posh end," he said. "I never knew it very well."

"This is all new. It was built on the site of that convent. The one they bombed."

"Blimey!" Jerry shifted in his chair. It rolled slightly and he realised it was on wheels. He cackled at it. "Was I injured?"

"You could say that. You were catatonic."

"Black or white? Or both?" Jerry thought he saw a tail disappearing up the chimney. He accepted the information without question. "It's a family trait. Like the Ushers. Wasn't it?"

"Like the bloody Draculas." Una Persson's amusement was admiring. "Pulled through just in time, as usual, haven't you? You've missed all the work and can enjoy all the fun."

"Oh, good." He yawned. "Is this your place, major? Or is it a new town hall?"

"It's your palace, old son. Built by public subscription. All the British nations, bar one or two, chipped in."

"So the war's over." He stood up and the chair shot away across the smooth floor and struck the far wall. He was still a little shaky on his pins. "Well, it's very kind of them. I didn't think I was that popular."

Una hid her pleasure behind an expression of mock severity. "You wouldn't have been, if it wasn't for the fact that, for the past decade, you've done absolutely nothing. You're the stuff heroes are made of, Jerry."

"Yeah? What's London like, these days?" He walked to the huge bay.

"There's a great deal to be done yet," said Major Nye. "Those skyscrapers over there are just the beginning. They'll have high-level moving pavements going between them eventually. And gyrocopters and airships and everything. Just as you visualised it."

"The City of the Future," said Jerry breathlessly. "Is it all for me?"

"And anyone else who chooses to live here." Una joined him at the windows. "Otherwise the rest of the world's regressed somewhat, though there aren't many people complaining. This will be your monument, where past and future come together. London's independent now, too, you see. It has no authority over anything but itself. It's a free city, a mercantile, cosmopolitan neutral zone, a symbol."

"A meeting place for artists, scientists, merchants," continued Major Nye. "*In Xanadu did Kubla Khan...*"

"Cor!" exclaimed Jerry. "Is it going to have a dome over it, too? A power dome?"

"If that's what you want."

"I can't just say what I want, surely? Who's the boss?"

"You are, Jerry." Una Persson's eyes were shining. "Happy Birthday."

"I get the whole of London?"

"Why not?"

"Nobody else," said Major Nye with a small grin, "wants it, really."

"Cor!" The shawl fell from his shoulders. He was

still in the uniform of the 30th Deccan Horse. "An O'Bean Utopia!" Major Nye went back to the mantelpiece and got his headdress for him. Jerry put it on as he stared through round, delirious eyes at the golden city of marvels beginning to rise from the ruins. Then he peered in the direction of the demolished Ladbroke Grove Underground Station. "There seems to be a lot of people coming up the road."

They stood on either side of him.

"We'd better get you upstairs," said Una, brushing at his back. "Onto the balcony."

"It's only fair. They'll be wanting to see you. You represent the future for them, you see. The wonderful tomorrow."

"Tomorrow? I don't get it."

"You will. They're not ready for it yet. Not personally. But it's comforting to be able to see what it will be like if they ever do want it."

Between them they escorted the astonished Cornelius from the room, through the double doors, up a wide staircase and into an even larger hall where the French windows had been opened onto the white marble balcony.

From below came cheers. A large crowd had gathered, clad in the costumes of a hundred nations, in plaids and lace; in kilts and pantaloons and britches and trousers and trews and dhotis; saris, sarongs, of silk and satin, chitons, chardors and cholees, frock-coats of cotton and felt, capes, cloaks and kaftans in moiré, astrakhan, corduroy, and gaberdine, bowlers, boaters, Buster Brown and pillbox caps, turbans and kaffiyehs, buskins, moccasins, mukluks, wellingtons, chuckars, brogues, slippers, sandals, plimsolls, pumps and trepida in colours more varied and dazzling than the rainbow's. And Jerry saw skins of every shade, African, Asian, Anglo-Saxon, Latin and Teutonic, and the faces of all these representatives of the races were turned to him and, when he waved, they waved back.

"Hi," said Jerry in some awe, "fans."

He saw a small figure break through the crowd and move across the street. "Miss Brunner?"

Did she turn and present two fingers to him? He could not be sure, for now the procession was passing the palace.

"Bloody hell!" said Jerry. "What is it? A carnival?"

"It's in your honour," said Una with great satisfaction. "They're deputations from every British state."

"Just like the Jubilee!"

"More or less," said Una, "though things have perhaps changed a bit."

Precedence had been given to the knife-wheeled Celtic chariot driven by a lady in a sky-blue smock who hailed him with her long spear, but she was followed immediately by the ceremonial elephants, festooned in scarlet and gold, jade and silver plumes of ostrich, peacock and bird of paradise, with intricately woven shawls, tassels and jewelled tusk rings, some of them bearing enormous howdahs on their backs—howdahs of bronze and gold or carved from rare woods and set under with mother-of-pearl...

"Those belong to my master," said Una proudly, "the Maharajah of New Marwar. He's one of the most powerful monarchs in Britain."

... and some of the elephants pulled monstrous carriages, not unlike ornate railway coaches, the windows curtained with green velvet, the metal glowing with brilliant enamels, containing the families of the rulers of Surrey, Sussex and South Dorset. The rulers themselves, maharajahs and rajas in traditional military uniforms similar to those worn by Jerry and Una, rode at the head of their lancers and their riflemen, their splendid infantry, veterans of Dorking, Bognor Regis, Lewes and Hastings, swords raised in salute to the Lord of London. Next came the mandarins of Liverpool and Morecambe, in glinting rickshaws, coaches and sedan chairs, their retainers waving dragon banners, beating gongs and playing pipes as they marched and danced their superb acrobatic steps; the great Captains of Birmingham and Bristol in vast open Cadillacs, sporting the blazing flags of New Trinidad and Old Jamaica, accompanied by masked troops playing drums of every description, by lovely black drum majorettes, by batmen and panthermen, all style and dash. Then came the great clans of Scotland, with wailing bagpipes and rattling drums, plaids bright enough to dim the sun, the green-kilted warriors of Eire and Cymru, the Coal Dancers of the Federation of Miners' Republics, bearing their bowler-hatted Chief Executive on their shoulders; the Lancashire Free State leaders, carrying their own banner, the great red-and-yellow tapestry with their famous slogan *Wigan Won the War* woven into it; there were more Irish Hussars, and Scottish Mounted Rifles, Australian Light Horse, Canadian Artillery, Welsh

Irregulars, Wessex Roughriders, regiments of horse and foot from South Wiltshire, East Kent, North Yorkshire, West Wickham, all carrying flags of their states, some of them wearing uniforms whose origin was thoroughly obscure to Jerry, who knew nothing of recent history; some of the mascots and totems—skulls, pieces of furniture, sheep, dogs, goats, bulls, portraits, items of clothing, children, mummies—were equally mysterious. There were Briganti, Iceni, Trinovantes, Cantiaci, Catuvellauni, Coritani and Cornovii, with red-gold bracelets and bears and braids and burnished shields of brass and bronze, with glittering M16s on their backs, with horned helmets, huge beards and fierce eyes. There were Mercians and Northumbrians, with blood-red banners and dark helms, mounted on bucking motorcycles decorated with chrome and gold and semi-precious stones and, after all seventy-two British nations had displayed their military strength, there followed the pipe bands of Surrey and Inverness, the brass bands of Fazakerly and Bradford, the steel bands of Ashton and Shepton Mallet, many of the tunes recognisable, many others hauntingly alien—a great wailing of sitars, saxophones, syrens and serpents, a banging and beating of bongos and congas and kettledrums and tablas, of gongs and cymbals, of xylophones and glockenspiels, the thrumming of guitars and mandolins, violins, banjos and double-basses, maraccas, mouth-organs, cowbells, sleigh-bells, tubular bells, songs and chants and shouts in fifty different dialects, all of them full of wild, innocent joy, for this was a celebration of peace of which Cornelius and his

London were the concrete symbols.

"The king! The king!" they cried. "For he's a jolly good fellow!" they sang, and "Auld Lang Syne!"

Jerry was weeping as he waved back. He turned to old Major Nye who smiled behind his moustache.

"Am I really the king? Or just a play-actor?"

Major Nye shrugged. "Does it matter? Elfberg or Cornelius. You are their ideal. Wave to them, Your Majesty!"

Una came close, murmuring: "It's an honorary title, with very little actual power. But the honour really is considerable."

"But what are my duties?"

"To exist. It would be foolish to make a king who had any concrete responsibilities, particularly after the trouble the world's been in. It's all titular, though you do have the whole of London to play with. Anyway, nobody else wanted the job."

"Not even Frank?"

"Almost nobody else."

Jerry continued to wave. "I don't know about you, Miss Persson, but it's the best offer I've had so far."

"You've never been one to resist a bit of glamour."

"It's more the security I like."

He waved violently at the airships, keel after keel, making their stately way across the sky. "I wish Catherine could see this. Is she about?"

"She's still sleeping, I'm afraid," said Major Nye. "We didn't like to try waking her until you…"

"Of course. But King Pierrot must win his Queen

Columbine now. It's only right. Catherine would expect it of me. I've never let her down before. Pierrot's been waiting for centuries, hasn't he?"

Major Nye looked baffled. "I thought you were playing Harlequin?"

"I wasn't suited for the part. I changed. It was quite natural. No danger."

A shadow fell across the balcony and for a moment an expression of terror appeared in Jerry's eyes. Then it vanished. He turned, arms outstretched. "Hello, Mum."

"Cor! Wot a scorcher!" Mrs Cornelius was sweating as only she could sweat, her huge bulk dripping with diamonds and pearls. She sported an ermine-trimmed robe of scarlet silk, a huge feathered hat. "D'yer like it? I 'ad it run up special for yer corernation. Loverly turn art, innit?"

"Lovely."

The procession was over. The sound of it began to fade near the top of Ladbroke Grove, heading towards Notting Hill.

Frank stood behind his mother. "Congratters, old son." Rage flitted in his eyes. "Feeling all right now, are we?"

The roar of the crowd below began to rise higher and higher and drowned whatever it was Jerry had been hoping to say.

10. THE MIRROR; OR, HARLEQUIN EVERYWHERE

London, England: the time is Christmas Eve, probably during the nineties, and from the black night sky drop flakes of soft snow, covering roofs and walls, trees and streets, giving to the air a silence, a taste at once damp, fresh and salty; and with the flakes, from the huge darkness, there descends a fluttering, indistinct figure whose feet touch the flat top of a tall, deserted building, the new Derry & Toms. The figure darts for the shadows, even though the roof garden is closed for the season, but the footfalls, which leave light prints on the surface, together with the slap of the snow on the broad rhododendron leaves, disturb the birds there and they move in their sleep. Overhead we hear a distant bass drone, as if a flying machine departs.

Wrapped in a cloak of red velvet trimmed with green moiré, the hood covering the head, a black domino mask disguising the features, the figure looks this way and that, then slips towards the exit, leaving more footprints behind it. As the figure moves, the cloak falls back to reveal the varicoloured costume of Harlequin.

Harlequin flits down the darkened stairs to the emergency doors, takes out a key, unlocks them, pauses, as if drawing breath, then enters a side street bustling with cheerful life: gas-jets roar over stalls and under stoves, some for light, some for heat: there are braziers, crimson and black, of jacket-potatoes and hot chestnuts; there are pans of pies, apples, toffee, cakes and fried sausages; all for sale, all cheap: fish and chips, barley sugar twists, humbugs, gumdrops, bullseyes. Huge, scarlet faces hang over the wares, shouting, laughing, crying. "'Ot codlins. 'Ot codlins!" Father Christmas pads along the narrow space between the stalls, ringing his bell, while his costumed imps caper here and there, handing gifts to any children they meet. "Plump turkeys! Merry Christmas! Merry Christmas! Best pippins!" A sweet for a girl, a sprig of mistletoe for a boy. "Carp! Carp! Merry Christmas!" And the breath steams from their lips, muffled in collars and scarves, to join the boiling mist from the pans and cauldrons which, in turn, meets and melts with the falling snow so that the air immediately above the stalls glows like a yellow aurora. "Roast goose! Salt beef! Merry Christmas! Merry Christmas!" Dogs bark, horses neigh, children scream for the joy of it all.

Harlequin moves quickly into the broader canyon, the renewed Kensington High Street. Here, beneath arcades created by overhead pedestrian galleries climbing, step by step, into the black-and-white sky, among elegant towers with windows of glittering gold and silver, whose tops are lost high above, between moving sidewalks, packed with shoppers, are the warm lights of more stalls:

stalls piled with vegetables, with meats, toys and sweets; stalls burdened with fowl and game, salmon and trout, pine branches, bunches of heather, holly and laurel; and behind the stalls are coffee houses, where men and women of every nationality—Hindus, Russians, Chinese, Spaniards, Portuguese, Englishmen, Frenchmen, Genoese, Neapolitans, Venetians, Greeks, Turks, descendants from all the builders of Babel, come to trade in London—seek the warmth alike, joining there in friendly intercourse; chophouses, where merchants exchange Christmas gifts and clap one another upon the shoulder—"Merry Christmas!"; pie shops, whose windows are heaped with beef puddings, steak-and-kidney pies, treacle tarts, sweating and smoking in great white enamel basins and trays; bazaars and emporia bursting with rich, mouth-watering smells, crammed with customers still upon their Christmas hunt, while from the other side of bright frosted windows, in the public houses, comes the sound of pianos, pianolas, fiddles, harmoniums and accordions.

God rest ye merry gentlemen, let nothing ye dismay...

Harlequin passes on, muffled in the cloak, head hidden by the hood, between a little knot of boys and girls gathered round a lanthorn pole, their shadows huge on the snow, to sing:

Good King Wenzslaslas looked out
On the feast of Stephen

When the snow lay round about
Deep and crisp and even...

Already other children stoop to gather the snow in mittened hands, knead it into balls, throw it at one another, laughing, screaming, yelling fit to burst...

Bring me flesh and bring me wine
Bring me pine-logs hither.
Thou and I will see him dine
When we bear them thither.

... Omnibuses rattle by, lights ablaze, top rails crackling like so many Christmas stars; carriages, rickshaws, cabs and cars. "Merry Christmas! Merry Christmas!"

Page and monarch forth they went,
Forth they went together.
Through the rude wind's wild lament,
And the bitter weather.

A mass of loose snow suddenly tumbles into the street, covering the children who shriek with delight and look up.

Sire, the night is darker now,
And the wind blows stronger...

A mighty airship moves slowly between the towers, its engines idling to produce the sound of a slow, gigantic heartbeat, while tiny silhouettes look down from the yellow illumination of the observation galleries to catch glimpses of the rich world below.

Fails my heart I know not how,
I can go no longer...

The 19.00 is bringing in the last of the Christmas mail, proceeding with such stateliness that snow is able to form on the top of her hull; she resembles a huge Yuletide pie. The bells of St Mary's Kensington ring out from the church in the shadow of the archway formed by two fourth-storey pedestrian roads:

Ding dong. Ding, dong. Merry Christmas.

Mark my footsteps, good my page,
Tread thou in them boldly...

Ding, dong.

And another bell joins in, held in the hand of a fat greatcoated figure with a huge white cap nodding on his head, a tray depending from his broad shoulders by cords, a huge grey muffler around his neck. "Mince pies! Tasty mince pies! Merry Christmas!"

Harlequin dodges the revellers who come round the corner from Church Street dragging two or three of their number on a broad, flat sledge. The sledge is stacked high with wicker baskets, a Christmas tree, balloons and bunting. Up the hill runs Harlequin while the snow grows thicker and thicker and the traffic moves very slowly, hooting, jangling, creaking, squeaking, engines revving, horses snorting. Over-excited dogs bark and snap at Harlequin's heels. Harlequin ignores them. Old ladies pause in their black fur coats to press coins into the hands of bright-cheeked small boys. "Merry Christmas! Be good to your pa, look after your ma!" And whistling delivery lads ride their big bikes along the pavement, scoring the snow with thin black lines, swerving amiably to avoid dancing Harlequin who is almost at Notting Hill Gate where crystal towers glow green and red, black and gold, blue and silver, overlooking a plaza where a fair is in full swing, with sparking dodgems and dazzling roller coasters, merry-go-rounds and whips, rattling and banging and smashing and crackling; with rhythmic wheezing music of the calliope, with the hot smells of oil and steam and sweet cooking fat, the bawling voices from the megaphones in the hands of the sideshow men. "Roll up, roll up, roll up! Merry Christmas! 'Ere we are again! Merry Christmas! Ten for a tanner. 'Ave a go, luv. Merry Christmas! Anyfink on the top shelf, George! Merry Christmas!" The fairground is full. Holidaymakers from the world over patronise it, for London is the centre all travellers hope to visit, the only city of its kind, where representatives of hundreds of independent nations meet to trade and to treat and to take advantage of the city's entertainments, to gape at its marvels, for London lives again as the City of the Future, a wonderland to visit but not to make one's home, rich with vice, and art, and cunning; radiant, articulate and wise. There are ships at anchor in the docks—ships from Shanghai, Toronto, Cape Town and Makhnograd, from Manhattan, Cardiff and Rangoon, from Darwin, Singapore and Freetown and a hundred states besides—there are airships at their masts over White City, bearing the flags of still more nations. The world is made up of thousands of such tiny states, most no bigger than Surrey, some no bigger than London which, itself, is independent, maintained by the pragmatism and the sentiment of a million survivors of a half-forgotten Age of Empires.

"Merry Christmas! Merry Christmas!" Down the main street, between the plaza on one side and a court of frozen fountains on the other, comes the huge sleigh with Santa Claus at the reins, drawn by six white ponies in green and black harness, with scarlet plumes on their heads, nostrils flaring, eyes flashing in the light from the huge triple globes on standards at intervals along the concourse, their rays diffracted by the falling snow. The crowd cheers. People pause to look. Harlequin crosses in front of the sleigh, just in time, dodging into the comparative peace of a narrow, northbound street. Little houses lie on either side now and in the window of each is a splendid Christmas tree alive with candles and bunting. From the doors come the smells of log fires, of roasting goose and capon and turkey and guinea fowl, of puddings on the boil, of beef and ham and sausages and pork pies, pickles and sugar plums, carp and codlins—all enough to tempt the palate of the most jaded libertine—but Harlequin hurries on. "Merry Christmas!" call the red-cheeked old men as they turn into their gates. "Merry Christmas!" sing the housewives and older daughters, in aprons and headscarves, opening their doors to their loved ones, their friends and neighbours.

"Merry Christmas!" cries the tall airship pilot, home for the holiday, his kitbag over his shoulder. "Merry Christmas!" reply the postman, the baker, the muffin-man.

But Harlequin replies to none of them, running on down the winding snowy street, darting in and out of the shadows cast by the sputtering lamps. Now dark figures leap from a gateway, dressed as knights, a dragon, a Fool, a Saracen:

> And a mumming we will go, will go, and a
> mumming we will go;
> With a bright cockade in all our hats, we'll go with
> gallant show!

It is the mummer's play with *St George and the Dragon*, taking their entertainment from house to house, to anyone who wishes to see it. The Fool blocks Harlequin's path, cap and bells a-jingle:

> "Alas, alas, my chiefest son is slain!
> What must I do to raise him up again?
> Here he lies before you all,
> I'll presently a doctor call,
> A doctor! A doctor! Are you a doctor, sir?"

Harlequin dodges to one side of the Fool, smiling, waving, on down the street. Harlequin comes to a crossroads between tall buildings. High above lights still burn in windows, illuminated clocks display the time, a board flashes the schedules of the airship and the Super-Concorde flights and black shapes of family flying machines drift across the glare. At the corner, beside a lamp post, an old man smiles at Harlequin, turning the handle of his plunking barrel organ. A monkey in a velvet jacket and cap shivers on his shoulder. The man's voice is as old and as steady as Stonehenge. "A pleasant Yuletide to you, Arlekin."

Harlequin bows and runs on. In the distance now, at the bottom of the hill, is a glory of twinkling electric bulbs decorating a magnificent building whose front aspect dominates Ladbroke Grove. Of porphyry and jade and marble and lapis lazuli, the building is a palace from a dream, built by a genie for Aladdin. In all this magical city there is nothing more vibrant than the Palace in the Enchanted Dale. It glows so that, from here, it seems the snow avoids it, or is melted before it can settle, yet the white lawns surrounding it deny this and here, too, the water of the fountains is frozen, reflecting all the colours which blaze from the house. The snow has settled on the hedges and the walls, it lies heavy on the shoulders of the statues and the ornamental beasts, on pathways and flower beds, shrubs and tubs, the poplars, cypresses, oaks and elms, all erected on the site of the legendary Convent of the Poor Clares Colettine where so much of Old London's history was made. Set back from the bustle on the hill, the palace seems a zone of tranquillity in all the Christmas merriment—but there is merriment here, too.

Harlequin darts through open gates which are decorated with Christmas wreaths, along paths, over hedges, through clumps of trees, across lawns, to stand at last at the side of the palace and peer through the holly-framed windows of the ballroom where red velvet curtains have been tied back to reveal a magnificent Christmas tree dominating a crowded hall. The dark green pine is trimmed with globes of scarlet and white, bunting of silver and green, a golden star. The hall itself is hung with laurel and holly wreaths, with ivy garlands, with mistletoe, and lit by hundreds of tall candles in crystal chandeliers. The warmth and the light pour into the garden where Harlequin hesitates and studies the guests. It is a masque that Harlequin witnesses, a masque that draws the hidden figure closer as if yearning to join. Harlequin sees all the old familiar characters of the mummer's play, of mime and pantomime, of folklore and traditional tale—Widow Twankey, Polichinelle, Abanazar, the Demon King, Mother Goose, Jack Frost (a genuine albino with crimson eyes), the Green Knight, Scaramouche, a rather lost-looking Pierrot, Hern the Hunter with his stag's antlers; a Fool, in motley with bladder, and bells, St George, Captain Courageous, Gammer Gurton, Buffalo Bill, Peter Pan, the Babes in the Wood, Cinderella, Britannia, Dick Whittington, and someone dressed in a Harlequin costume almost identical to Harlequin's own; Queen Mab, Prince Charming, Robin Hood, Robinson Crusoe, Sleeping Beauty, Puss in Boots,

Pantaloon, Goody Two Shoes, Hereward the Wake, Puck, Gog and Magog, Lady Godiva, King Canute, Blue Beard, Dick Turpin, Hengist and Horsa, the Three Wise Men, King Arthur, John Bull, the Fairy Godmother, Cock Robin, Father Neptune, Jack-o'-Lantern, Sweeney Todd, Doctor Faustus, Jenny Wren, the May Queen, Humpty Dumpty, Old King Cole, Sawney Bean, Springheeled Jack, Charlie Peace, Queen Elizabeth, Mr Pickwick, Charley's Aunt, Jack Sheppard, Romeo and Juliet, Doctor Who, Oberon, the Grand Cham, a Dalek, Old Moore, Falstaff, Little Red Riding Hood, Beowulf, Renyard the Fox, St Nicholas, Boadicea, Noah and Mrs Noah, Jack the Giant Killer, Mother Hubbard, Beauty and the Beast, the King of Rats, Yankee Doodle, Nell Gwynn, John Gilpin, Baron Münchhausen, Alice, Sitting Bull, Ali Baba, Little Jack Horner, Asmodeus, Mother Bunch, Sinbad, Dame Trot and her cat; there was a badger, a bull and a bear, a wolf, a cow, a sea-serpent, a dragon, a hare, a cock and an ass, old men dressed as young women, old women dressed as young men, girls dressed as boys, boys dressed as girls, so that another observer might have thought he witnessed some innocent Court of Misrule.

Harlequin held back from entering, partly because of the false Harlequin within, partly because in all that company only Columbine was not present. Laughter washed from the hall as a band played a sprightly Lancers and the guests danced in long columns, up and down the ballroom, round and round the tree, clapping and whistling, leaping and pirouetting, fingers on hips, wrists raised, bowing, prancing, arm in arm, hand in hand, shouting with merriment and good humour: the ballroom shook to their feet as figures in elaborate silks and velvets, in laurel, in Lincoln Green, in cloth-of-gold, in brocades, in motley, in animal heads, in scarlet and black moleskin, in hoods, capes, cloaks, tabards, doublets and hose, in leather and lace and living plants and flowers, in painted wood and padded fur and polished metal, masks and powder cosmetics, wigs and false noses, silver- and bronze- and gold-gilding, whooped and giggled and bent their bodies in the ritual of the dance.

The windows rattled, the log fire blazed, the candles flickered, the creatures of folklore, mythology and fable capered and shouted. Harlequin retreated.

"Better the myth of happiness," Harlequin murmured, "than the myth of despair."

Then Harlequin had slipped away, to climb nimbly up a trellis at the side of the palace, swinging onto a balcony and through a window already open. Snow blew into the darkened room as Harlequin closed the window and drew from a sash wound twice about the waist a traditional wand, crossing rapidly to the white bed in which lay a golden-haired girl dressed in a daffodil-yellow ballet costume—Columbine, already masked, but pale, breathing sluggishly, fast asleep. Harlequin seemed sad, looking down on the girl for long moments, cocking an ear as the music rose from below, hands on hips, indecisive. Then Harlequin skipped a few steps, almost involuntarily running to the door to look out—a wide landing, a marble balcony, the ball below—back again to the bed, taking one of Columbine's cold hands, kissing it as a single tear crept from beneath Harlequin's domino and fell upon the flesh. And where the tear had fallen it appeared that the skin grew warmer and that colour spread along the bare arm to the soft shoulders, the neck, the wonderful features of Columbine.

Then Harlequin kissed Columbine upon her gentle lips, stood up and placed the tip of the wand upon her breast and Columbine opened her eyes. They were blue. They were bright. They were kind.

"Merry Christmas, my own, dear Columbine."

"Merry Christmas."

There came a noise from the marble landing beyond the door. Two guests—Britannia and the mock Harlequin—went by. Harlequin moved to close the door, hearing a little of their conversation and smiling at its familiarity.

"He'll always fall on his feet, it seems—but I think he knows he hasn't really earned the position." Britannia spoke sharply, trying to adjust an uncomfortable sword and shield carried in one hand so that she might with the other clutch her punch. The shield was decorated with a Union Jack and the motto: *Honi Soit Qui Mal Y Pense*. She supported an elaborately plumed helmet of engraved silver and red horsehair, a scarlet-and-gold coat, with epaulettes, and her skirts were made up from the old arms of Britain: lions and harps for the most part.

"He thinks he has," said quasi-Harlequin peering over the balcony and almost losing his triangular hat, "that's the worst of it. He's all cocky again, as usual—never seems to realise how much other people protect him."

"You can't say you've actually protected him, Frank." Britannia was amused. "I, on the other hand, did my level best to look after him…"

"I've offered him dozens of really good opportunities in the past, Miss Brunner."

"I suppose that's where we both went wrong. All the opportunities were in the past…"

Singing rose from the hall below:

> *Peace on Earth! How sweet the message!*
> *May its meaning bless each heart,*
> *And today may all dissension*
> *From the souls of men depart.*

Britannia accepted the false Harlequin's arm. "I suppose we'd better join them." They began to descend the wide staircase.

"Merry Christmas!" cried Major Nye in the armour of St George (he had always felt a strong sentimental enthusiasm for *Where the Rainbow Ends*). "Merry Christmas, Miss Brunner! Merry Christmas, Frank." He waved an arm which clashed faintly. "Food at the buffet. Anything you like. Drinks at the bar. Hot punch. Name your grog!" His pale eyes twinkled. He clanked back into the milling crowd.

"I suppose all this devolution has its virtues, after all," said Miss Brunner. She dropped her sword. Frank picked it up for her. "I, of course, was a firm believer in centralisation. However, your brother ruined that. We were partners at one time, but there was a division."

"I remember," said Frank, "I got shot!"

"Did you? Poor boy. Now I'm reconciled. I'm a schoolteacher these days, did you know? For the Maharajah of Guildford's children actually. Seriously, I'm beginning to think that it was a good idea to slow the pace, absorb things better. There isn't much of the century left. Of course, we still have the moral superiority, don't we?"

Frank turned his masked face so that he could see the buffet. He licked his lips.

"It's a bit medieval, I suppose," continued Miss Brunner nodding agreeably to Bishop Beesley as he went by with Mrs Cornelius in tow. Bishop Beesley had come as Widow Twankey, Mrs C. as Mother Bunch, "but none the worse for that, by and large."

"Yeah," said Frank with a certain relish, "they're thinking of re-introducing the Black Death next year."

"This isn't really the season for cynicism, Frank, dear." She drew him towards the tables. "Now, what shall we have?"

Frank picked up a plate. "What about some devilled bones?"

"Spare ribs, aren't they? I suppose it's appropriate." She began to gnaw.

Mr Koutrouboussis arrived at the buffet panting and exhausted. "Phew! You need a lot of energy for this!" He had come as Aladdin's wicked uncle, Abanazar, with a dark, pointed beard fixed to his chin and heavy robes of green satin sewn with gold astrological symbols, a monstrous turban on his head. He studied the fowls, the cold meats, the blancmanges, the jellies, the flans. "It all looks so delicious." He handed a plate to Prinz Lobkowitz who wore an Elizabethan Oberon costume and whose mask glittered with real gems. "We've met before, I think. Merry Christmas to you."

"And to you, sir. Our host seems a trifle under the weather." Prinz Lobkowitz chose some olives.

"Perhaps hosts never can enjoy themselves as much as their guests. There must be so many anxieties. Were you at the last party?"

"During the Peace Talks? An absolute disaster."

"Doomed to failure, one could argue. A worthy attempt."

"To maintain the old order. Isn't that what most peace talks are about?" Prinz Lobkowitz smiled. "It's a natural enough instinct, surely."

"Ah, you would know better than I about such things." Abanazar rubbed his hands and picked up a dish of plums.

"It is true," said Oberon, "that I have been a politician all my life, and an idealist for most of my career, if the search for perfect compromise can be dignified by the description of 'ideal'."

"It is better than anything I ever possessed," Koutrouboussis told him sadly, spooning at a plum or two, "save for a passion, once, for a young girl. But she evaded me, though for some time she was mine. Do you understand women, Prinz Lobkowitz?"

"Oh, women, women, there are far too many different

ones. You speak of the romantic kind?"

"I am not sure. Romance remains a mystery. I enjoy power, however. Women are said to admire men who enjoy power."

"They use them often enough, that is true, to further their own romantic dreams. The more a man loves power for its own sake, the less he interferes with their fantasies, while at the same time he is able to indulge them. Such relationships were once quite common, when I was younger. They seem to work excellently. And yet you have never experienced one, with all your ships and oil?"

"Never. I suppose I was too direct. She obeyed me, but only up to a point. She disappointed me. She would not commit herself as much as I had hoped."

"There you have it. She saw you as committed to your power and therefore thought she would be free, that she need not give too much of herself to you. It was you, Mr Koutrouboussis, who disappointed this young woman."

The Greek tugged absent-mindedly at his false beard. Parts of it came away in his fingers. A peculiar knowing light burned and faded in his dark eyes. He fumbled in his robes and withdrew a cigarette case, offering it to Lobkowitz, who declined. "I wanted her very much." He said again: "She evaded me."

"My friend," said Prinz Lobkowitz sympathetically, and chewed a pickled walnut.

A large crowd was now approaching the table. Prinz Lobkowitz and Mr Koutrouboussis wandered away.

Sebastian Auchinek arrived with Mitzi Beesley.

Sebastian Auchinek was not quite right as the Demon King, though the costume itself was splendid, with a long pointed tail and real horns. He held his pitchfork gingerly, anxious not to hurt any of his fellow guests. Mitzi Beesley was a depraved Peter Pan. "The English have always needed queens," he was saying. "They are useless without them. Queens created the Empire, after all."

"Half the greatest explorers were—" began Mitzi.

"I'm not sure that's quite what I meant."

Mitzi giggled. "But Herr Cornelius isn't a queen. He's a king. Or is he a king *and* a queen?"

"His trouble is that he's all things to all men—and women too. Perhaps he doesn't know himself. It's probably the secret of his success."

"He doesn't seem too pleased with that success." She craned to catch a glimpse of a darting white costume.

"I agree he seems ill."

"Hello, Father," said Mitzi. "You make a lovely widow."

"Thank you, child." Bishop Beesley was a picture of dignity in his flounces and ribbons, his huge hat, his rouge. He had already been twice mistaken for Mrs Cornelius. He continued his conversation with Colonel Pyat, a Saracen King in golden armour. "My motives were questioned probably because I was always a trifle unorthodox. I hoped to show people the way—back to decent standards. I did my best to be up to date at all times. I did not reject technology, nor did I turn my back on drugs."

Mo Collier, as Robin Goodfellow, had been standing at

the bishop's elbow. "I read one of your sermons. It was great. *Cocaine in the Treatment of Sinus Infections*. Remember?"

"Not too easily."

Mitzi joined the conversation, glad to help her father. "It was just before *Salvation through Sugar*," she said. "The Mars Bar Messiah, they called you." She became sentimental, recalling former greatness. "The Orange Fudge Oracle. The Chocolate Cream Cleric. The Hershey Bar Bishop. The Man Who Brought the Tootsie Roll into the Pulpit. The Turkish Delight—"

"There was so much to do," said the bishop. "Some of the details have become a trifle hazy now."

"Sort of set into the blancmange of the past." Mo was in a rare philosophic mood. "Stuck to the sides of the great jelly mould we call Life."

"The Smartie Saint," continued Mitzi. She began to pant. His eye had fallen on her.

Dazed, Mitzi dropped back. To escape the dreamy Robin Goodfellow beside him, Bishop Beesley gathered up his skirts and followed her.

Mo was tasting some cream. Dubiously he licked his lips. "Does it go off?" he asked a nearby Karen von Krupp, who said, without taking her attention from her companion, "That'll be your epitaph, Mr Collier."

"… but I can't hope to survive for ever in this environment," Miss Brunner was telling Karen von Krupp, who wore her Beowulf outfit rather well, in spite of her age and frailty. "All I wanted was to create a little peace and quiet for myself. People kept interfering."

"Ja," said Karen von Krupp. She was quite drunk. "Ja, ja, ja."

"Simplification had always been my goal. Naturally, I had to synthesise a great deal of information. The world had to be broken down into the proper bits in order to produce a programme suitable for processing by a reasonably sophisticated computer..."

"Ja, ja," said Karen von Krupp. "Ja, ja, ja."

"You thought she embraced the world," Professor Hira (as Polichinelle, with peculiar protruberances on chest and back) was no longer calling himself Hythloday. He was talking about Miss Brunner, unaware that she was behind him. Mr Smiles knew; he looked awkward as the Green Knight. They had made him leave his green-painted shire-horse with its blood-red bridle in the stables where, unbeknownst to him, it was fighting with the two lions which had drawn Miss Brunner's chariot as far as the front door. "She did not! She crushed it, forced it into a little square box; packed it in a hurry, too. Some try to understand the world, while others seek to impose their understanding on it. Unfortunately, Mr Smiles, these latter folk are those least equipped to perform the operation. Like Frankenstein, my dear Mr Smiles, they produce a monster."

"I'd considered coming as Frankenstein." Mr Smiles brightened behind his black beard which he had, unsuccessfully, also tried to dye green, "but I gathered it wasn't suitable. Too modern or something. Or too general? And yet Doctor Who is here. Is everyone supposed to be part of British folklore tonight? Frankenstein, I should have thought…"

"I think so." The little Brahmin physicist was disappointed in his audience. "Although I'm Italian, aren't I? Pulcinella? Punch?" He chuckled. "Or Vice, if we're getting down to basics. We're all part of the same zany Cavalcade, eh?"

"I'm not sure about that. They made me leave my horse outside."

"Harlequinade, then. Where is Harlequin?" Professor Hira sought about him in the crowd. "Or what about Masquerade? Or is it a Morality Play? You're the Englishman, Mr Smiles. You tell me what it is we're in!"

Mr Smiles sipped his spiced rum. "God knows," he said. "A bloody madhouse."

Mrs Cornelius had somehow got hold of part of Old King Cole's costume. She still wore her skirts of green and brown, but she had a crown askew on her head, a white beard hanging around her neck. She spotted Hira and was delighted. "Oo! There yer are! Where yer bin 'idin', eh?"

Punch blushed.

"I jest bin talkin' ter Robin 'Ood," she confided to Mr Smiles, putting a hearty arm about her lover, who gasped. "I arsked 'im where 'is mate wos—you know, ther monk." She screamed with laughter and her crown threatened to fall off her head altogether. "As usual I got me pees an' kews mixed up. Where's yer mate? sez me, Wot mate's that, madam, sez Robin 'Ood, Oh, yer know ther one, I sez— Wot's 'is name? Then I remembered, you know, didn't I?

Triar Fuck? sez me. Then Robin 'Ood straightens up like a telegraph pole. Forgive me, madam, 'e sez, but I don't believe as 'ow I 'ave the where-wival!" She flung back her head and just saved her crown as she shook with mirth. "Get it? See? Robin 'Ood ain't a bloke at all. It's a bloody woman, innit! Ah, har, har, har! They always bloody are in fings like this, ain't they?"

Professor Hira was baffled as usual but he managed to laugh with her through long practice. "He, he, he. Oh, very good!"

Robin Hood herself strode by, equally baffled, causing Mrs Cornelius another outburst. Lady Sue Sunday had lost Helen Sweet again.

"It's traditional, see," explained Mrs Cornelius to Professor Hira. The band had begun to play an Irish jig. "Oo, come on!" She seized her lover and dragged him back towards the tree where most of the guests were dancing again.

Lady Sue found Helen Sweet, as Little Red Riding Hood, talking to Simon Vaizey. The elegant playwright had almost not come, since he wanted to wear his own Pierrot costume, but he had compromised and come as the Fool. "… Through dreaming towns I go, The cock crows ere the Christmas morn. The streets are dumb with snow," he was saying to a rapt Helen. "I've long since given up any hope of finding *my* Grail, dear. I haven't the brains. Well, God give them wisdom that have it; and those that are fools, let them use their talents."

"I'd suggest you try using them elsewhere, Mr Vaizey,"

said Lady Sue jealously. "Nice to see you again. I'd heard
you were dead."

"I couldn't miss the party, could I?" Simon Vaizey
stole away.

Jerry Cornelius, moving gracefully amongst his
guests, bowed his Pierrot bow, elaborate and strange,
passed Simon Vaizey and winked, reached his seat of
honour. In his black-and-white Pierrot costume, his make-
up, he bore an aura of sadness with him which no amount
of capering and smiling could dispel. He sat down with
a sigh, long and limp in the marble chair at the farthest
end of the hall, just below the musicians' gallery, from
which dripped bunting, laurel, holly and ivy, so that he
was half-hidden by decoration. Above his head the band
was playing traditional music—fife, tabor, pipes and the
beat of the snare dominated everything while the guests
whirled about the tree in a haze of green and gold, scarlet
and silver. He was feeling that loneliness most painful
when one is amongst friends; and there was more than
a touch of his old self-pity. He pursed cherry lips and
whistled, against the harmony above, a Commander Cody
and His Lost Planet Airmen song, *I'm down to seeds and
stems again blues...*

"Merry Christmas, Jerry!"

Flash Gordon found him, brushing aside the bunting,
sympathetic and unwelcome as usual. His hot, doglike
eyes were about the only recognisable thing behind his
thick make-up, his long golden wig (he had come as Lady
Godiva). "You'd have been much better as Harlequin,

Jerry." Evidently he believed that his friend was sulking. "Somehow the part doesn't suit Frank."

"I used to be," Jerry crossed his billowing legs, "but Harlequin somehow metamorphosed into Pierrot. It happened in France, I think. Don't ask how. I used to believe I was Captain of my own Fate. Instead I'm just a character in a bloody pantomime."

"It's not too bloody now, at any rate." Flash always tried to look on the bright side. "Everyone's cultivating their own gardens. I didn't tell you about my new strain of peas, did I?"

"I was never much interested in gardening," Jerry told him, doing his best to be friendly to Flash.

Flash laughed. "No! You liked blowing things up. You and Mo Collier. Blowing things up."

"Of course," Jerry continued, "I'm grateful for what everyone's done." He reached out to pat a slightly hurt Flash on the heavily sweating right hand. "But all I wanted was Catherine back. They could have had everything else. There's no point without her. It's all my fucking fault, Flash."

"You shouldn't feel guilty." As someone whose main relish in life came from feeling guilty, Flash was unconvincing. "You shouldn't blame yourself."

"I'm just pissed off. I've ruined it, as usual. I can go anywhere I like in the city. Do anything I like. See anyone I like. Disguises are easy. Nobody bothers me. But all I want to do is stay home and make love to Catherine."

"Well," said Flash speculatively, "you could always…"

Jerry shook his head. "It's not the same."

"I'd agree with that!" Flash's eyes grew rounder and hotter with reminiscences. He realised, suddenly, that he was being selfish and did his best to return to more general topics. "They say that's the trouble with Utopia. You get bored. While there were big countries to fight, or big corporations, or just very powerful people, it was easier to be an individual." He sighed artificially. "Now everyone's an individual, eh, Mr C? It's taken a lot of the fun from life, I'll tell you."

Jerry was surprised to find himself agreeing with Flash. He nodded. "It's horrible, winning. With everyone on your side. It makes you edgy. And I've run out of things to do."

"You've done a lot for everyone. I'm grateful. We're all grateful."

"It's nice of you to say so, Flash," Jerry looked down as a small black-and-white cat rubbed its thin body against his leg. He picked it up and stroked its head. It purred. He smiled.

"That's what you need," said Flash encouragingly. "A pet. You've cheered up already."

"I love it." Jerry spoke in some awe. "That's what I need. Love."

"Everybody loves you, Jerry. Well, almost everybody."

"It's not being loved, Flash, that's difficult to come by. It's loving."

"You love everyone. Everything."

"That's my trouble. Oh, I wish I could find a way to wake Catherine up. She was my lodestone. Past, present and future. Reality, if you like—myth, too—of hope, of reconciliation, of peace and freedom." He had to raise his voice for the music was growing louder and louder, the shouts of the guests noisier and noisier. "She's my ideal, Flash. Nobody else will do. Have I said all this before?"

Flash came closer, to make himself heard. His breath was warm in Jerry's painted ear. "Not in so many words. You've been a good brother to her, Jerry, in your own way. You've looked after her, even though she hasn't been able to give you much in return."

"I was willing to destroy the world for her."

"That's real love all right," said Flash. "That's the test, isn't it? Still," he smiled nervously, "I'm glad you didn't."

"I thought I had."

"Oh, not you, Jerry. Never!"

Jerry put his chin on his fist. Pierrot defeated.

"I'll go and get something to eat. Do you want anything?" Flash moved away, rubbing at the make-up on his face. "This stuff's going to bring on my blackheads something rotten. See you later, Jerry."

Gathering his blonde locks about him, Flash sidled for the buffet tables.

Jerry saw Harlequin break from the dancing crowd and run towards him. "You ought to get a spot of grub down you, Jerry," said Frank. "You're looking like the bloody phantom at the feast. Enjoy yourself, boy! What price entropy now, eh?"

"Oh, piss off," said his brother, and stroked the cat.

Frank seemed unmoved by Jerry's rudeness, perhaps because he was very drunk. His mask was higher at the left than at the right, his hat was too far back on his head. "You're not sleeping enough, these days, are you?" He staggered and leaned against the back of Jerry's marble chair. "You ought to try to get a bit more shut-eye. Mind you, you shouldn't need that much, considering all you've had in the past... On the other hand, sleep isn't cumulative, you know. That's the irony, isn't it? Tiredness, of course, is. You get worse and worse. That's what's wrong with speed. Less and less real, in a sense. You've been pushing yourself beyond the limit. All these new schemes... these potions you've been cooking up in your lab..."

"You don't look that well, yourself."

"I've given too much of myself away, Jerry. It was always my trouble."

"You've never given anything away in your life. Sold it, more likely. Blood and souls..."

"Steady on, old son. Noblesse oblige!" Frank burped. "Pardon." He was gleeful, evidently sensing that he had got through to his brother. "I could let you have something to get you moving again. A few mills of—hic—tempodex." He made a plunging motion towards his arm. "Back on your old form? No danger!"

"I'm all right here. If you could find a drug to perk Cathy up, that'd be more useful. After all..."

"No recriminations! We agreed. Anyway, it's not in my interest, is it?" Harlequin smirked. "Not with you in your position and me in mine. Now, if you were to give me more power..."

"I haven't got any bloody power!"

"Well, influence, then…"

"You can't transfer influence, Frank."

"I dunno. I've been experimenting…"

"I wish I'd never bought you that chemistry set when we were kids. It's been nothing but trouble." Jerry stared moodily over his brother's head. The music had stopped again and the guests were surging towards the buffets and bars, parting like the Red Sea on either side of the tree. "This is all your fault. Not mine."

"Oh, come on now. Do me a favour, Jerry. You were the one with the big ideas. It was just carrying on the family business. What's born in the blood is bred in the bone. We're all victims of history."

"That's why I was trying to get rid of history." He rose from his throne, now that he could see a clear path ahead, and left his brother standing beside the chair, running a grey hand over the cold stone.

"You want to get yourself a proper job, old son," called Frank. "This is no work for a man!"

Jerry ignored him. Already the guests were beginning to move back into the centre of the ballroom. His mother approached, holding a plate on which an entire trifle staggered. "'Ere yer are, Jer—wanna bit?"

"No thanks, Mum."

"Good fer yer." Evidently she had been sick down her dress and had cleaned it inexpertly with the beard she now held in her other hand.

Prinz Lobkowitz rescued him. "What a nice little cat. What's its name?"

"Tom," said Jerry, "I think."

"And the costume! Perfect." Prinz Lobkowitz quoted knowingly, probably Verlaine.

"Ce n'est plus le rêveur lunaire du vieil air—
Sa gaieté, comme sa chandelle, hélas! est morte,
Et son spectre aujourd'hui nous hante, mince et clair.
Et voici que parmi l'effroi d'un long éclair
D'un linceul.
Sa pâle blouse à l'air, au vent froid qui l'emporte,
Ses manches blanches font vaguement par l'espace.
Avec le bruit d'un vol d'oiseaux de nuit qui passe,
Des signs fous auxquels personne ne répond."

"Oh, I wouldn't say that," said Jerry. He pushed on, the crowd growing denser. Major Nye leaned against a pillar talking to Karen von Krupp, St George in conversation with Beowulf. "The British, you see, have an ability to shuck off their civilisation in an instant and become, for as long as it suits them, wild beasts. It is the secret of their survival—it is what makes great explorers, mountain climbers and killers. They do not belong in Europe. They never belonged in Europe. Their instincts have always led them to more savage parts. It was civilisation brought the British down—as civilisation crept across the globe like rabies, they were forced to turn on one another and, for a long time, make a savage environment of their own land. You take my meaning?"

"*Ja*," said Karen von Krupp, "*ja, ja, ja.*"

A great mound of vegetation, Jack-in-the-Green, that

had been Herr Marek, the Lapp priest, was confiding in a whisper to Cyril Tome, who was now setting puzzles for children's television and who had come as a somewhat anaemic Hern ("more a Hernia," as Lady Sue had said to Helen Sweet when they had arrived). "I've been haunted, you see, for years by the knowledge that I am the slave of a machine existing somewhere under ground. It has forced me to simplify my language so that it can communicate with me better. I *could* attack it by using complicated and poetic language, but it takes reprisals, killing or maiming not me but my friends—in railway accidents, planes and car crashes, lift failures, and with electric shocks. I have to think of others, but I must warn them, somehow, too. In order to do this I have resorted to complicated subterfuges..."

"Merry Christmas!" Mitzi Beesley raced past, pursued by her grunting father. "Now," he breathed, "now we'll see!" He had his skirts to his knees as he chased her. She disappeared behind the tree.

"The failure of the second half of the twentieth century was to absorb the achievements of the first half," said Dick Whittington (ex-prime minister M. Hope-Dempsey), "particularly the rarer malt whiskies." He was speaking to Eva Knecht, also a principal boy. She had come as Prince Charming. "You are drunk," she said. "Would you like to tie me up?"

Jerry could see that the party was beginning to lift. Stroking his cat he continued on his way through the throng and reached the wide stairs just as the band began to play Dr Hook's 'Queen of the Silver Dollar'.

It was a beautiful Christmas, thought Jerry. The nicest he had had. Slowly, he mounted the stairs, pausing to look back at his happy guests, at the snow falling outside. It was getting quite late. He looked for Frank in the hall, but the Harlequin costume was nowhere to be seen. He shrugged and continued up the stairs, tripping once over his long satin trousers.

He had reached the landing and was on his way to his own apartments when he heard a noise from behind Catherine's door. He paused, made to enter, then changed his mind. Almost in panic he began to run along the landing to his own rooms, dashing through the door without bothering to put on the lights, dumped the little cat on his bed, and went to the trunk in his study, rummaging through it rapidly until he found what he wanted. "Wait here," he told the cat. It was best to take no chances.

Needle gun in hand he returned to Catherine's room. "Who's in there?" He kicked open the door and walked in.

Frank stood at the end of Catherine's bed. He had removed his mask. He had a loaded hypodermic in his hand. He was looking tired and ill, like a sick vulture. "I don't feel very well," he said. "Look. She's woken up."

Catherine, in contrast, was in the peak of health. Her skin glowed, her eyes were bright, if a little dazed. She and Una Persson were propped on their pillows, in one another's arms. Catherine was entirely naked, her Columbine costume scattered across the floor. Una was naked save for her Harlequin's mask. She did not seem to realise that she was still wearing it.

Frank fell to his knees. Una pulled a smoking S&W .45 from under the bedclothes. "I'm sorry, Jerry. I've shot your brother. He was going to…"

"That's all right." Jerry put his needle gun in his baggy pocket. Joy mounted within him, slowly. "How long have you been awake, Catherine?"

"Not long. Una woke me."

"I'm very grateful, Una," he said, "for all you've done."

"Ugh!" groaned Frank from the floor. "She's two-timing you, Jerry. Ugh! Both of us!"

"I don't think so," said Jerry, smiling tenderly at both of them. "Are you?"

"I must be going." Una Persson's smile was just a fraction late, but it was a good, brave one. "Leave you two alone."

"Oh, no," said Jerry. He sat on the bed beside her, still looking at Catherine. "Please stay."

Una stroked her hair. "I was just saying goodbye." She looked at her wrist. "What's the time? My watch has stopped."

"About midnight, I think."

"Good. I can catch the last flight out."

"You're welcome…" Jerry said.

"Ugh." Frank's voice was fainter.

"I'm still a working girl, you know." Una climbed from the bed and, walking around her victim, began to pull on her own Harlequin costume. "I'm sorry about the mess."

Frank groaned. His chest was crimson.

Una tucked her slapstick into her sash. "I didn't mean to kill you. It was the shock. You shouldn't have dressed yourself up like that. I thought you were me for a moment. What were you trying to achieve? Imitation isn't art, you know, Frank."

Unclean blood fell down his chin. "Merry fucking Christmas," he said, "you bitch. Both of you. All of you." Clutching himself he began to sidle across the floor. "Oh, fuck. Oh, fuck."

"He'll be all right, I expect," said Catherine to reassure Una. She reached out and took Jerry's hand, squeezing it. Jerry sighed. "He's always making a lot of the things that happen to him."

Frank reached the door and crawled through it into the light of the landing. "God help us, one and all."

Una went over and closed the door. "You'll want to be alone. I've told her everything you've done for her, Jerry— and all that's happened." She bent to fluff at his ruff. "Pierrot wins Columbine, at last. It's taken hundreds of years."

Jerry could see that Una was close to tears. He stood up and helped her on with her red-and-green cape. "Let me know if there's anything I can do."

"Your work's over," Una said, "but mine's not finished yet. Otherwise I'd give you a run for your money. Pierrot couldn't wake her, you see. Only Harlequin has the power to do that. Pierrot has no power—only charm." She kissed him briskly on the cheek. "Cheerio, you little bugger." She paused by the bed and bent to kiss Catherine's lips. "Merry Christmas, Columbine."

"Oh," said Catherine. She looked from her brother to her friend.

Una reached the window, opened it and stepped through. Cold air filled the room. A few flakes of snow settled on the sill. Then she had gone, Harlequin returned to the night, and the window was shut. There came a sound, like the crying of hounds, but it was either made by the guests below or came from the traffic in Ladbroke Grove.

In the ballroom it seemed that the Christmas Party had taken on fresh life as wave upon wave of laughter rose up to them. "Merry Chrissmas! Merry Chrissmas!" they heard their mother shout. "Merry fuckin' Chrissmas!"

Then the music started up and the palace shook to their dancing feet.

Jerry pulled off his huge trousers but kept his flowing blouse and his skull-cap on. He knew how much his sister liked it. He got into bed. He touched her vibrant skin. They embraced. They kissed.

From outside, from below in the whiteness of the garden, a light voice was raised for a few seconds in song:

For in you now all virtues do combine—
Sad Pierrot, brave Harlequin and lovely Columbine...

There sounded a bass drone, then silence.

Jerry rolled into his sister's soft arms and the two were joined together at last.

"Catherine!"

"Jerry! Jerry!"

A crack of light appeared from the door as it was pushed open and a small black-and-white cat entered. It jumped to the foot of the bed and began to wash liquid from its paws. It looked up at them and purred.

All in all, thought Jerry, it was going to be a very successful season.

EARLY REPORTS

What wonders now I have to pen, sir,
Women turning into men, sir,
For twenty-one long years, or more, sir,
She wore the breeches we are told, sir,
A smart and active handsome groom, sir,
She then got married very soon, sir,
A shipwright's trade she after took, sir,
And of his wife, he made a fool, sir.

The Female Husband, c. 1865

Old England, once upon a time,
   Was prosperous and gaily,
Great changes you shall hear in rhyme,
   That taking place is daily.
A poor man once could keep a pig,
   There was meat for every glutton,
Folks now may eat a parson's wig,
   For they'll get no beef or mutton.

What Shall We Do For Meat!, c. 1865

Now the trial is o'er, and the Judge did say
Mistress Starr, you have lost the day,
And five hundred pounds you'll have to pay
    For tricks that are play'd in the Convent.

Funny Doings in the Convent, c. 1865

All the world will mount velocipedes,
    Oh won't there be a show
Of swells out of Belgravia,
    In famous Rotten Row;
Tattersall's they will forsake,
    To go there they have no need,
They will patronise the wheel wright's now
    For a famed Velocipede.
The dandy horse Velocipede,
    Like lightning flies, I vow, sir,
It licks the railroad in its speed,
    By fifty miles an hour, sir.

The Dandy Horse; or, The Wonderful
Velocipede, c. 1865

Three men they say on that fatal Friday,
    At four o'clock on that afternoon,
Those villains caused that explosion,
    And hurried those poor creatures to their doom.
They from a truck took a barrel of powder,
    A female, Ann Justice, was there as well,
And in one moment death and disorder
      Around the neighbourhood of Clerkenwell.

Awful Explosion in Clerkenwell, c. 1865

I am the famous dancer, Harlequin.
I've shown my postures and my grace sublime
In every epoch and in every clime.
Wherever Youth and Beauty gaily meet
I am the dancing pattern of their feet.

Harlequinade, c. 1865

The myth of the golden past gave way to the myth
of the golden future but, for a short time in the 90s
and then the 1960s we enjoyed the myth of the
golden present.

—M. Lescoq,
Leavetaking, c. 1965

TUNING UP (5)

"Who are we today, then?" Miss Brunner leered at Jerry over her pint. "Che Guevara?"

Jerry hesitated at the door of the Blenheim Arms. The pub had a special extension for the evening. It could stay open until midnight. It was very noisy. It smelled strongly of mild beer. It was packed with celebrants. It was warm. "Happy New Year," he said. He closed the door of the local behind him.

"That suit's very lightweight for the weather, isn't it?" His brother Frank took Miss Brunner's lead. "On our way to Bermuda, are we?"

"I don't feel the cold," said Jerry. He knew that he looked smart in the suit, even if it was rather thin, and he hadn't bothered to wear an overcoat because he was only popping into the pub from across the road where he was staying with his mother. Gradually, however, he became self-conscious. He approached the bar. They were all in tonight. All facing him. Mr Smiles wiped froth from his moustache. "The trousers are a bit baggy, aren't they?"

"They're meant to be baggy." He felt in a pocket for some money. The pocket seemed the size of a sack.

"Stop taking the piss out of him," said Catherine. She wore blue denims and a dark green sweater with a picture of Dr Hook and the Medicine Show on the front. "I think it's very sexy, Jerry." She opened her shoulder bag, looking for her purse, but Mo Collier was ahead of her. He waved a fiver at the barman. "Usual?" he asked his friend.

"Why not?" Jerry had forgotten what his usual was. He was attempting to regain lost ground by cultivating an air of insouciance. He looked Miss Brunner up and down: black strap-overs, fishnet stockings, skirt just above the knee, square-cut jacket with heavily padded shoulders. Perm. Earrings. "That's a sweet costume. Are we going as historical figures? Where did you hire it?" He was lame.

She shook her head in genuine disappointment. "This gear cost a fortune and you know it. You can do better than that."

But she tugged for a second or two at the back of her jacket and raised his spirits.

Frank said anxiously, looking at his wristwatch: "We'll have to drink up. The coach'll be here any minute." They were all going down to Brighton to celebrate New Year's Eve at Mr Smiles's new hotel. He had spent the last ten years in Rhodesia, where he had made a fortune, and was anxious to renew old acquaintanceships. Frank wore a red polo-neck sweater, purple bell-bottoms and a black velvet blazer-style jacket. He held a double gin in one pink hand.

"Still teaching at St Victor's, then, are we?" Jerry asked

Miss Brunner. "Having our way with the tweenies?"

"That's defamation if ever I heard it." She spoke without much conviction, almost amiably. Even though she had been prosecuted for her sexual activities at the school she had not only managed to get off all the charges but had somehow managed to become headmistress of St Victor's Primary School. Her attempts to reintroduce corporal punishment, though, had not been all that successful. Increasingly the parents of the children were from the upper middle classes—people who had moved into the district as their incomes declined, who sustained their position in the world by selling their houses in Chelsea, South Kensington and Belgravia for large profits and buying cheaper houses in North Kensington, with the result that rents had risen all round, though the authorities tended to be warier of residents who might now be the sons and daughters of rich people, or literate radicals, rather than working-class youths. There were distinct, if superficial, improvements. Black men were hardly ever beaten up in public by the police any more (this distressed the new arrivals) and the police had increasingly come to see their new rôle as the protectors of Rate Payers from Non-Rate Payers (those whose rates were included in their rent and paid by the landlord). Street fighting in North Kensington had declined and street music and street theatre had increased, but the police did not discriminate between these activities: all were likely to cause annoyance to the Public (Rate Payers) and were dealt with with equal ferocity. According to the methods favoured by the individual officer, friendly banter would be employed, an attempt to 'jolly' the victims into giving up without a struggle, or outright threats and violence would occur from the start. Miss Brunner approved of the police's new attitude but mourned the days before parents became sophisticated and could now recognise, pursue and pillory the poor paedophile. Not everyone gained from the New Liberalism. Ten years before, hardly anyone had heard of her particular passions, except her little charges and their hopeless parents who had been content to recognise her authority, as they recognised all authority, with a dumb and wholesome fear and, amongst the more spirited, like the Cornelius children, a little primitive and easily handled blackmail. As well, the older and more knowing they became, the less interest she took in them. The seventies were increasingly difficult years for Miss Brunner. In her opinion children were growing up far too early.

"I still fink 'e shouldn'ta moved me wivvout arskin'," Mrs Cornelius was complaining. She sat at a little corner table, behind two pints of stout, talking to Colonel Pyat who sipped his vodka and nodded intensely at almost every word. He was dressed in an old fur coat, part of the stock of second-hand clothes at his Elgin Crescent *Glory of St Petersburg Vintage Fur Boutique* which was doing such excellent business, these days; time had given him wealth, a seamed and baggy face, a decadent Dalmatian, which wheezed on a leash at his feet. Mrs Cornelius had recently been given accommodation in the basement of a house in Talbot Road and was shortly to be moved to an identical

basement in the house in Blenheim Crescent whose second
floor she had occupied for so many years. Frank had sold
the family flat for a handsome sum to a young doctor and
his wife and had told his mother that the council would be
bound to find her a new home when they saw the condition
of the basement, which was very damp. However, it had not
taken her long to get comfy and now she didn't really want
to move. She wore a vast ragged coney coat, a present from
the colonel. She saw Jerry at the bar and waved him over.

"'Ullo, Jer—yore lookin' very dapper—they put yore
dole money up? Har, har, har!" She shook, looking to the
others for confirmation of her drollery. "Her, her, her, ker-
ker-ker-ker…" She had developed the local cough almost
to perfection. Jerry picked up his whisky and swallowed
it down. His mother felt in her handbag and produced a
tenpenny piece. "Ker-ker-ker—shu—hu—shove some—
ker-ker-ker—money in the jukebox, love. "'Ere yer are!"

Reluctantly he came over to take the coin. "What d'you
want to hear?"

"Oh, you know best. One o' yore fav'rites. Wot abart
that 'Oo lot?"

"Don't like 'em any more."

"Rollin' Stones, then."

"They haven't done anything worth listening to in ages."

"Chuck Berry!"

"Come on, Mum! He's gone completely commercial.
Years ago."

"There must be someone yer like, Jer. Ya used ter 'ave
all these 'eroes."

"They've all gone off. Or died." His smile was wistful. "I haven't got any heroes any more, Mum—at least, nobody you can hear on the average jukebox. Not these days."

"Well, give us some Gary Glitter. I like 'im. Or Alvin Stardust. Or the Bay City Rollers. They're like The Beatles, ain't they?"

"Why not?" He pushed his way through the crowd to the glowing jukebox. He put the money in and pressed buttons at random. He returned to the bar and gave his mother a thumbs-up sign as Paul Simon began to sing something miserable and only barely revived.

"Oh, I like this," she said, "it's one of the old ones, innit?"

A plummy voice rose to challenge the music. The bishop was drunk again. "We gather today to celebrate the deaths of enemies and to mourn the deaths of friends…"

"Go on, Dennis!" shouted Mrs Cornelius. She was always kind to the old has-been.

"'E must be on 'is ninth crème de menthe," said Mo Collier, grinning at Jerry. Ex-lay preacher and Boy Scout leader, Dennis Beesley had once run the local sweetshop but had sold it years before. Rumour had it, he had eaten all the profits. He had taken part in many neighbourhood activities, had organised the North Kensington chapter of the Monday Club, been chief representative for the Union Movement, the Empire Loyalists and, until lately, the National Front. He was still regarded by some residents as a political sage, in spite of the mysterious scandal which had led to his being expelled from both the Boy Scout movement and the National Front. His daughter Mitzi, who had looked after him since his wife had run off with a black Methodist preacher from Golborne Road, was also in the pub, being chatted up as usual by half a dozen or so of the lads, though she was showing more interest in the owner of the nearby all-night supermarket, Mr Hira, known as 'The Professor' because of his constant references to his university degree.

Dennis Beesley continued his oration, cheered on by several regulars. "... to execrate those whom we hate and to praise those whom we love. From the highest and noblest of motives are brotherhoods such as ours formed so that we may comfort one another, huddling close, turning our backs on the terrifying darkness of Eternity, lifting our quavering voices in hymns of praise to the Great Idea, the Desperate Hope." He raised green liquid to his full, sticky lips. The red blotches under his cheeks clashed badly with the crème de menthe. He drew a breath. "My dear friends, let us now kneel to stroke one another's heads, to murmur reassurance, to pretend to divine commitment, to rage, for a short while, against the Unacceptable, to complain of our wrongs, to seek scapegoats for our own shortcomings, to protect the indigenous people of these isles against the encroaching hordes of the Children of Israel, against the Yellow Peril, the Black Invasion, the Asian Tidal Wave, the Red Menace, the Brown Betrayer, the Olive Exploiter and..." He frowned as he drained his glass.

"And the Great White Whale," suggested Mr Hira, putting his arm round Mitzi's waist. Mitzi rubbed herself against him. Beesley burped. "Thank you," he said. His flesh turned to a shade of green much paler than his drink. He shut his mouth suddenly and rolled urgently towards the lavatories.

"Hurry up," Frank called after him, "or you'll miss the coach."

"Such a shame," said Miss Brunner. "They ruined him, unfrocking him like that—or un-knickerbockering him, is it? The elders made far too much of it. He was only after their bullseyes."

"Definitely the post-war answer to Walt Disney," Major Nye was saying enthusiastically to Catherine. "I love him. I've enjoyed them all. Ten Thousand and One. The Clock and the Orange. Barry Lindsay. He can do no wrong in my eyes."

"I've always thought his pictures have everything except a good director," said Jerry, not for the first time.

"Yes, I know," said Catherine. "You've mentioned it before." She meant no harm, but she crushed him. He drank another whisky.

Mrs Cornelius came flat-footed to the bar. "'Ow old's that Miss Brunner nar? She was a stoodent teacher, wa'n't she, w'en you woz at school? Must be fifteen years, eh? Still at St Victor's, is she?"

"Still there." Miss Brunner had heard her. "I'm headmistress now, you know."

Mrs Cornelius was admiring. "I've got ter 'and it ter yer." She winked at Miss Brunner and jerked her thumb towards her son. "Carn't yer do somefink abart 'is appearance? Ain't yer still got some inflerence over 'im? 'E used ter be such a smart dresser—all the trendy colours, all bright an' sharp. Nar look at 'im. Looks as if 'e's garn on a bloody safari! Looks like a bleedin' clarn at ther circus wiv them trahsers! Ah, ya, ha, her, her—ker-ker-ker-ker!"

"The world caught up with me," said Jerry, "that's all. Anyway, I never liked going with the crowd."

His mother hugged him and stopped herself coughing. "There, there! Don't let yer ol' ma git yer dahn. No offence meant, Jer."

"None taken, Mum."

"That's the stuff. There's not a lot o' 'arm in yer, Jerry. I'll say that!"

"What you drinking, then?"

"'S'all right—ol' money-bags is payin'—'ave one on the Fur King o' Elgin Crescent! I did okay stayin' wiv 'im, eh?"

"You certainly did."

"I've never gone short o' beaux," she said. "Whatever else 'as 'appened ter me. Men've orlways fancied me. An' I, I've gotter admit, 'ave orlways fancied them." She shifted on her massive legs. "Ker-ker-ker."

"I don't know how you do it, Mum," he said as she shouted for service. "You'll still be going in a hundred years."

"Two bloody 'undred!" She winked at him. "Vodka, port an' lemon an' whatever 'e's 'avin'," she told the barman. She indicated her son.

"Double brandy, please," said Jerry. He thought he might as well get something out of an evening which had so far been more than a little depressing.

"Is 'at right," said his mother, "abart you goin' off all

them pop stars yer used ter like?"

"They never fulfilled their promise, did they?"

"An' Georgie Best and Muhammad Ali and them others?"

"Same went for them. They all seemed to let me down at the same time."

"Funny, reely, wiv Caff takin' up with all that, nar. Wot yer like nowadays?"

"Nothing much. I've lost faith in heroes."

"Ah, well. Yer orlways did 'ave yer 'ead in the clards. Come darn ter Earf a bit now, eh?"

"Looks like it."

Catherine put her arm through his. "Don't needle him, Mum. Everybody's picking on him tonight."

"She wasn't," said Jerry. "Not really."

"Buyin' 'im a bloody drink, wa'n I?" His mother was defensive. "You wos orlways too protective to'ards 'im, Caff. Let 'im stand on 'is own two feet—'e's old enough an' ugly enough nar!" But Mrs Cornelius was smiling as she carried the vodka and port back to her table.

Jerry sipped his brandy. He offered the glass to her. "Want some?"

She nodded and took the drink. "You coming with us to Brighton?"

"Depends how pissed I get. It's the worst New Year I've ever had. I feel so lonely. I'm really depressed, Cath."

"That's not hard to see. Whenever you wear the wrong clothes for the weather I can tell. Clothes are a dead giveaway, aren't they, to how a person's feeling? If you like we can go back to my flat. I don't particularly want to spend God knows how long in a smoky coach, singing rude songs—besides the roads are almost impassable, apparently. Heaviest snow of the century. We could see the New Year in together."

"What about your girl friend?"

"She's working. Gone abroad for a few days. She knows about us, anyway." Catherine squeezed his hand.

He was profoundly grateful. "Why not?" he said casually.

The door of the pub opened and cold air blew in. There was a glimpse of the frozen street. A bulky figure stood there. He was dressed in a vast dark overcoat, with a black muffler over his face, a fur cap on his head. In the odd light from the pub the tall dog at his side seemed to have red ears and eyes.

"We're off!" cried Frank with delight. "Off into the countryside. A-hunting we will go. Tantivvy, tantivvy!"

Jerry saw a small black-and-white cat run from the warmth of the bar into the chill of the street and had an impulse to stop it, but the newcomer was shouting now: "All aboard what's going aboard!"

Hooters, whistles, rattles clattered and cawed and shrieked as, baying, the party surged out into the old year's last night.

CODA

But Harlequin's domination has waned ... In the
modern world he is pale and lost, the frustrated
Pierrot. Columbine has become a gold digger,
Pantaloon is gaga, and the Harlequinade itself
which used to be the core of the Pantomime,
the mythical world into which all waited for
the particular scene to be transformed, is now
separated off as a quaint little period piece.

—Randall Swinger,
'The Rise and Fall of Harlequin',
Lilliput Magazine, December 1948

OVERCROWDING—THE INCREASING STRESS IN NORTH KENSINGTON

North Kensington's Golborne Ward is the most severely overcrowded area in all London. Here 40% of the people live at a Housing Density of more than 1½ people a room. Kensington is one of the four London boroughs in which "signs of increasing stress can be seen through the effects of overcrowding". These are some of the stock facts to emerge from the Milner Holland report of housing in London.

Kensington Post, 19 March, 1965

MRS C. AND FRANKIE C.

"They say in the paper that we are on the brink of a new Ice Age," said Colonel Pyat hopefully, casting a gloomy, Slavic eye over his ranks and ranks of old fur coats, evening capes, stoles, cloaks, hats and gloves. Spring had just arrived and with it the normal slackening off of business which always depressed him. He had long since ceased to believe in the future.

"Stop broodin' yer silly ol' bugger an' 'urry up," said Mrs Cornelius cheerfully. Her old eyes glittered behind a barricade of cream and powder. "Ker-ker-ker. We still got ter call fer Frank." Out of loyalty she wore his latest gift, though the weather was unusually mild. They were on their way to the People's Spring Festival, organised by local community leaders on the Westway Green below the motorway flyover to the west of Portobello Road. Mrs Cornelius was excited. It was to be Jerry's first public appearance with his rock-and-roll band, the Deep Fix.

"Mind you," she said as an afterthought, "these fings

orlways start late, if at all. Still, it's up ter us ter be on time, innit!"

"I hate it," grumbled Pyat. "Jungle music. Teddy Boy noise."

"Cor! You are art o' touch, incha!" She snapped her fingers and rocked from side to side, wafting lavender water and scented powder. "Y've gotta be wiv it these days—trendy, far art, too much, rock an' roll!"

She swayed through the door into Elgin Crescent. It was a busy Saturday in the market. Colonel Pyat glanced viciously at the Indians, with their cheap cheesecloth shirts and dresses, who were doing such a roaring trade. There was the usual confusion of locals trying to shop in a hurry while visitors moved slowly and uncertainly along the narrow street between the stalls, wondering why so many people scowled at them. Most of the money they brought to Portobello Road stayed in the district for the few hours that the antique-dealers and stall-holders remained there. Colonel Pyat followed Mrs Cornelius from the shop, locking the door carefully behind him. He, too, wore an enormous fur coat. The day was miserably bright and sunny.

Together they pushed their way up the Portobello Road, through the trinket-sellers, the street-musicians, the purveyors of craft-goods, the racks of denim and cheesecloth, the mass-produced patches and buttons and belt-buckles, the greengrocery stalls, the sellers of Indian metalware, of beads, flutes, drums, posters, army uniforms, handbags and purses, weapons, Victoriana, until they reached Frank's shop, which was currently dealing in stripped pine. Frank waited reluctantly outside, holding a brass candlestick in each hand, part of his old antique stock. "If I sell 'em for that," he told a small man in a pork-pie hat, a camera and a black blazer with four metal buttons on the cuff (evidently a German), "I shan't make any profit, shall I?"

"Fifteen?" said the German.

"Sixteen," said Frank, "and that's final."

"Done," said the German awkwardly.

"You're so right," said Frank accepting the money. "You won't regret it. That stuff appreciates, some of it."

"Come on, Frankie," said his mother, pulling at him. "Yer can't stop dealin', can yer, yer little cunt?"

He was offended. "At least someone in this family's making their own living."

They trekked on until they reached the railway arch and, immediately after it, the motorway arch, where dozens of small stalls were set out selling the accumulated junk of the twentieth century. They skirted the stalls even as their eyes automatically shifted across the wares, rounding the corner to the big patch of grass where a crowd of young bohemians and their children had already gathered outside the graffiti-smeared walls of one of the motorway bays. This bay had a chicken-wire fence strung between its columns and a sign, already much attacked by weather and local children: WESTWAY THEATRE. Within the bay old railway sleepers had been arranged in banks to form seats. On the wall behind the seats were three murals, one by Cawthorn, one by Riches and one by Waterhouse. Somehow the murals had escaped the ravages of the rest of the theatre which had long ago collapsed as a result of calculated lack of local government support. The council had been reluctant to allow the project in the first place and had made sure it would not flourish by bringing in an administrator from outside the district and making sure that he had no power, no money and no encouragement. After a while enthusiasm had broken down into a classic series of disputes between a variety of splinter groups and an attempt to produce a free theatre for the district had failed. But, for the first time in over a year, it was to be opened—or had been opened—by the people who had originally started the scheme with their free Saturday concerts featuring Quiver, Brinsley Schwartz, the Pink Fairies, Henry Cow, Mighty Baby, Come to the Edge and Hawkwind, until the police, in support of seven Rate Payers, had managed to put a stop to them—and Jerry and his band were to have their chance at last.

Mrs Cornelius, with the dignity of one who was related to an artiste, Colonel Pyat in tow, Frank in the rear, went through the gates, calling out to her son who sat dreamily on the little stage trying to put a new plug on his amplifier. "'Ere we are, then! Give us a number, lads!"

Mo Collier grinned at her in some shyness. He had plugged in his bass and was plunking at it. No sound came from his own amp. He turned a couple of knobs and a screeching rose and fell. He made another hasty adjustment. "'Ullo, Mrs C. You're a bit early, aincha? We don't start till 'alf past two."

"It is now exactly a quarter to three," said Colonel Pyat.

He tapped his wristwatch as if it were a barometer.

"Sod," said Jerry. He looked through the chicken wire at the gathering crowd. Behind it a number of policemen were beginning to line up. He finished with the plug and fitted it into the board. A red light flickered on his amplifier. He was surprised. He took his Rickenbacker electric twelve-string over to the amplifier and pushed the jack-plug lead into the socket. He played a chord. Mo winced. "We'd better tune up."

Terry the drummer suddenly came to life behind the kit and played an erratic roll before subsiding again. He looked like the dormouse in Alice in Wonderland. They had all had several tabs of mandrax and had become very stoned to help quell their nerves for their performance. Jerry began to pluck at his many strings, staring vaguely at Mo, who plucked back. Gradually they got their instruments into some kind of uniform tuning. Mo nodded towards the centre of the stage where hardboard had been placed across a gap (there had been two attempts to burn down the theatre during disputes between different radical groups). "Watch out for the 'ole, man."

Jerry nodded absent-mindedly. He was visualising the enthusiasm of his public. He had a glazed, harried look.

"All right, Mick Jagger," shouted Frank in his poshest voice, "let's hear you!"

"Ker-ker-ker," said his mother.

Jerry approached the microphone and began to chant into it. Nothing came through the PA. He staggered back towards the amplifiers. Elsewhere various people were fiddling with other pieces of faulty electrical equipment. Jerry had a word with his friend Trux, who was holding a wire in one hand and scratching his head with a screwdriver.

"Ker-ker-ker."

People were beginning to file into the theatre now, although the stage was so arranged that the band would play facing the people who sat outside on the grass. Some of the organisers of the event had not yet turned up. There had been a problem involving fresh disputes with a group of Rate Payers; the organisers could be seen on the far side of the green, gesticulating, deep in conversation with a number of middle-aged men and women with arms folded in front of them and expressions of extreme distaste on their faces as they looked first at the crowd and then at the stage. Once or twice a policeman wandered over and talked to a long-haired man in a fairisle pullover or had a word with a thin-lipped Rate Payer.

Jerry went behind the stage into the connecting bay, which served as a dressing room. He was beginning to feel much better. He accepted a joint from a girl whom he remembered vaguely. Her name was Shirley Withers and she had offered him a warm look such as he had not received for a very long time. He felt taller, slimmer, more handsome. He grinned at her. A promising grin. He began to move with some of his old grace, the guitar resting casually on his hip. He went back on stage and plugged in again. He played a fast twelve-bar progression. He knew he was playing well. He nodded to Mo and Terry and began to jump up and down as he played. Some people were already clapping and cheering.

Mo put a final turn on his A string and inclined his head in a brief bow. Mrs Cornelius, Colonel Pyat and Frank Cornelius sat down in the front row. Jerry did not look at them. He was looking at his Fame.

Unexpectedly, they all started more or less together, going into a fast, standard boogie rhythm. Jerry danced towards the mike. He had never felt so happy. At last he was able to emulate all his earlier heroes. Perhaps he could become a hero himself, only he wouldn't let people down the way the others had. The crowd was his. He stepped up to the mike and opened his mouth.

The crowd roared.

It was the last thing he heard before the floor gave way beneath his feet and he fell into the shallow pit below.

He was far too drugged to feel any real pain, or even much concern, as he lay on his back looking up at the dim patch of daylight above, at the broken Rickenbacker on his chest, listening to the waves of laughter and applause from the audience, to Mo's bewildered bass, to Terry's inappropriately determined drum solo. Then he passed out for a moment or two.

He felt sick and miserable when he woke up. Shirley Withers was in the hole with him. She was trying to lift him upright. He saw his mum peering over the edge.

"You okay, Jer?"

"I'm fine. I can carry on now." He knew his chance had disappeared. "Your guitar's *ruined*," said Shirley. "Have you got another?"

345

He shook his head. He got to his feet, the pieces of smashed wood still hanging around him by the strap. He climbed out of the hole and blinked. The police had closed in on the crowd. A fight had started. Two panda-car constables were already on stage. Frank was talking to them.

"Pigs!" shouted Jerry weakly. He turned to Terry. "Keep playing. Keep playing."

"They turned the power off," said Mo. He sat down cross-legged and buried his face in his hands.

"Don't let them stop your music!" Jerry addressed the confused crowd. "You've got rights. We've all got rights."

"No need to make any more trouble, sir," said one of the constables. "How's the head?"

"Piss off!" said Jerry. "It's a plot. Why'd you bloody have to interfere?"

"We've had complaints. I've nothing against this sort of music myself. I like it. Not that you could play any now, could you, old son?" He indicated the broken Rickenbacker. "So there's not a lot of point in making a fuss."

"I haven't had a go yet," said Jerry mournfully.

His mother moved to his defence. "Lay off the poor littel sod—it was 'is turn to do 'is act. 'E's bin waitin' years fer the chance, an' you 'ave ter go an' spoil it!"

The constable backed away from her. "We didn't damage the stage, madam."

"Pigs," said Mrs Cornelius with some relish. "Mother-fuckers!"

"It's all right, Mum," murmured Jerry.

"I'm on your side entirely," Frank was saying to the

other constable. "If I had my way I'd ban this sort of thing altogether. I'm a Rate Payer."

"Put 'em all up against a wall and shoot 'em," said the constable with relish, then, as one of the organisers approached, "I'm really sorry about this. We're just doing our duty."

"Are you sure you're okay now?" said Shirley. Her eyes were worried rather than warm.

"Fine," said Jerry, "um…"

She anticipated him. "Got to go now. See you around. Bye, bye."

"Bye, bye," said Jerry.

"You were very good," said Mrs Cornelius. "Wan'e, Kernewl?"

But Colonel Pyat, a huge, frightened hamster, was already on the other side of the barrier and making for home.

"I'm a Trader *and* a Rate Payer," Frank continued. "I've lived here all my life. I remember when this was a quiet, decent neighbourhood."

Mrs Cornelius gurgled sceptically. "Wot? Oh, yeah. So fuckin' quiet yer couldn't get a bloody taxi ter take yer 'ome. They woz shit scared o' Nottin' Dale. They wouldn't drive yer beyond Pembridge Gardens! An' the coppers used ter patrol in threes. I remember one year they barricaded the Nottin' Dale coppers in their own nick and they couldn't git art till the people let 'em art!" She eyed the constable with fond speculation. "We woz famous in them days," she said, "for bein' fierce. They're all soft nardays—coppers *an'* yumans."

"Listen," said the policeman with some heat, "they

wanted to send the SPGs in—then you'd 'ave known what for!"

"Took pity on yer, did they?" said Mrs Cornelius contemptuously. "Ruddy little squirt."

"Now, then, madam…" He reddened, seeking support. "Arthur…"

With a quick, cunning movement, Mrs Cornelius stuck out her varicosed leg. The constable yelped and fell head first into the hole. Mrs Cornelius took her son by the arm. "C'mon—let's go an' 'ave a cup a tea. Yer'll make it yet, Jer—I know yer will."

The sleepers and the dope had begun to take effect. Jerry's eyes were watering. As his mum led him off the stage, he burst into tears.

AUCHINEK

Sebastian Auchinek's expensive white suit thoroughly outshone Jerry's cheap one. They sat together, side by side, on a long deep tan ottoman, in Auchinek's elegant, sparsely furnished, Sackville Street office. Big windows admitted cool sunlight as if it were exclusive to the establishment. Auchinek was hatless. Jerry wore a broad-brimmed fedora. "Sam Spade? Right?" said Auchinek pointing at the hat.

"Philip Marlowe," Jerry told him. "*The Long Goodbye.*"

"Right! Beautiful." Auchinek returned to his commiserating mood. "But they're not cheap, are they, Rickenbackers?" He spoke reverently. "£500?"

"About that," said Jerry. He had got his guitar from a friend who had done Sound City's entire stock in 1973, loading two pantechnicons in half an hour on a Sunday morning in July.

"And," said Auchinek smiling, "of course it wasn't insured?"

"No."

"You people!" Auchinek wore a waistcoat of pale blue

leather, its edges trimmed with metal studs, a lilac shirt, a yellow cravat. Somehow all he seemed to lack was a green parrot on his shoulder. "So, Jerry! What can I do you for?"

"I wondered if you could get us some gigs. We did very well at the Westway, until the accident."

"Heavy rock?" Auchinek rose sadly and went to his desk. He looked significantly back over his shoulder as he picked up a black plastic box which looked as if it had cost much more than anything in silver. "Heavy rock? It's not my scene. Solo singers, yes. Orchestras, yes. Boy and girl singing acts, yes—soul trios, quartets, quintets, sextets, septets, octets, yes, yes, yes, yes. Soul, soul, soul, soul—that's your basic day-to-day demand anywhere in the country or on the Continent, Las Vegas, you name it. Soul isn't just a popular fad—it's the genuine commercial music of a decade. Black or white, it makes no difference. Country music, rock-and-roll groups, reggae—nothing compared to soul. Jerry, you haven't got a bad voice— make it sweeter—get together with some other guys, maybe some gals, and do some harmonies—a good funky bass, a touch of wa-wah, even a taste of fuzz, nobody's objecting to that. It's fine, gives it body, texture—do you know how many records I've produced myself?—you don't have to give up your principles, just alter your angle a little. Mainly it's the songs, see." He began to sing in a low, lugubrious voice, hunching his shoulders, awkwardly moving his hips. "Baby, baby, baby, you broke my heart in two—now two hearts beat as one, but they're not having any fun, 'cause both those hearts belong to me! See? Lovely stuff." He made a cryptic windmilling motion with his arms. It was on the strength of this motion that Jerry, for the first time in his life, had developed racial prejudice while watching *Top of the Pops*. He had discovered that he hated black people. Then, after another week or so of watching similar acts, he decided that he hated white people, too. Now he was hating Jews. He wondered just how much disharmony *Top of the Pops* was responsible for. It was surprising what music could do for the racial situation. However, he was desperate enough to continue trying to reason with Auchinek, his only contact in the commercial music business.

"I can't do it. But we thought of this idea—Music from the Spheres—astronaut music that's come from the stars— it's a good gimmick. We tell the kids it was given to us by space people, see. Like *Chariots of the Gods*, you know."

"*Gramophones of the Gods*? Jerry, a gimmick's as good as the thing it's promoting. Okay—yes, good gimmick— but did the astronauts send us soul music? Maybe they did. You prove it. If the music isn't soul—if it isn't what people want to hear—it doesn't matter how good a gimmick you've got. It's the Number One Rule, Jerry. I've told you before."

"But that stuff's just so much Muzak. It's piped music for supermarkets. People didn't want to hear The Beatles till they heard them, or Hendrix, or The Who."

"They heard them—they liked it—therefore it must have been what they wanted. My point!"

Jerry accepted the Camel Auchinek offered him. "But

mythology, see? Everyone's into mythology. I was reading this book—*The Mythical History of Britain*—yeah?"

"Fabulous…"

"It reckons we're all descended from the Trojans…"

"Trojans? I thought we were all descended from Martians. Maybe Trojans was their word for Martian?"

"You're probably right," said Jerry.

"So what about the Martians?"

"An album—the mythical history of England up to the present day."

"So?"

"Couldn't you interest someone?"

"Certainly I could interest someone. With my muscle, Jerry, I could interest anyone. Fabulous history of England?—fine—as rock music—the sort you like?—not really—as folk music?—who cares?—as soul? Very good! Good orchestrations, nice lyrics, nice arrangements, easy swinging rhythm—lovely—but King Arthur? A soul opera of King Arthur? Maybe, maybe. You are thinking of King Arthur? Like Wakeman? That's nice, the Wakeman. Exactly what I'm talking about. But it's been done. Can it be done again? With a new angle? Well, maybe. But Wakeman isn't The Miracles, if you see what I mean. A market, I grant you. A good market. But not a really solid market. Not so safe as soul. So what else were you considering? Let's spell it out, eh? Talk it through. Fine? Trojans? Who's heard of Trojans, these days?"

"We could make it Martians, as you suggested—gods as astronauts, the Bermuda Triangle—something up to date. The same stuff—but more modern…"

"Yeah, but that's mythology—the Bermuda Triangle is *science*. You don't want to get them mixed up, Jerry. There's too much confusion already in the world today. Still, not to split atoms, eh? Okay. Martians. Bermuda Triangle, Scifi, right? Far out. Okay, the market's getting big enough to stand it. Super. Fab. So far so good. So we have a Soul Opera about the Bermuda Triangle—"

"Or Jaws Superstar," said Jerry wildly.

"Sharks? Sure, maybe. Giant sharks. Updated Moby Dick, with good music. Why not? We do a film. We all go out to Bermuda for a few weeks. Why not? Sure. Come to me with something on tape, some notes. Good. I'll listen to it. I'll take it down to the country with me. If I like it, I'll sell it. Can I say more?"

"But I need a new guitar first. If you could lend me the bread…"

"You still have that Equity card since I got you the film extra work?"

"Yes."

"Then I can help you earn some money. Una's new show."

"Playing guitar?"

"They don't need a rock guitarist. Not another one. A good part. The show's about Frankenstein, see, and what it means in moral terms today—beautiful songs." His hands windmilled over one another.

"But I haven't had any acting experience."

"You don't need it."

"And I can't sing soul songs."

"You don't have to. You yell. Rock-and-roll experience is perfect for this part. You scream. You jump and up and down. With these teeth in. You get three appearances, maybe more. A night, I mean."

"Who am I?"

"Who are you? You're the vampire. I should have thought of it before. I apologise. Okay? Want it? The pay's good. Get your name on the programme. A start in a career. Look at *Hair*, how many people made it from that! Look at *Jesus Christ Superstar*? And *Godspell*?"

"Oh, blimey," said Jerry.

"Contacts. You'll have a new guitar in no time. A break. Una'll be delighted."

"You hate me, don't you?" said Jerry.

"Hate you? What's hate? I disapprove of you, because you're a talented boy who doesn't know what's good for him. You frustrate me, Jerry. You do. You frustrate me very, very much. So what's it to be? The vampire? Or back to busking on a borrowed banjo? Down the garbage chute or up the golden escalator?"

"I'll try the vampire," said Jerry.

PERSSON

"You were splendid." Una Persson leaned over a drowsy Catherine and lit Jerry's cigarette for him. She climbed across their bodies to be on his left. They all lay together in Una's king-size four-poster. It was early afternoon. "You're a natural actor." Una was talking about the movie rushes she had seen earlier that day at the studios. The film was her own first starring rôle (a remake of *Camille*) and by encouraging Jerry (who played Armand's friend) she seemed also to be encouraging herself.

Lying between the two women Jerry was in his element. His emotions were mixed but all pleasant. He felt they were three sisters sharing a delicious conspiracy, that he had two mothers, two concubines, two loyal friends; moreover he became still more cheerful when they ganged up on him, to take the piss out of him, to dress him up, to have their way with him. Perhaps it was their affection for each other which turned him on most, the fact that they were able to relax with him and therefore make him relax in turn. They enjoyed going out together, forming a little exclusive club whose erotic secrets only the three of them would ever know. Depressed, they were able to comfort one another; happy, they were able to infect one another.

"And you're better than Garbo." It was true. "Much better. You're a bit like her in looks, but your range is greater."

Una lay back on her pillows, fingering her breasts as she absorbed his praise.

"You can out-act anyone, Una." With a luscious sigh Catherine ran her soft hand down her brother's chest and stomach. "Ah! I don't know how I get the work at all! I can't act for toffee. Still, six weeks in panto's better than nothing. We start rehearsals next month. It's hard to get into the Christmas spirit in September, mind you." She rubbed her own stomach. It rumbled. "Cor, I'm starving. Breakfast time."

"It'll be teatime soon," said Una. "I've been working since six o'clock."

"I'll get some tea, then," said Catherine agreeably, running her fingers through tangled blonde hair. "Did you pick up the tickets from the agent?"

"Three one-way Class 1 berths on the *Alexander Pushkin* sailing next week for New York. We'll have to fly back."

Catherine put her dirty feet on the white carpet, stood up and took her pale brown Janet Reger négligée from the back of the door. "It'll be nice to see the old house again. And a good time to go." Like her brother, she shared with Una an enthusiasm for American Gothic wooden houses.

"Will they let us sleep in the same cabin?" Jerry asked as his sister left. "Do you think?"

"I've arranged it. They think we're ballet dancers. It's okay."

"That's the Russians all over. One rule for the ballet dancers and another for everyone else. I wonder what it'll be like." Jerry's Russophilia was only equalled by his romantic love for the United States. He could think of nothing more marvellous than travelling to one place on a ship belonging to the other. He had often remarked on the strong similarities between the two nations and believed this similarity to be the cause of their rivalry.

Una indicated the print on her wall. It showed the famous eighteenth-century actor John Rich in his rôle of Harlequin. The caption above the print read *Harlequin Dr Faustus in the Necromancer* and below it was a verse:

> *Thank you Genteels, these stunning Claps declare,*
> *How Wit corporal is yr. darling Care.*
> *See what it is the crowding Audience draws*
> *While Wilks no more but Faustus gains Applause.*

"I told them we were putting on a new production," Una said, "but I didn't tell them you were playing Columbine."

Jerry patted his stomach. With success, he was expanding.

"I'm not sure I'll get into the dress. Can't I be Harlequin or the Pierrot?"

She shook her head. "It's not your turn."

He giggled as she took him in her arms.

NYE

"You're Noël Coward, if you want to be." Major Nye stiffened his shoulders. "I can't say fairer than that. You've the figure, now that you've lost a few pounds, the voice, the looks—or can have. What d'you say, old chap?"

It would be Jerry's first real star part in the West End, but he remained reluctant to begin a new commitment. Una would be back from America soon and Catherine would have returned to the provinces. If he took the rôle it would mean quite probably that they would not be together for several months.

"I don't know an awful lot about the thirties," he said.

"Twenties, actually, this setting. *Bitter Sweet* with an all male cast. As he'd have liked it himself. You're not worried?"

"Not about that. So it's Brylcreem and six-inch fag holders, eh?"

"That's a bit superficial, old boy, but you've got the mood—it's what the public's desperate for…"

Major Nye had become an impresario late in life, with

his run of successful nostalgia shows on stage, screen and television. Series like *Clogs* and *Mean Streets*, set during the depression in Northern towns, had shown people that things had been worse than they were now and taken their minds off their current troubles, while musical versions of *King of the Khyber Rifles*, *Christina Alberta's Father*, *A Child of the Jago* and *The Prisoner of Zenda* were all still running in West End and Broadway productions, as well as in touring companies (Catherine was currently playing Rupert of Hentzau in one of these).

"The traditionalists are going to be a bit upset," Major Nye continued, pausing by a railing and staring out to sea. He had come down to Brighton especially to meet Jerry who was just finishing a run as Harlequin Captain MacHeath in the revived *Harlequin Beggar's Opera* which Jerry had himself suggested to Major Nye after Una Persson had given him the idea. The revived full-blooded pantomime was just one more of the major's successes in England and America. "But we're used to that by now— and we're doing more for them than anyone else, even if we do take liberties occasionally. Still, it's the literary bods do the complaining, not the public, and it's the public that matters, eh?"

"Every time," said Jerry. He waved. Elizabeth Nye, the major's daughter, who had first interested her father in the stage, was running along the promenade to meet them. She was playing Columbine Polly Peachum to Jerry's Harlequin. "Hello, Jerry. Hello, Daddy. Is lunch still on?"

"If you're interested, my dear." He looked

questioningly at Jerry. "Spot of lunch, then?"

"Lovely," said Jerry. "Have you asked Sebastian about this?"

"No need to bring in agents until the last minute. They only confuse things. I didn't know you were still with him."

"He's useful," said Jerry. "Anyway, I feel sorry for him. His musical interests have taken a turn or two·for the worse."

"He didn't move with the times," said Major Nye. "Lived in the present too much, in my view. Couldn't see that the wind was changing. Of course, I never expected anything like this myself. I started, you know, doing modest little music-hall evenings with amateur performers. Now we're dragging up every damned traditional entertainment since Garrick's day—and before. We'll find we've got mass audiences for *Noye's Fludde* next season, at this rate."

"The eighteenth-century satirists thought the Harlequinade was going to be the death of the theatre." Jerry had pursued his usual research. "They thought Shakespeare and Jonson were done for—pushed out of business."

"Nothing ever kills off anything else," said Major Nye comfortably, pointing his stick at Wheeler's across the road. "Nothing invented ever dies. Fashions change. But it's always there, waiting to be revived according to the mood of the times. History is retold by every generation, always slightly differently—sometimes very differently. Funny stuff, when you think about it, Time."

"I've never thought about it," Jerry said.

A BUNDLE

Jerry sat in the studio mock-up in his elegant evening dress smoking a sophisticated cigarette, copying his successful Coward rôle but looking more like a Leslie Howard, sardonic, quizzical, as he turned to the camera and said:

"Once upon a time it meant something to be the owner of a car. It put you above the common herd. Now Rolls-Royce brings back meaning into motoring—" the camera pulled away from the close-up in order to show the whole scene—"with the mini-Phantom."

"Cut," said Adrian Mole, the director. "There's a phone call for you, love. That was beautiful. All right, lads and lasses, you can go home now. Everything's perfect."

Jerry climbed from the cramped seat and moved stiffly from the studio. In the office one of the bright, competitive girls who worked there handed him an instrument. "Hello?"

The voice was indistinct, accented, anxious. Colonel Pyat.

"Your mother, Jerry. She is not at all well. She wants to see you."

"Is she in hospital? St Charles?"

"No, no. She wouldn't let them take her. Still in Blenheim Crescent. You haven't been to visit her lately and I think she's upset."

It was more likely that Colonel Pyat disapproved of him, thought Jerry. "Thanks, Colonel. I'll go and see her right away."

"I've looked in, but I have the shop to run. I'm all alone, you see."

"Don't worry. Has the doctor been?"

"I haven't spoken to him, yet. But I think it's serious. She could be—oh, well, you had better look for yourself."

"Does Frank know?"

"Frank, too, has his business. He's going to try to pop round this evening. Catherine we can't find."

"She's on tour." Jerry was surprised by his lack of annoyance, his spontaneous feeling of concern for his mother.

The evening clothes were his own so he did not need to change. He went straight to the car park where he picked up his real Phantom. He nodded to two young girls who recognised him as he drove into the street. It was surprising how popular he had become since he had allowed Auchinek to give him the 'conventional' image. It offered reassurance, of course. He touched the stud to lower his window and threw his Sullivan's cigarette into the street. He looked bitterly at his eyes in the driving mirror. He had always hated reassurance. Reassurance was death.

He reached Shepherd's Bush and headed up Holland

Park Avenue, turning eventually into the maze that was now the Ladbroke Grove area, all diversions and one-way streets, coming at last to Blenheim Crescent. Opposite his mother's basement, which was identical to the one she had temporarily removed to in Talbot Road, was the fortress of the new housing estate, built on the site of the Convent of the Poor Clares and named after the order (Clares Gardens, though no garden was in evidence anywhere). He found a space close to his mother's flat and parked. All the meters had been smashed, though he didn't benefit, however, since he had his resident's parking permit. He still lived in Kensington, in the more exclusive Holland Park area. He locked his car carefully, knowing the habits of the local kids, and descended the makeshift wooden steps of the basement. The wooden door was unlocked. He went in, recognising the familiar, comforting smell of mildew and stale food.

"Mum?"

A fairly feeble cough came from the back room, where she slept. He made his way through the débris of her living room, with its ancient furniture, its scattered magazines, its unwashed crockery, its dead flowers, and entered the bedroom which smelled of disinfectant, camphor, mothballs, rose water, lavender water, urine, stout and gin, a combination which never failed to fill him with nostalgia.

She lay in the iron-framed bed, beneath several quilts, propped on a variety of dirty cushions and pillows, in full make-up, so that it was impossible to tell from her skin how she was, though her eyes were uncharacteristically dull.

"Hello, Mum. Not too good, I hear."

Somehow her jowls and her baggy pouches seemed to be one with her disintegrating cosmetics and gave the impression that the face beneath it all was that of a child. She had rarely seemed so pathetic. He drew up a cane-bottomed chair and sat beside the bed. Because it was conventional, he held her hand. She pulled it away with a throaty chuckle. "'Oo'd'ya fink I am—Littel bloody Nell?" Her coughing began strongly but quickly grew faint. "Ker-ker-ker…" She reached, unable to speak, for the glass on the bedside table. He handed it to her. She drank. It was neat gin, Jerry guessed, by the smell on her breath as she handed the glass back.

"I've 'ad it, Jer," she said. "You know 'ow old I am?"

She had always kept it a secret. He shook his head. She was delighted. "An' yer never will," she said. "Know 'ow old you are, do yer?"

"Of course I do. I was born on 6 August, 1945."

"Thass right. They let orf ther bloody A-bomb ter celebrate. Most people on'y ever got fireworks—an' they 'ad ter be pretty fuckin' posh, an' all!" She eyed his costume. "Nice. I orlways knew you'd make it, in the end. You an' Caff. Frank's doin' okay, too—but 'e never 'ad much imagination, did 'e? Not like ther rest'v us."

"Yeah," said Jerry, nodding. He took out his silver cigarette case, offering it to his mother. With some difficulty she removed a cigarette and put it between her lips, drooping as always. Jerry lit it. He lit another for himself. She coughed a little but soon stopped.

"Well," she said, "I'm dyin'—it's why I was so keen to

see yer. Got yer in'eritance, in I?"

"Oh, come on, Mum, don't be daft." He tried to smile. "Besides, you haven't got a penny. It's all gone on wild living."

"It *'as*, too!" She was proud. "Every bleedin' shillin'. They didn't need no bloody inflation when I was arahnd!" A brief cough and Jerry thought he saw her wipe blood from her lip.

"Shall I go and fetch the doctor?"

"No point." She tapped the side of the mattress. "There's a box under me bed. You know—me box. You 'ave it." She reached into her several layers of cardigan and nightdress and removed a key from her bosom. She pressed it into his hand. "Open it later. There's yer birf certificate in there an' a few ovver fings, but not much. Yer farver…"

He passed her an ashtray, a souvenir from Brighton, so that she could put her cigarette down while she coughed.

"… wanna know abart 'im?"

"I didn't think you knew much."

"More 'n I've wanted ter tell up ter now. I got a lot of it from me mum and me sister." She chuckled and the dewlaps shook, threatening to break away and fall on the quilt. "Bloody funny story. It goes back ter the year dot. I dunno wot 'e'd be—yore great-great-gran'dad, maybe— any'ow 'e was born abart 1840 an' married this, er, Ulrica Brunner. Ker-ker-ker. They 'ad these kids—where is it?" She felt under her pillow and withdrew a sheaf of tiny slips of paper, sorting through them. "Ah. I've bin workin' it art, see. Yeah. Katerina, Jeremiah an' Franz. Well, Katerina married this Hendrik Persson geezer—a Dane or

Dutchman or somefink—but on'y just in time—she woz awready up ther spart—by guess 'oo—"

"Jeremiah," said Jerry with a sinking feeling. He had come to expect coincidences in life since he had begun to study the history of the Theatre.

"Yeah," said his mother. Then she realised what he had meant and shook her head. "Nar! Not 'er bruvver—'er *dad*." She winked at him. An ancient owl. "Give us some o' that Lucozade, love. And put a drop o' gin in it." He poured some of the yellow liquid into her gin glass. She sipped. "Ur! Innit 'orrible? Well—ker-ker-ker—Katerina 'ad 'er baby an' this Persson feller thort it wuz 'is an' corled it, believe it or not, Jeremiah—in honour of 'er dad, see? Well, Franz marries a cousin corl'd—" she picked another slip of paper from the sheaf—"Christina Brunner, right? An' they 'ave some kids, one of which is anuvver Cafferine, an' Jeremiah goes ter live wiv 'is married sister an' from wot me mum sez they 'as it away an' a little girl's the result—anuvver Ulrica. Then 'er bruvver goes ter Russia or somewhere an' changes 'is name ter Brunner or Bron or maybe Brahn, see. Any'ow 'e meets this Cafferine Brunner later and they gets married, not knowing then that 'e's 'er uncle. They 'ave free kids they corl Frank, Jeremiah an' Cafferine an' 'e goes off again, back ter Russia. Frank marries a Betty Beesley, Jeremiah marries some German bint name o' Krapp, an' Cafferine marries a cousin corled, believe it or not, Cornelius Brunner, an' she got one in the oven off 'er bruvver before she trips dahn the aisle. In the meantime Ulrica's grown up an' married anuvver

Russian corled—this is funny—Pyat, but, from wot we worked art, she'd 'ad a kid by *'er* dad an' it was brought up fer years wivart knowing its mum an' dad till someone tells it—it's registered, see, as Frank Brunner. Eventually Frank Brunner marries Jenny Beesley an' they 'ave two boys an' a girl. The girl does well for 'erself, goin' on ther stage, legit, an marryin' inter the foreign royal fam'ly—Princess Una von Lobkowitz, no less. An' then ther boys marry a Mary Greasby an' a Nelly Vaizey an' settle darn in Tooting or somewhere sarf o' ther river, but Jerry's a widower in ther meantime, wiv a fair amarnt o' Krapp money, an' there's two kids—Alfred and Siegfried—'oo 'ave ter change their name ter Krapp an' go an' live with ther fam'ly in Germany, while Jerry comes back ter England an' marries a Greek girl, daughter of ther shippin' millionaire Kootiboosi or somefink. They 'ave free kids—Francesca, Joacaster an' Constant—an' live up Campden 'Ill somewhere. Francesca marries a bloke called Nye an' goes art ter India wiv 'im where she dies in childbirth—one son, Jeremiah. Joacaster marries a cousin, Johannes Cornelius, an' goes art ter Sarf Africa, an' they 'ave a little girl, an' Constant marries a Katerina Persson an' they 'ave a little girl an' all, 'oo's up ther stick a monf after 'er first period, if wot I 'eard wos right, with 'er dad's daughter, Honoria—which *might* be me—in fac' I'm pretty sure it is. Well, you know a bit abart yore dad—'e wos moody—'e married me, I'll say that, though a good deal older'n me, but corled 'imself by 'is secon' name, Jeremiah, for ther weddin' an' I never woz sure it was legal—'e scarpered o' course an' fer a long

time I thort it woz 'cause o' ther coppers. Anyway, you free
come very close tergevver, though yer might not 'ave all
been 'is, or any of yer—yer could've bin 'is bruvver-in-law
Frank's, 'oo I sor a lot of 'cause 'e—ther one wot married
me—was orlways travellin' or lockin' 'isself away—or,
I must be honest, *my* dad's, if it woz me real dad or me
mum's—the ol' goat. 'E wos a kernewl, too, yer know, in
Mexico, it woz, an' ovver places. Any'ow me sister Doris
married a bloke corled Dennis Beesley an' I sor a fair bit
o 'im while she woz doin' war-work an' me ovver sister,
Renie, married yore little mate Mo Collier's dad Alf—nice
bloke 'e woz, killed in Germany 1946, somefink ter do wiv
ther black market, wannit? Anyway, there woz a lot'v ups
an' darns rahnd abart that time an' I don't blame meself,
though no-one'll ever know exactly 'ow 'oo's related to
'oo—except we're sure as eggs related—we woz orlways
a close family. Sammy, 'oo died, was Alf Collier's bruvver,
an' they 'ad a Brunner, a Persson an' a Cornelius or two
in there somewhere, an' all. Well, ther's on'y a few *main*
fam'lies in this distric', ain't there? Like over in Nottin'
Dale they got abart free clans—'Arrises, Fitzgeralds and
Bensons—it's ther same wiv ther Corneliuses, Cornells an'
Carnelians rahnd 'ere—along wiv ther Brunners, Perssons
an' Beesleys, though they woz never much compared ter
ther Corneliuses 'oo really run these blocks for a 'undred
years or more—since the Convent woz built an' there was
on'y that an' The Elgin 'ere a 'undred years ago or so. An'
they did well for themselves, some of 'em."

"Where did they come from, Mum?" Jerry asked.

"Ireland? There were a lot of Irish moved in here, didn't they—because of the convents?"

"Some finks Ireland—but this area's orlways 'ad a lot o' immigrants in it—Dutch, Italian, German, Swedish, French—it's a common name. English an' all. Wot abart *that* fer a tale o' scandals, then? Incest on top a bloody incest, eh? D'yer believe it?" Her eyes glittered.

"Every word," he said. "I'm glad it's cleared up the mystery of my birth."

She bawled with laughter. "Yer sarcy sod! Ker-ker-ker."

"Others did well for themselves, did they?" He frowned. His mother never took him seriously.

"Oh, yers. One got a knight'ood, one opened a department store, anuvver started a rest'rant—gold mines, ships, factories, greengrocers—yer've on'y got ter name it! There wos a doctor or two an' all—an' some of ther girls married inter the English aristocracy. They spread all over, ther Corneliuses!" She gasped and laughed again. "Like muck! Like a fuckin' plague, eh? Har, har, har, ker-ker-ker-fuck!"

Blood really was coming from her mouth now. Jerry helped her sit upright. Her body shook. Her skin sagged as if she shrank within it. "Oh, fuckin 'ell. Oh, fuckin' 'ell. Jerry. 'Ere, did Caff tell yer?" She struggled. Her eyes ran with tears; her make-up smeared. She looked like an eight-year-old. She was full of fear. "Did she? Don' let 'er 'ave it, Jer."

"Have what, Mum?" He was distracted, holding her in one arm and trying to reach for the glass of Lucozade with his free hand. "Eh?"

"Ther baby…" Her frame reared in his grasp. "Yore fuckin' bastard baby." She began to cough but was too weak. Her body quivered. The fear fled. She grinned. "Yer got ter larf, incha?"

"Drink this, Mum. I'll go and get the doctor." He was weeping. He knew she was dying.

She cuddled against his chest, like a baby animal. She sighed. It took him a few moments to realise that she had not breathed in. She grew cold. He kissed her stiff, lacquered hair, the powder of her face, and then he was calm, standing up, pulling the sheet to her chin, kneeling to feel under the bed and pull out the box.

It was too dark to see properly in the bedroom and he did not like to turn on the light. He carried the cheap wooden writing chest into the other room and put it on the table in the window. He looked out, over the top of the area, through railings at the blocks of new flats. He shrugged and used the key to open the box. It folded back into a surface on which one could write, each half of the surface being the lid of a section. He pulled up the top flap, using the little loop of string his mother had nailed there, in place of the original tag. There was a bundle of papers amongst the cuttings of advertisements, beauty treatments, anecdotes his mother had accumulated or inherited from her mother. They stretched back more than a hundred years, to 1865. He took out the bundle and set it aside. He opened the bottom flap. There was a fairly new book there which he had bought while researching his part of a year or two earlier. It was called *Pantomime, A Story in*

Pictures, by Mander and Mitchenson, published in 1973. He was puzzled. It was not like his mother to keep any book, let alone this one. Perhaps she had intended to sell it. He turned his attention to the bundle. He was very close to breaking down.

He fingered the papers, secured by rubber bands. He turned to call back into the cold, dark bedroom. "Don't worry, Mum—old Corneliuses never die—they just fade into someone else. There's too bloody many of us, eh?"

He was certain that he had heard her chuckle. He jumped up and went back to look into the bedroom, but she had not moved. She lay dead in her bed.

He returned to the table. He pulled the bands from the bundle. The bands were so old that they had perished and fell away beneath his fingers.

He found some photographs, very faded, of himself and Frank and Catherine when they were children. They had been at Brighton and had had their photographs taken in a booth, poking their heads through holes above cut-out figures so that it looked as if they were three pierrots, with children's faces and adult's bodies, on the pier. Their mother, standing beside them, looked far more innocent than her children, just as she looked now. She had been thinner, then, too. He found a marriage certificate for his mother's wedding. *Honoria Persson married to Jeremiah Cornelius at the Parish Church in the Parish of Tooting in the County of London on 22 July 1944 according to the Rites and Ceremonies of the Established Church after Banns by me, Wilfred H. Houghton, Curate.* At least he seemed legitimate, he thought. He could find no birth certificate for either his mother or the three children, though she had said his would be there. Perhaps she had been thinking of the marriage certificate. He found ticket stubs for his first appearance at the Prince of Wales Theatre as the vampire in *Soul of Frankenstein*, which had run for a week. He found ticket stubs for Catherine's early appearances in the Jupiter Theatre repertory company, where she had met Una Persson and Elizabeth Nye. There was a Royal Première programme for *Queen Christina*, the successful follow-up to *Camille*, which his mother had attended in full regalia, outshining anything the Royal Family could produce. There was a programme for *Twelfth Night*, decorated with a Heath Robinson jester and a phrase from the play—*A great while ago the world begun, With hey, ho, the wind and the rain. But that's all one, our play is done, And we'll strive to please you every day*—in which Una Persson had appeared as Viola and he as Sebastian. There was a number of other programmes and tickets, all of them connected with the careers of himself or his sister. There was a film company hand-out, giving the synopsis of a bad science fiction film in which he had appeared for a few seconds, as an extra, and on this had been scrawled a peculiar doodle, apparently in his own hand. He could remember nothing of it. He held it closer to the light from the window, trying to see if it made any sense at all. As he lifted it, his brother's staring face appeared, grinning at his with comforting malevolence.

Jerry got up from the table and went to let Frank in.

He opened the door, lifting the handle so that it would not scrape on the floor as it usually did. "She's dead," he said.

"Catherine?"

"No, Mum."

Frank made a small, unpleasant sound and went to check.

Jerry again picked up the dirty hand-out:

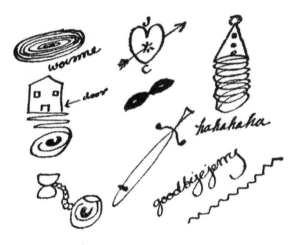

He screwed it up and let it fall on the floor, then he called goodbye to his sobbing brother and left the basement, climbing aboard his Phantom, on his way to find Catherine. He turned on the stereo. The Beatles were singing 'Hello, Goodbye' again. The sky was dark grey. He switched on the windscreen wipers. It was raining heavily. He, too, had begun to cry by the time he reached Greyfriars Bridge, on his way to Blackheath, the bearer of bad news for the mother of his unborn son.

APPENDIX I

The following is reprinted from *The Nature of the Catastrophe*, London 1971:

This chronology begins with the convenient date of 1900, but there is evidence to support the existence of a Jerry Cornelius even in pre-Christian times (the first significant reference, of course, is the famous one in Virgil!) just as there is evidence to say he did not appear on the scene until much later. We are not here suggesting, for instance, that a child of one year could have been a spy during the South African War. The chronology merely lists well-supported references to Cornelius. It does not propose that they can possibly refer to the same individual!

The Compilers

1900

18 December

Birth of a boy, christened Jeremiah Cornelius, at the Bon Secours convent, Guatemala City. Mother died: father unknown. He lived in the convent until the age of about six when he was transferred to a monastery school some distance from the city. (Letter to David Redd of Haverford West from Sister Maria Eugene of the Bon Secours convent, who died in 1960.)

1901
25 January
Boer War double agent known as 'Cornelius' caught and shot by a party of Boers under Commandant Pretorius, about two miles west of Jericho, Transvaal. (Dispatch from Pretorius to Kruger.)

1903
9 April
Log of the SS *Maureen Key* reports picking up an English-speaking seaman in Bay of Biscay about noon. Seaman was adrift in small boat and was incoherent. Name: Jerry—possibly Cornell or Carnell, Carmelion or Cornelius. Was handed over to port authorities in Bilbao but disappeared shortly afterwards having stolen a coat and a piece of meat.

14 October
Catholic mission in Djelfa, Algeria, contracts plague of unknown origin and all die. Scrawled on the side of the confessional are letters JE CORNELIU, plainly recently written by the monk who had been acting as Confessor when overcome by the disease. (*Le Monde Catholique*, 30 October.)

1904
24 January
Programme of the Empire Theatre, Leicester Place. The

Grand Spectacular Tableau, No. 7 on the bill—'The Treasure Island of Monte Cristo': the part of Edmund Dantes played by Mnsr J. Cornelius. At No. 10 on the bill Mdlle Marguerite Corneille, Comédienne.

14 October

The St Petersburg uprising. A list of arrested "foreign elements" issued by the Okharna (secret police) includes a Jeremiah Cornelius (thought to be a pseudonym). It is unclear whether he was deported or executed. (Burns Collection.)

1905
November

Reports from the Carpathian Mountains in Romania that a bandit—"perhaps an Englishman"—called Jeremiah Cornelius has been operating there for more than a year, organising several bandit gangs into a single force. (Records of Transylvanian Central Police Bureau now at the Austrian War Museum, Vienna.)

1907
16 February

Reference to a Jerzy Cornelius in list of thirty prisoners tried by military court as Socialist Democrat terrorists, St Petersburg. All found guilty and shot. (Burns Collection.)

8 July

Rouveniemi, northern Finland. A gang of criminals thought to be Russian nihilists rob several banks, a post office, several shops and are thought to have escaped by train. One suspect, a Russian

Jew calling himself Bronsky, claimed that the leader of the gang was known only by the name of 'Cornelius'. The Russian thought the leader was probably a Swede. (*Dagbladet*, Sweden, 12 July.)

8 October

"A young man of well-bred appearance, speaking Danish with a French accent, giving the name of Jeremiah Cornelius and his country of origin as Australia, formally accused of indecent assault by Miss Ingeborg Brunner at the 11th Precinct Police Station, Göteborg, last night. So far police have failed to arrest the accused." (Dispatch sent by Thomas Dell to *Sydney Herald*.) The story was not published, although a subsequent cable informed the newspaper that Miss Brunner had dropped the charges. (*Sydney Herald* correspondence files.)

12 November

The journal of Yüan Shih-k'ai, Commissioner of Trade for the Northern Ports, China, notes the employment of a Captain J. Cornelius, described as "an American soldier of fortune", to "help in the training of officers for the Peiyang Army", Tientsin. It appears that Yüan Shih-k'ai's commission was later countermanded, but that an appeal to the Empress Dowager reinstated Cornelius, though his position with the Peiyang Army became poorly defined. When, in 1909, Yüan was dismissed from office, his American protégé, on leave in Shanghai, disappeared. (*The Journals of Yüan Shih-k'ai*, edited with an introduction by Prof. Michael Lucy Smith, Collett Press, 1942.)

1908

19 February

Calcutta. Aurobindo Ghose of the extremist Nationalist Party records that Tilak, leader of the party, sent "a Eurasian called Cornelius with a message" to Congress leader Gokhale, a moderate. Gokhale never replied to the message which, Ghose thought, contained some suggestion of a secret meeting, but Cornelius was later arrested in a waterfront brothel where he had disguised himself as a woman. He was charged with the attempted assassination of Gokhale's close associate, Shastri. "A meaningless action," comments Ghose. There is no reference to the result of any trial. (Ghose, India's Lost Opportunity, Asia Publishing Co., Bombay, 1932.)

13 April

Afghanistan. Dispatch from Colonel R.C. Gordon commanding 25th Cavalry Frontier Force. Rumours that dissident hill tribes are united under a quasi-religious chief who appears to be of European or Eurasian ancestry and is referred to variously as Elia Khan, Shah Elia or Cornelius. "A tall man with burning eyes who rides better than any tribesman and who has already cost us some fifty men, including three lieutenants and our Risaldar Major." Colonel Gordon asked for reinforcements but died with the rest of his post when it was wiped out two days later. (Michelson, 'Lords of the North West Frontier', Strand Magazine, April 1912.)

1909

30 March

A man known only as 'the English assassin Cornelius' is

arrested in Innsbruck after hurling a bomb at the Kronprinz Frederik of Statz-Pulitzberg whose horse reared in time so that the bomb missed and exploded in the crowd. The assassin later escaped under circumstances which indicated help (or even orders) from someone highly placed in the government. (*Daily Mail*, 2 April.)

17 May

Secret dispatch from Captain Werner von K. (probably Koenig) dated Linz, 17 May, to Ludendorff of the German General Staff, Berlin: "I am sending to you Herr Cornelius, who has convinced me that he can supply much exact information concerning our good neighbours!" (Records in Berlin Military Museum Document PRS-188.)

1910

29 January

Gustav Krupp writes to his chief ordnance technician Fritz Rausenberger: "You were quite right to employ the Herr Doktor Cornelius. His efforts have contributed greatly to the speedier development of our new gun. Please convey to him the firm's congratulations." (Krupp correspondence files.)

1911

22 May

Passenger list of the SS *Hope Dempsey*, leaving Southampton 22 May, bound for Rangoon, via Aden, Karachi, Bombay and Madras, gives a Mr Jeremiah Cornelius (who later disembarked at Port Said).

August

Sir James Keen, an amateur archaeologist exploring ruins in Chad, reports meeting a fellow Englishman in the town of Massakori. "A tall, youngish chap, very brown, affecting native dress and living, apparently as the sheik's chief lieutenant, with one of the tribes of armoured nomad horsemen. He was civil, but reticent about his origins, offering me only his local name, which I did not catch. However, I learned the day after he had left that he was regarded by the French as one of the most painful thorns in their sides and that the garrison at Fort-Lamy had orders to shoot him on sight, no matter what the circumstances. I was informed that his name was Gerard Cornelius and that he was a deserter from the Foreign Legion." (*The Lost Civilisations of Africa*, Harrap, 1913, p. 708.)

2 November

Report of Lieutenant Kurt von Winterfeld, commanding a company of Protectorate Troops stationed temporarily at Makung on the Njong River, Cameroons, states that a European called Cornelius was shot while attempting to steal the steam launch serving the garrison. He had passed himself off as a German trader in order to board the vessel, but von Winterfeld suspected that he was an English spy. His body fell into the water and was not recovered. (*German Imperial Year Book for 1911.*)

1912

7 March

The Bight of Biafra. The *Santa Isabella*, a Portuguese schooner, hailed by a European sailing a dhow. The European gave his name as Cornelius and offered to work his passage to Parades, the ship's home port. In Parades Cornelius was believed to have transferred to the *Manité*, an American barque bound for Charleston via Boston. (Log of the *Santa Isabella*.)

1 June

Captain Simons of the *Manité* records loss of the seaman Cornelius overboard three miles off Nantucket in heavy seas. (Log of the *Manité*.)

13 November

Discovery of a cabin, recently built, on Tower Island, Galapagos, by crew of an Indian fishing boat blown off course and seeking shelter. No sign of cabin's occupant. Indians frightened, left island as quickly as possible after one of them, a half-caste known as 'Cortez', had taken an empty metal box bearing the lettering 'Asst. Comm. J. Cornelius, Sandakan'. (Journals of Father Estaban, San Lorenzo mission, San Domingo, Ecuador.)

27 November

An English engineer Jeremiah Cornelius offers his services to help in the completion of the Panama Canal but cannot produce satisfactory references. He is not employed. Later, parts of the canal near Cristoban are dynamited. Colombian guerrillas are suspected. Manager of the Company hears rumours that Cornelius is working with the Colombians. (Records of the Panama Canal Co.)

1913

5 April

United States troops in Nicaragua attacked by a well-organised band of 'nationalist' terrorists in several areas around Lake Nicaragua. US marines in Granada are wiped out and all arms, including several artillery pieces, stolen. Interrogation of suspects reveals that the terrorists are said to be led by an American, Jerry Cornelius. (Records of US Marine Corps.)

30 October

Peking. The missionary Ulysses Paxton mentions a conversation between himself and Liu Fang of the Methodist Episcopal Church. Referring to the possible conversion of the military leader Feng Yü-hsiang (later to be known as the "Christian General"), Liu told Paxton that a certain "Father Cornelius" had been responsible for Feng's interest in Christianity. Neither Paxton nor Liu knew of a missionary of that name in the area, though Liu had heard it said that the so-called "White Wolf", a remarkably intelligent and powerful bandit leader who had taken to roaming north-central China in the wake of the Second Revolution, was rumoured to be an ex-Catholic missionary called Kang Na Lu ("Acting with High Resolve") or Cornelius. (*Devil against Devil* by Ulysses M. Paxton, Grossett and Dunlap, NY 1916, p. 179.)

1914

Summer

The White Wolf, pursued by Feng's and other armies, is killed in Shensi during a pitched battle between his men and 'government' troops. Feng weeps beside the corpse and repeats the name 'Cornelius' over and over again. "Later he ordered the body burned, but it had been stolen, presumably by survivors of the White Wolf's band." (*North China Herald*, 25 August.)

1915

May

Rumours of the White Wolf's reappearance in Kansu. In Kungchang Mission, Father King, an American priest, lends rail fare to a fellow missionary, Father Dempsey, who claims to have been the captive of a bandit gang. Father King notes the initials J.C. on the other priest's bag. Father Dempsey claims that the bag belonged to a fellow missionary, Father Cornelius, who was killed by the bandits. Father Dempsey boarded train for Haichow and Father King comments on his surprising fitness, his apparent youth, his brilliant eyes. (Letter to Father King's sister, Maureen O'Reilly of Brooklyn, 8 June.)

3 August

During the famous Okhotsk Raid (thought to be inspired by Germany), two of the attacking gunboats were sunk before the defender's batteries were put out of action. The commander of a Russian launch heard the name Cornelius shouted several times during this engagement and gathered that this was the name of the officer in charge of the raid. He assumed the name to be German (although Germany continued to deny responsibility for the raid long after the end of the war). Upon the surrender of the garrison, the attackers disembarked, imprisoned all military personnel, and looted the city of most of its food, treasure and arms. The name Cornelius was heard by civilian witnesses who thought it referred to the tall man in elaborate Chinese dress who wore an ivory mask, carried no weapons, and appeared to supervise the pillage of Okhotsk. (*Report of the Official Committee Investigating the Fall of Okhotsk*, St Petersburg, March 1916, pp. 306–9.)

1916

4 February

Sale by Henrik van der Gees of Samarana, Java, of his estates (inc. rubber plantations and tin mines) throughout the East Indies. To: Mnr Jeremiah Cornelius, a Dutch banker. The estate was the largest singly held property in the East Indies and was sold for a disclosed sum of eighteen million guilders. (Samarana Land Office records.)

17 August

The Cornelius estate made a public company, the managing director being a Francis Cornelius, believed to be the brother of the purchaser who has returned to Rotterdam. The chairman is given as a Herr Schomberg of Sourabaya. (*Die Gids*, Batavia, 20 August.)

1917

14 July

Parish register for St Saviour's Church, Clapham, records the marriage of a Captain Jeremiah Cornelius, RFC, to a Miss Catherine Cornell, respectively of Nos 32 and 34 Clapham Common South. Captain Cornelius was on a forty-eight hour leave and returned to France immediately after the marriage. (Note: There is no record of a Captain Jeremiah Cornelius having served with the Royal Flying Corps.)

1921
6 May

The Interior Department of the USA leases naval oil reserves at Teapot Dome, Wyoming, to the Jeremiah Cornelius Company of Chicago. Various accusations in the Press (notably the *Philadelphia Enquirer*) concerning the allegations that the founder of this company is none other than 'German Jerry' Cornelius, a notorious racketeer often considered to be a more dangerous, though less notorious, character than Dion O'Banion, of whom he is a known associate. Thomas Redick of the *Enquirer* disappears, presumed killed. The Cornelius Company continues its activities, although it denies any connection with criminal elements and claims that its president is "travelling in Europe". (*American Mercury*, 15 October, 1923, p. 38.)

1922
1 March

The Munich Riots of February/March. Arrested as a "socialist agitator" by the police, a J. Cornelius. Tried 3 March and imprisoned for thirty days before being expelled from Germany on his failure to produce papers proving his citizenship. (Munich Court Records.)

September

Rout of Greeks from Asia Minor by Kemal Pasha greatly

facilitated by the tank company commanded by Major Cornelius, a South African soldier of fortune. (*Daily Mail*, 3 October, *The Sin of Pride* by Victor Manning.)

December

During the March on Rome a Geraldo Cornelius prominent in the Fascist takeover of power (for a short time he was editor of *Il Popolo d'Italia*) until assassinated "almost certainly on Mussolini's orders" in December of the same year. (*Threatened Europe*, J.P.H. Priestley, Gollancz, 1936, p. 107/8.)

1923

July

Lithuanians capture Memel from the French garrison installed by League of Nations. "The plan was successful almost certainly because of the work of the Dutch adventurer Cornelius." (French commander quoted in *Le Figaro*, 12 August.)

1924

21 January

Death of Lenin. A suspicion that he was assassinated on Stalin's orders voiced in the English-language *Exile* (14 February), a White Russian newspaper published in London and aimed at arousing sympathy for the émigré cause. Count Birianof wrote: "Various Russian expatriates were approached by those who were plainly agents of the Bolsheviks and told that they would be given the opportunity to 'eliminate' the Red leader. It was so plainly the kind of trap we have become used to that all émigré organisations gave orders to their membership to pay no attention to the schemes. However we have reason to believe that a Levantine gentleman, originally of Kiev and familiar in the Whitechapel area as 'Cornelius the Nihilist', made it known that he would be willing to do the deed. Whether 'Comrade' Lenin died of natural causes (a guilty conscience, perhaps?) or whether he was killed, we shall probably never really know. However, if he was killed it was almost certainly by Cornelius acting on the orders of General Secretary Joseph Vissarionovich Dzhugashvili (who prefers to hide behind the name of 'Stalin')—a man with a greater lust for power than even his fanatical master knew! And what has happened to the nihilistic Jew? Dead, himself, by now, if we know anything at all of Bolshevik plots and counterplots."

1926

27 February

Otto Klein shot on the steps of the Regensburg Opera House. After preliminary investigations, Regensburg police ordered the arrest of a tall, dark, slender man of about thirty going by the name of J. (possible Johannes) Cornelius, a known member of the NSDAP. (Mackleworth, *The Return to Barbarism*, Gollancz, 1938, p. 18.)

18 April

Ernst Auchinek tried for the murder of Klein; strongly denies that he has been known as Cornelius or that he has any connection with the NSDAP. He was hanged a month later. (Mackleworth, ibid., p. 22.)

1927

22 November

Leon Trotsky records a meeting with "the man generally known as 'Cornelius'" in Siberia, where they were both exiled. "I was curious to meet this mysterious fellow, of whom I had heard much from Stankovich, in particular. He was undernourished and poorly dressed for the winter, but his eyes were hot enough to melt snow and he seemed singularly self-contained. I met him only for those few short moments before he was led away, but I had the impression that he was almost enjoying his imprisonment." (Letter to Manfred Schneider, 5 June, 1930.)

1928

April

Mount Chingkangshan, between Hunan and Kianri. Mao Tse-tung has retired here after his recent defeat of September 1927. He is joined in the spring by Chu Teh, who brings with him an occidental sympathiser called Cornelius. Mao and Cornelius discuss tactics for several days and Mao is much impressed by the man's knowledge of China, as well as his grasp of Communist theory and its application to the special problems of China. Mao offers Cornelius a position in the army he is planning to reform, but Cornelius disappears that night and there is some suspicion that he may, after all, have been a spy of the Kuomingtang. (H'ang Lean-li, *Two Paths to Freedom*, Routledge, Kegan Paul, London, 1940, p. 807.)

January–December

All Cornelius properties sold up in US and Britain.

1929

November

Wall Street Crash. "Situation not improved by the sudden pulling out of Cornelius interests from many major companies." (*Wall Street Journal*, 26 November.)

1931

December

Japanese invasion of Manchuria. British minister in Tokyo telegraphs London: "Would suggest preparedness re rumours Japanese aided by English fascist associated with Russian émigrés here. Could prove embarrassing for us as basis for potential propaganda. The Englishman is said to be called Gerry Cornelius. Suggest you ascertain origins, etc., and speedily cable any information to here." (6 December.) The telegram was acknowledged but its contents ignored. (*Imperial Policy in the Far East*, 1909–1939, C.W. Nolan, Samson and Hall, 1950, p. 506.)

1932

12 April

Body of a young man about thirty found in Thames near Hammersmith Bridge. Several stab wounds in the throat. A gold and ormolu striking watch marked *Thos. Tompion, London, 1685* on its inside case and on the inside of its outer case *Jerry Cornelius from his dear friend Southey, Keswick 08*, the only object discovered on the body. The engraving is of little help in identifying the body since it evidently cannot be addressed to so young a man. Records show that no such watch has been reported stolen. No further evidence comes to light and the case is closed for the moment. ('London Keeps Her Mysteries', *Union Jack* magazine, August 1934.)

1934
1 July

Secret message from Himmler to Hitler on morning after extermination of Röhm and SA supporters: *All cleansing operations successful. Only the Jew-lover Cornelius remains to be tidied away.* (*Night of Terror*, Barry Hughes, Scion Books, 1951, p. 64.)

1935
March

One of the 'freelances' used by Mussolini in the Abyssinian campaigns of March is listed as Cornelius, a Dane. (*The Times*, 29 March.)

10 August

Arab Nationalists meet in Cairo for the third Secret Congress at which Comintern representative is present. Representative used name 'Cornelius'. (Adad, *Arabia Reborn*, Daker, 1962, p. 76.)

1937
18 December

Palestine. Jews and Arabs clash outside Qasr-el-Azak. British special patrol discovers corpses morning of 18 December. Among the bodies are those of two Europeans. One carries a revolver of unusual design and with no maker's name or registration marks. An inscription on the barrel reads "From Catherine to Jerry". The other corpse is that of a woman, very like the man in features and colouring. She has a similar gun with the inscription "From Jerry to Cathy" on the barrel. "The odd thing was that they seemed to be fighting on opposite sides." (Report of Lieutenant Robert Gavin, Special Police, Palestine, quoted in Fennel and Harvey's *British Political Policy in the Middle East 1900–1950*, Benson and Bingley, 1958, p. 569.)

1938

14 September

Madrid. "An offer was made through a Dutchman called Cornelius to supply us with 5,000 Mauser rifles and about a million rounds of ammunition. The Dutchman also offered tanks, planes and so on. We believed that he must be representing a foreign government but he insisted that he was an independent dealer. He demanded 50,000 dollars (US) for his 'wares' which, of course, at this stage we were unable to raise. We learned later that he had sold the guns to the Falangists and that they had proved to be in a dangerous state of disrepair and caused a number of casualties before being abandoned. We concluded that the Dutchman had unconsciously done us a favour in preferring to deal with our enemies and we drank his health!" (Palero, *The Betrayal of Spain*, Independent Publishing Association pamphlet, 1948, p. 12.)

1939

5 January

Czech Ambassador in Copenhagen writes to his government in a dispatch: "I strongly recommend that you accept Herr

Cornelius's terms and ensure speedy delivery of the arms he mentions." (A.P. Peters, *The Day Before Doomsday*, Viking, NY, 1960, p. 56.)

3 March

Ivan Jeczakowski, the Polish industrialist, acting as agent for his government, pays two million American dollars to the Brazilian arms dealer Geraldo Corneille on delivery of fifty British Mk 1 infantry tanks, in Warsaw. (A.P. Peters, ibid., p. 72.)

6 July

Passenger list for the SS *Kao An*, a Panamanian passenger steamer, leaving Southampton, includes a Mr and Mrs J. Cornelius, a Miss Christine Brunner, a Mr S.M. Collier and a Mr Gordon Ogg, all bound for Macao.

22 September

The British tanks sold by Corneille to Poland develop technical faults and are abandoned after one engagement with the German Army near Lodz. "We placed too much reliance on them. They seemed to fall apart around us," reports the colonel in command of the regiment. (A.P. Peters, ibid., p. 106.)

1940

20 August

Assassination of Trotsky, Mexico City, by a Russian using the name of Jacques van den Dreschd of whom Trotsky had written just before his death: "He claims to be a friend of Cornelius, whom I met briefly in Siberia. At certain times I felt they could almost have been brothers—particularly about the eyes." (Letter to Maria Reine, August 1940.)

1946
Summer

Nuremberg War Crimes Tribunal. During their trials von Ribbentrop, Göring and Streicher speak repeatedly of a witness who will come forward in their defence. He is referred to sometimes as 'Herr Mann' and sometimes as 'Cornelius'. After being sentenced to death, they claim that Cornelius has betrayed them. Unsuccessful attempts are made to trace 'Cornelius' but the only person of that name seems to be one of Himmler's astrologers believed to have committed suicide soon after the Fall of Berlin. (*The War Crimes Trials, Nuremberg and Tokyo* by Walter P. Emshwiller, Reilly & Knap, NY, 1949, p. 1003.)

1948
11 February

Assassination of Gandhi. Police seek "a one-armed man called Cornelius" in connection with the crime. Cornelius believed to be an Eurasian living in Delhi. There is some information suggesting that he was a collaborator with the Japanese in Burma and that he has an Indian wife. All investigations prove fruitless. (Mehda, *What Killed Gandhi?*, Indian Publishing Company, Bombay, 1954, p. 40.)

1949
14 March

Jerusalem. Israeli commanders interview a captured

Egyptian spy Cornelius. He dies during questioning. (Uncorroborated report in *Freedom*, 12 October: *The Needless Agony* by Sandra McPhail.)

1953

May

Kenya. "One of the captured Mau Mau who had almost certainly been involved in the massacre of the Gordon family claimed that they had been led by a white man who had dyed his skin and posed as one of them. This man, said our prisoner, had been directly responsible for the rape of the two younger girls and their subsequent dismemberment. Several stories of this kind were circulating at the time but no evidence ever came to light to confirm or, for that matter, deny the rumours, though one of the Mau Mau leaders came up with the name of Jerome Cornelius, a businessman of Afrikander extraction, who had been lost in an aircrash the year previously. If a white man was directing Mau Mau operations in the Muranga district—which seemed to us highly unlikely, to say the least!—he must have made himself scarce soon after our big operation of June and July when the Mau Mau were virtually wiped out for the time being." (James B. Bayley, *The Darkening Continent*, Union Movement pamphlet, 1956, p. 7.)

1954

3 June

Angkor Wat, Cambodia. The bodies of five French soldiers discovered in a temple. They had been tortured. The sixth soldier was still barely alive. The torture was evidently the work of Cambodian terrorists calling themselves the Cambodian

Liberation Army. Before he died, the sixth man claimed that the terrorists had been led by a European whom they called Cornelius (Campaignes en Cambodie, Versins and Henneberg, Gallimard, Paris, 1963, p. 98.)

1955
18 July
Algeria. French intelligence contacts FLN officer who uses the pseudonym 'Cornelius' and gives information which leads to the death and capture of nearly twenty important members of the FLN. (Peter B. Saxton, *The Sun is Setting*, Howard Baker, 1969, p. 103.)

30 July
Nicosia, Cyprus. Eight Cypriot terrorists are captured by British troops in the Hotel Athena. Before the captives can be transported to prison a counter-attack takes place and they are rescued. The only survivor of the raid is Corporal John Taylor who says that the raid was led by a masked man whom one of the captives addressed as Cornelius. (*Daily Sketch*, 1 August.)

1956
October
Suez Crisis. "It was rumoured that Eden had received a report from a Foreign Office man in Cairo called Cornelius. The report advised immediate occupation of the Canal Zone. This report, so it was said, was what finally decided Eden to give the necessary orders." (Sir Hugh Platt, *The Defence of Suez*, Collins, 1960, p. 17.)

10 November

Budapest. Russian and Hungarian secret police seek an Englishman believed to have taken an active part in the uprising of 23 October. He is sometimes called Cornelius. For a while the police place much importance on his capture and interrogate all imprisoned foreigners as to his whereabouts, but suddenly stop their investigations and no more is heard of him. (Richard Geiss, *They Went to Hungary*, Hodder and Stoughton, 1958, p. 400.)

1958

September

China's Great Leap Forward. European refugees cross from China to Hong Kong. Among them is a Jeremy Cornelius, half Chinese, half English, who disappears before he can be vetted by the authorities. (*Hong Kong Times*, 21 September.)

1960

Spring

The Ladbroke Grove Murders in London. Within three months eight women disappear. All live in Ladbroke Grove. Two of them are found dismembered in the grounds of a disused monastery in Kensington Park Road, the others are found in Hyde Park. All corpses have the initials J.C. carved on their foreheads and the work is thought to be that of a religious maniac. The last corpse found has the slogan "J.C. loves C.B." carved into its back. Moses Collier, a labourer, confesses to the murders but further investigations and questions prove that he is mentally unbalanced and could not have been responsible for any of the murders. The case remains unsolved. (R.W. Eagen, 'The Killer's Mark', *Weekend*, 4 July, 1966.)

1961

Summer

The war in the Congo. White mercenaries fighting for the Congolese are commanded for a while by a Major Jerry Cornelius, apparently a Belgian deserter. Later Cornelius disappears, believed killed by UN troops. (Alexander Charnock, Twilight of Africa, Hutchinson, 1965, p. 607.)

1962

20 November

The Cornelius Realty Company of Key West buys large areas of land in Florida at a time when values are relatively low because of the Cuba Crisis. After the crisis is over, the company resells the land at 100 per cent profit and then dissolves. (*Business Month*, January 1963.)

1963

24 November

Dallas, Texas. Police seek a Jerry Cornelius in connection with the assassination of President Kennedy. It is believed that he is an associate of Lee Harvey Oswald and a young man known only as 'Shades'. The young man, it is rumoured, was heard boasting in a Houston bar that he was Kennedy's killer, not Oswald. After a fruitless investigation police conclude that Cornelius and 'Shades' are inventions of Oswald. (*Time*, 11 December.)

1964

Spring

Sudden takeover of various large department stores in London and London suburbs by the Torrent Group of Companies. The Torrent Group is described as a partially owned subsidiary of the Cornelius Development Corporation of Chicago. (*Business Journal*, 15 June.)

1965

Spring

The Deep Fix, a pop group, go to No. 1 with 'Felt for You, Velvet for Me'. "There's few would argue that lead guitar Jerry Cornelius is the group's real guv'nor and maybe the best white blues guitarist ever." (Chris Marlen, *Melody Maker*, 19 April.)

30 June

Bomb explodes in Alford Street, Dover, Kent. Several bodies found but none identified. The house was owned by a Mr J. Cornelius, believed to be one of those killed. (*Kentish Times*, 5 July.)

14 August

Thailand. A meeting of Chinese trade representatives with Bangkok businessmen. The intermediary is a 'Mr Cornelius', a Belgian industrialist. (*Eastern Trading News*, 25 August.)

22 September

Death of a youth in Kilburn, stabbed in broad daylight in High Street. A gang of youths was seen running away from the scene of the crime. An identification bracelet on the young man's body gave the name Jerry Cornelius. Police asked relatives or friends of the dead man to come forward but so far nobody has done so. (*West London Times*, 29 September.)

1967

12 December

"Police raided a flat in Chepstow Villas, Notting Hill Gate, last night and seized what they described as the biggest ever drug cache to be found on private premises. The occupant of the flat, a Mr Jerrold Cornelius, escaped from custody and has not yet been found. The police wish to interview him in connection with their inquiries. The drug cache included marijuana, hemp, cocaine, heroin and purple hearts as well as methadrine and dexadrine." (*Guardian*, 13 December.)

15 December

Conference of Black Panther leaders in Kingman, Ohio. Minister for Special Activities is given as Jerry Cornelius—"something of a mystery man even in Panther circles". (*Newsweek*, 20 December.)

1968

13 January

The highjacked TWA Boeing 707 which crashed in the sea off Trinidad had a J. Cornelius listed among its passengers. There were no survivors. (*International Herald Tribune*, 15 January.)

17 December

Multiple crash on the M1 motorway near Luton. One of

those killed in the Phantom V he was driving (and which was in head-on collision with an articulated truck) is a Jerry Cornelius, described as "a young fashion designer". (*The Sun*, 18 December.)

(*Note:* Although the compilers have discovered other references to people who might be Cornelius since the last entry above, they have not yet been able to check the authenticity of these references and therefore prefer not to include them as yet.)

APPENDIX II

"What's the hour?" The black-bearded man wrenched off his gilded helmet and flung it from him, careless of where it fell ... "We *need* Elric—we know it, and he knows it. That's the truth!"

"Such confidence, gentlemen, is warming to the heart."

The Stealer of Souls, 1963

"Without Jerry Cornelius, we'll never get it. We need him. That's the truth."

"I'm pleased to hear it." Jerry's voice was sardonic as he entered the room rather theatrically and closed the door behind him.

The Final Programme, 1968

APPENDIX III

The captions to chapters in this novel are advertisements and headlines taken from the following sources, most of them published 1975/76: *Jane's Weapons Systems, Interavia, Official Detective, Crime Detective, True Detective, Official UFO, Guns & Ammo, Titbits, Weekend, Guardian, Daily Mirror, Horology Magazine.*

The first four chapter headings referring to Harlequin are taken from productions staged between 1716 and 1740 by John Rich at Lincoln's Inn Fields and Covent Garden. The fifth is from Charles Dibdin's Covent Garden production, Christmas 1779. These classic pantomimes consisted of a dramatic 'opening', in which the main characters all wore oversized masks, on a theme usually taken from folklore, Romance or Classical Mythology—and which lasted for the first quarter whereupon, at a moment of tension in the plot, the characters would be transformed magically into members of the Harlequinade, to act out their parts in a fantastic, musical, satirical and symbolic manner and bring the whole entertainment to a satisfactory resolution. There were some 400 pantomimes of this kind staged in the 170 years between Rich's first production and the start of the modern pantomime which began to take its place from the 1870s and had almost completely superseded it by the 1890s.

The Broadsheet quotes at the beginning of the Coda section are almost all taken from John Foreman's excellent two-volume collection of facsimile broadsheets *Curiosities of Street Literature* (London, 1966).

Muzak is a trade name for piped music used in restaurants, supermarkets, bars and other public places.

A NOMAD OF THE TIME STREAMS

The Warlord of the Air

It is 1973, and the stately airships of the Great Powers hold benign sway over a peaceful world. The balance of power is maintained by the British Empire—a most equitable and just Empire. Yet, moved by the politics of envy and perverse utopianism, not all of the Empire's citizens support the marvellous equilibrium.

Flung from the North East Frontier of 1902 into the future, Captain Oswald Bastable is forced to question his most cherished ideals, discovering to his horror that he has become a nomad of the time streams, eternally doomed to travel the wayward currents of a multiverse. Bastable falls in with the anarchists of this imperial society and sparks a course of events more devastating than he could ever have imagined.

TITAN BOOKS

A NOMAD OF THE TIME STREAMS

The Land Leviathan

Oswald Bastable visits an alternate 1904. Here, he discovers that most of the Western world has been devastated by a short, yet horrific war fought with futuristic devices and biological weapons. An Afro-American Black Attila is conquering the remnants of the Western nations, destroyed by the wars, in an attempt to bring civilization and social order.

The Steel Tsar

Bastable encounters an alternate 1941 where the Great War never happened and Great Britain and Germany became allies in a world intimidated by Japanese imperialism. In this world's Russian Empire, Bastable joins the Russian Imperial Airship Navy and is subsequently imprisoned by the rebel Djugashvili, the 'Steel Tsar', also known as Joseph Stalin.

TITAN BOOKS

THE ETERNAL CHAMPION SERIES

The Eternal Champion

John Daker hears in his dreams the call of another world. When he answers, he discovers his true name, and his destiny: he is Erekosë, the Eternal Champion, called upon to resolve the perpetual struggle between Reason and Chaos.

Summoned by King Rigenos of Necranal, Erekosë regains his rightful place as leader of the human army in the fight against the mysterious Eldren race. He swears to destroy them all, but realizes too late that it is the humans, and not the Eldren, who pose the true threat to the Multiverse…

TITAN BOOKS

THE ETERNAL CHAMPION SERIES

Phoenix in Obsidian

John Daker, in the form of Count Urlik Skarsol, is summoned from the side of his beloved Ermizhad to Rowenarc, the City of Obsidian. He knows not what his task is to be, nor who called him there: only that his destiny is inextricably linked to that of the mighty Black Sword…

The Dragon in the Sword

In the dimension of the Six Realms, where the ice caps have melted, the planet is flooded and the dying sun casts little light. John Daker, in the form of Prince Flamadin, traverses a strange water-world seeking a resolution to the immortal struggle between Law and Chaos.

TITAN BOOKS

THE CORUM SERIES

The Knight of the Swords

The Queen of the Swords

The King of the Swords

The Bull and the Spear

The Oak and the Ram

The Sword and the Stallion

TITAN BOOKS

THE CORNELIUS QUARTET

The Final Programme

A Cure for Cancer

The English Assassin

The Condition of Muzak

TITAN BOOKS

THE MICHAEL MOORCOCK LIBRARY

Elric of Melniboné

This first volume collects the classic 1980's comic
adaptation of the Elric of Melniboné novels by fantasy
legend Michael Moorcock!

Bear witness to the story of Elric, Lord of Melniboné; his
dark cousin—the evil Yyrkoon; their dark magics; and
their terrible struggle for rule of the fabled Emerald Isle.

Elric: Sailor on the Seas of Fate

Forced to flee his city of Melniboné, Elric and his
sorcerous blade, Stormbringer, journey to the edge of a
black sea where he begins a voyage that will bring him
face-to-face with all the champions time can summon…

TITAN BOOKS

PRAISE FOR MICHAEL MOORCOCK

"The most important successor to Mervyn Peake
and Wyndham Lewis"
J G Ballard

"Michael Moorcock transcends cool.
He is beyond any need for cool."
Neil Gaiman

"His imagination sweeps the reader along.
Amongst the best Moorcock has written."
Sunday Telegraph

"A Moorcock novel through and through: exhilarating,
funny and deeply peculiar. It's been years since the Who range
put out anything as smart and engaging as this."
SFX

For more fantastic fiction, author events, exclusive excerpts,
competitions, limited editions and more

Visit our website
titanbooks.com

Like us on Facebook
facebook.com/titanbooks

Follow us on Twitter
@TitanBooks

Email us
readerfeedback@titanemail.com